Revenge of the Akuma Clan

BENJAMIN MARTIN

TUTTLE Publishing

Tokyo | Rutland, Vermont | Singapore

To The People of Kumejima

Published by Tuttle Publishing, an imprint of Periplus Editions (HK) Ltd.

www.tuttlepublishing.com

Copyright © 2013
Benjamin Martin

Library of Congress Cataloging-in-Publication Data in process

ISBN 978-4-8053-1274-2

Printed in China

Distributed by

North America, Latin America & Europe
Tuttle Publishing
364 Innovation Drive
North Clarendon, VT 05759-9436 U.S.A.
Tel: 1 (802) 773-8930 | Fax: 1 (802) 773-6993
info@tuttlepublishing.com
www.tuttlepublishing.com

Japan
Tuttle Publishing
Yaekari Building, 3rd Floor, 5-4-12 Osaki,
Shinagawa-ku, Tokyo 141 0032
Tel: (81) 3 5437-0171 | Fax: (81) 3 5437-0755
sales@tuttle.co.jp
www.tuttle.co.jp

Asia Pacific
Berkeley Books Pte. Ltd.
61 Tai Seng Avenue #02-12, Singapore 534167
Tel: (65) 6280-1330 | Fax: (65) 6280-6290
inquiries@periplus.com.sg
www.periplus.com

Indonesia
PT Java Books Indonesia, Jl. Rawa Gelam IV No. 9
Kawasan Industri Pulogadung, Jakarta 13930
Tel: (62) 21 4682-1088 | Fax: (62) 21 461-0206
crm@periplus.co.id
www.periplus.com

First edition
17 16 15 14 13
7 6 5 4 3 2 1   1308RP

CONTENTS

SOMEWHERE IN JAPAN

With the setting sun's final rays blocked by layers of rock, the only illumination in the slimy cavern came from the green moss on the ceiling. Insects scurried along the few bits of ground free of mud as the sole occupant stared intently at a wooden statue. He perched on a fallen stalactite, his black hair nearly as dirty as the ripped black jacket hanging loosely on his shoulders.

"I should have left you to rot in the police warehouse," the boy said, crouched in a corner, his once proud arms wrapped around emaciated legs. Weeks alone had turned beautiful and often superficially cheery features into a drawn and haggard scowl. Weeks of skulking in barely habitable holes had made his injuries fester. Weeks of plotting had given him an air of intensity that neared the brink of sanity. His wild eyes peered past his tangled hair to the lifeless wooden statue, as if his intensity alone could coax an answer.

The little wolf statue remained still, despite the fact it was no longer missing a paw. Chul Soon had replaced the missing piece, yet his brother still sat there, looking pathetic. Unlike the others—their statues destroyed in the fire—Natsuki had cut off Chul Moo's arm before he was turned. When the fires raged he had not been whole. Without all the pieces, the fire could not consume him as it had the pack. Yet there was no triumph in the statue's survival. The wooden featuresbetrayed his brothers' thoughts. There was no rage, no thirst in them. Instead, some pitiful emotion stared back at him.

"Weeks of trying to find out where they put the statue. All the work to get you out. And still nothing. You are as useless as ever. The one beneficial thing you ever did for us turned out to be the destruction of everything. You led us to the... to *him*."

With a sudden smile that did nothing to soften his hard features, Chul Soon jerked closer to the small statue. The wood looked nearly alive in the garish moss-light. Greasy hair swayed as sharp teeth moved to the statue's pointed ears.

"Oh, I know," he whispered. "You still want her. And I want him, if in a different way. We will have them together. But first, a new spirit. We need to go hunting, brother."

Chul Soon had escaped the warehouse basement behind the Nakano supermarket. The storm drain he had found when he first scouted the new lair had saved him.

'I was right to keep it from Jahangir,' he thought, compulsively checking his surroundings. The thought of his mentor sent new pangs of rage through him. 'I will find someone stronger. Someone I can use to destroy *him*.'

With night deep around them, Chul Soon slipped silently through the dark Japanese forests. His goals clear, he became a shadow with a statue, unseen by even the most observant creatures.

After the destruction of his pack, Chul Soon had fled. Thinking himself the only survivor, he had run like a dog, his tail between his legs. It had taken him days in Himeji to realize it had not been his fault—that Jahangir had been the weak one. He had let them down. It took even longer to realize the blame also belonged to Chul Moo. He had brought them Rie. His obsession with the girl had brought them to the attention of the Matsumotos.

By all rights, he knew he should have run straight to the others. He should have gone and told them all that had happened. He should have shouted to all who would listen that there was a new Jitsugen Samurai. But no. The gaijin would be his. Chul Soon would be the one to end that problem, and the only way he could guarantee that was if the others only found out about it after.

Many painful days before in Himeji, Chul Soon had found a newspaper about the fire in Nakano while stalking a stray cat. He recognized the opportunity at once and began searching for more information. A member of his pack was still alive. One of the other ōkami had escaped the Matsumotos' fire at the warehouse. Though he was recognizable as a foreigner, Chul Soon remained hidden among the city's many tourists. Safe, he formed his plans.

It took him days to sneak back into Nakano. David and Takumi were observant. With their lackey ghost, they patrolled every night. Since he disappeared around the time of the fire, Chul Soon could not show up during the day as a human. He knew the policeman Yonamine and special investigators were still looking for the animals that had attacked Masao Matsumoto and Misaki so he could not rely on his wolf form for cover. He grew so hungry trying to sneak into town that he almost let his hunting instincts overwhelm him. Luckily, his rage was stronger than his stomach. Chul Soon waited until he could place all the Matsumotos, Yonamine, and even the two overly observant strangers that were supposed to be undercover investigators. He crept into town, often sliding through muddy rainwater troughs next to rural roadways, until he was back at his old haunt. It took him three days to find the wooden shard in the burnt out basement. It was such a tiny sliver, but by its absence, the missing piece had kept the wooden statue from burning to dust.

Of course, the wooden bit turned out to be the severed paw of the pack member he had hoped for least. Chul Soon had made it out of Nakano nearly starved. A few mice and a nature photographer came along at just the right time. The mice fed his body. The man fed his spirit. He was annoyed circumstances forced him to leave the man alive. His disappearance might lead to suspicions that would only make his upcoming task all the more difficult.

Back in Himeji, it took Chul Soon all his self-control to keep from over indulging. The large city offered him enough cover to feed, and for the first time in his life, he was free of observation. Direct observation, he had to remind himself. Without Jahangir, his resources were limited. He could not access his accounts without tipping off certain other relatives. If he spent too much time on the streets, someone would notice and report him. Japan was a safe place. Everyone followed the rules.

Chul Soon waited and read. The local papers told of the remarkable wooden statue that survived the fire. They covered the single missing piece and the fire investigation. Oddly, the newpapers never published a picture, and they dropped the story soon after.

Despite stealing papers and watching café televisions for news, it was the Matsumotos who finally led him to the statue. A few contacts he had with the local obake tipped him off that Ryohei was back in town, watching a specific police warehouse. With more than a little help from the same obake, Chul Soon was able to lure Ryohei away just long enough to slip in, grab the statue, and get out.

Seeing his brother sitting on a shelf had shocked Chul Soon. He had almost left him there, alone with his sad eyes. After running from hole to hole for another three days to make sure no one followed him, his initial surprise had turned to annoyance, and then anger. The statue drew back the missing piece from Chul Soon's bag on the second day. His brother's statue was whole. He could bring him back, but should he?

"I'll at least have some help..." Chul Soon mused as he stepped back into the dank cave. "You will right your wrongs, brother, even if it kills you."

It was easy. All he had to do was get his brother a new spirit. In the meantime, he would figure out the much larger problem of manipulating Chul Moo into helping to kill *all* the Matsumotos. Chul Soon let go of his hold on humanity, giving himself over to the primal instincts at his core. Yellow fangs enclosed the statue.

"Time to go see some old friends," the black-haired wolf growled around the wood. Together, they ran through dark and secret places.

NEW YEAR'S EVE

No one chooses how they come into the world. I was certain there was nothing I could do, no choice, no control. I was so angry. Angry all the time. It was not in my nature to internalize, and so anger became hate...

The soft winter moonlight reflected off the small white hills around David Matthews as he walked along a familiar path through the Matsumoto Forest. He paused to brush a flake of snow from his blond hair, his hard blue eyes carefully observing every detail of a familiar pine. His bare feet moved quickly through the cold slush between the trees. He had recently turned fourteen, but his height and western features made him appear several years older to his Japanese friends.

David was more than a Junior High student in a foreign land. He was the inheritor of a tradition thousands of years in the making, yet he felt himself to be much the same as when he had arrived in Japan just months before. Of course, the excess childhood fat that had defined so much of his previous life had melted away in face of the tough Matsumoto training. Even without them, the life of a normal student would have eventually gotten him into better shape. Maybe. David smiled as his path curved around a thick tree. Most of his classmates were not under threat of constant sword duels, as he was whenever he stepped outside his room. One four-walled room and school, the only places he could truly relax, not that school was very relaxing. He also had to admit that his other half would probably scare the pants off just about anyone at Nakano Junior High, that is if he did not cute them to death first.

Kou, the tiger god within him had also grown in the last two months. Since helping to wipe out the ōkami lair in downtown Nakano, Kou had grown to nearly six feet long from tail to snout. He had refined an air of fierceness that allowed him to convert his usual kitten-like personality and big eyes into something far more dangerous.

The kami was as much a part of David as his own thoughts, as much as any part of his body. Transforming, David left a thick winter kimono behind and let Kou paw through the soft new snow. One of the benefits of having a kami within him was that as long as they had paws and fur, they could stay quite comfortable in the falling snow.

Above, an unintended squawk alerted them to a small gray bird hurtling from among the white tipped tree branches. Kou sat back and looked up, his tongue slid out with an unconscious movement he had picked up from David. His black tongue licked his furry lips as the little missile dived unsteadily at him. The baby phoenix spread its small wings in an attempt to airbrake. Veering off, the unstable bird flopped into a pile of snow in front of Kou.

"*Still having trouble landing?*" the tiger asked aloud in his purring Japanese. "*What if you break your wing again? Injured animals do not stay off predators' menus for long.*" David chided Kou as the tiger's mind conjured visions of the little gray-feathered bird becoming their next meal. Around them, the snow melted from the heat Reimi radiated.

"*I don't get to fly as much as you run. And Takumi isn't around to help me,*" the phoenix said, her voice high and lilting.

"Speaking of Takumi, he asks that you try to stop running into trees. He keeps coming back sore." David's blue twinkled in Kou's eyes as the tiger's mouth and throat formed his own voice. Ever since that day at the Matsumoto Shrine, David had gained the ability to speak and understand Japanese perfectly. It was a necessity—while most Japanese studied some English, few spoke it fluently.

"*He never lets me change,*" she pouted. "*You two are lucky. You can speak with each other, while I am cut off from Takumi. Anyway, Happy Birthday. Natsu and Rie should be on their way.*"

"*Everyone will be on their way,*" Kou said. "*The New Year's Shrine ceremony will start soon.*"

"And my birthday was two weeks ago," David added.

"Reimi!" Natsuki's voice floated along the path behind them.

"*Oops. Looks like I'm in trouble. She doesn't like it when I fly off. I'm harder to follow than you are,*" she said sulkily.

The little phoenix sprang out of the puddle and pumped her wings. She flew just high enough to clear Kou's head and land between his shoulders. Reimi wobbled precariously as she tucked her wings in. Kou grudgingly allowed her to wait there for the girls. Although he was not cold, he could easily feel the warmth that spread out from where Reimi sat on his back. The phoenix exuded a heat that changed with her mood. Happy as she was, Reimi would have burned a lesser being than a tiger god.

The two kami were far from being completely comfortable with each other, but David insisted Kou try to be nice—despite the tiger's instincts to go for a taste of the little bird.

'Remember the last bird you ate? You still had feathers stuck in your teeth when you transformed,' David thought. Kou replied by reliving the memory of the hunt, which made keeping Kou from slinking off for a snack even more difficult.

Natsuki and Rie appeared from behind a stand of trees, the pair huddled together against the cold. Natsuki was the tallest girl in their class, yet was still shorter than David. Her newly-cut short black hair hung around her ears, glowing with moonlight reflected off bits of snow. Her features were so much softer than the hard angry lines David had remembered when they first met, but that only served to hide the strength of her will. Rie had kept her long black hair and it shone faintly in the moonlight. More willowy than ever, she still radiated a kind of graceful power, albeit tinged with an occasional shadow.

"I can't believe you two aren't cold. It's freezing out here," Natsuki frowned, pulling her coat tighter as they approached the adolescent tiger and gray bird. "Your sister says 'Happy New Years' by the way. Just got her email."

"I feel like my contacts are freezing," Rie said, stamping her feet. David cringed at the reminder of his failure. Though Rie never seemed to blame him, David still felt responsible for her abduction by the Jeong brothers. Chul Soon, and perhaps even Chul Moo, were still out there somewhere. His only condolence was the certainty he would see them again.

Reimi took the opportunity to jump onto Kou's head, interrupting his thoughts as she opened her wings to fly the last few meters to Natsuki. Kou snapped at her tail feathers as they flew by, just out of reach of his fangs. His tail twitched in annoyance and a low rumble began in his throat. Catching her as easily as she caught thrown swords during practice, Natsuki pulled Reimi into her jacket, sighing at the extra heat.

"How come I don't have a personal heater for a partner?" Rie asked, smiling at Kou. The tiger shook a bit of snow from his fur and blinked.

"So how many people will be here tonight?" David asked, curious about his first New Year's Eve in Japan.

"A bunch of people from town. There will be other gatherings of course, but this is the biggest Shrine in Nakano, and the only one with a bell," Rie answered, her voice light on the cold breeze.

"Shouldn't you two change back to your human forms? I mean, what if someone sees you. I have Takumi's clothes."

Despite her words, Natsuki did not appear too eager to give up Reimi's fiery heat.

Reimi popped her head out, saying *"Fine, but only if you let me go flying later. We never get to practice."*

"That's because I end up climbing twenty trees when you do," Natsuki said. "I'm not some flying squirrel." Though her words were true enough, Kou easily saw the smile playing at the corners of her mouth. Chuckling with their tiger growl, Kou loped off to his clothes. Though he had a special set of armor that would transform with him, he could not very well run around in tiger striped armor while groups of outsiders were on the Matsumotos' Estate. In a blink, Kou had David's clothes in his mouth and was gone. Natsuki left Takumi's clothes behind a tree and walked away with Rie.

David was the first to rejoin the girls. Jumping out from a tree, he smiled at Natsuki's foot, an inch from his face.

"Tsk tsk," David shook his head seriously. "You really shouldn't go around kicking everything that jumps out at you. I mean who else with my skin and hair color would be around here?"

"That's why she stopped," Takumi said in a voice newly deepening. Shorter and slighter than David but coiled and strong as a snake, Takumi ducked out from behind a tree. His thick winter kimono melded into the dark shadows of evening despite the white snow behind him. "She still has better control than you. Sorry about Reimi, she really wanted to fly."

"We better go. It's almost eleven-thirty," Rie said. With a smile, she took the lead, weaving through the familiar trees of her ancestral home.

"Good. Kou might be warm, but I'm freezing," David said. Appearing naked in the snow was not fun for him after being warm and comfortable as Kou.

Covered in white, the clearing looked completely different than it had the last time David visited it. The bright colors of fall were gone, but so too was the crater. After its destruction when David had saved Rie, the Matsumotos had expertly re-built the shrine in secret. Waiting before the Shrine, Masao and Yukiko Matsumoto stood with Natsuki's parents. On the right side of the clearing, tents had been set up with some of the lo-cal restaurants offering variations on toshikoshi soba, a tradi-tional New Year's Eve noodle dish. David spotted several of his classmates crowded around the tents, enjoying the warmth of the steaming food and lights.

Masao turned the instant they stepped out of the forest's shadows. He touched a small box next to the stairs leading up to the new Shrine. A gentle glow sprang from rows of lighted lanterns that marked a path through the trees. With a gesture, Yukiko led the way left from the Shrine. Hidden among the trees, a snow covered pagoda blended into the forest. The lan-terns encircling the wooden structure added a warm glow and illuminated a large bronze bell.

"What's that?" David asked.

"It's a Buddhist tradition to ring a bell one hundred and eight times before midnight. Though not Shinto, it has become a tradition here. Everyone will have a chance to ring the bell. It's a way to purify ourselves before the New Year," Masao said, leading them around the pagoda to a set of stairs. Behind them, David realized the rest of the townspeople had followed and were lining up for their turn to ring the bell. Kou chided him for not paying better attention to his surroundings. They were both relieved to note that the local school bully, Koji, had not shown up.

After Masao, Natsuki, and the rest of the Matsumotos went, David walked up the stairs and grabbed the rope he had seen the others use. The rope pulled a chained log that he swung forward. When the log hit, the bell rang with a loud, solemn peal. David shivered as the vibrations washed through him.

'It's like something really is gone. I guess my old life is over, isn't it,' David thought as he walked back down the stairs.

*'It is, but in return we both have a new life to live. A powerful
one, full of meaning. Together, we are a Jitsugen Samurai, the culmination of hundreds of years of tradition. Traditions are an important
way of learning from the past. Let's go find some toshikoshi rat before
midnight strikes.'*

'We'll go hunting later, I promise,' he thought in reply. 'You
know, most people would be concerned if another voice answered their every thought. But I'm glad you're here.'

Within him, the kami growled in pleasure as they walked
back out of the forest in search of food. As the last bell tolled at
midnight, David felt other possibilities, the other ways his life
might have turned out, fade away with the deep, low sound.

Rie found him a bit later staring off into the forest. Noting his
still familiar vacant look, she pulled him gently toward the
Shrine.

"Talking to Kou again?" she whispered. "Come on, we
have to pray to our ancestors for a happy New Year."

Though he had been talking to Kou, David felt on edge.
The Matsumoto forest usually felt like home, but with the
snow covering familiar paths, the whole place felt different.
David followed Rie after one last look into the forest's depths.
As he neared the Shrine's steps, his mind drifted back over the
many times he had been there. The accident that had left him
possessed by a Japanese god, his triumph during their Golden
Week games, Rie's possession by an evil spirit, and his success
at bringing her back all flashed before his eyes. Then Takumi
appeared beside him and jerked him out of his revere.

"Here take this. It's good luck," he said, handing him a
small brass coin with a round hole in the center. David recognized the five-yen coin. "Throw it in the box, and then follow
along."

Takumi bowed to the Shrine then took his own coin and
threw it into a small box. Reaching up, he shook a thick white

rope, which rang two large brass bells. Then he bowed twice, clapped his hands twice, and bowed again. Turning, he moved aside for David who repeated the movements, a bit unsure what to think about it all.

'You know, I was brought up in a semi-religious family. Is it okay to do this without really knowing what it means?' David thought, hoping Kou would answer.

'You know by now that there is something to the Japanese legends and traditions. What harm can it do to ask your ancestors for a good New Year? We must be mindful of those who came become before us. The Matsumotos, kami, and even your ancestors may prove to be powerful allies if only we ask.'

Thoughtful, David looked up from his last bow and caught a glimpse of Ryohei, the Matsumoto Estate's resident obake floating around one of the trees up the mountain. With a wink to him, David turned away to make room for the next group of people.

"So what happens now?" David asked. "In America we usually make a lot of noise, have fireworks and stuff. It's strange having an almost somber New Year's."

"Some people will probably do fireworks in town," Natsuki said, smiling. "Most will just go home and spend their time quietly. *We* are going for a hike."

"A hike?"

"Yep," Takumi said. "Though I guess I could let Reimi fly."

Takumi and Natsuki, partners through her bond with his kami, walked off. David just caught Natsuki say, "You better not go off and leave me with just your clothes," before they were out of view.

As David began to follow, Yukiko motioned to him and Rie. After ensuring there was no one around to hear, his host-mother bent close.

"Make sure you keep your senses open," she said, unusually stern. "I'm sure that last week was not a lone event."

"Don't worry. Kou's on it."

"Come on, let's go" Rie said, pulling him after Takumi and Natsuki.

An hour later, David sat with the other three young samurai high above the Matsumoto Shrine. The walk up the snowy mountain had been quiet. David had matched Rie's pace, but he could not help but think on Yukiko's words.

'If there is another attack…' As they reached the top, their silent conversation ended. Instead of Takumi and Natsuki as they expected, there was only a small open area surrounded by pine trees at the top of a cliff. The area was quiet, though they could hear some of the conversations floating up from below. David tensed.

"Relax," Rie said. "They're probably just making out over in the woods."

In response, Natsuki dropped out of a nearby tree, causing David to whirl and summon his Seikaku, the powerful dual-nature sword that he could summon at will.

'If only Jessica could learn to be that quiet,' David thought with a wistful sigh. Even dropping from a tree, the girl who was normally so loud at school had been eerily silent. His sister had struck up a fast friendship with Natsuki after her visit. Every other day he had to translate another note between them or send messages over Skype. 'At least I get to hear what she's up to again.'

"Reimi's around here somewhere," Natsuki said. "And we were not making out." To emphasize her point, she punched David hard in the arm. Though he could have dodged, he let her connect, and then followed up with a backhand to her forehead. It might had turned into an impromptu sparring match, but then Reimi distracted them with an aerial somersault that nearly ended with her smashed into a tree.

Below the cliff, the warm lights of Nakano Town glowed just past the Estate's trees and the main road to Himeji. Takumi reappeared and helped them unpack the few supplies they had brought up the mountain. David smiled at the awkward distance he tried to keep from Natsuki.

A bit later, Rie stirred beside him on a log, and David again wondered why they had not become partners. Kou had no answers for him. Whether it was because they had just broken their bond with Natsuki, or for some other reason, he was just as free as he had been for those first few days he could talk to Kou. Their glimpse into just how strong and important the connection between Jitsugen Samurai and partner could be tainted their enjoyment of that freedom. Murmuring something too quiet for him to hear, Rie sat a little closer.

'*Females.*' Kou thought the word almost like a curse. David chuckled. '*They are difficult to hunt. Why are we sitting up here freezing? We could be hunting or lying in a tree.*'

Rie shivered beside them. Although prepared, David saw that the others were just as cold as he was.

"How long are we going to be up here?" David asked.

"A few more hours," Takumi said. He stared out over the cliff into darkness, while Natsuki stole occasional glances toward her partner.

"Kou and I will be right back. We're going to get some firewood." David stood, and loped off into the trees. Once they were out of sight, David transformed, sighing as Kou's tiger fur insulated them from the cold. Light over the deep snow, Kou was able to round up enough wood for a fire much faster than David was, despite his lack of opposable thumbs. Kou's animal senses, so much more potent than David's, also ensured no stray beasts would ambush them again. In just a few minutes, Kou had a stack of wood next to their friends.

'I could use a bit of your fur right about now,' David thought as he braced himself for the change back to human form.

'*Why not? We used to get mixed up. Maybe we can put some fur on you.*'

'Some things best not left to chance. What if we make a mistake and I end up orange haired forever?'

'It would be an improvement.'

David growled at his other half and willed himself into his human form, pink skin and all.

"Good thing I was a boy scout," he muttered a few minutes later as he moved the last twig into place.

After a few tries, David coaxed a feeble flame with a few matches from Natsuki's bag. Afraid the faltering sparks might die; he leaned in to blow on the flame. A sudden gasp made him turn just as something small and dark rushed past him.

The fire erupted into an inferno that heated the entire area. Surprised, David rolled away from the flames as the girls scooted back from the waves of heat. Takumi was gone.

Looking into the flames David saw that Reimi was no longer a small gray bird. Instead, an iridescent whisper of fire resolved into twinkling eyes and beak. Fluttering in and around the flames, Kou suspected she was feeling as he felt stalking through the forest. Reimi was free and at home. Laughing, David sat again with Rie, and together the three students watched the phoenix play in the flames. Sometimes she seemed nothing more than another flicker of heat, while at other times she was a shooting star of red feathers and flame. The flames began to wither after consuming nearly every bit of the wood Kou had gathered.

"I'll go get some more," David said, getting up.

Rie pulled him back down. "No, don't. You'll miss it."

With a last few sputters, the flames died as melted snow erased the last embers. A small gray head poked its way out of the mush. Shaking herself off, Reimi hopped out of the sludge and over to Natsuki.

"That was fun. We should do that more often," she squeaked.

"If I had known all you need is a bit of fire to enjoy yourself so much I would have slept in front of the kotatsu burner instead of having to try to follow you up trees!" Natsuki said laughing.

With a look at David, Reimi fluttered out of view. David followed after with Takumi's clothes. They made it back just in time to watch the first sunrise of the New Year peak over the hills above Himeji.

"You know," whispered Rie as the sun's rays hit them, "it's the year of the Tiger."

BACK TO SCHOOL

Choices... I had spent my whole life avoiding them. It was always easier to follow, to do what others wanted me to do. Yet it was always there, the nagging feeling that something was wrong, that I could be more than I was...

Although it was a holiday, David did not expect to escape their usual morning training. Most of the time, David and Kou looked forward to the mental and physical challenges of their practices. Still, they were pleasantly surprised when they returned from the mountaintop and Yukiko announced they all had a day off from their usual routines. Natsuki stayed for breakfast before heading home to spend the rest of New Year's Day with her parents. The Matsumotos and David enjoyed the traditional New Year's bento lunch boxes called osechi that Yukiko had ordered months in advance, and then relaxed for the day.

David understood a little better all the preparations that had gone on before the holiday. Yukiko had mobilized everyone when not training to clean out the entire house. Instead of spring-cleaning, the Matsumotos wanted to be sure that everything was ready for a new year. David had especially enjoyed helping to make mochi. With the twins and Natsuki, David had helped smash steamed rice into sticky goo. They had filled some of it with sweet beans to make a very tasty treat. Rie had taken three big rounds of mochi, stacked them, and topped them with an orange. The offering was a center-piece at the Shrine, and David finally understood what all the plastic decorations he had seen in stores were supposed to represent.

With the work done, the entire family was able to relax. Later in the day, the mailman arrived with a stack of postcard greetings for the family. David was surprised to receive a stack of his own from classmates and other students at the school.

'I'm embarrassed. The only presents and letters I sent were to my father and Jessica. I didn't send any to our class-mates—and I don't even know half of these people.'

'*It seems you are more popular than you thought,*' Kou growled from within him. '*I'm sure Jessica will enjoy the picture of you and the twins you sent. I bet she'll scratch out your face and focus her hunt on Takumi.*' David took the opportunity to growl back.

Though David's father and Jessica had visited a few weeks before, they were still unaware of his life as a Jitsugen Samurai. It had been easy enough hiding the changes from his oblivious father, but it had been far more difficult to hide them from his sister. David knew his father cared, but also knew that very few things could hold his interest for long. Fortunately, Jess had been more interested in telling David about her friends back home than in prying into David's life.

It helped that she grew silent whenever she saw Takumi. With secrecy so essential to his and the Matsumotos' sur-vival, David could not afford to let his family know about Kou. It was safer for them that way. With a sigh, David went to find Takumi so he could ask what to do about his lack of greetings for other students.

Outside the main house, David jogged toward the forge, a low building that bordered the traditional Japanese garden behind the main house. With a burst of speed, David leapt over the small stream that ran through the Estate. The recent snows had frozen the top layers, but he could still see water running below. He had cleared the stream so many times that he was shocked to find himself wet, cold, and gasping for air beneath a layer of ice.

Struggling, he convulsed in the shallow water. His whole body bumped against the rocks as something dragged him closer to the pond in the center of the garden. He twisted against the pull on his leg. His arm caught a tree root and gave him just enough leverage to turn his face, but the ice kept him from getting any air. With a shock of panic, he smashed his head through the ice just long enough to pull in a quick gasp of air.

A strong jerk dragged him back under. David pulled hard with stomach muscles developed by hours of sit-ups. He caught sight of a translucent blue form in the water before his head banged against a rock and he had to straighten out.

'A little help here?'

'I did the last one. I will let you have this hunt.'

'Just cause there's a little water.'

David growled, and shut his eyes against the water. He moved faster through the water as his body relaxed. He mentally followed the tingling flow of energy to the core of his being. There, he sensed the remaining metal that had impaled his heart so many months before at the Shrine. Calling it forth, his Seikaku appeared in his hands. As they entered the pond, David had enough room to maneuver. Even as the squirming little kappa tried to drag him to the bottom, David lashed out with the wooden form of the Seikaku. The transparent form that had held him dissolved into the surrounding waters.

Free, David swam under the bridge then used his Seikaku to poke through the ice. A hand helped him out of the water. To either side of him, Rie and Takumi sat on the bridge, having watched the whole ordeal.

"Fine. I do the dishes tonight," Takumi said, his voice grim as he looked to his sister. David knocked water from his ears.

"You two bet on me?"

"Of course," Rie said with a sweet smile. "Takumi thought it would take you another couple of minutes to get free."

David shivered in the cold and then punched Takumi.

After only a few days off for the winter holidays, school started back up again. Nakano's second years faced the busiest semester of their academic calendar. In addition to the usual competitions, tests, and activities, the second years would be going on a school trip to Kyushu in only a few weeks.

With Chul Moo's disappearance and Misaki's death, Class 2B was smaller than before. Many of David's schoolmates were still in shock from the Jeong brothers' disappearance and the deaths over the past months, including the fire that had raged in the warehouse. When David arrived for the first day of class, their homeroom teacher Mr. Moriyama also told them that Yuuto had transferred to another school. Although he gave no reasons, David, Takumi, Rie, and Natsuki all assumed it had to do with the aftereffects of the ōkami's domination over him. Both Yuka and Yuuto had become loud and sometimes even obnoxious in class after the Matsumotos and David had freed them the previous semester.

Yuuto especially had been a paradox. Always exhausted in class, he made every teacher's request seem as if it was a personal affront. Sometimes this came out as a lack of reply, other times as yelling or rude outbursts. The only thing he had kept up with was sports, but even then, he would go on as if directed by some plan no one else could see.

Although disturbed and guilty over Yuuto's departure, David was still happy to be back at school. Only a few months before, he had felt isolated and lonely, but over time it had become more like a second home. The myriad cultural differences that had kept him off balance were still there, but with the language barrier gone, they no longer kept him from making real connections with his classmates. While he was still far from mastering Japan, Kou had provided him with the tools to improve. Slowly, he was making friends among his classmates and enjoyed spending as much time as possible with them.

David's classmates and even the Matsumotos had become far more willing to deal with his occasional mistakes and differences since he could explain where he was coming from. It also helped that Kou acted as a check for him. Always present within his mind, Kou could often sense problems coming and help David avoid them.

'If only random monsters would stop attacking us.'

'They were all weak. Though I guess it is only a matter of time before Chul Soon sends something worse.'

With their initial preparations and meetings done for the morning, Class 2B began heading for the beginning of semester ceremony. At the beginning of every semester, the entire school met in the gym to listen to speeches from their teachers and fellow students.

Realizing he was zoning out again while talking to Kou, David said, "I'm just glad I haven't had to give a speech yet."

"It's not that bad. You just have to talk about how hard you're going to try this semester," Naoto replied.

"Yeah, or talk about what you did during the break," Shou added. "That's what I talked about last year when my turn came up."

"Such an over-achiever," Naoto said.

'*Naoto acts like you do with Jessica. Is Shou his brother?*' Kou asked.

'No. Just friends.'

"What did you two end up doing?" Shou asked. David jumped at the question, his head snapping to look at the shorter boy.

"We were at the Estate with everyone else," Takumi said, covering for David. "Not all of us get to go on ski trips during winter break."

'Yikes, I thought he meant us for a minute there. Takumi is getting way too sneaky.'

"Hey! My Dad got a promotion. He wanted to celebrate or something," Naoto said, rubbing his hair with one hand and looking away. David noticed his shoes and belt were new, and the hand in the hair gesture was one hundred percent embarrassment.

'*Naoto seems to be a bit uncomfortable with his new home life. I think he was used to hating everything.*'

'I bet he's wishing he had studied more. Now that his parents are loaded they are going to want him to go to a good school!'

Naoto and Shou eyed David as he began laughing. They were used to him zoning out at random, something that had started after Kou had awoken. His friends even ignored the occasional times he finished or started conversations that made sense to no one else. It was the more overt strangeness that still caught his classmates off guard.

All of Class 2B had noticed the odd things, like when he twitched his head at sounds no one else could hear, but they strove to ignore it. Unfortunately for David, they had all met Jessica. The fact his sister had fit in so well, even without speaking any Japanese, had shown them David's weirdness was not just because he was a gaijin.

David had become good enough at sports, classes, and with his friends, that they overlooked a number of quirks.

They were especially accommodating when their own grades improved from his homework help. Only the twins and Natsuki knew that the strangest of his quirks were due to his possession by a kami. Kou shared his mind, an alien presence that never completely faded.

Not all David's classmates welcomed him and his changes with open arms. A cadre of third years led by a boy named Koji had marked David for humiliation during his first month. Several more run-ins had only stiffened Koji's resolve to end David's newfound popularity. The incident had only isolated Koji, making him more dangerous.

David shrugged off thoughts of Koji and returned his focus to walking down the school halls. Kou pulled at David's attention until he noticed that their group had grown. Natsuki was keeping pace near Takumi as they all walked together. It was the closest he had seen them in public since the previous year.

'I am just glad we don't have to deal with Natsuki all the time anymore. She's so much more civil this way.'

'*You cannot fool me. I know you miss having a partner, even if you pretend to like the freedom more. Do not worry, we will find someone worthy.*'

"Here," Natsuki said, handing David a folded bit of paper. "What?"

"It's a list of the best songs right now. Jess wanted to know what music she should download, right?"

"You know, if you're going to be pen pals maybe you should practice English rather than send everything through me," David replied.

"She's your sister," Natsuki said smiling. "Besides, it's fun giving you more work."

With an innocent grin, Natsuki led Takumi and the others into the gym. David sighed and thought of his sister as he waited for the bottleneck at the gym entrance to clear. It took everyone a few minutes to find and change their shoes at the entrance, so he read over the list. At the top was AKB48, an all-girl group with nearly one hundred members. While it was true he had noticed many of his classmates listening to their music, he did not want to point his little sister toward their idea of fashion.

Once everyone was in the gym and had lined up by class and year, the ceremony began with greetings and bowing led by the vice-principal. After about an hour, the ceremony ended and their teachers released them to their normal classes.

Back in the classroom, their homeroom teacher Mr. Moriyama explained that most of the beginning of the semester would be devoted to getting ready for their school trip to Kyushu and the Cultural Festival just after. The rest would be getting ready for finals.

'Great. Tests, homework, and monsters for who knows how long. Maybe we should just sneak off and go hunt Chul Soon.'

'If we had done as I suggested, we could have tracked him. By now, he must be too far gone for me to hunt. We will just have to hope the monsters they send do not injure your cub mates.'

Class 2B's schedule for the next two weeks had them focusing on all things Kyushu. In Social Studies, they learned about the history of the most southern of the four main Japanese islands. They also studied the geography of Kyushu's Prefectures and the history of Nagasaki and its exposure to Western culture through the Dutch. In science, they covered the region's unique animals and plants, while in Japanese they studied dialect differences.

After school, David joined with the twins and Natsuki in the gym. David laughed at their shivers and complaints about the cold. Just a few weeks before, the team had sweated through each practice complaining about how hot it was. With the change in weather, the entire team had invested in new Yonex HeatTec clothing to keep in their body heat. Even Takumi muttered as he zipped up a full tracksuit. David's choice of shorts had most of his teammates wondering again if he was sane.

On the courts, they all worked through their usual warm-ups and drills. Takumi and Natsuki's constant practices together on the Estate showed most when they played together. Few could challenge them because there was such synchronicity in their movements. Their badminton playing, more than anything else, began the rumors that they were dating, though no one dared whisper such things around either of them.

After badminton, David walked the few kilometers back to the Matsumoto Estate with his friends. He opted for a human dinner, much to Kou's annoyance, then joined the others for evening practice.

Unlike in the mornings where the focus was on physical martial arts, David spent most of his evening practice time repairing the damage he did to the forest trees while practicing with his Seikaku. It took him nearly double the time to fix or create something than it took for destruction. Masao never smiled when he assigned tasks, but David suspected he enjoyed giving exercises that were ever more intricate.

Since the Matsumoto's swords were in high demand and with Nakano villagers often seeking Masao's advice as the local Shinto priest, there was also significant enough traffic on the Estate to require the extra time David spent fixing his accidents. Yukiko reminded him of the fact when she came back with a giant radish that still had a rather large wood shard in it. David fixed the vegetable, then left Rie and Natsuki in the forge so that Kou could run with Reimi through the Estate.

"Don't forget to write about the kappa," Yukiko called after. David groaned.

"Yet another page in your own Jitsugen Samurai Diary," Takumi said. "You can title it 'My heroic near-drowning.'"

David lunged after his host-brother, but he disappeared into a puff of smoke as Reimi took wing. Growling, Kou chased after the gray bird.

≡

A TRIP TO KYUSHU

*Of course, every time my thoughts strayed, every time I
thought I could be more, he was always there to remind me of
what I was. His only concern was revenge. I wanted to sug-
gest following, but I was silenced as if dead...*

As school and the Estate settled into routine, David almost felt
like a regular student again. Excitement for the school trip
built up among the second years. The worries about being unable to locate Chul Soon, the monsters that kept attacking, and
the statue that the police had found were constant but distant
concerns. If only Koji would graduate, David would love being at school.

The next few weeks sped by. David and Kou eliminated
two more weak monsters during their usual patrols around
the Nakano valley, but caught no scent of the one enemy they
most wanted. With a mix of reluctance and excitement, David
gave up the responsibility of protecting the valley as his classmates headed north.

David woke up half way through the flight. Getting onto the
plane had not been a problem. Unlike when he tried to enter

the ocean, no sense of unease or distress had overcome them on boarding the plane at Kansai International Airport.

"Damn, it wasn't enough," Rie said, cursing David's ability to heal so fast. She rummaged through her bag. The sense of otherness and fear that had hit them when the wheels left the ground came back to him as a kind of echo of the initial assault. He vaguely remembered Rie pouring a handful of pills down his throat as Kou convulsed in their shared mind.

Beside him, Takumi sat smiling and watching the clouds outside his window. Reimi, daughter of fire and wind, seemed to have had no problems leaving the ground. Kou on the other hand was a tiger, and was bound to the earth.

David's throat was coarse and dry, but he managed enough head movement to see Rie struggling to get her bag from under the seat.

"It's alright," David said, choking on his words a little. "The panic is gone… I can't hear Kou." He sat up straighter as his throat and mind cleared, his strangled senses struggling to take in the other passengers. Their classmates sat arrayed around them in their regular winter uniforms. David shuddered. 'It's been months since I've been without him. I… I'm alone.' It took David several minutes to compose himself enough to ask, "What happened?"

"As soon as we left the ground you started panicking so I gave you mom's pills. It should have been enough to knock out a normal person for a few days. Are you sure you're okay?" she asked.

"The feeling is there, but I think I can handle it," David said, frowning at the stale cabin air. "I think that's why Kou is keeping himself separated, so I won't feel his full panic. What's worse is the itch. It's this drive to get back to land."

"That's probably why I didn't have a problem," Takumi whispered. "Reimi is cut off from my mind, so I wouldn't be able to feel her panic even if she did. I do feel the itch though. It peaked a while ago but now it's fading a little."

"We must be getting close to Fukuoka," Rie said. Ahead the monitors changed to a map with a little airplane showing that they were over the ocean. David sighed and sat back, trying not to think about the distance between him and land.

The instant their plane touched down at Fukuoka International Airport, David relaxed in his seat. Around him, the rest of Nakano's second grade chattered about the rest of the trip. Moving an entire grade was such a logistical nightmare that David was surprised they made it onto the plane, let alone all the way to Kyushu.

Fukuoka was at the northern part of the huge island of Kyushu, one of the four main Japanese islands. As they got off the plane, all the students had to squeeze into narrow lines to keep the terminal walkway clear for the bustle of passengers moving between gates. David looked around at the few shops. He could see the security gate in the distance.

'Wow, this is almost as big as Phoenix's airport,' he thought.

'I wouldn't know… but I'm glad we are back on land. I'd prefer never to go through that again,' Kou mumbled as he peeked back into David's mind.

'Well, there's still the return trip.' Kou growled and withdrew again to sulk.

Nakano Junior High's teachers checked the line of students to ensure everyone was present, and to quell bits of restlessness after the flight. In addition to their homeroom teachers, Principal Yogi, three tour guides, and the school nurse were also present. After the rest of the passengers finished debarking, David followed along with everyone else as they wound their way to the baggage claim. They had all packed lightly, but the cold weather necessitated larger bags than they could carry on.

A rumble washed through the female students as they moved past automatic doors and chill wind blew in. It was colder than it had been back on the mainland. Since skirts were still part of their winter uniform, several of the girls started hunting through their bags for extra jackets to wear over their uniforms.

"Glad we don't have to wear skirts too," Naoto murmured.

The boys around him nodded their agreement. They were all warm in their usual black slacks, but with the added warmth of heavy uniform jackets. Unlike their summer uniform, the winter uniform jacket was all black with buttons in the middle and a high flat collar, similar to a naval dress uniform. The girls on the other hand wore their usual blue summer skirts with thick blue shirts and white sailor scarves.

Once everyone made it outside, their flag toting tour guides headed down a set of stairs to the subway. Their teachers watched as everyone gathered around the automatic ticket machines. Though his abilities allowed him to read Japanese, it was the first time David had ever attempted to buy his own train ticket.

"Come here," Rie pulled at the corner of his sleeve. "You look just like the first time you got off the plane from America."

"Sorry, those route maps were not made to be easily understood," he replied. "Who designed this thing anyway? There are a million buttons. Besides, I never rode trains back in the States." With Naoto telling everyone nearby about David's dilemma, Rie helped him sort through the process before the class moved on without him.

While waiting for the train, students and teachers took pictures for the school album and for the projects they would all have to do on their return. Then, to make sure everyone got on, each class lined up in front of a mark on the ground denoting where the doors would open. When their train came, David hurried on with the twins and Natsuki.

Just as the doors shut, David caught a glimpse of something out the doors. Rie too, looked at the same place, and then turned her gaze on him. He shook his head as the train picked up speed. Whatever he had seen disappeared as advertisements outside the windows began blurring into a stream of bright color.

"I can't wait to get to the hotel. It is supposed to be really nice," Natsuki said.

"Yeah, it's too bad we had to go to school this morning, then spend the afternoon traveling. It's like we're losing a whole day!" Naoto complained.

Not long after, the students got off and found their way up to the ground level. Tantalizing smells from a bakery hit them as they left the escalator. David caught several of his classmates moving toward a shop across the way before the guides were able to herd them to the exit. When they emerged, they were in front of a busy intersection with the Miyako Hotel across the street.

Once in the hotel they began the first of several planned ceremonies. Each one was well marked in the schedule booklet that every student had to carry. There were so many people they ringed the wide balcony on the upper level of the lobby. Mizuki stepped forward as the first designated representative, said a few words on behalf of the rest of the students, and bowed. The hotel manager then gave a speech about the hotel, asking the students to be mindful of the other guests.

'This is the kind of thing I could expect on any school trip, except everyone's so quiet. It's so formal,' David thought.

'*This otherness you feel, it is similar to what we feel near the ocean... but so much weaker.*' With the ceremony done, the students broke up by class. David continued his inner conversation with Kou as he met up with Takumi. Moriyama-sensei handed out keys and arranged David's class into rooms.

David, Takumi, Naoto, and Shou were all crammed into a small but well-appointed room. Teachers were interspersed along the hallway, with the girls separated into their own rooms. Once everyone settled, each class met to go over the next day's schedule.

'This is nothing like school trips back home. I can't believe we are staying in such a nice hotel. And the manager! He accepted having almost a hundred students running around at the same time in stride, like he does it all the time!'

'*He probably does. I seem to have vague memories of various groups of students moving around together from the Zodiac Tiger. I am sure they get school groups through here all winter.*'

That night, Kou dreamt of snow, sucking David into the random firings of the animal part of their shared mind. For the first time, David saw himself standing beside Kou, both forms separate and real. Then darkness reached into their combined dream and he remembered no more.

David and Kou were less than pleased to find Takumi attempting to wake them with his old violent method. It took all of David's will to remind Kou that they could not transform and take a bite out of their well-meaning host-brother.

'Think of what it would do to Reimi,' David thought in his half-asleep muddle.

'*Exactly,*' Kou purred. '*Fresh bird.*'

The feel of his tail twitching under the sheets woke him enough to wrap an iron control around Kou's predatory instincts. He knew he should have avoided bringing up Reimi when Kou was so close to transforming, but with Takumi shaking him awake it was a near thing.

Although they often got up at four at the Matsumoto Estate, David was normally able to rest his body by transforming into Kou at night. With all the students around, David was unable to let Kou take over, which deprived them both of the restoration they normal got from switching bodies. His classmates might freak out if they awoke in the night to see an adolescent tiger prowling their crowded hotel room. With a bit of concentration, David ensured nothing else transformed and the tail was quickly gone.

Frowning, David pulled himself together and followed the others to the top floor for breakfast. The hotel served both Western and Japanese style breakfasts, so he took both pancakes and miso soup. Though Shou gave him an odd look, it was nice to get a taste of home, and the soup helped warm him.

After breakfast and some quick packing, the second years met in the lobby for their farewell ceremony. The class bowed and thanked the manager for their brief stay. David followed Rie as everyone shuffled outside. Their tour guides met them just outside, leading the students to two buses. Smaller than their American counterparts, the buses were just big enough to fit all three classes.

Class 2B split between the two buses. David was able to stay with his group of friends, while most of their not-quite-enemies ended up on the other bus. Mizuki, the class representative, and her cohorts' exclamations of how happy they were to be on the good bus did not die down until the guides shut the door, drowning out their noise.

David felt a pang as they drove through Fukuoka. A large city surrounded by low mountains, it reminded him of the valley back home in Arizona. Phoenix was a place that, according to the Matsumotos, he would never be able to see again. He remembered the pain he had felt when Masato Matsumoto had told him he could never return. He also remembered his slow acceptance. At least his family could visit. Sitting back, he listened to their new bus guide as she talked about Fukuoka and otherwise attempted to keep the students entertained. David's thoughts centered on his family, and the email Jessica had sent just before he left for the trip. She had complained that all she had to look forward to was a trip to Catalina Island in California in the next year. Natsuki's promise to send her souvenirs had barely consoled his little sister.

'I'll have to send a postcard later today,' David reminded himself, settling in for what proved a long, if interesting, bus ride.

The buses stopped once at a small park where the students were able to throw a few snowballs at the members of the other bus, though they were still low and the snow was scarce. The bus guide spoke throughout their ride, talking about various aspects of Kyushu as they drove south. Only Hidemi, Rie's quiet, bookish friend took notes for their guidebooks. David rested, confident in Kou's indelible memory. Eventually, they arrived in Nagasaki.

The buses pulled over long enough for the students to jump out, and the bus guides led them up a set of wide high stairs to a restaurant overlooking a river. There they enjoyed crunchy fried ramen with a thick stew called "chanpon." The restaurant served the food on round turntables so everyone could get to it. Groups of students sat around the large tables enjoying the food and chatting about the rest of the day to come as they watched the boat traffic in the bay below.

After lunch, the students assembled outside again. David gathered with his friends as the second years broke up into four groups, each led by one of the bus or tour guides and a teacher. David scowled as he realized that since they were the smallest class they would be in their own group while the two other classes would be broken into three groups. Together, Class 2B turned a corner and found themselves at the bottom of a hill. Rising before them was a street that looked like the setting for a performance of Charles Dickens' *A Christmas Carol*, complete with a church at the top. David raised his eyebrows in surprise as their guide started talking about how the area had been one of the first to open to foreigners.

As they walked, David realized that most of the buildings housed touristy stores. A little old lady managed to attract a few of his classmates as she tried to sell odd trinkets and jewelry. Laughing David was reminded of Sedona, a little tourist town in northern Arizona. Sedona had the exact same mix of old buildings and peddlers.

'I guess some things are truly cross-cultural,' David thought as Moriyama ushered Shou and Tsubasa away from the old lady.

The group spent the next hour walking around a place called Glover Garden. A collection of old merchant buildings from the 1800's, it was unimpressive to David who had seen old style buildings with their tall thin doors before. For the rest of his classmates, however, it seemed to be a first. Despite the history around them, David soon found that the girls were mainly interested in hunting down the heart-shaped paving stones hidden around the property. David had never seen his host-brother go quite so still as when Natsuki pulled Rie away to go look for one of the stones.

"What's that all about," David asked as the girls ran away.

"Dreams of love will come true if you touch a stone," Naoto answered, yawning as he looked over a railing to the bay below.

David noticed that in addition to their other groups of classmates a few other schools were out and about the area. It was interesting to see how their school uniforms differed. As he watched, he thought he caught a girl in a gray uniform look at him, but when he turned back for a better look, she was gone. Shrugging, David followed his classmates toward the exit. The girls giggled behind them. The usual animosity between the class representative's group and Natsuki and Rie's friends was overcome by their common interest in the potential power of the heart stones.

On the way back down the hill, Moriyama let the students peek into a few shops. Shou and Naoto appeared before David holding matching black key chains with "I love Badminton," and "I love Track and Feild" respectively. One whole half of the store seemed devoted to the same design with different sports on everything from shirts to cups. They seemed proud to have found trinkets in English.

"'Track and Field' is spelled wrong," David said, laughing. Naoto shrugged and smiled, heading off to pay at a register. David's two friends had a kind of war going to see who could fit the most key chains and phone straps on their pencil cases.

As the rest of his group looked through the stores, David found he was alone outside a cake shop. Turning, he nearly ran into a short Japanese woman holding a tray of cakes. She had moved so close to him without his noticing that the shock nearly made him summon his Seikaku. His heart racing, he covered his shock with a polite bow and moved away. The woman moved with him.

"Listen but do not react," the woman said. David peered down at her, unsure if he should head for Moriyama-sensei. Something about the woman seemed off.

'She is standing too straight, too serious for a cake seller who has to bend over a register all day,' Kou warned.

David slid his foot behind him, moving into a fighting stance.

"No need for that. I'm from a mutual friend. Continue your watch. We have reports that Chul Soon may be on Kyushu. He was your classmate. He knows about your school trip. Some of us think he may try to attack while you're away from the Estate."

"Wait who are you? How do you know about…"

"David," Moriyama called. David's teacher was at the bottom of the drive, the rest of his classmates around him and ready to go. David looked back, but the woman was gone. With a shiver, he headed after his group.

Class 2B spent the next hour walking the streets of Nagasaki. They peered past restaurants and walked through what looked to David like a Chinatown. Moriyama and their tour guide led them across a small channel and through a gate with a sign proclaiming they were entering Dejima Island. The whole way he felt watched. His skin crawled. The cake lady had unnerved him.

David and his classmates wandered through the reconstructed Dutch buildings of Dejima. Much of it was like a museum but there were enough hands-on activities to keep them interested. They even found a spot where they could play with old-fashioned badminton paddles made of wood and leather. As they walked, Takumi took pictures with one of the school cameras. As he stopped to snap a picture of an old school room, David scanned the rest of the tourists, hoping and fearing he might spot Chul Soon. Instead, he spotted a few of the gray uniformed students he had seen earlier in the day.

"Where do you think they're from?" Kenta asked from beside David and Takumi. Tall and beefy, the fourteen year old often went over-looked by David and his friends. Though he had seen him often enough in the library, David had rarely talked to the student council member, assuming he was one of Mizuki's friends.

"They're from Okinawa," Tsubasa answered. Tsubasa seemed like the least likely person to befriend Kenta. He was much, much shorter, and so thin he looked to be almost bone. David smiled. He knew Tsubasa from the badminton team. Although he was at a disadvantage due to his height, he was quick. His passive face watched everything with intelligence, be it on the court or in class. Kenta's raised eyebrow was enough to get Tsubasa to continue. "I was looking at the hand generator display and a group of them came in. I guess one of them was into technology too and we got to talking. They're doing almost the exact same trip we are. I wouldn't be surprised if we see them a couple more times."

David shrugged, but before he could turn away, Kenta spoke up, saying, "Do you two want to come with us? I saw a big cannon around the corner and it looks like the rest of your group wandered off."

Looking around, David realized the others were gone.

"Sure," David said. Together the four walked off to find the old cannon, David alert for any sign of his enemy. Kou prompted him to speak so their observant classmates would not notice his search. "So why are you on the student council too, if all you're interested in is the technology club?"

"Because people asked me to. Not everyone wanted Mizuki, and even those that did decided it might be better if she wasn't the only voice for our class," Kenta said with a laugh. They spent about half an hour exploring the various paths, models, and rooms before they found the rest of the class. An enthusiastic guide had pulled them into a presentation on the second floor of one of the buildings.

Since time was limited, Class 2B stopped for lunch at a convenience store and took one of the local streetcars to their next stop. David just had enough time to choke down a tuna sandwich outside the museum's entrance. The other groups seemed to have spent their time more efficiently, and had already eaten by the time 2B arrived with their shopping bags.

Inside the Nagasaki Bomb Museum, David wandered through the exhibits with Kenta, Tsubasa, and his friends. The instant they passed the ticket counters, David felt out of place. The old style clock near the entrance, stopped at the instant the bomb went off, sent a chill through him that stayed past the strikingly lit ruins and twisting towers of steel. There was an aura to the place. It spoke to a part of him he had never been aware of before. Each piece in the bomb museum evoked a deep sense of sadness and loss. Despite the burnt lunch boxes, human hand fused to stone, and other horrible things, the tone was not anger, but instead a will to show the price paid in war. David felt the importance of ensuring such weapons are never again used.

As they wandered through the museum, their group began spreading out as his friends moved to different exhibits. David followed the sound of someone speaking English and shivered as he entered a room with low benches and videos of survivors telling their stories.

"It's like there are ghosts telling us their stories," Kenta whispered as he left the remaining group to watch one of the videos. Beside him, Takumi tensed as David moved toward the corner of the room. Like David, he could see that it was not just the old-timers' stories that made it feel like there was someone else there. In the corner they were approaching, a young man, almost transparent, stood looking through a wall, a sad expression on his face.

The obake looked up at them as they came closer but made no move to attack. With a jerk of his chin, the obake gestured to a video of an old man talking about his lost comrades.

"Don't forget what you saw here," the obake's wilting voice said in English, his tone pleading for someone to hear him.

"I won't," David whispered. With a sudden look of surprise, the obake turned its long gaze on David. The apparition stared back with a curious look, as his western features grew ever more defined. Then with a solemn nod, the apparition disappeared, just as the obake that had attacked Natsuki had disappeared when David pierced it with his Seikaku.

"What did he say? I didn't catch the English," Tsubasa asked, cutting off Takumi before he could ask the same thing. Together David and Takumi turned on their lone classmate.

NAGASAKI GHOSTS AND KASTELLA CAKE

Such a large part wanted to give in. I guess that is why I was so unhappy. Spending every minute in struggle is taxing. Every second was a test straining nature against desire. It was easier to let myself be carried away by instinct, but every hour I refrained was proof of the possibility. Still, I always chose to succumb. The constant anger aimed at myself then, was because deep down, I knew all I truly had to do was make a different choice…

It was harder than David thought it would be to find a secluded place in the museum. It took five minutes of prowling the first floor before they found an alcove isolated enough to pull Tsubasa aside.

"You can see ghosts?" Takumi hissed once they were alone.

"Sure, I've been able to see them for months. Apparently, you can too. How come? I figured it out by accident," Tsubasa said. He turned the same curious stare he always had while researching motors, gadgets, and computers in the school library on David. "What did the obake say before he disappeared?"

"You'd better go first," David said, reminded that he was supposed to keep everything to do with samurai and spirits secret. Tsubasa just stared back. "Fine, the obake asked us not to forget what we saw here. He must be the one who died while standing before the window. His friend was standing right next to him yet he survived. The ghost wanted to make sure someone would remember what his friend said in his video message."

Tsubasa stared back at them as if expecting more of an explanation, but shrugged his shoulders. David might have sighed in relief but something about the boy's look said he had not given up on getting answers.

"You know I'm in the electronics club right? Well we are always building stuff, playing with circuits. Well a year ago Kenta and I decided to try to make x-ray glasses. You know, kids' stuff. We ended up with a kind of mirror that had an electrical current running through it. I had it at home, and when I looked in the mirror, I caught a glimpse of an old man. When I looked up, my grandfather was standing right there." Tsubasa turned and gestured as if his grandfather would show up right next to them all. "He had died about a year before that, so it scared me, but three times since I have seen ghosts, and even talked to them. Kenta didn't believe me, but we still worked on it together. I guess once you see one, you can see them all. So what about you two?"

"Ah, well I've always been able to see them," David said. "Takumi too, I think the one in here had been waiting for someone to hear him. He must have been satisfied when I acknowledged him. You should be careful though. Not all the ghosts you meet are nice."

Tsubasa's stare told them he remained unconvinced. David sought for something to say that might ensure their classmate would keep quiet, but the rest of their class began walking up the long curving exit ramp. Tsubasa followed David's gaze to the giant cruise missile hanging from the center of the room, then shrugged, and headed off after the others. With the Matsumoto secrets somewhat safe for the time being, David and Takumi followed behind.

'It's a good thing Natsu wasn't with us,' David thought once they were outside the museum and following their guides through a series of parks. 'She still freaks out when she sees Ryohei. She wouldn't have liked the obake in there.'

'*Definitely. I think we should convince Tsubasa to let us borrow his mirror though. The other Matsumotos could benefit from being able to see Ryohei and other ghosts,*' Kou replied within David's mind. He had kept quiet since the plane ride, but David could tell the young tiger was getting restless. They had both grown used to being able to transform every night. David missed the feeling of wind through his fur, and the increased senses were addictive. As they walked, Natsuki and Rie fell into step alongside them.

'*You don't have fur. All you have is that peach fuzz you call hair.*'

'Dude, not cool. You have fur, and when we're a tiger, I can feel it just the same as if I did have fur.'

The second years walked through a large park with several statues that their tour guides explained, and then viewed a bit of ground from the explosion excavated and preserved behind thick glass. David focused so much on trying to read every movement Tsubasa made that he missed most of the scenery. As they walked past a stand of trees, David froze as Natsuki, Rie, Takumi, and Tsubasa all stopped at the same instant. He saw Natsuki start to cringe away even as the rest of his classmates walked on, oblivious of whatever had stopped his friends.

David ran ahead. The ground fell away before them as concentric circles focused on a tall monument in the center of a wide clearing. Off to the side, the ruins of a building stood surrounded by grass and paved stones. As the rest of the second years walked down toward the center, listening to their tour guides, David realized what the others had seen before him. Throughout the entire area, there were translucent apparitions milling about in old uniforms and clothing from a different era.

Just ahead, Natsuki's skin had tuned sickly pale with fright. She was just shy of bolting. Beside her, Takumi had closed his eyes in concentration as he focused on not turning into Reimi. When Natsuki had been his partner, Kou had transformed to comfort her whenever she had become distraught. As her new partner, Reimi would want to do the same, though having Takumi transform into a phoenix would be horrific for their covers as normal students. David stepped forward warily.

"Don't worry, we will keep you safe," David whispered from behind them. "They aren't here to hurt you. Look, they are all just sad. I think they just want someone to recognize they were here, and not forget. Stick close to Takumi. Things will be fine."

About halfway down the path, Tsubasa turned, his gaze sweeping the area everyone else would have thought vacant. When he turned past the girls, his casual eyes took on a knowing look. David was thankful his observant classmate did not wait to ask more questions, but instead followed the other students. Below, Moriyama gestured for them to hurry as the class lined up for a picture.

Before they could move, a little girl in an old-fashioned kimono appeared before them. She was small, cute, and as transparent at a light breeze. David hid a smile as Natsuki attached herself to Takumi's arm in fear.

"Will you remember me?" the little girl asked in a barely perceptible voice, her words laced with sadness fostered by years of unanswered questions.

David noticed a tear glisten in Natsuki's eye, and she nodded. With a radiant smile, the little girl danced away on the wind, disappearing among the trees. Although there were still many other obake about, Natsuki relaxed a little.

Realizing what she was doing, Natsuki extricated herself from Takumi's arm. They made it to the center of the clearing for a picture before the epicenter monument without any of the other obake stopping them. Their guides soon led them out of the area.

The incident rattled David. It reminded him that this school trip could turn from a string of fun new experience to something far more dangerous if Chul Soon or one of his allies showed up. Resolved to be more vigilant, he continued walking with his classmates.

A short distance from the clearing, their guide led them up a long flight of stairs that ended before a fountain. A tall bronze statue rose in the distance, taller than the cascading water. Past the fountain, they walked through more ruins, statues, and monuments, closing on the giant statue of a man sitting, one hand raised to the sky, pointing with two fingers. As they approached the statue, David saw the same gray uniformed students he had seen throughout the tour, ten of them, standing before the statue as a photographer took their photos.

"That's not a very big class," Rie said.

"They're from a small island way east of Okinawa," Kenta replied from Tsubasa's side as the class lined up.

Mizuki stepped forward to read a speech, and then led the class in bowing before the statue to pay their respects to those who had died. Once the ceremony was complete, their teachers and a grizzled cameraman arranged them by class before the statue so that he could take their picture. As they jostled into position, David noticed one of the gray uniformed girls staring at him. Instead of disappearing when he looked, she held his gaze. With long black hair, almond eyes, and an intense expression she was both beautiful and somehow different at the same time. Before he knew it, the camera flashed and she was gone.

'Great, I'm going to be staring off into space on the photo,' David thought as they finished. A few classmates away, he caught Rie give him a look that made him feel oddly guilty. 'She must have seen me staring.'

'*Of course she did,*' growled Kou. His inner tiger provided mental images of Rie's curious glance. It was as if Kou was his personal TiVo, playing back every twitch of her features in exacting detail. Despite her neutral features, thanks to Kou David saw the muscle movements that marked her emotions shift from concern, to surprise, and then annoyance.

Rie left him alone as their teachers herded them en masse to the waiting buses. During the hour ride, David thought about the intriguing girl and wondered why she had stared at him with such intensity. It took a little persuasion, but as he had with Rie's reaction, Kou recalled the strange girl's face for him. The memory evoked a strange sensation in him, and he puzzled at it as the bus pulled away from an underground parking lot.

Later, their tour buses pulled off a scenic coastal road to the Kastella Cake Factory so they could shop for souvenirs.

"Kastella is supposed to be really good," Takumi said from the seat beside him. "I hope they let us taste-test."

"Let's go find out," David replied, sure they'd be safe enough in the rural tourist trap.

Inside there was a whole range of snacks and novelties from Nagasaki prefecture. Most items were individually wrapped snacks, a convenient way to buy for a group. Their teachers and tour guides followed a Kastella worker into a back room, leaving the students to browse and buy on their own.

"The teachers get samples and coffee," Rie said as she and Natsuki appeared next to David. "Come on. Let's go find something for mom and dad."

Together, they tried the different varieties, all of them delicious, even when they strayed from the more ordinary flavors. With Takumi, they picked a few cakes while Natsuki bought her own for her parents and friends.

"Ryohei is going to be seriously frustrated," David whispered as they sampled a lime cake. The family's ghost always looked on with a sense of loss when they ate in his presence.

"So lime or honey for the badminton team," Natsuki asked coming over with two medium sized boxes. Rie turned to consult with her, and David returned to trying the various mini-squares of cake.

David rolled his eyes as Naoto walked by, his cheeks stuffed with cake. The gesture was lost on his classmate so he headed over to join Takumi as he followed Natsuki and Rie through a section of crafts.

"You're not going to buy that, are you?" Mizuki asked from the next aisle over in a casually cruel tone. David peered around his host-brother and saw Hidemi holding a small fox. The quick look of anger that shot across the calm demeanor of his classmate shocked him. Kou played back the exchange for him again. She had indeed been at least interested in the little statue. Ahead, Natsuki started yelling at Mizuki for making fun of Hidemi. They got so loud, so fast, that Takumi had to drag Natsuki outside so that the shop employees would not kick them out.

David selected and paid for two items for his sister and dad, since food would not survive the post, and then hurried after his friends. Outside, David saw Natsuki's temper was fading as she talked with Takumi a bit away from the buses. David started walking over, but the look on Takumi's face made a half-formed thought whole. David covered his shock by turning and walking to the end of the lot, where a fenced observation point overlooked the sea. Kou purred as the sun began to fall below the horizon.

'You finally put together all that tension between them. We've known for a while that they like each other.'

'But it's more than that isn't it? Takumi does like her. All their awkwardness... We should get them to date.'

'And you think you won't still be stuck in the middle?' As they pondered the issue of Takumi and Natsuki, David felt Kou's animal instincts strain against their prolonged need to stay human. They had to fight to remain in human form as their instincts drove them to transform and run free as a tiger.

"Snap out of it. Your eyes are orange," Rie whispered from beside him. "Sure, someone might just think it's a trick of the light but you can't transform with the whole class around you."

"Thanks," David said with a smile and a wink. "We needed a distraction."

"Oh, you mean aside from your new Okinawan friend?" Rie asked with a quiet voice. Before he could answer, she turned, leaving him alone above the sea. He turned to call her, but felt a tug on his collar. In an instant, he was over the railing, falling toward the rocks beneath.

"Stupid owl statue," David grumbled as their bus rode up a mountain road. Both buses of students had watched as Moriyama scolded him for playing on the railing. His uniform was full of dust and two rips. The little statue he had bought for Jessica had somehow scrambled up his back and tried to pull him to his death. It took more than a miniature owl to kill him, though from its screeches of 'Die! Human, Die!' he was sure it thought it had the upper hand. Still, he had to summon his Seikaku and smash the crazy little bird, no easy task among the pillars supporting the overlook where his classmates had been.

By the time he had destroyed the possessed souvenir, Moriyama had already started a search for him. Ashamed at the surprise attack, and angry at having to pretend he had lost his balance, he sulked all the way through their entry ceremony at the next hotel.

Unlike the last hotel, this one had an open tatami mat area like the flooring in the Matsumoto Estate. Instead of beds, there was a futon in the closet for each student. Like large quilts, the futons were little more than a layer of padding over the firm rush mats beneath. Since none of the rooms had their own showers, everyone had half an hour scheduled just for bathing at the community baths before dinner.

"There's only the public bath here," Daiki said after David failed to find more than a toilet in their room. He had new roommates this time, and they all looked like they would have preferred a non-dusty roommate. "Umm. You'll want to make sure you shower off well before you get in."

"I'm looking forward to it. The hot springs baths are supposed to have healing properties from the minerals in the water," Kenta added.

David had grown accustomed to the Japanese style of bathing while living with the Matsumotos. He was fine with showering outside the tub, then sitting in the warm relaxing water. It was nice after his long training sessions with the Matsumotos. The Plateau Hotel's bath, however, was a bit of a shock.

There were two giant baths for the men and women, separated in different rooms. A long row of showerheads was against one wall complete with stools and soap so that each person could shower before going over into the pool-size hot tub. Although more than a little embarrassed, David soon realized that his other classmates ignored everything else around them, and that it was his western upbringing that made the experience awkward. Thick steaming fog made the whole process easier and the hot water was relaxing after the long day walking Nagasaki's streets.

'Let's just hope kappa don't live in hot springs. I so don't need to fight an invisible water spirit while naked.' For once, Kou agreed.

五

AMUSEMENTS
AND HISTORY

*Of course, this time I made the wrong choice... again. I told
myself I was pressured into it, but like most things we tell
ourselves... Well, with a plan outlined, part of me was excited
for the hunt. I could not help thinking there might still be a
chance, if I could just get rid of him...*

Although David had expected his classmates to stay up late
into the night, chatting or trying to sneak out, it never happened. Sure, they talked for a bit, but after the busy day they
had and with an even heavier schedule planned for the next
day, they were all asleep just after the scheduled ten-thirty.
Without being able to recuperate in their tiger form, David was
having unfortunate flashbacks to the constant exhaustion of
his first months of training. After scribbling out a postcard for
Jessica and his father, and then redoing them in English, David
drifted off to sleep.

The next morning, the students ate a large Japanese style
breakfast with miso soup, rice, fish, and several local side
dishes. They had another quick ceremony in the hotel's lobby,
and then were out the door and on the bus. David was able to
secure the very back seat with Takumi. Since Natsuki and Rie
were just in front, David took the time to tell Takumi about the

woman's warning and the owl attack. He almost stopped when his host-brother started laughing.

"What should we do? Maybe I should sneak off and try to lure Chul Soon out, if he is really here."

"If he is on Kyushu," Takumi whispered, "he'll come for us. If you leave, Reimi and I won't be able to keep the rest of our classmates safe. I know you want to go hunt him, but we can't put the rest of our class at risk."

They discussed other options, but soon their buses pulled onto a large ferry. As they crossed the loading ramp, David felt a heavy sense of unease descend upon him. It was not as bad as the flight, but he could see the ferry was still connected to the port. As he fought the roiling tension from Kou, their tour guides ushered them out of the bus and up toward the passenger areas. While they exited, Moriyama handed out packets of stale shrimp flavored snacks. Their use became clear once they were on the upper levels. Seagulls darted around the boat catching the snacks mid-air.

David remained inside as his classmates braved the cold to feed the gulls. Sure enough, as soon as the boat began pulling away, the tension shifted within him to an instant panic. It took a long time for Kou to withdraw, but David was able to recover enough to walk outside and join his classmates about halfway through the trip. On the weather decks, students and other passengers threw the shrimp snacks and in return, the birds twirled and dove through the air after them. The more adventurous birds would even fly in and pluck the snacks right from the screaming students' hands. David watched in amusement, and handed his own packet off to Naoto, who was trying to lure the birds onto Shou's head. Then he saw Takumi.

His host-brother stood alone and away from the other students. His face was pale as he followed the birds. As David got closer, he realized Takumi's strange appearance was not just from the intensity with which he looked at the other birds but that his eyes were a darker gray than the water running by swiftly below them. Startled, David realized that Reimi was very close to breaking through.

'She must be able to sense the other birds around her.' Kou's lack of reply struck David, but he managed to turn his attention back to Takumi.

Although there was no mental connection between boy and bird, Takumi and Reimi could still sense the world around them while in the other form. Even if they were unable to access each other's senses or talk, they could still see the world through the filter of their separate existences. Takumi had trouble describing it, and since David and Kou were connected, they did not have to worry about out of body experiences when they changed. Still, David could tell that Reimi wanted to transform and join the darting birds. Takumi's hands were turning bright white with the pressure he was exerting on the boat's guardrail. David checked to ensure no one was watching them, and then made a quick decision.

"Go around the corner and change. I'll cover for you and hide your clothes," David whispered.

With a look of great relief and gratitude, Takumi popped around the corner. David knew they were taking a chance, but he also knew that if the pressure Reimi was exerting on Takumi was half what Kou could do, then it was better to let them fly. As soon as David turned, he saw Reimi, the small gray phoenix. She looked up at him with wide deep eyes, the color bright red as if flames smoldered within.

"I know it's been awhile since you've been able to fly, but be careful please! And no showing off. There are a lot of cameras over there. Make sure you're back so Takumi can get changed," David whispered. Anyone watching might have thought David had gone insane talking to a bird, but David knew Reimi was more intelligent than anyone but Kou.

"It's not my fault you two are on this trip. If you had stayed home I could have done my regular flying," Reimi said sweetly, blinking her fiery red eyes.

"You are so much like Natsuki," he replied, exasperated. "You'd better take off before she finds us. She's going to be pissed."

With another blink and shuffle of sleek feathers, Reimi opened her gray wings and hopped up onto the railing. She swayed for a second before tilting forward toward the water. Her wings caught and she rose high into the air on the turbulence behind the boat. David smiled, and then hid Takumi's clothes behind a bench. Walking back around the corner he ran right into Natsuki.

"Where is he, she?" asked Natsuki in a harsh whisper. Rie just behind her. David glanced back and up.

"Reimi couldn't let the seagulls have all the fun," he said, deciding to enjoy his decision, rather than worry over it. As if accentuating his point a gray blur swooped in among the white birds and snatched a snack from a Mizuki's hand. She screamed and backed all the way into the boat's interior.

"At least there's no fire," Rie said.

Natsuki looked as if she was going to burst, then let out a loud laugh and sat on the bench to watch Reimi fly. Rie sat beside her, an odd expression on her face.

"How come you're not mad? You always got mad at me when Kou summoned you without warning," David whispered, curious and more than a little annoyed.

"It's different with us," she said.

After a few more dives, spins, and other aerial stunts, Reimi tilted her wings and curved around behind the boat. She landed awkwardly on the railing, and then hopped down onto Natsuki's lap. The little bird seemed to smile, her eyes blazing white-hot for just an instant.

"That was fun, thank you Natsuki. I am sure Takumi is a nervous wreck. Tell him not to worry. Also, thank him for the chance to spread my wings a little. It's the first time I've been able to fly over water, pretty scary!" the phoenix said in her haunting voice.

After nuzzling Natsuki one last time, she hopped over to David, allowing him to take her and Takumi's clothes to a nearby restroom. A few minutes later, Takumi emerged and they were able to join their classmates unobserved.

With the ferry approaching its destination, the second years threw the last of their bait over the side to the still swooping birds.

Less than half an hour after leaving the ferry behind, their two buses pulled into a giant parking lot and stopped next to a line of similar tour buses. Beyond the lot, brightly colored walls and towers failed to conceal the rollercoasters of every type stretching into the sky.

Despite the other tour buses, there was almost no one in sight as the students made their way into Greenland Amusement Park's first promenade. It was as if the park had cleared out the whole place just for Nakano Junior High's use. After receiving tickets for lunch, their teachers released the students to go and have fun, with a strict return time.

After a quick ride on a free leg coaster, David surveyed the rides, stalls, and people around them. The park was not as empty as it had first seemed. Here and there, other uniformed students ran around in small groups. David even spotted a few gray uniforms among the more common blue and white.

'Seems like the Okinawa kids are here too,' he thought to himself.

'*You're going to be left behind. The rest of your friends are almost to that other metal contraption you call fun,*' Kou answered, prompting David to run off toward a ride called the Corkscrew.

'Welcome back.'

As they went through the rides and attractions, everything from huge coasters to gondola rides and archery, David saw more and more of the gray uniforms. Everything was fun enough, though some of the rides were difficult for him to fit into since he was so much taller than most of his other classmates. The thrill of dives and spins paled against his memories of the fight in the warehouse and the other dangers he had faced.

'It's the same prey- I mean kids that are following you. They change up between getting to the rides before or after us but they are following.'

'Could it be Chul Soon?' David asked as he tried to catch the other students' faces. The operator opened the door then and they were ushered into another giant spinning wheel.

By unspoken consent, David's group decided to wait for lunch until just before it was time to leave, that way they could get as much done as possible before they left. After a particularly rickety old wooden rollercoaster, Rie sidled up to David.

"This is so much fun!" she said, her face flushed with excitement. "It's my first time on rollercoasters. Guess what? I heard Mizuki got so scared after the first one she refused to go on any others. So much for the Class Representative!"

"You know, I had forgotten," David said smiling. "I used to be afraid of rollercoasters. I never went on them until a few years ago. We went to a place by my house for my birthday, and since I was the birthday boy, they dragged me onto the biggest coaster there. It scared the hell out of me, but it was also exhilarating. I guess after what we've been through anything they can throw at us here is pretty tame."

"I can almost imagine the old David sitting scared in a cart before it plummets," Rie said wryly. "I guess he really is gone isn't he? That's okay though. I like the new you. And so do a few other people."

Turning David saw a group of girls from another class eyeing him and giggling as they pretended to examine a game. One of the girls turned away from the rest and walked over.

"Picture time!" she said in enthusiastic, if muddled English. David was jammed in a small kiosk with the group as they maneuvered him around. Kou growled within as the flash stung their human eyes, and David had to concentrate to ensure they did not transform. Then with more giggles, they pushed him out of the booth. They let him stumble away and rejoin his own group as they concentrated on digitally editing the prints and adding cute graphics before they were printed. Kou's growl shifted from annoyance to amusement.

'Now you are going to have your picture stuck on a bunch of girls' pencil cases, complete with little hearts and all their eyes enhanced to look like yours.'

With his own growl at Kou, David rejoined the others. Naoto looked at him but said nothing.

'If I didn't know better I'd say he was jealous!' David thought.

"Ha! You got snatched by the pikura girls," Tsubasa said with a smile. "Maybe we can lose them in the maze."

The wiry boy turned toward a two-story building that looked as if there had been at least an attempt at making it look scary. With his tracking and martial arts training, David was confident the indoor maze would be easy enough.

Inside the building was an interesting explosion of glow-in-the-dark colors. Every few meters, there was another set of doors and a quiz question. While it was entertaining for the group to watch whoever answered the question wrong to try to open a locked door, the path led them in a relatively straight line at first.

The second floor was a different matter. Darker than below, it was more like an old bomb shelter with twists, turns, and a low ceiling. David hung back, allowing the girls to take the lead, as they seemed the most excited by the maze. Just as David was losing interest, a strong hand grabbed at his black uniform jacket and pulled him away from his group.

Twirling and on the edge of summoning his Seikaku, David found himself face to face with the beautiful young girl he had seen the previous day. Her gray uniform seemed to blend with the low lighting and dark walls. A shadow was across her face but her bright eyes shown out like lanterns. They were in a small space, inside a divider accessed by a gap between it and a wall. He was surprised to note some kind of perfume on her that, while he could not describe, was intoxicating.

"Uh, hi," David said, while he gulped in breaths of air in an attempt to steady his racing heart and Kou's fighting instincts.

"I've been watching you. You're different from most of your other classmates, and not just because you're a gaijin." Leaning in, her voice became a bare whisper. David froze. She was so close in the small space. "I need your help. Someone is after me. Someone that I think you could handle." Her hand brushed against his side.

'Chul Soon.'

"David?" Rie called from out in the maze. Before he realized what was happening, David was back out in the maze just in time to catch Rie walking around a fake wall. "Come on, everyone is already outside, where were you?"

"I, uh, I guess I got lost," he replied, glancing back. He saw the barest flicker of gray as the mysterious girl disappeared. Rie studied him.

"Either you're lying or you're an idiot. I'm not sure which I'd prefer," she said, turning for the exit.

Outside the maze, the rest of their group was trying their hand at a hammer bell while they waited for him. With only twenty minutes to go before they had to leave, the students headed toward the entrance for lunch. David tried to spot the Okinawan students, but even Kou failed to find them. With everyone fed and the last stragglers accounted for, they took one last picture before a giant superhero statue and headed out.

As everyone on the bus began discussing the virtues of the various attractions, David pondered the strange girl's words. Kou replayed the memory of their encounter as they rode through the Kyushu countryside. The bus took them through towns, farms, and mountains as they made their way south and east. The rice fields gave way to buildings and the Nakano students were suddenly in the midst of another large city. Beside him, Naoto pointed to the outer walls of an ancient Japanese castle through gaps in the tall buildings around them.

The Nakano Junior High School tour buses pulled into yet another parking lot behind a long line of other buses. Unlike at the amusement park, there were people and tourists everywhere. From the parking lot, a large expanse of grass and a dike spread out before them. As David got off the bus, he saw the tall walls, first of stone, then wood, that formed a square around the double-towered keep beyond. The walls looked as if they could have been larger versions of the ones at the Matsumoto Estate, only newer.

"For the arrows," Tsubasa said as David stared. "The holes in the wood are so the defenders can still shoot."

"I wonder if the Matsumoto Estate ever had them," David whispered to Takumi. His host-brother tilted his head in the Japanese form of a shrug.

As David's attention returned to Kumamoto Castle, he felt Kou awaken within him. It was the same feeling he had gotten when they had seen a portion of the Zodiac Tiger's memory in Kyoto. His vision blurred and the parking lot disappeared. Thick smoke obscured the keep. His perspective had also changed, he was lower to the ground, and his senses fed so much information to his mind that he had trouble understanding the flood.

As he slinked forward on his four powerful legs, men in old leather and wood armor ran past him. Approaching the walls, David saw a group of scared but determined men rushed out of one of the gates to meet the samurai. These new men had dark blue uniforms and guns instead of swords and arrows. The men knelt, their rifles shaking as the samurai rushed them. There was a flash of muzzle fire and the line of samurai broke. Another force galloped from the trees to join the riflemen. Among their horses was a cart of supplies. Together the two forces fought their way back to the high inner walls. Where no one had been an instant before, an older man in richly adorned military suit stood. He bowed.

'They do not realize who they follow,' the old man said. His voice was tired. 'I have been unable to lure the yūrei out. Fighting a war, I did not want to fight, just because one monster has found high walls behind which to hide. I have sent letters, but the new government does not understand the true history of Japan yet. There is no room for my kind of warrior anymore, no room for the Jitsugen Samurai.'

'*Do not despair young warrior,*' came the deep, growling, and powerful voice David had heard only once before. Just as when Kou spoke in tiger form, David heard the words as if they were from himself. Yet this was not Kou's voice, it was older and more powerful. '*Together you and I shall go defeat this abomination. Then you may relax, reassured that another will come if your suspicions about who is behind this are true.*'

David was struck by the desire to call out to the old man, but he disappeared. Before him, a large black-haired stallion looked down with deep, intelligent eyes before his perspective shifted back toward the castle. Together the two animals surged forward. They ran past men of both sides unopposed. Finding their way through high twisting walls, his enhanced vision took in the rifles pointing through slits all along the way. The horse and golden tiger somehow made it unscathed to the giant keep. Already several buildings around them were on fire, but the main structure was intact. Imperial Guards were everywhere, sorting through the new supplies and helping the injured from the recent sortie. David wanted to turn from the arrow and sword wounds, but his body took in the sights with sickening clarity, the scent of blood straining the tiger's restraint.

The horse and tiger did not stop until they were at the top of the highest tower, a feat given the steep staircases. There, in a room that overlooked the siege below, stood an unassuming man. As the horse reached the floor, the man turned. His skin was translucent and his eyes were dark orbs. David remembered the way Rie had looked after her possession, his stomach twisting at the memory. The yūrei smiled wickedly, its lips a vicious curve of ripped flesh. Taking a sword from a dead guard, he attacked.

By the time the yūrei had made it across the room, the horse was gone and an old man was standing in his place. A bright sword, a Seikaku, was in his hands. The battle was fierce. David had been studying swordplay for months. He had seen Masao Matsumoto wield the blade faster than he could follow, yet here was something so beyond that it was inconceivable. Both moved with inhuman speed. But even as they fought, the memory began to fade from David's mind.

Blinking, David was back where he had been before the vision. Kou purred loudly within his mind, yet nothing else seemed to have changed. With a frown at the Zodiac memory, he followed Rie toward the same walls Kou's predecessor had entered with the old man.

Inside, little was recognizable from the memory. The wooden structures were new, rebuilt after fire, and modern souvenir shops and museums replaced old battlements. As they approached the keep, their tour guide talked about the hundred wells, the history of the place, and local legends. He smiled to himself when they spoke of the siege during the Satsuma Rebellion and the destruction of the keep from fire.

'The old horse, he must have been Saigou Takamori, the leader of the Satsuma Rebellion. They arrested him, so he likely defeated the yūrei and lived. I wonder if their duel is what really destroyed the old keep,' Kou thought.

After walking through a wide tunnel with thick wooden support beams, they exited into an open space before the main keep. There, each class once again lined up for a group photograph. This time, David did not see the Okinawan girl.

'If only our classmates could see our Tiger Armor. It's so much cooler than the plastic those guys are wearing.'

'If you had reason to wear your Tiger Armor then we would both be in trouble, wouldn't we,' Kou replied, chuckling a little within David's mind.

'We might need it if Chul Soon shows up.' That thought killed their mood as they moved toward the keep.

It was an interesting exercise, David thought, walking up the narrow steps and among the exhibits within the keep. The whole interior of the castle had been converted into a museum. As he wandered, David compared the pictures, relics, and rec-reations to what he had seen in the Zodiac Tiger's memories. Kou helped make the comparisons by calling up specific im-ages from the newly accessible memory. At the top, David met his classmates as they crammed into a narrow space with wide views of the castle grounds and Kumamoto city beyond. With the railings ringing the center staircase, the top floor was no-where close to what he had seen in the vision. Beside him, Nat-suki and Takumi smiled together as they looked out at the walls and turrets below.

Slowly, so as not to draw their attention, David brought his hands to his face. As soon as he had them in focus, David quickly snapped a string of photos with the school's Canon D6. As soon as the first one went off, David could see Takumi begin to turn. Loud, high-speed shots clicked off, and David wondered if his ears had started improving. Before Takumi could register what he had done, David hopped the closest railing and ran down the stairs with a wide smile.

'Let's put some of our hard-earned speed to use.' Kou growled in pleasure.

David and Kou had decided to make it their mission to get Natsuki and Takumi to start dating publicly so that they could move past all the awkwardness. While they obviously cared about each other, Takumi and Natsuki were touchy whenever

David did something that might bring their "relationship" to the attention of the rest of their classmates.

'I don't get why they don't just start dating,' David thought has he weaved between the other museum-goers, Takumi hot on his tail. David cleared the entirety of the stone steps outside only to land before their homeroom teacher. Berating him for running, Moriyama-sensei led him to the giant tree to wait for the rest of the students. David gave Takumi an orange-eyed wink as he handed the camera to Moriyama. The camera was there for the official scrapbook. After viewing a few of the pictures at David's insistence, Moriyama smiled and laughed. Takumi looked murderous, but David was off the hook.

Since they had spent the whole morning on the ferry and at Greenland, the students only had an hour at the castle. As they got back on the bus, Takumi whispered, "I'll make you pay for that."

"Don't worry, it's not like you were kissing or anything. Though you should have. I'm sure she would have liked it," David whispered back. A pained look of embarrassment washed over Takumi's usually stoic features.

'*He can fight ōkami, obake, and oni yet he cannot even consider telling the girl he likes how he feels. You should be careful or he might realize you're putting the attention on him so that he doesn't ask you-*' Kou's thought was cut off as their bus left the castle. Another long ride on their way to the next hotel.

'That's not why I'm doing it. I mean it's not like I have any potential girlfriends or anything. Not that I'd even want one.'

David and Kou continued their internal discussion as their tour guide told them about the areas they passed through. Beside him, Takumi remained deep in thought, while the rest of the bus listened, studied, or played with their friends. For his part, David's thoughts drifted back to the girl in gray.

At the next hotel, there was an actual open-air bath so they had an hour and a half before dinner to work on their homework and bathe. The boys were given the first forty-five minutes, so after stowing their bags they headed back downstairs to shower, then headed out to the huge bath. Unlike before, where the bath was inside, this time they had to run naked through the frigid night air to get to the water. Once they made it in, they found the water barely warmer than the air.

With such a disappointing bath, they were happy to give it up well before their time was up and returned to their rooms to finish their work. Every night they had to turn in their guide books with various questions answered so they could prove they had paid attention and learned something. With the rest of their time, they began to plan their skit for the recreation period on the last day.

As David readied his futon, he made a mental note to get a new souvenir for Jessica. With Kou already fading out, he began to drift off, yet he was not surprised that the strange girl in gray came to mind. He wondered if he would see her again.

六

SKI PATROL

I should have realized it back then. Love can never start with deception and violence. How many before me have gone to battle for love only to find that it was not for another that they fought, but for themselves...

The next morning, Class 2B woke again at six, and the students were soon preparing to leave the hotel. Since there were other students in his room, David was safe from Takumi's promised reprisal, though he was sure it would come eventually.

For their fourth day, the second year Nakano Junior High School students traveled by bus to Oita Prefecture. High in the mountains, they passed snow covered rice paddies and small groups of houses until they arrived at their destination. Thick curtains of fog hid the mountain before them, and the only things they could see past the large building in front of them were the swinging ski lift chairs disappearing into the mist. Although no one had brought snow clothes, inside the warm lobby, attendants directed them to locker rooms, where the students changed into matching outfits, boots, and skis. An attendant guided David to a separate counter where he received a different set. Out of all the students, he was one of three who already knew how to either snowboard or ski. During the planning sessions, David had pulled the gaijin card and

convinced Yukiko to get his teachers to let him go snowboarding instead.

David attempted to fit in and follow Japanese custom, but
as the incident with the camera proved, his attempts were not
always effective. He had begged Yukiko, and she had agreed
to ask his teachers to let him go snowboarding. The twins had
tried to convince her to let them switch as well. Since the class
was only for skiing and they had never gone before, their pleas
had not worked. While David had been far from athletic growing up, he had learned to snowboard while on a trip with his
father's TV station. While he had never gotten past the basics,
he was far more comfortable with the idea of being on one
board than two.

David was careful not to smile as an attendant led him
aside to get his snowboard. Takumi's glare was particularly
epic.

'Takumi usually keeps better control over his emotions.'

*'I wouldn't want to hunt him right now. He still has not forgiven
you for that picture.'*

'Maybe if I wipeout into a tree they'll all feel better,' David
replied as he caught the stares of his other envious classmates.

With many stares following him, David slid over to the lift
with a push from his free foot. He just caught the rest of Class
2B gather around their instructor and begin stretching as he
reached the ski lift line. The last thing he saw as he faded into
the low clouds was a few specks tilting their skis between par-
allel and triangle positions.

It took David one trip down the first half of the mountain
to remember his s-curves. He was delighted at how his hard-
won balance made snowboarding almost easy.

*'Do not become distracted by the snow-slider. We must stay
alert.'*

David acknowledged Kou's concerns, but it was hard not
to slide into a zone where nothing but the speed mattered. As
his body relaxed, the board seemed to move on its own, letting

him navigate around the other skiers and snowboarders. Despite his warnings, Kou purred with excitement as they gained more speed than he had ever achieved before. His second time down, the class was higher on the slopes, so David stopped to watch and help, as some of his classmates were having trouble staying up. He was surprised that even Rie and Takumi were having problems. Even with the same training David had received, they were not prepared to think about balancing on long pieces of fiberglass just to stay upright.

While David helped Kenta re-attach a ski, he saw Rie slip and fall. He moved to catch her, but somehow Hidemi was there first, catching her before Rie could hit the ground. It was an agile move for their class's resident genius, but David caught the bit of her face that was still visible stiffen as she helped Rie back up.

'Rie must have been heavier than she expected,' David thought with a laugh. As soon as he got Kenta's ski back in place, he shifted his weight and slipped away. In order to test the extent of his ability with his board, David took the second lift to the top of the mountain. Although he had never gone down the more treacherous slopes back home, he figured he could handle it, or at least heal fast enough to make it down the mountain without too many problems.

On the lonely ride up, David's mind wandered. Something about Hidemi's expression bugged him. His training with Masao had taught him to analyze the world, to ask questions and seek answers that could explain how things truly were. His interest pulled Kou from the Zodiac Tiger's memories, and together they sought a reason for their interest.

Unbidden the image in his mind shifted from Hidemi. Kou growled. The girl in gray was in David's thoughts so much that Kou was becoming annoyed. No one had ever occupied David's mind quite so much, and what was in David's mind, affected Kou's as well. As David approached the lift drop off, he shrugged aside the errant thoughts and concentrated instead on lifting the front of his board and positioning himself so he would not fall down like fool during the exit.

At the top of the hill, he slid away from the lift to a small area next to a stand of trees. David sat, sinking into a drift of fresh snow. Beside him, the back edge of the mountain tapered away into a wonderland of trees and clean, fresh snow. David reached forward to brush white mush from his quick-lock bindings.

'I'm sorry, okay? You don't have to give me the silent treatment,' David said as he peered through the fog, thinner at the top than it had been lower down.

'We are being watched,' Kou replied. David jerked his foot back out of the binding and joined Kou in re-checking the area.

Sure enough, David spotted a lone figure hiding down the opposite slope of the mountain, away from skiers and prying eyes. Whoever it was wore the same rental outfit that David and the rest of his classmates had received before the lessons. As David studied the figure, he adjusted himself so he could escape down the more populated slope. Seeing David about to leave, the mysterious figure stood, pulled back her hood, and waved at him.

Without stopping to consider any further danger, David tilted the edge of his board around a barrier rope and propelled himself across the slight decline. He slid toward the girl from Okinawa slowly, watching all the while. Soon tall forest trees surrounded him, cutting them off from the top of the mountain. He slid to an easy stop a few feet from the girl and noticed she was shaking, though it did not appear to be from the cold.

"Quick, behind the tree," she said in a harsh whisper. David smiled at her dramatic tone and moved under the shadow of a tall pine.

"So what is it that you want? I don't even know your name." David moved closer, drawn by curiosity and his quickened heartbeat. She looked to be about the same age, though it was always difficult for David to gauge just how old Japanese people actually were. Her eyes were soft and inviting, despite the fear that seemed to be radiating throughout her entire body. She moved closer to him, her hand reaching up for his face.

Her cold fingers brushed past his cheek, setting it aflame. With a shockingly strong grip, she brought his head closer, as if to whisper in his ear. David just caught her stiffen in fear as his back exploded in lances of pain. A sudden weight on his back drove him past the trembling girl. Sharp claws of pain drove into his shoulder and ribs.

"She's mine," growled a voice, carried by hot fetid breath close to David's ear. With the extra weight, David and his attacker scooted forward on his snowboard. Since only one of his boots was still in the bindings, he was unstable, barely able to guide the board. They slid away from the girl, even as his back arched in pain. The claws dug deeper and David pounded at the thing on his back and angled the board toward a small drop off. Gaining speed, he regained a measure of control and balance.

Struggling against the weight, David's hands met thick course fur as he battled the ōkami that had attacked him. He slammed his free foot into the bindings, and then pushed with his toes on one foot while picking up the others. Warping the snowboard beneath him, he turned in a quick circle as a huge tree loomed before him. With a crash and an even greater blast of pain, David slammed the ōkami into the tree back first.

Falling forward, David punched the bindings on his board, releasing his feet. In midair, David twisted, the claws pulling out of his back as painful as having fingernails extracted one at a time. The cold snow turned red beneath him as David's blood seeped into the frosty ground. Beside the tree, a reddish brown ōkami, bigger than even Chul Soon had been, shook its snarling wolven features, clearing its head from the impact.

Looking back, David saw the Okinawan girl. Her back was pressed against the tree and two much smaller ōkami growled at her, snapping when she tried to move past them. They looked identical, gray with streaks of the same reddish brown the monster before him had.

David shuddered as the wounds on his back began to heal, thankful that his Jitsugen Samurai powers made it quick. Still, he felt the full pain from both the injury and the healing process. The claw marks were deep enough that it would take several minutes before they would stop hurting.

Gathering his wits from the surprise attack, David's jaw set in determination. Kou roared within in outrage. He searched within himself for the familiar place where his true sword, the Seikaku, resided within him. Finding the molten globe of metal in his chest, he willed it to take the shape of a sword, summoning it before him. To anyone watching David, it would have seemed as if he closed his eyes and let his arms fly away from his sides. Then with inhuman speed, his arms were in front of him, holding a nearly transparent metal blade that caught the sun's rays off the snow and threw them in a myriad of patterns.

In less time than it had taken his attacker to blink, David was prepared to defend himself. The monster before him growled in anger, attacking with large claws and fangs. David blocked with his sword. The massive ōkami rained heavy blows, and David could hear the rest of the small pack hassle the girl.

Determined, David focused his mind on his Seikaku, his eyes shifted to orange as Kou took ever more control over their movements. Working together Kou and David began to open up shallow cuts along the ōkami's body.

The ōkami's skin was so tough that even with a sword sharper than any normal katana it was difficult to inflict any real damage. Kou also had to defend David's body from the ōkami's razor claws as David focused on directing the sword.

'We are lucky he isn't transforming into his human form. He's incredibly powerful,' David thought as they evaded a slash to their knee. Without his armor, he was vulnerable to the ōkami's attacks.

'*He must not have brought a sword or gauntlets. He did not expecte a fight, or at least not one he could not have won as a wolf,*' Kou replied as they managed to slice deep enough to cause damage. The ōkami howled in outrage. Building on their success, David began to attack joints, weakening the ōkami's resistance and will. A gasp of pain sounded from the girl.

'We need to end this.'

David dropped the tip of his blade, creating an opening near his left shoulder. With a rumble deep in its throat, the ōkami's paw slashed out to take advantage of what seemed like a mistake. Kou roared within, David's eyes blazing brighter as they checked their movement and sent the Seikaku slicing upward. The glistening steel drove halfway through the wolf's paw. A quick sawing motion finished it. With the ōkami momentarily stunned with pain, David brought his sword down. The wolf spasmed as the strange metal cleaved it between the ears.

Even as the wolf began to collapse, David changed the sword to its elemental form, and drove it with all his might into the center of the beast. With a howl the ōkami turned into a smaller wooden statue. David left his blade touching the ruddy wood just long enough to ensure the severed paw popped into place.

'Can't let what happened to Chul Moo happen again, can we,' David thought as he turned his attention to the other two ōkami.

David took in the situation in an instant, registering the ōkamis' placements and threat levels. The girl pressed against a tree, her palms flat beside her, digging into the rough bark. Before her and on the right, one ōkami growled. Shivers of rage racked through its fur, making the hairs on its back rise in waves. Beside it, the other wolf was subdued, mewling and looking between the girl, its twin, and the statue behind David.

Hours of drills with the Matsumotos had given David and Kou the ability to take in everything about a situation, and then act. After a moment of hesitation had nearly led to the death of both his host-siblings, David had worked hard to increase his decision making speed while trying not to sacrifice his judgment. The result of his training was a far more confident and self-assured person than the one who had watched Chul Soon bite Takumi.

David slashed before the growling ōkami even realized it was under attack. Since it was not fully grown, and was not concentrating on fighting, David's Seikaku passed through its neck, the vicious head rolling to look back at him with hate. David changed his sword to its elemental form again and soon had another statue.

Turning, David paused. Instead of the expected attack, the last ōkami sat with its ears angled in sadness. With one last look at the girl, it rolled over as if playing dead. David did not even bother changing his sword. With blinding speed, the wooden Seikaku's point stabbed into the ōkami, a perfect yet smaller statue replacing the whimpering wolf.

Looking up, David saw the girl, frozen with her hand out, as if to stop him, a peculiar look on her face. Then, shaking her head, she turned to David and smiled. Before he knew what was happening, she was there, pressing into him, her light arms and delicate hands wrapping around him as her bright eyes gleamed with gratitude and happiness. Then her soft lips were pressing against his and there was nothing else in his universe than the strange girl from Okinawa. His entire being, past, present, and future, became that moment. All thought blanked from his mind. Even Kou was silent as she pressed against him. Then she was gone, leaving David alone and dumbfounded as she jogged away.

"What's your name?" was all he could think to yell.

"Manami! Amuro Manami!" she called. "If you come to Okinawa, look me up!" Her voice faded as she disappeared from view.

Checking the area, David was shocked to see a boy stomping toward him through the snow, his skis in his hands. David tensed as he recognized Tsubasa beneath his large snow goggles.

'How much did he see?' David wondered, afraid he already knew the answer.

'*Maybe everything. Should we dispose of him?*' Kou asked.

'Really? That's your plan? Kill off one of my classmates and hope no one notices?'

'*My, you are uptight. It is almost as if a cub you just met licked you, and then loped off without trying for a bite or two. Let him guide the conversation, then go from there.*'

David watched Tsubasa as he approached, trying to gauge what the other boy had seen and how he would react. David considered him a friend but could not say he knew the boy well. He knew Tsubasa was suspicious of him and the Matsumotos after David saved him the previous fall and after the incident with the obake the previous day. David remembered the blood from his back in the snow. He ducked behind the tree and rolled to clean off his jacket, then kicked snow over the spots of red. He could do nothing about the rips in his jacket, but they were not large.

"It's a good thing I found you and not… well, not someone else," Tsubasa said with a smile. He pointed back where Manami had disappeared. "You're going to have to tell me how you do it."

David froze, uncertain about what Tsubasa had meant. Had he just seen the last bit, or had he seen David decapitate a wolf as well?

"Better hurry. The principal sent me to remind you time is almost up. They're going to come looking for us soon," Tsubasa said.

David knew he was right. The teachers had given him a strict timeline. If he did not check in, they would send the entire ski patrol after him. He made a quick circle, locating his snowboard and the statues. He froze again as he realized one of the statues was gone.

"Your new girlfriend, Manami, was carrying the other wolf statue when she took off. I have to admit she was pretty cute. How did you meet her?" Tsubasa asked, stopping near him. David's eyes bulged in surprise.

'Why would she take an ōkami statue? And why the one that gave up?' he thought.

David recovered somewhat and muttered something about Okinawa while reaching for his snowboard. He gathered the two grotesque wooden statues, looking around for a method to destroy them. One was small enough to hide in his jacket, but the larger one was bigger than a basketball.

"I won't tell her," Tsubasa said.

"Huh? Oh, yeah. Thanks," David said, confused but too worried to think too deeply about Tsubasa's words. He began the short hike to the top of the mountain. Near the top, he caught a whiff of smoke that he had missed before. Around the edge of the mountain, there was a small hut with a fire in an old oil barrel. Looking around, and with Tsubasa in tow, David dashed over to the fire, dropping the statues into it.

"We better hurry or we'll both be in trouble. I'll race you down," Tsubasa called, already running for the ski lift. David ran after, catching up to him only after Tsubasa had attached his skis. "See you at the bottom."

With a grin, Tsubasa jumped forward, dropping down the steepest part of the mountain. With a curse, David dropped his board and slammed his large snow boots into the bindings.

Hearing them click, he was after Tsubasa without even stopping to attach the runaway board strap.

It was soon clear that despite Tsubasa's wiry frame, he was an excellent skier. He flew through the icy moguls with practiced ease. He was however, human, and like most humans was concerned about his safety. David on the other hand knew that even if he smashed into a tree he could recover.

A soaring jump brought David down right next to Tsubasa as he negotiated a difficult curve. Surprised, Tsubasa swerved and almost lost his balance, but David grabbed a pole and had him righted even as they came upon a steep drop.

"You know you're going to have to tell me about that sword of yours, right? I mean after the ghosts, the deal at the warehouse, meeting strange girls, and you chopping wolves to bits, I think you owe me," he called.

David cringed, stopping even as Tsubasa tipped his skis down and disappeared with a smile. By the time David caught up, they were already passing the first lift exit, and entering the more populated areas around the bunny slopes. Just ahead of him, Tsubasa slid to a stop, their classmates just beginning to gather before leaving. David pushed his right foot forward, throwing up a plume of snow as he skidded to a stop, his heels balancing against the mountain.

Guilt ripped through David as Rie's gaze found him. Her smile made him burn with dread and guilt. Tsubasa had seen the Seikaku. Then David remembered Tsubasa had also seen Manami kiss him. He could feel his face burn from more than the cold. His emotions, so strong and foreign, were so uncomfortable that Kou withdrew from his mind.

"I win," Tsubasa said, then, in a low voice added, "I'll keep your secret for the rest of the trip, but then I expect answers."

Rie tried to get David's attention, but he avoided her as their class headed to lockers to change. David explained away his lateness to Moriyama-sensei, telling him it was due to a rock and subsequent introduction to a large tree. In payment for his ripped jacket, David had to stay in after lunch while the rest of the students enjoyed another hour of skiing. David spent the time trying to figure out what to do with Tsubasa. Masao had hammered into them how important secrecy was for his survival, and in just one afternoon, he had managed to expose his powers to two teenagers.

七

FOG BRIDGES AND
STUDIOUS SHRINES

*Even without a body of my own, my consciousness still clung
to some aspects of reality. Fixed in place, it was like the personal prison I had deserved for so long. I felt every lick of the
fire, yet I was unable to hide from the pain in death's escape.
Something kept me, bound me...*

David and his classmates arrived at their next location after a
short bus ride. The attraction was a long pedestrian suspen-
sion bridge spanning a deep gorge. Although known for its
view, a thick rolling fog obscured the gift shop and ticket
booths.

As their group approached the bridge, a white metal tower
arose out of the dark fog with two massive cables extending to
anchors on either side. Students vied for positions over gaps in
the fog so they could see the stream rushing by far, far below.
As they walked, David noticed Takumi edge back toward the
end of their group, fading into the fog as the other students
hurried ahead, eager to cross and get away from the biting
cold over the gorge. As soon as it was just the two boys among
the fog, Takumi smiled. An especially thick cloud of fog rolled
by and when David could see again, Takumi was gone. A uniform lay crumpled on the girded flooring before him.

"Reimi is becoming a bad influence," David muttered as he gathered the clothes and stuffed them into his jacket. "Wasn't Takumi the one who used to harp on keeping things secret?'

'We should have snuck off before getting on the bridge. We could go try to find a rabbit down there.'

David hurried to catch up with the rest of the students, but Natsuki found him first. She studied the gray clouds and a darker gray swept by their heads. Continuing on, they passed a guard marking the center of the bridge. Once he was out of sight, Reimi continued her aerial acrobatics overhead, making Natsuki laugh, clear and loud through the echoing canyon. Despite himself, David smiled as Reimi dived, brushing her head with a wingtip.

He was glad for the distraction, and, even more so, for the fact that Rie seemed to be too busy to notice they were gone. He was not sure he could hide his guilt and embarrassment from his ever-observant host-sister. It was different with Takumi. Despite his usual attempts at stoicism, Takumi would understand there had been nothing he could have done. Rie might not. With Kou sharing his memories, David relived the fight, the shock of the kiss, and the feelings it had brought forth in him. The surprise at having Tsubasa confront him, demanding explanations of secrets that were not his to share, troubled both boy and kami.

They made it to the end of the bridge. Their classmates huddled in groups, trying to stay warm. A few played in the open area, while others stared longingly at the bridge, their way back to the warmth of the buses. David let his classmates head back first, content to dwell on his own thoughts. He missed Natsuki, standing beside him, eying him. As soon as the other students were out of hearing, she leaned in close, pulling David toward one of the bridge pilings.

"What did you do?" she hissed. Natsuki ignored David's shocked expression. "Come on, I was Kou's partner. We spent so much time together I would have to be a dolt not to know your moods. Besides, we're friends. Now, you have that I-did-something-bad look. What is it?"

Cringing at the transparency of his feeling, David asked Kou, 'Should I tell her?'

'She will find out sooner or later. Maybe she can give us some advice on how to tell the Matsumotos.'

'Right, you know we are going to regret asking her for help. She's going to lord it over us for weeks,' David thought. Aloud he said, "It's complicated. There was an incident on the mountaintop."

David proceeded to tell her about the strange girl, the fight, the missing ōkami statue, and Tsubasa. At Kou's prompting, he added, "And she kissed me. Not that I wanted her to or anything. It wasn't my fault. Really!"

"You're on your own with that one," Natsuki said, laughing. "You should tell the others as soon as possible, but perhaps after the trip. We will be back on the Estate tomorrow. Just try not to give yourself away with that dour expression of yours. I'm sure, well, never mind. If it were Takumi in your place…"

For the briefest moment, David saw the hard gleam that had been so common in Natsuki's eyes before she had partnered with Reimi. Then, they were past the guard in the center. David heard the barest flap of wings and Reimi was back on the bridge, her talons wrapping around a metal railing.

"This is going to be tricky. Natsuki, why don't you watch our backs, I mean keep watch and David can take the other side while I transform. Just make sure you tell Takumi to hurry. And no peaking Natsu."

Before Natsuki could finish her swipe at the little bird, Reimi was jumping toward the floor of the bridge. Her face frozen, Natsuki had just enough time to look away before Takumi appeared with only the fog to hide him. He donned the clothes David surreptitiously threw to him.

"We need to have a chat with Reimi when we get back," Natsuki huffed as she bowled past Takumi. With a grin, the boys followed her.

'I'll tell everyone as soon as we get back,' David thought. Having decided on a course of action, he was in a far better mood. 'I can't change what happened. Actually, it turned out pretty well given the circumstances. They will just have to deal with it.'

'*I agree, except I still think we should take care of the nosy one.*'

"You mean Tsubasa? I'm worried too… I hate having to keep all these secrets sometimes. I mean if I could just tell Jessica, things would be so much easier. With how much she talks to Natsuki and even Rie now, it's hard not to let something slip. I've had to edit two of Natsuki's notes already.'

'*You could tell her about the kiss. No secret-*'

'No way.'

Later, the thrumming beat of a taiko drum welcomed the students to their last hotel. To their right a deep river rushed by, disappearing into a distant canyon. On the opposite bank, a strange collection of buildings crouched in upon the water. David could not help but stare. He was reminded of the movie *Spirited Away*, a famous Japanese animation that told the story of a mortal girl who became imprisoned at the spirits' baths. The movie's creator had surely drawn his design for the outside of the baths from the sprawling hotels and industrial buildings supplying the hot water for what must be innumerable onsen.

Almost every student stared as the sun set and lit a multitude of small flames in the many windows among the buildings. The beating tempo of the drums changed, quickening to a more familiar and furious sound. One of the Class 2C students had taken over and started the taiko they often played at school concerts while the hotel people watched in appreciation, and what looked like a bit of fear for the drum.

The hotel Hizenya was their largest sleepover place yet. For the first time they did not have to crowd to make enough room for all the students during their initial welcoming ceremony. The lobby was a glass walled monstrosity that warmly welcomed them all. Early as it was in the evening, it took them a good half an hour for everyone to find their rooms at the far end of the hotel.

David stayed with Takumi, Naoto, Shou, and Yoshiki. Since it was the last night, their room assignments matched the performing groups for the evening's recreation period. Yoshiki was the only one David did not know well. Quiet, the boy had not made much of an impression on him over the last eight months. They enjoyed their last bath. The facilities were separate and indoors so both boys and girls could use the full hour allotted. Dinner was a tour de force of traditional Japanese dining. By far, it was the most spectacular dinner, even after three nights of elaborate food. When even Takumi was full, the second years returned to their rooms to prepare for evening recreation.

The next day, it took all of David's willpower to drag himself out from Kou's feline lethargy and trod off to breakfast with the other students. They ate with the other classes and then boarded the bus for the more than hour and a half trip to their last destination. David eyed Rie and Natsuki as they boarded the bus together. He relaxed when Rie came aboard following after Natsuki laughing, and then stiffened as he noticed she was laughing along with Tsubasa, who came in just behind her.

David's concern drew in Kou as they both speculated about what their conversation could be. The two people who knew about the previous day's events were both uncomfortably close to Rie. Though he could not quite decide why, the thought of his host-sister finding out about Manami filled him with dread. She sat down next to him.

"Okay so what happened? It's like you never came back from snowboarding yesterday," Rie chided. "Natsu went through a whole story about how nothing strange is up, which means something definitely is." She gave David a couple seconds to respond, but when he failed to, she leaned closer to him instead. "I miss training. We usually get to... Anyway you don't usually avoid me, so what's up."

Around them, the rest of the seats filled up. Before David thought up an answer, the bus lurched away and the guides started speaking. David just caught a spark of hardness around her eyes before Rie took a deep breath and looked away. She started writing answers to questions in her trip book, and David got the impression she was trying to ensure her contacts did not melt away in her annoyance.

David breathed a sigh of relief. 'She's just wondering why I keep avoiding her... I'll just tell her about it when we get back and things will go back to normal.'

Their last stop for the school trip was Dazaifu Shrine, a place famous for its educational protection spirits. Students from all over Japan sought prayers, luck, and good fortune by visiting the shrine, either in person or by proxy. As part of the second years' trip, they would leave wooden tablets that had been prepared by the third years with all their hopes for their coming high school entrance exams.

After walking from the bus parking lot along a street lined with food shops, they arrived at a large red torii gate marking the start of the shrine property. Together they passed along manicured paths with ancient trees girdled by sacred ropes and paper. They washed their hands at a large spring, ladling warm water onto their palms and into their mouths to purify them before entering the shrine proper.

At the gates, they rubbed wooden bulls' heads for luck, shiny with the polish of uncounted hands. After passing under the massive arch, they entered a wide square. The shrine was at the far end, with stalls along both sides selling fortunes and good luck charms. David and the rest of the students filed up to the Shrine to bow and throw coins. With their group activities done, they were given time to pray on their own, shop, and wave at the video cameras that were sending their pictures over the web.

Since he had not been raised in Japan, David had a different view of luck and fortunes than his classmates. Although from a semi-religious family, his father's focus on science had left little time to instill more than the vague traditions at church. David had gotten the impression that his mother had started their going to church, and Dr. Matthews kept it up as a way of keeping alive her memory. His father had taught him enough about the world, however, to doubt luck and prayer. David and Jessica preferred to rely on their own skills and minds to find the answers to the unknown. While his friends, even Takumi and Rie, went hunting for charms to help improve their grades, David drifted, closing in on the outskirts of the square.

"I think Koji-senpai will like this one better than that fox," Mizuki said, in her usual bossy tone. David scowled at himself for missing the class representative's group, and backed away.

'Better to get him one of the arrows,' David thought as he enjoyed Kou's visual suggestions about where and how they could deliver it.

As he turned away from the group, David found himself face to face with someone he never thought he'd see again. Manami looked just as shocked to see him, her dark cheeks reddening in embarrassment as she looked for a way out. David was beside her in seconds, her arm locked in an iron grip built from badminton and kendo. Looking behind, David saw a few others in the gray uniforms he had come to expect from the Okinawan students, those on almost the same tour as his class. Without a word, David guided her, firmly but kindly, out of the square to another smaller and empty area just off the corner. To the left was a low stone bridge and walkway, across from them a light brown and white building with a steep Japanese-style roof that stood vacant.

"Damn, damn, damn!" she said. "I should have known your class would be here too. I let my guard down once-"

"Quite the way to greet someone you left with a kiss," David replied. He was excited, curious, and wary all at once. Too many questions burned through his mind to be coherent, so he opted for flippancy.

"I was hoping you'd remember that," Manami said with a sweet and alluring smile. It was David's turn to blush then. "Look, I'm sorry I took off like that but I was in a hurry. I mean you're cute, I would have preferred spending the rest of the day making out with you, but I am on a school trip. And, well, you had just sliced up the three ōkami that had been hunting me."

"Wait, you know about ōkami?" David asked.

"Sure, they're all over Okinawa. They don't transform much, but it's why I suggested you visit. Well, aside from the fact I wanted to see you again." Manami smiled and David felt his heart leap.

'She's distracting you. What about the statue that she took? Why were the ōkami after her in the first place? How did she know they were after her and that you could help her?' Kou pressed, trying to pull David's thoughts back into focus.

"Look, I'm sorry to run off but I should be meeting up with my teachers," Manami smiled again and then her warm lips were on his mind blanking out. It was not until he noticed the hand on his arm tense that he opened his eyes again. Unlike before she had not disappeared as he feared. Instead, she stared in surprise. "Uh oh."

David turned, following the hard focus of her gaze until he saw its target. Rie and Tsubasa stood together at the entrance to the square. Rie's eyelid twitched, rage overcoming her features.

The smell of ozone filled the air as Rie's hair flew out in waving tendrils. It called to mind the obake that had attacked Natsuki the previous year. The apparition's long waving fingers were disturbingly similar to Rie's anger. An electric surge filled the small square with a resonating power that was both oppressive and energizing. The tension in the small square crescendoed, and then disappeared in an instant. Out of nowhere, an overly large gray rabbit with beady red eyes and long yellow fangs appeared on top of Manami's head.

Chaos erupted as Manami started flailing, trying to brush off the huge animal as it attacked her head with its powerful legs and sharp teeth. Rie stared in shock at the rabbit she had somehow summoned. Beside her, Tsubasa stared for an instant before the image of a girl running around with a rabbit on her head sent him into a fit of uproarious laughter. He looked between Rie and Manami as if he could not decide whose expression was more hilarious.

David disappeared from the square. Kou's hunting instincts overwhelmed them. In full view of both Manami and Tsubasa, he transformed into a tiger and pounced. Seeing Kou with his mouth wide and fangs bare, Manami bolted. She clawed at her head as the rabbit's long ears flung around. She only made it two steps before Kou had her. His furry weight pushed her to the ground as he scrambled up her back to get at the rabbit. An instant later, Kou had the crazed rabbit in his jaws. A quick shake quieted it.

Ignoring the others, Kou carried the carcass off a few feet. Rie, Tsubasa, and even Manami stared at him in shock. The instant Kou killed it, the rabbit shrunk to a more normal size. At the same time, Kou seemed to gain a month's worth of growth all at once. Plopping down, Kou began to gnaw on the remains. Manami tried to slink away but froze at a growl from Kou. When she stopped, he returned his attention to his kill.

After a last crunch of bone, Kou primly wiped his chops with a paw and sauntered over to Manami. Along the way, he sent a nod to Rie, indicating she should join them.

"So it seems we have more than a few questions and problems to deal with, and not much time to deal with them," Kou said.

Rie glared at Manami, who returned the look with a broad smile before turning her attention back on Kou.

"So you are a Jitsugen Samurai, a real one, not one of those crummy imposters that ran things all those years ago. When I saw you I just thought you were a shifter, turns out I got way luckier than I had any reason to hope for," Manami said, reaching out to touch Kou's fur. A simultaneous growl from Kou and Rie kept her hand at bay.

"What did you do with the third statue?" Kou asked. David was too confused, too shocked, to take over. While Kou was just as confused about what had happened, he was clear about his distrust of Manami, where David was not. Not to mention David's clothes were a good three meters away.

"Ah, well about that. I hate to do this. I really am thankful after all. But you see that's just one question I can't answer right now. Kisses," Manami said with a smile and a blown kiss at Kou. Then with a flash that blinded them all, she was gone.

'She threw something. Quick, look, there she goes,' David thought, seeing a flash of gray disappear back into the main square.

"It's no good, she's already gone," Tsubasa said, pointing behind him to the square. "I assume you don't want to make a scene. We have to get back ourselves soon. We haven't been gone long but the teachers will notice."

Rie seemed to compose herself, and then looked down to Kou.

"David you better be listening in there… I want an explanation as soon as we are back at the Estate," Rie said, her yellow eyes staring down at Kou. Turning, she focused on Tsubasa. "I don't know what you know or think you know but

I can't tell you anything. If you keep quiet until we are back I'm sure my father will answer some of your questions, otherwise Kou will have to make you another statistic."

"A statistic?" Tsubasa asked, confused.

"Yeah, haven't you heard? Animal attacks are on the rise." Rie was so straight-faced that even Kou looked up at her with an incredulous face. "And as for you, stop cowering inside of Kou and change back before someone sees a tiger running around the Shrine."

Kou transformed as Rie slipped a new pair of contacts in to hide her yellow irises. Tsubasa hummed to himself as he helped block David's body enough so he could get back into his uniform. The transformation took David and Kou longer than it had taken in months since they were both so preoccupied. He was just in control enough to say, "Don't Look!" when Rie's head started to turn in what he was sure was annoyance. He still had orange fur in some awkward places.

When the three of them returned to the square together, Natsuki and Takumi joined them with inquiring glances. Since Rie was unwilling to explain what they had been up to, David spent the whole of the bus ride surrounded by questions and covert stares that he was unable to answer.

Since they arrived at the airport with plenty of time to spare, David even had to deal with Takumi and Natsuki trying to pry answers from him as he wandered among the various omiyage stalls. It did not take Takumi long to realize Natsuki was more aware of the situation than he was, which prompted him to be all the more emphatic in his questioning. Tsubasa's friend Kenta seemed curious as well, but David spotted him shrug and walk away, content after a quick chat with Tsubasa. David was so hesitant around Rie that she broke her silence as the plane taxied.

"We will talk at the Estate," she said, just before pouring half a bottle of sleeping pills down his throat. She gave him so much it took five punches to wake him up after they landed at Kansai airport.

DEBRIEFING A SORCERESS

*When it began, it was as if I was being called home after a
long journey. I was aware but my senses were crude. When
it began, it was an agony of rushing input and forgotten pain.
I felt again the fires burning, but this time, instead of strip-
ping away my sanity, the flames made me whole…*

When the second years made it back to the Nakano train station after the two-hour ride from the Kansai Airport, family,
teachers, and fellow students were waiting to meet them. A final ceremony marked the trip's official end. The second years
lined up one last time. Mizuki, of course, spoke for 2B in between the representatives from the other two grades, and after
the Vice-Principal and PTA chief. As the students started to
break up, Rie ran over to her father to inform him about the
trip. Without any outward sign of the surprise that was sure to
be rushing through him at her words, he gazed around at the
other students and families until he spotted Tsubasa. He
headed toward the young boy as soon as Rie finished.

Once David and the twins were in the car with their bags,
Masao revved his Mercedes's engine and started for the Matsumoto Estate.

"Wait until we get home. I'm going to have to hear this
from the beginning," he said, preempting David. They sat in

silence, and were soon curving through the forest outside the Matsumoto gate. With Masao driving, the trip was quick, and more thrilling than many of the Greenland rides. Yukiko was waiting for them as they pulled up next to the house. Masao let her sate her initial interest in their trip, but soon asked her to ready some tea while the three students disposed of their bags. Together they met in the main room around a kotatsu, a low table with a heater and blanket to keep them warm in the cold winter weather. "Alright David. You had better start from the top."

David cleared his throat. He strived to be as clear and concise as the edited Jitsugen Samurai diaries he had read the previous year as he told them about the trip.

"What exactly did she say?" Masao asked, cutting past Rie's sharp intake of air as he described his first meeting with Manami. She watched David, attempting to extract every detail from his posture and features.

"It's unusually blurry. She said something like 'You're different, and not just because you're a gaijin. Someone's after me and you can help,' and then Rie called for me and she was gone," David said. Masao nodded for him to continue. As the most difficult part came up, he paused.

'Do I have to tell them everything?'

'You know the answer to that. It's no big deal. I lick things all the time.'

'You are absolutely no help.'

"Well, she kissed me," David managed to say. It was a strange mix of emotions for him to deal with, and he was sure the Matsumotos could read all of them on his face. The elation and pride it stirred within him, the fact it had been his first kiss, and that he had enjoyed it. Could they also notice the surprise and guilt, and all the other confusing bits running around in his head?

"There would not have been much you could have done," Yukiko said, noticing Takumi's expression as David finished talking about the fight at the ski resort. "Without a weapon you would have had to transform to fight, something that might have given even more away than David's sudden swordplay. At least we can give Tsubasa an excuse for that without letting him into all our secrets."

"Actually," Rie said, hesitating under her father's cold gaze. "That's not everything that happened."

With glares from Masao and shock from Yukiko, Rie told them about the events of earlier that morning at the Shrine. She told them how Tsubasa had pointed David and Manami out to her as they left the main square. She told them what she had heard with perfect recitation, until her own part came into play. Then her voice lowered to a bare whisper.

"I lost control. I have no idea how it happened but somehow I summoned an animal."

Masao wiped his forehead with a silken cloth as he dealt with the extraordinary news he was hearing from his children. On just one trip, they had succeeded in revealing secrets that had remained hidden for centuries.

"So let me summarize. Tsubasa now knows about ghosts and ōkami and that David can transform into a tiger, and possibly that he can summon a sword. And that you," he said, turning to Rie, "can summon animals. What is more, you helped an ōkami kill off her enemies and abscond with a statue. That ōkami is as good as reanimated. All the while, you revealed to a third pack that a Jitsugen Samurai exists. Did either of you listen to anything I have said about secrecy over the last year? David cannot survive if evil comes at him in force. Even with all of us helping, if David falls, Japan is defenseless."

As David and Rie shrunk under Masao's diatribe, Yukiko leaned in, gracefully refilling Masao's tea.

"Now look who is not listening. Yes, there may have been better ways to do some things, but it is partly our fault. We could have dealt with Tsubasa earlier. We should have realized that his interest would have been piqued after the warehouse fire. With a mind like his, he was bound to keep searching until he found his answers. Who knows, he might end up being a useful ally for our children.

"As for the rest, we do not know for certain that girl was an ōkami. David reacted no differently than you to his first kiss and none of us knew what would be the side effects of Rie's possession. It seems Rie retains her connection to the spirit realm as you had hoped. Not only do we have a Jitsugen Samurai and a shape shifter, we now have a majo as well. On top of all that, it looks like our…friends have been trying to watch for Chul Soon as they promised."

It was obvious that Yukiko's words only partially mollified Masao. David hid a sigh of relief as everyone's attention turned to Rie. He wondered again who the cake lady was. Not that her warning had come to anything. It was also the first David had heard of lasting effects from being a yūrei.

"From what we've read," Yukiko began, "when the yūrei summoned an oni it created a bridge between your body and the ancient prison where the monsters were locked away by the Zodiac Kami. Many layers bury that prison. Part of your soul still remembers the path through some of them.

"Unfortunately," Masao cut in, "we know nothing about majo that have been created in this fashion. The book in which we found the ceremony to release you had nothing about the man after the corrupt kami was cut out. We will have to see if we cannot find more about him."

"Wait. If you've never heard anything about this before, maybe it was just a freak accident or something," Rie said. A chill swept through David as he remembered the rage on Rie's face just before the rabbit appeared in the square.

"Majo are well documented throughout Japanese history," Yukiko said. "Though the popular stories have exaggerated or even made up much about what we now call witches, there are several reliable references in the library. Often they are born with an innate understanding of the paths through the layers. Rare is the person who gains access from dealing with kami. Most uncommon is the majo that forges their own connection."

"See, I always knew she was a witch," Takumi said, already moving away from Rie's high punch.

'Well that hasn't changed at least,' David thought.

That night Kou ran. Aside from the brief fight with the rabbit, it was his first chance to be free in a week. Kou and David reveled in their animalistic abandon, though Kou's new growth threw off their control. They figured his tail was only a few centimeters longer, but it was enough that their paws did not always go where they intended. It took twice as long as normal for Kou to hunt since he was so clumsy, and it did not help his mood that Ryohei hovered along after them chuckling.

Despite spending nearly the entire night as a tiger, David woke refreshed, his time as Kou rejuvenating him far more than the hotel futons had. Despite his enthusiasm, David's usual five kilometer run with the twins and Natsuki left him winded after a week without practice.

They worked through their complete basics, leaving off the more advanced training since their muscles were a bit rusty. They went slow, taking longer since they did not have to be at badminton practice until ten. While Takumi was just as energetic as David, both Natsuki and Rie seemed to drag, unable to recuperate as easily as the possessed.

Masao surprised them by allowing the samurai to practice at their own pace. Since Masao never let them off, David was sure his host-father had plans for them after badminton. Natsuki joined them for a long breakfast, and they filled her in on the details from the trip. Walking to school, Natsuki and Rie huddled together chatting seriously while the two boys followed behind. Takumi looked as if he was pondering whether to exact his revenge for the photos, but it seemed he opted for security, and avoided speaking about anything that should not be overheard. Though Yukiko had softened Masao's anger, he had been adamant that they work harder to maintain secrecy.

Near the Police Station, Natsuki finished her conversation with Rie and motioned to David. "Your sister is mad you didn't email her last night," she said, brandishing a print out. "She got your card though, I think. You'll have to translate the rest for me."

David sighed but knew the news of the gifts he had gotten for his sister should mollify her.

'I don't know why you insisted on getting her a zodiac charm. You humans have gotten us all mixed up. For all you know her sign is a rabbit...mmm rabbit.'

At school, the first and third years bombarded David and his classmates with questions about the trip. There were plenty of normal experiences for them to talk about, so they were able to satisfy most questioners before Tsukasa-sensei, their coach, started practice. The second years on the badminton team also presented their senpai, the third years, with key-chains they had bought while in Nagasaki.

Once practice started, David threw himself into badminton drills. The repetitive motions and the quick speed the shuttles flew at him helped to limit his expanded awareness, and although the fact she might be an ōkami bothered him, he was unable to force the memory of Manami from his mind. Still, Kou delighted in pulling a bit of his attention to Rie, who caught his gaze from a few courts away. He smiled as the team's rotation brought them closer together. When she drew opposite to him, Rie hammered him with all her strength and skill, forcing him to reply in kind.

His muscles sore and energized, David followed the twins and Natsuki from the locker rooms. Tsubasa was waiting for them outside the gym. The lanky boy smiled and waved. In his hand, he held the same cloth shopping bag Kenta had held on his way to the ōkami lair the previous year. Whatever was within had sharp lines that made the bag bulge in odd places.

"So nice of your dad to invite me over today," Tsubasa said as they approached. He had discarded his badminton clothes for his school uniform, in which he somehow looked more like a computer technician than usual.

"Of course, why don't you walk with us," Takumi said. Although caught by surprise, it was not the first time Masao had neglected to tell his children his plans. Together the five students walked through Nakano town back to the Estate. To their surprise and gratitude, Tsubasa avoided talking about the school trip, and instead filled them in on the technology news he had missed that week. His classmate's calm exterior impressed David. Waiting to find out how much he had seen felt as if Kou was trying to claw out of David's skin. Takumi had assaulted his parents with questions when they revealed the truth behind the bedtime stories of the Jitsugen Samurai, yet the shorter boy seemed to be taking everything in stride.

The longer David thought about it the less surprised he was. In class, Tsubasa would calmly pursue his answers, revealing knowledge only when thought out. In badminton, what Tsubasa lacked in power and speed, he made up for by being crafty and clever.

When they arrived at the Matsumoto Estate, Takumi showed them to the main room, and then left with Rie to find their parents. David and Natsuki sat with Tsubasa while they waited. Beside him, Natsuki adopted the calm and graceful manner she reserved for adults and more recently, around Takumi.

'I wonder how much he knows. Hell, I wonder what Masao-shihan is going to tell him,' he thought as he waited. 'Tsubasa just has this empty curiosity about him.'

'*The better question: Is he going to leave here,*' came Kou's prompt response. '*Masao is serious about secrecy. Tsubasa could be a huge liability.*'

'Yukiko-san hinted he might be useful. It would be nice to have a few more friends. I mean we have friends at school, but just like with Jess, without knowing someone's full story, it is hard to stay connected.'

Tsubasa just stared around the room, unaware of the internal conversation across the table. As time passed, David watched Tsubasa's calm exterior start to crack. His training and Kou's tiger awareness allowed David to spot the tightening muscles in his neck, the ridged posture, and his darting eyes. His slight movement away from Natsuki showed that, above everything else, her unusual manner unnerved him the most. Noticing the move, Natsuki gave Tsubasa a killer, knowing smile. It wound him up so much that he jumped as Yukiko entered with a tray laden with tea.

'It's a gift,' David thought. 'Natsu is pretty creepy sometimes.' Kou growled a chuckle.

Unassuming, Yukiko entered, the picture of Japan's past. She was graceful, with intelligent eyes that surveyed Tsubasa, but did not warn him of the skills she possessed. The spiraling steam from a teapot sent a warm scent of green tea through the chilly room.

"Natsuki-chan, be nice," she said. "Relax. No one is going to do anything to you. You are our guest. Masao will be along. He was working in the Dojo and needs to put away his knives."

Tsubasa relaxed as a smile touched the edge of her mouth. The atmosphere in the room turned more comfortable as the students warmed their hands around cups of green tea. Natsuki smirked and sipped at her tea. After an interval long enough to throw the boy off, the head of the Matsumoto Family entered in a thick winter kimono and sat at the end of the low table across from Tsubasa.

"Well, tell me what you know, and then I will judge what to do with you," Masao said. David noted a bit of Grandpa in his words. Although he sounded stern, there was an undercurrent of amusement that Tsubasa missed.

"Um," Tsubasa said, swallowing a surge of nervousness. "Well, I know there are ghosts and ōkami. I know David can call a sword out of thin air, and can turn into a tiger. I saw Rie make a rabbit appear out of thin air. They can all see ghosts, and without the technology Kenta and I used. I think David had something to do with the warehouse fire too. Now I know you must have destroyed some ōkami since the statue they found matches the ones I saw. The thing I don't get is how he," Tsubasa pointed to David, "went from super gaijin to cool in less than a year. Whatever it is, I want in.

"Besides, I think I can help. I still have the obake mirror. Kenta and I started working on adapting it to see kami and other things, but we never got a chance to test it. I was the only one to see an obake in it, so even Kenta doesn't think it works. Maybe I could try to make it see other stuff."

Tsubasa was so excited he seemed to miss the implied threat in Masao's words. The drop in temperature was enough to warn David of Ryohei's impending appearance. Beside him, Natsuki stiffened a little before the sliding door opened again and Takumi came in, followed by Ryohei, the Matsumoto Estate's resident ghost.

"Wow, they're like twins," Tsubasa said.

"So I keep hearing," was Ryohei's wavering reply. Masao arched a single brow, looking between the boys and the empty space from which the voice had come.

"Good, you found him," Yukiko said, welcoming Takumi and Ryohei.

"Very well, one last thing before we break all the rules," Masao said with a sigh. "I assume you brought your mirror?"

With a smile, Tsubasa withdrew a clunky mirror with wires and a control knob on the side.

"I know it's not very pretty, but it's just a prototype. We were trying to make x-ray glasses, but stumbled on this. Then we started modifying it to try and see kami after Yuuto asked us to."

"May I?" Masao asked. Tsubasa jumped up and started adjusting the controls.

"Ryohei is it? Nice to meet you," Tsubasa said, bowing to the ghost, who smiled and bowed in reply. "Would you mind standing behind Masao-san?"

After Ryohei was in place, Masao held up the mirror, turning it in his hand to see behind him.

"Nothing," Masao said with a frown.

"Here," Tsubasa said, pressing a button on the side of the mirror. With a crackle of electricity, the image on the pane shifted, Ryohei's translucent visage appeared next to Masao's solemn face. Masao lowered the mirror and turned. There for the first time, Masao saw the ancient Matsumoto ghost.

九

REBIRTH

From one cage, one prison, to another. My escape from the bondage of the wooden statue led me straight back into the service of my dear brother. After that hell though, I was only too happy to play the role he wanted of me. We began preparations to leave…

Waking up in the pre-morning darkness had once been the bane of David's existence on the Estate. The long runs and kendo practices were still demanding but he was adjusting. He was familiar enough with the Matsumotos' martial arts basics that he could focus on perfecting each muscle movement instead of worrying about which move came next. The repetition of punches, blocks, kicks, and sword strikes helped center and prepare him for the day.

'Just think. It used to be just Takumi, Natsuki, and us here,' he thought to Kou as he moved a wooden practice sword over his head.

'Yes, now Rie has returned and Tsubasa is joined with the samurai,' Kou growled. David stopped the heavy sword, working to control its most minute movement. *'That bit of wood used to move you. Now you have the strength to put it where you will.'*

'They are, aren't they? Samurai? Masao calls me a Jitsugen Samurai because of you, but all of them work just as hard to protect us and the rest of Nakano.'

'To protect Japan.'

Beside him, Tsubasa tried to copy David's movements. Where David could stop precisely, the newest student often slowed his wooden stave until it stopped or over shot his target. When they finished with individual practice, Tsubasa and David faced one another to begin one-step fighting drills. After bowing, Tsubasa attacked with a basic over-head strike and David used a basic defense.

"The point of these one-step fights," Yukiko said for Tsubasa's benefit, "is to work on spacing, footwork, and on bringing forms into a less ritualistic practice."

Beside David, Takumi and Natsuki worked together, while Rie practiced with Masao. It was a rarity to have Masao train with them, but with Tsubasa, the numbers had become uneven. Since Takumi was the senior student, he gave the commands for each drill.

As Takumi called the next encounter, a sudden shock raced from the center of David's chest. The metal form of his Seikaku appeared in the air before him even though he had not willed it into existence. By habit, his hands moved to catch the gleaming blade. Pain, like a wave of fiery heat, ran from his fingertips as he gripped his sword. The fire grew in intensity as it raced toward his chest. The agony of an inferno drove him to his knees, even as Tsubasa's un-checked practice sword swung over David's head. His own wooden sword clattered to the ground.

With everyone standing over him, "Chul Moo is back," was all David managed to gasp through the pain. Every fiber of David's body knew the truth of it, even as the shock receded.

'We did expect Chul Soon to find a way to reanimate his brother,' Kou added, still growling at the pain. *'Perhaps not quite so fast, but ever since the theft it has been inevitable.'*

Even Masao was baffled, however, at the pain the connection between David and Chul Moo had caused. It took the elder Matsumoto days of sorting through the library to find instances of Jitsugen Samurai being aware of the return of a previously defeated foe. Past Jitsugen Samurai had long ago learned to destroy the statues resulting from the banishing of an evil spirit, and over time the details of what could happen to the statues left intact faded from collective memory.

"When you banish a spirit with the Seikaku, your sword retains a link with the physical statue you create," Masao said at evening practice a few days later. "Converting it to your elemental form gives you a power over it. What you felt may have been the last vestiges of that connection. When Chul Moo was brought back to his human form, the connection broke."

"So will David retain any power over him? Or is it gone now that he's no longer a lump of wood?" Tsubasa asked, fascinated by the powers and connections surrounding the Seikaku. The idea of the metal acting as a conduit between human and kami seemed to give him endless theories to test.

Although it was unprecedented to have so many aware of Japan's true past, so too was David's situation unique. After two days of thought, Masao had introduced Tsubasa to the secret history of the first Emperor, Ninigi. The condition of the introduction to their secret world was that Tsubasa had to train just as diligently as the other samurai did. Young as David was, Masao and Yukiko had decided to err on the side of having too many allies. The benefits of secrecy they had so impressed on David were limited since at least one ōkami pack already knew of David's existence.

In the evenings, Tsubasa worked at improving and developing new technologies to help the Matsumotos. Ryohei often floated along with him, standing in as his test subject. Occasionally, David left his work transforming the Estate's trees to help him develop a kami detector. Their original version, the one that Jahangir and the Jeong brothers had hoped to turn to their own use turned out to detect variations in obake, rather than kami. Though useful for detecting ghosts that had recently fed, and thus how friendly they might be, it was far from practical in a fight.

Rie spent most of her evening practices trying to learn to control the latent effects of her time as a yūrei. She roamed the forest for hours alone trying to summon even an insignificant creature. Despite her best efforts, no new animals popped into existence.

Yukiko also worked to find out what had happened to her daughter. Every night that Rie practiced summoning, Yukiko searched the Matsumoto Library.

"Kou's size jumped because he absorbed the energy contained within the spirit Rie summoned," Yukiko said after emerging from the library one evening. "Unlike the oni David killed, the rabbit did not come through a Devil's Doorway. Since it was not an evil spirit sealed away, Kou was able to draw its power into himself."

"So if Rie learns to control her summoning, Kou will be able to keep eating spirits?" Takumi asked.

"A giant tiger would be a lot more noticeable than Kou is now," Tsubasa said, gesturing to the tiger that was still only about as tall as his knees.

"I do not think just any spirit would give itself up to me. The rabbit was a natural prey, it knew it had lost, and surrendered itself to me. The same might not be true of others. Either way the point is moot, unless Rie stumbles upon some key that will let her access her power," Kou said, his bright orange eyes looking to Rie.

'She looks troubled. I'm sure she's been trying to summon something, but can't. It must be frustrating, like the first couple times I tried to summon the Seikaku,' David thought. Kou's eyes changed to blue as David took control of their body. He winked at Rie.

With the new information, they continued their evening practice. Rie concentrated on finding some way to summon a spirit, while Takumi transformed so that Kou and Reimi could race through the forests. Tsubasa followed Masao back to the workshop, already adjusting wires in his mirror.

While everyone on the Matsumoto Estate worked to improve their skills, their normal lives moved toward the end of the school year. Before the end, however, they still had one last major event. The cultural festival in early February was a culmination of the year's work. Every subject put out displays and the students began preparing performances so parents could see what they had learned. Some classes, like English, made them fill out their notebooks and hand them in. Other classes had specific projects that they had to complete.

"I wish I could just whip out my Seikaku. I'd have this box done in no time," David whispered to Takumi as they worked on a Monday afternoon.

"I think the lack of joints and nails might give you away," Takumi said laughing.

Together they used traditional Japanese tools to try to shape stiff pieces of wood into the proper shape. The saws were tricky to work with. The wide, double sided blade attached to a short pole seemed better suited to cutting down a small tree than on such small pieces of wood. The whole process was a pain. Nonetheless, all the students worked to try to get the perfection Tsukasa-sensei demanded. Just like on the badminton court, he settled only for their best.

Each homeroom class also had to put together a performance for the presentation part of the festival. The teachers would select the best performances to perform, but they all had to prepare. During one of the homeroom periods, Class 2B met to discuss who would do which part for their assigned skit.

"This year for the cultural festival, we will be doing an adaptation of *Momotaro*, also known as Peach Boy. For those of you who aren't familiar with the story, it is an old legend where a couple asks the gods for a son. One day, a peach appears and out pops a boy. That boy later leaves to go fight monsters on Demon Island. We have enough parts for ten of you, with one director, and the rest working on sets and props," Moriyama said from the front of the class. "I'll let you select the director and the lead. The rest will be by chance."

As the classroom exploded in murmurs, David sat back and relaxed. *Momotaro* was a Japanese fairy tale he already knew. During his first month in Japan, David had been essentially illiterate in Japanese, but during a lonely foray into the school library, he had found a very small selection of books in English. Most of them were children's books since the language would be easy enough for the level of the students studying English at the school.

'Maybe I'll be one of the monsters on Monster Island," David thought to Kou while the rest of the class started talking about who should direct.

'*As long as you're not the dog. Having to pretend to be a dog would be an embarrassment. At least you know something about how monsters fight. You could portray one pretty well,*' he replied.

'Kenta and Tsubasa should work on props. I bet they could pull off some pretty good special effects-'

'*You know, David, you really need to get better at paying attention to the outside world when we talk… or should I call you Momotaro?*'

David growled Kou's growl as he walked the corridors of Nakano Junior High. After a brief discussion, his class had elected Mizuki as director. She had then suggested Daisuke for the role of *Momotaro*, but a bloc of girls had shot her down. With a majority, they had quickly started putting their own plans into effect, electing David to the role before he had finished talking to Kou. The rest of the period had been a blur of selections and rewrites to the script. The girls seemed determined to make it into a romance, and the new director seemed to be the only one with less say in matters than David had.

"We should be spending our time looking for Chul Soon and Chul Moo rather than worrying about some stupid play," David said once they were away from their classmates.

"There wasn't time to tell you this morning, but mom says we got another note from our 'friends.' They suggested the Jeong brothers skipped the country since they've had no luck tracking them since the sighting in Kyushu," Takumi said. Though it was serious enough, he could not help smile at David's plight. All he had been stuck with was a role as one of Momotaro's animal helpers. "Anyway, I have to pick up the scorecards from Tsukasa-sensei's room. Later."

"What *friends*," David grumbled, annoyed that no one had warned him, and that he still did not know who the cake lady was.

'*You're mad because you'll have to spend every free period preparing for the play and follow Mizuki's direction. If you think about it, I'm sure you'll figure out who the woman was.*'

David stopped. Of course, with Kou in his head it was easy enough to see the connection. "The Crown Prince. He has people searching for Chul Soon," David said. "And I have every right to be annoyed. The twins, Natsu, even Tsubasa all voted *for* me."

It might have been a voice, sound, or some other sense, but David turned, aware of something wrong with the world. His long training with the Matsumotos had refined his understanding of how his body interpreted things. With Kou's help, he stalked animals, and like when they walked as a tiger, there was an unnatural silence about the place. He was about to come up on the secluded area behind the gym, where only a lone forest road gave the area any utility. It was the place where he had once broken his hand trying to punch Koji.

Things might have ended when they succeeded in humiliating him, when they beat him up, but then he had become a Jitsugen Samurai. Still, Masao had been clear. David was only supposed to use his new skills to defend. He knew, though, that things would not fade away. Koji was too wrapped up in his own rage. Like an ōkami, he was stubborn, strong, and none too smart.

'You're wrong. The ōkami are cunning. Don't tempt us to underestimate them by grouping that bully with them.'

"Hello Koji-senpai," David said as he stepped around the corner and mentally acknowledged Kou at the same time. He bowed respectfully. The boys and lone girl around Koji came from the toughest family situations. Most rarely came to school, but none was as vicious as Koji. David's avoidance of Koji's last plot had stripped away most of the other third years' support, leaving Koji with just a few lackeys left. One of the boys seemed to deflate a little. Koji's anger only flared warmer.

"Your condescension won't help you now. We don't want you here. Go back to America," Koji said. David heard the fast footfalls coming and frowned. The others heard as well, and moved to intercept the newcomers. Three of the larger boys backed Rie and Tsubasa against a wall. It was then David realized he was the tallest, biggest there. In the months since coming to Japan, he had grown and developed in an impressive way. "Awww look. David's girlfriend and boyfriend showed up. I wonder if this is their little love spot."

The other boys chuckled, but backed away from Rie. Those who knew her reputation were wary. The twins never flaunted their abilities, but most students knew about the Matsumotos' athletic and martial skills. Others whispered because of her disappearance during the time when so many of their fellow students had been attacked. Rie had supposedly transferred to a school in Hokkaido, only to return soon after. She came back more driven, and for those who were honest with themselves, scarier.

"Why don't we just leave them out of this? Koji-senpai, you wanted to have a private discussion right? How about we go over into that forest and you can talk," David said, eying Rie. She gave him the slightest shake of the head, but it was enough for Koji.

"Look! She doesn't want him to go. How cute. Boys why don't you keep her and their lapdog company while I go have a chat with this… thing," Koji said laughing. He turned, and pushing David before him, headed for the forest.

MOMOTARO FIGHTS

It felt good to have a body again, and it was not as difficult as I expected to follow Chul Soon's plans. As we made our way through China, it seemed natural and easy to fall back on my instincts. There was plenty of prey, and without the prosperity of Japan, it was easy to take what—whom—we wanted...

Once David was past the first trees, he felt a familiar flow of strength begin to run through him. The forest was their element, Kou's home. Koji could not know how just being among the trees roused and energized an Earth Jitsugen Samurai. The older boy was smiling, his anticipation revealed as a dark giddiness on his features. When they were out of view of the rest of the onlookers, David abruptly turned.

"So what is it, exactly, that you want? You aren't going to touch me, and if you did you would just mark yourself as a bully to even more people," David said, his hands by his side. "You might end up hurting yourself again, which I'm betting isn't your purpose either. So is there any way we can end this?"

His face contorting in rage, Koji lunged. From his stance, David guessed he had begun training in aikido.

'*So much for your genius plan to try to talk him down,*' Kou thought as David moved. '*Now how do you plan on finishing this without revealing your training?*'

'Really? No trust?'

David let his actions respond. He pivoted his left foot as his right swung behind, body changing so that he was to Koji's side, rather than in front as the first punch came in. As the older boy passed by him, David struck. Using his fingers and feet, he touched a hundred points before Koji could take more than a step. Each hit was only strong enough to be register, without doing any damage. David stood still as Koji stopped and turned, bewildered. He attacked again.

David caught Koji off balance by shooting his arm out instead of side slipping as he had before. He hit Koji's forearm with his right hand while catching the older boy's wrist with his left. David slid forward along Koji's outstretched punch. In one fluid motion, David was behind Koji with his arm locked. A tap to the soft area behind his knees had Koji on the ground.

"See, this is the problem with bullies. There is always someone better," David whispered into Koji's ear. "You were right. I was pathetic when I got here. But guess what? Now I'm not. So here are the new rules. You shut up, leave everyone else here alone. You graduate, and then go to your next school and become a model citizen. Otherwise–"

"What, you'll tap me to death? You let me go, you're dead," Koji growled.

"I wonder if your aikido sensei knows you've been using your new skills to beat up kids… I bet he'd love to hear about that. As for those taps, any one of those could have done this." David released one of Koji's arms just long enough to push Koji's head toward a rock. Jerking him to a stop a foot above, David bent down and smashed the rock to pieces. Though it broke his hand, and pain shot through his arm, David controlled himself, locking Koji back in place before he could react.

"See? If you aren't a good boy, I'll come and find you. It won't be at school, and there won't be a crowd. It will just be me, alone, in the dark… and then people will wonder where Koji went. But they won't wonder for long because no one cares about bullies. Now, I'm going to let you up, you are going to leave and pretend you knocked me around. Then you're never going to bully another person, ever."

David let Koji stand. He could still see the fire in the bully. Wrapped in shadows, David let Kou come forth, shading his eyes orange as he growled low in his throat. Kou's aura seemed to go out before them, knocking into Koji even as an obake's aura weakened its prey. Koji froze in fear, and then turned, running back through the trees. David's sense of victory faded as a chattering sound grew around him

"It's your turn."

When David rejoined the others he told them about Koji and about the crazed pack of rats that had attacked him just after. They all agreed it was an incident to keep from Masao, though Kou was keen on detailing the many possessed rats he had eaten. While David had crossed a line, they were all glad to have dealt a blow to Koji's pride.

"I'm glad you were able to take care of that one. I think I almost summoned another animal on Koji's head," Rie said. "Though, I do wish you had called us to help take care of the rat demons. You can't keep all the fun to yourself."

David tried to work out if Rie was being serious or not. He had not considered the pack of huge gray rats with long yellow fangs and sharp claws fun. He had ruined yet another school coat. The rats had chewed it to pieces before Kou could get them all. The confused look on David's face sent Rie and Natsuki into a laughing fit.

"I think David is going to enjoy the rewrite a little too much," Natsuki said, eyeing David with an evil smile through her mirth.

"That's right, I don't think he's heard about the rest of the casting," Takumi said with an even bigger grin. "Since it is on Valentine's Day the girls demanded Moriyama-sensei let them add a love interest for *Momotaro*."

Despite his best attempts to find out what he meant, the others refused to tell him what he had missed. In frustration, he let Kou take over and run the rest of the way to the Estate.

When David finished his evening exercises, during which Masao had him break a tree into boards then rebuild it three times, he found an email waiting from his sister. Before he could open it, she popped up on instant messaging. After letting a stray comment slip, David spent the next ten minutes trying to describe the fight with Koji without letting drop any of the Matsumoto secrets. Cursing his inability to tell her the truth, the calendar by the computer gave him an idea.

"Can you do me a favor for Valentine's Day?" he asked. David spent the next half hour after making his request, reading about every boy Jess knew as she speculated about the upcoming holiday.

'I don't like Jess thinking about boys so much.'

'*At least your plan to distract her worked. And you got her to agree to send you that stuff.*'

'Yeah, but in return I have to translate all these boy questions for Natsuki.' David shuddered and began typing an email to Takumi's partner.

Each day went faster as they devoted more class time to practice for the play. David's nervousness built along with his classmates' grand preparations. Whatever divides there had been among class 2B, they seemed to have dissolved as everyone threw themselves into the play. With the Jeong brothers out of the country, his attention was ever more on the expanding number of lines, scenes, and stage positions he had to deal with.

Soon, Valentine's Day was upon them and their class scheduled for the second year slot. Although a Sunday, performances were set for the morning, and the homerooms were open for the subject displays. David hurried with the rest of his classmates to finish last minute preparations. The students had one-half of the gym, while the parents and families filed into the other half. After several welcome speeches and the first few skits, Class 2B left to prepare for their turn.

'This is worse than before we attacked the lair. I can't believe I have to do this in front of the entire school.'

'At least you do not have to worry about forgetting your lines. They're easy, and I can help you remember if you forget.'

With a shudder, David slid into a dark corner to change into his first costume.

"And now, Class 2B will be presenting a special Valentine's Day rendition of Momotaro," Miu, the announcer said as David's heart pounded off stage. The curtains opened.

On stage, a painted backdrop depicted an ancient Japanese countryside, with twisting rice paddies surrounded by mountains. Together, Natsuki and Daisuke were dressed as an old farm couple. They wore the traditional baggy pants and brownish stripped jackets of old Japan as they worked with fake Japanese tools. Beside them, raised cutouts of blue waves marked a fake river.

"Oh it's such a hot day," Natsuki said.

"It wouldn't be hot if we had a son to help us in the fields," Daisuke replied, pointing his fake beard at Natsuki.

"It's not *my* fault we never had children. I wish I had a son," she said.

As the old couple sighed and worked, a giant peach rode in from the side of the stage. Kenta and Tsubasa had rigged it with a remote, allowing them to make it seem as if the peach was washing down a river toward the couple. When the peach was just before them, it stopped.

"Look, a peach," Daisuke said. "Let's eat it. I'm hungry."

As the pair approached, the peach split apart. David popped out of the middle. He was dressed in a mawashi, the wrap used by sumo wrestlers, and nothing else. The girls had managed to keep a straight face when, against his protestations, they insisted on it on the grounds of historical accuracy. In the original story, the boy had popped out naked.

"I am Momotaro," David said in a loud voice. "I have been sent to be your son, for you have worked long."

"For joy! A son!" Natsuki crowed. "But such a strange looking boy. No one will ever like him." The last words had been one of the few additions Mizuki had been able to add, despite a large amount of support to have them taken out.

Together Natsuki and Daisuke walked off with the peach as the curtains closed. Offstage, David pulled on shorts, a jacket, and belt. His classmates had designed the costume based on a happi, the traditional festival wear. The white shorts were a bit too short for his taste, but again they had insisted. The outfit left his arms bare and he was pleased to note he looked a little like the character Goku on *Dragon Ball*. Hidemi took the opportunity to throw a little more flour into the wigs that Natsuki and Daisuke were wearing.

When they were ready, the couple went back onto the stage and pretended to work like before. Then the curtains opened again. Momotaro entered from the side carrying oversized vegetables.

"Thank you Momotaro," Daisuke said. "You have been here alone with us for many years. A friend recently died. Her daughter will come to live with us."

Rie entered wearing a kimono and bowed. Despite the pressure of the performance, David could not help but smile. Her graceful stride perfectly matched one of Yukiko's brightest spring kimonos. Then, just as suddenly as she had come, the lights all blanked out and she was gone again.

"Parents. I must go to Demon Island. The oni have abducted the girl, and I must save her," David said as the lights came back on.

"We knew you would have to leave someday," Natsuki said. "Here, take these four skewered rice dumplings and go rescue her."

David marched off the screen to applause as the curtain closed again. Students scrambled to change the background to a beach with a boat and an island in the distance as others added a Japanese pennant to David's costume. Beside him, Takumi, Naoto, and Shouta were dressed as animals.

"You know, you look good as a bird," David said to Takumi, wincing as Mayu rammed the pole for the pennant against his back.

"I still don't like the plan our classmates concocted. At least it's you and not Daisuke," Takumi said, adjusting his wing in annoyance. "This is not how bird wings are."

Miu, hearing Takumi's remarks turned red and hurried away.

"Now look what you did," Mayu growled as she left David and hurried after her friend.

Back onstage, the curtains opened to the new background and Shouta dressed as a dog. He pranced around the stage until David entered with a swagger. Seeing David, Shouta ran up to him, yapping "Wan Wan!" Japanese style.

"Where are you going?" Shouta asked.

"I am going to Demon Island. The monsters have done many bad things, and have a great treasure, we must stop them," he replied. "Will you come with me and fight?"

"Sounds a bit dangerous for me," Shouta said, squatting and scratching at his ear with a paw.

"I'll give you a rice snack if you come," David said, showing a skewer with the four rice dumplings on it. The dog jumped excitedly around him and then followed David off-stage. Without warning, Takumi swung across the stage on a cable and harness Tsubasa had rigged for him. He kept up a "Chirp Chirp" for the audience though his swinging was wild. David entered with Shouta in tow.

'Yikes, I hope that cable doesn't break,' David thought as he came on stage.

'Tsubasa knows his trade. It was fine in the rehearsals.'

"Hey, a bird," Shouta called. "Can I eat that too?"

In response, Takumi dropped, smashing into Shouta as he swung on his cables. Reaching up, David was able to steady Takumi, and then release him.

"Where are you going?" Takumi asked once he composed himself. "Did you know you have a mongrel following you?"

"This is Dog. Together we are going to Demon Island. The monsters have done many bad things, and have a great treasure, we must stop them," David said over Shouta's growling.

"Demon Island? Sounds like fun, can I come too?" Takumi asked.

"Sure. Here is a rice dumpling. Let's go!" David said.

Together the three marched offstage. Naoto loped into view in a monkey costume. His enthusiastic performance had the student section laughing, and soon even the parents were clapping.

"Banana? Banana? Give me a banana," Naoto said when David entered again.

"I don't have a banana, but I have a dumpling," David said. "If you come with me to fight on Demon Island, I'll give you one."

"OK, but why will you go to Demon Island?" Naoto asked.

"The monsters have done many bad things, and have a great treasure, we must stop them," David replied again. Together they marched off as the curtains closed. The background changed again. It became a jungle island, fronted by a large gate. Kenta placed a boat cutout and waves near the edge of the stage.

'I still can't believe I'm supposed to do this in front of the entire school. And Rie! She must be so embarrassed, I can't believe Mizuki set this up.'

'It must have been the best way for them to get back at both of you. I don't know why you're so worried. The last time went well enough.'

'Because she's my host-sister. And her extremely deadly father and brother are in the same room. And because it's embarrassing.'

Before David could complain more, someone pushed him onto the stage. With the three animals in tow, David entered.

"We have arrived. Dog, go see if you can open the gate," David said.

Before the dog could protest, Takumi as a bird, hopped to the gate.

"It's locked," he called.

Three monsters approached from off-stage. David frowned. The monster that Kaeda was supposed to be playing was different from the one he had seen during rehearsals. It was far bigger and wielded very real looking Japanese nightsticks.

"Quick! Let's eat the dumplings, then we will be strong enough to defeat the monsters," Naoto called. All four ate the rice dumplings then turned to the monsters. As planned, David drew his fake wooden sword, and advanced on the lead monster while the animals went for the other two. David knew something was wrong before the first swing. The face behind the monster suit was not Kaeda's face. What was supposed to be cardboard was hard wood.

'It's Koji. You should have finished him off when you had the chance.'

'I can't just kill a student, no matter how dumb they are.'

David slid under Koji's dual attack. Elbowing him, he dropped his useless prop sword, sliding around behind him. As Koji spun, David forgot about the rest of his classmates, about the entire school watching as he focused on his enemy. This time David did not hold back. The series of punches he gave Koji connected hard. Dropping the tonfa, Koji looked into David's serious gaze. David did not know it, but he was the picture of ferocity, with his hair on end, almost like Kou's fur. Koji ran. The audience laughed as the leader of the monsters turned tail. David even heard the laughter from his classmates backstage, and then Rie screamed, high and piercing. It was a sound he had heard only once before and had hoped he never would again. Before the other two monsters could react to Koji's disappearance, another, all too real monster, stomped onto the stage.

+ —

VALENTINE'S IN JAPAN

*From China we headed north. The way became easier the far-
ther we went. Though the border was secure, we had advan-
tages that the refugees and smugglers did not. As wolves, it
was a simple matter to sneak back into our Korea...*

'We can't transform, not with all these people,' David thought
desperately. In response, Kou withdrew from his mind. The
fanged lizard moved much faster than David had thought possible, and given Rie's scream, he was sure she had somehow
summoned it. In front of the entire school, and with cameras
rolling, David did the only thing he could.

"Run!" he called to the other actors as he dropped. Takumi
was aware enough to grab Naoto and Shouta and pull them
away. The second he passed from the audience's view behind
the low paper waves, David summoned his Seikaku in its
wooden form. His body protected it from the other two students
playing monsters. They backed away from the komodo dragon
as Takumi pulled the others to the far side.

Rolling, David popped back up, seemingly with his prop
sword in hand. In reality, the long curve of wood was a deadly
tool in a Jitsugen Samurai's hands. The monster's long fangs
dripped with saliva and sweat dripped from David's brow. The
effort required of him to maintain the Seikaku without Kou's

help shocked him, and he could feel the limits of his endurance and training approach. He moved swiftly, hands twisting as his arms rose. With a crunch, David brought the Seikaku down onto the center of the komodo's head.

The crowd yelled and clapped as the dragon was revealed to be nothing but paper. Momotaro stood alone on stage staring down at the wreckage of the paper monster.

'It was so real.'

'*There was a spirit in that husk. Rie must have summoned and bound it to some stray paper. It is old Japanese magic, more controlled than a true beast, but far less potent. Wake up, you have to finish the show, the clapping is dying off.*'

David glanced back at the audience. Before he could run off-stage, Takumi came out carrying Rie. Her eyes closed, she was limp in his arms as the monkey and dog followed after.

"Momotaro, the monsters are all dead. Where are the gold and treasures? All we found was this girl," Takumi said, jumping back into his scripted lines.

"Yeah!" Naoto added. "Where's this greatest treasure ever?"

David moved, placing his Seikaku in his belt, he sighed with Kou's return. He took Rie from Takumi the bird, and carried her to a cushion made to look like a rock.

"Here is the treasure for which I sought," David said. As he spoke, Rie opened her eyes. They shone with tears. David could read her guilt, remorse, and confusion at the summoning. A strange pain reverberated through him in response her hurt. "If gold is all you seek, there will be some among the monsters' lair, go and find it. Far more important are the relationships we build with those we care about. I was sent to bring joy to an old couple, and through me, they found their chief happiness was what they could accomplish together. I wonder only if someday I too will find my own other half."

At that point, the adapted script called for Momotaro and the girl to kiss. In practices, Mizuki and her cadre had enjoyed endless laughs making David hold Rie and pretend to bend close to her. Their discomfort had been a like a crazy magnet for their class. Since every class member could imagine the horror of having to be in their place, they enjoyed the knowledge that they were safe. But there, in that moment, David forgot the crowd watching. His whole awareness focused on the pain on Rie's face.

His hand reached for her and she stood, helped by David's strength. As he leaned in, the image of Manami with an evil rabbit on her head popped into his head as Kou returned enforce to his mind. With wide eyes, David fought against the pressure of Kou's will. Rie caught his eyes glow orange, but to the audience, David's body froze inches from Rie before he fell to the ground as if fainting. Rie's confusion only added to the moment as the audience erupted in laughter and cheers as the curtains closed.

'I am going to kill you,' David thought through clenched teeth.

'You have no idea what might have happened. We have a responsibility. Think. She's still dangerous.'

Around him, students were moving to clear away the props and hangings for the next performance. Rie turned without a word and walked stiffly offstage. With Kou withdrawing, David grabbed the paper komodo dragon and ran after her. Offstage, the rest of Class 2B met them. The girls, minus Mizuki and her friends, grabbed Rie and huddled around her, while the boys slapped David on the back and asked him about the scene changes. Takumi stood off to the side, throwing glances between the groups of boys and girls. David noticed that he was in his "self-control mode." Whenever he had strong emotions he did not want to show, Takumi tensed and his eyes started darting. The babbling of his classmates was broken off as Mizuki came up with Moriyama-sensei.

"They didn't even consult me and I was the director! There was nothing in the script about a last monster," Mizuki complained. "They didn't even kiss like they were supposed to."

"What was that about? It looked so real," Moriyama said, ignoring Mizuki.

"Ah, well that was my doing, I made a puppet. Mizuki didn't like most of our ideas but I did it anyway. The crowd really seemed to like it right?" Tsubasa said, covering for Rie's summoning. It was dark behind stage so no one noticed her yellow irises. As the others turned their attention on Tsubasa, Rie scooted away to put in a fresh pair of color contacts. She got them in just as Moriyama started leading them toward the exit so they could watch the rest of the performances. David wanted to talk to Rie, but the shuffling students kept them apart. He ended up next to Takumi instead.

"We will talk later," Takumi whispered as they sat to watch the third years' performances.

David was nervous through the rest of the show. The presentations ended and the audience began moving out of the school gym to the subject rooms, where parents could examine the displays at leisure. Before leaving to check on his classroom though, Moriyama stopped and caught David trying to slink away.

"David! Nice job today, your acting was so much better than during practices, very believable. I'm going to get a lot of praise for your work!" he said laughing. "Don't worry about Mizuki-chan, I like the changes Tsubasa, Kaeda, and you made. Very original." To the rest of the class he added, "Don't forget, we still have a homeroom class after your parents check out your work. And I expect a lot of chocolate."

Laughing he stepped away. In his place, a large portion of the student body assaulted David. They commented on everything from his costume to the fights, but they all ended with the fall. Everyone seemed to think it was a stroke of genius. After the first few comments, David could not help but smile, eliciting a smug purr from Kou. The boys seemed in awe of his acting while the girls looked for Rie so they could offer superficial sympathy. In the chaos, Takumi slipped away to meet and report to Masao and Yukiko. David's one advantage was that they all had somewhere to be. After a lot of embarrassed head scratching, he was able to extract himself from the press of students.

Alone, David headed across campus for his homeroom. Exiting the gym with other students and parents, he caught a glimpse of Koji outside. Seeing David, Koji's stepped back in fear. He gave a hurried bow, and then sped away with several frightened looks over his shoulder.

'What's with the taking over my body in the middle of a performance?'

'You were not thinking. So I had to do it for you.'

'But she was... the script... You had no problems before.'

'She was not in control. Have you already forgotten Grandpa's training? You must always be in control of your mind, or else others will control it, even me. Neither of us wants me to dominate your mind. It would defeat the point of having a Jitsugen Samurai. It would waste the Zodiac Tiger's sacrifice. Manami has shown me that your mind is not always clear around...'

"Now I know why people go tiger hunting," David growled in a low voice as they walked. His shoulders slumped and his hands went in his pockets as he resisted Kou's thoughts, unconsciously slouching into his pre-possession-at-a-shrine posture.

'For all you know Rie might have set an elephant on our head, then how would she have felt?'

There were few people around him since parents and students alike had hurried to the classrooms. The few remaining students had long ago learned to give David a wide berth when he reverted to gaijin mode. Though he wanted to fend off the logic of Kou's words, the reality of what had happened on stage began to wash through him. His hands started shaking, and he was suddenly aware of the adrenaline leeching out of his system. Without another word, Kou opened himself to David, allowing his presence and strength to wash through his human half.

'Masao is going to kill me. Using my Seikaku right there in front of everyone. Thank god we didn't transform.'

'Why you're welcome, I am a god you know, at least to the Japanese. Just tell them the truth, I'm sur-'

Kou was cut off as two girls flung a third into David's path. In horror, David felt far too much hair on the back of his neck stand as Kou's fur materialized over his skin. With a surge of will, he ripped himself away from Kou and focused himself on the girl in front of him. Kou snarled viciously within as David realized the girls had surprised Kou. The impossibility of it made him smile, even as his whole body seemed to forget to function for a few quick blinks from the girl's nervous eyes. Her features barely registered, but from her height and obvious embarrassment, he guessed she was a first year.

As he tried to speak, her mouth worked in small frantic movements that made no sound. She thrust a box into his hand saying, "Please eat this," and then sprinted away.

Kou snarled again in indignation. The mental image formed not at all complementary to the girl.

'You have deer on the brain,' David thought. His mind moved like sludge as he tried to process what was happening.

The other two girls took one look at David's shocked expression before giggling and running after their friend. Looking into his hands, he found a small red box decorated for Valentine's Day.

David was ambushed twice more before he made it back to the 2B classroom. By then, Kou had recovered and was a pit of mirth in the back of David's mind. He could just imagine the little tiger rolling around in a fit of the growling-coughs that were his laugh. David stashed the chocolates in his locker and changed out of the Momotaro costume, diving into the broom closet to extricate himself from the mawashi.

It was one garment he could live without ever wearing again. Only Kou's complete indifference to nudity had enabled David to get through the embarrassment of putting it on and having to wear it in front of the entire school. The worst part had been that he could not put it on alone, and had to get help from Moriyama. Still, Kou laughed at his embarrassment.

'In Japan, people often see, but do not look.'

Back in his school uniform, David headed downstairs for the second half of the cultural festival. Every subject had at least one display. David's shoddy wooden box was stacked with the other second years' constructions. Beside them were the first year's engravings and third years' electric cars. All around, parents wandered, looking for their children's items. David found the Matsumotos by the school trip display. The pictures, journals, and the newspapers everyone had written while in Kyushu hung on corkboards. David had to remind himself not to laugh when he saw the picture he had taken of Natsuki and Takumi in Kumamoto Castle enlarged and prominently displayed. It had caught them together in a natural moment, and David was starting to understand the meaning of the look on Takumi's face.

'You know, they actually look good together.'

Masao greeted David with a quick flick of his eyes, while Yukiko smiled at him. David looked for Rie but she was not with her parents. Instead, Takumi came over, and walked him down the wide hallways between classrooms.

"Whose idea was the changes? Can't say I missed the whole love scene they tried to make you do, though you deserve it after that picture," Takumi whispered as they passed the Cooking Club's tea ceremony. Miu waved to them at the door, trying to get them to go in.

"In a bit," David said with a smile to her. When they were past, he returned to their conversation in a whisper, his lips barely moving. "That was Kou's doing. Should I be running for the hills?"

"Dad seemed okay with how you handled Koji-senpai and the shihen Rie summoned," Takumi replied just as quietly.

"Oh you mean that giant komodo dragon of wimpiness thing? Yeah, we need to hear more about that."

Tsubasa and Kenta ambushed the pair outside the technology classroom, pulling them into a large and cluttered space where a few parents were examining robotic arms and computers.

"So we heard you already got some choco," Kenta said without preamble. "Hiroko-san said her friend heard that a first year gave you some homemade choco a bit ago."

"Did you really get some? I've only ever gotten giri-choco," Tsubasa said with a bit of awe.

"Well, yeah, a couple groups of girls ambushed me before I even made it back to change. I didn't look in the boxes yet though. What's the difference?" David asked.

"Later, we have to get back to our presentations, just wanted to know if it was true. Hope I get some," Kenta said.

"Oh, hey, thanks for the cover earlier," David whispered after Kenta left. "You were a lifesaver. See you at the Estate later?"

"Sure, no problem," Tsubasa said already focusing more on his computer than on David and Takumi.

Back out in the corridor David tried to ask Takumi about the chocolates, but his host-brother just watched him as if reappraising the boy he used to know as an out-of-shape, uncoordinated gaijin. Distracted, Miu succeeded in pulling them both into the Home EC room for a tea ceremony.

十二

HOMEMADE CHOCOLATES

On the surface, little had changed at home, yet there were subtle signs that the things Chul Soon had set in motion so long ago were bearing fruit. The whole world trembled at the growing pressure. Though those who lived there were kept in the dark, we could keenly feel our goals moving forward…

In the lunchroom, students sat with their usual groups of friends. As they finished heart-shaped pudding cups, conversations turned toward reviews of the performances and speculation on who would get chocolate.

'I'm getting kind of worried. They all seem very interested in getting homemade chocolate. And where is Rie? Let alone Natsuki. I haven't seen either of them since the performance.'

'*You're on your own with this one. Tigers don't do chocolate. Now a nice…*'

'Hello? Still with the deer? I'm eating.'

Although it was a weekend day, it was still a full school schedule, so students grudgingly finished lunch and headed for their usual cleaning duties. David helped a few other students clean out the lunchroom, and then joined Takumi in the gym for badminton.

"Where did all the girls go?" he asked as Takumi brought over a shuttle.

"They're freaking out over their chocolate. Come on, let's play."

After practicing for a bit, a couple of other boys from the team joined them and together they played a few games. Although he was always improving, David was still no match for Takumi. He lost his game against him, but won a close match against Tsubasa. When they returned to their homeroom, Moriyama was waiting for Class 2B.

"I know you're excited and everything, but hold out a little longer. We are going to go finish cleaning up after the fair, and then you can have the rest of the fifth period to do what you want. Sixth period is open reading or homework." It was clear from his expression he did not expect them to study. For the first time David noticed all the extra bags in the back of the classroom. Most of the girls had department store bags alongside their usual backpacks and duffle bags.

With the entire school working together, it took little over half an hour to clear out the displays on the first floor. The students were taking most of their items home, so their bags and lockers were soon full of more than chocolate. David made it back to the classroom first, so he started handing out the candy heart boxes he had asked Jessica to send him from America. He had kept them secret from even Rie and Takumi as a surprise. After putting one on each desk, he tried to slip out again, only to run into Natsuki.

"Where are you going?" she asked, her focus slipping to his bag. "Come on, it's one of my favorite days of the year. I get to see all you boys die of embarrassment when you get chocolate."

Natsuki wheeled David back in as the rest of the students started filing in. As promised, they had time to read or study. At their desks, most of the students were curious about the boxes of candy. When Moriyama came in, a few of the students started asking about them, so David ran over to explain. A few words in, Moriyama laughed and called the class to attention so David could explain the American holiday. Up until that point, David had assumed things would go the same as they did back home.

"Well, in America we just trade cards and candy back and forth to everyone, though a boy might give something special to the girl he likes. I guess if you have a boyfriend or girlfriend, you might go out on a date or to dinner, and then exchange a special present too," David said, suddenly aware he had the attention of the entire class.

"Wow, American boys have it tough," Mizuki said, so surprised she forgot to ignore David as usual.

"Right, well," David said being more than a little confused, "These are some traditional candies we give out. I got enough for everyone." David hurried back to his seat as groups of friends bent together to discuss the cultural differences. Next to Takumi, David leaned in as surreptitiously as possible and asked, "What do you do in Japan?"

"On Valentine's girls give boys candy," Takumi said. "Most often just giri chocolate, you know, store bought. If you get homemade chocolate you're lucky because it means they like you."

"Girls don't get anything?" David asked in surprise.

"Well, maybe in elementary," Takumi said through a laugh. "But that's what White Day is for. Next month boys give return presents, but for now, we get free food."

Then it hit him. The girls who had ambushed him *liked* him. The idea was so foreign he had a hard time believing it. As David sat trying to think through the horror of having to track the girls who gave him chocolate and explain he was not interested, Natsuki appeared before him and unceremoniously dropped the smallest square of obviously store bought chocolate possible.

"Don't think the candies get you off. Better get me something nice for White Day," she said in a loud voice as she continued through the boys. David hid a smile as he caught

Takumi watching her go from boy to boy handing out chocolate. Along with the rest of the boys, David got chocolate from most of his female classmates, only Kaeda and Yuka refrained, though they made a show of giving large boxes to Daisuke and Yoshiki. Hidemi popped up after a few minutes with a smile and a box of what looked like homemade chocolate.

"Don't read into it too much. I made some for everyone. As for you," she said turning to Takumi. "I'm still mad at you for knocking me over last year. You never did tell me the real reason you were in such a hurry. So here." She handed him a box similar to David's, only it was a quarter of the size. "Seen Rie?" David and Takumi both shook their heads and returned to their growing inventories of chocolate.

"Don't worry," David whispered. "I'll share."

Unable to help himself, Takumi laughed, and then punched him in the arm. "Like you will get more than me."

"Yeah, because I'm going to get the most," Naoto said, sliding into the conversation.

With a knock on the door, girls began arriving from other years and classes. After a few minutes, the female badminton team members arrived with things for all the boys on the team. With the exception of an occasional third year alone, most of the girls moved in small groups, like the ones that had ambushed David earlier. As some of Class 2B's girls left to give out their own presents, more and more girls seemed to show up. With every knock, David grew redder. With each "Looks good," and "Thank you," David could not help but be shocked by the variety of the girls and gifts coming at him and the other boys. He had never received even one special valentine's card back in the States.

The most embarrassing encounter was when the brawny girls' judo captain brought him an entire chocolate cake. She had stood in front of his desk and said only, "I've decided you can ask me out if you want," before leaving without an answer. The reactions from his friends and the other boys in the class ranged from Shou's jealousy to Takumi's incredulity and Tsubasa's pride. By the time Rie came back to the classroom, pink and red boxes covered his desk.

The walk back to the Estate was quiet. Tsubasa and Natsuki left to take their presentation pieces and chocolate home before heading to practice. Rie was tense and quiet in a way that reminded David of the time after he rescued her from the yūrei. Takumi spent the whole walk throwing covert glances at the bulging shopping bag David had begged off Natsuki.

David called, "Tadaima!" with the twins as they struggled out of their shoes in the Estate's entryway. He just managed to make it onto the raised floor when Natsuki's bag burst sending pink packages rolling around the floor. David bent to pick one up, but then noticed both Masao and Yukiko sitting at the low table in the room right of the entrance. With a sigh behind him, Rie began helping David gather his presents. Natsuki arrived soon after and together they all relived the events at school.

Masao examined each action, and questioned them on how they had made their choices. David caught the corner of Masao's mouth twitch as he glossed over his argument with Kou, though a light touch from Yukiko kept him from pressing. When Rie's turn came up, he noticed just the slightest shift of her attention toward him before she started talking about the events leading up to her summoning the shihen.

Offstage, Rie had been bound as she was supposed to be. Instead of having Kaeda, Yuka, and Ayaka dressed as monsters, however, Kaeda had returned to Rie to gloat about changing places with Koji. Just after, a much larger monster had appeared behind her classmate.

"Your boyfriend thought I would just roll over and leave things be. Let's see how he does with some real props," Rie said, repeating Koji's words and tone. She described his wicked grin through the mask as he had brandished his pair of real tonfa. Rie had tried to escape, but a cloth muffled her screams. Kaeda dragged her farther into the darkness. None of their classmates had noticed as the contacts covering her yellow eyes melted in rage.

"I saw Koji's face. He wanted blood. He left me and there was nothing I could do. I don't know how it happened, but the old paper props crumpled into a mass and turned into the komodo, and it stomped toward the stage." Rie shivered at the memory.

They continued the debriefing, but the ordeal was far less painful than David had expected. Yukiko checked to ensure they recorded their experiences for the library. David sighed as he finished his entry without anyone focusing on the most difficult questions.

'You've already done enough of that.'

'*Someone has to be the brains-*'

"I already called Tsubasa-kun," Yukiko said, as they finished. "I gave him the night off from practice. I think we will let all of you off the hook as well. Masao and I want to do some more research on Rie's... abilities."

Natsuki stood gracefully and with a firm hand drew a surprised looking Takumi out of the room, leaving David alone with Rie. She studied him, her quiet expression unreadable.

"Umm, I should probably put my stuff away," he said. Her features sharpened and her gaze turned to the pile of presents.

"Of course. I hope you enjoy the chocolate," she said, her voice controlled. She stood, and David looked to the pile of chocolates. When he turned back, she was disappearing around the far side of a shoji door. Even with the Matsumotos' training and Kou's indelible memory, he could not quite be sure if he had seen something red in her hand.

The rest of February sped by. At school, Koji became a model student. Whenever he saw David, he bowed low and hurried away. The change created new rumors about David, but his easygoing presence and the lack of visible bruises on Koji served to debunk the more outrageous of them.

To Takumi's great enjoyment, David had to live through several embarrassing encounters where he had to thank and then decline the various offers he had received. To his chagrin, some of the girls had only given the gifts as dares, while others ran away whenever he tried to talk to them. Even worse, Natsuki managed to translate a version of what had happened and send it to Jessica, which led to a whole slew of emails full of pointed questions and jokes. It got so bad, that Kou agreed to help him plot a fair revenge for White Day.

'*How about a rat? She never liked them very much.*'

'That will be perfect. Think you can catch one alive?'

'*Please.*'

'Just because you play with your food first, doesn't mean it can survive more than a few minutes after you land on it. Anyway,' David continued before Kou's growl could cut him off, 'any idea why Natsuki's all annoyed with me, I mean more than usual? I asked her this morning and all she did was jab at me harder!'

'*I was there. You are about as insightful as a rabbit.*'

The Matsumotos' morning practices were more intense than ever. Since learning he was possessed by a Japanese god, David had struggled to perfect his understanding of the Matsumotos' kendo basics. As his senpai, or senior students, the twins were in charge of teaching him. Whenever he thought he had mastered a move, either Takumi or Rie gave him new challenges as he worked with Tsubasa or Natsuki. Even with the strange awkwardness between him and Rie, when they had swords in hand they trained with intensity.

On the last day of February, Masao surprised him by announcing that he had advanced to the point where the twins could no longer guide his lessons effectively. At first, David thought the change might help remove some of the tension between him, Natsuki, and Rie, but then Masao continued speaking.

"From now on, David, you will train with Yukiko after basics," he said. "Tsubasa will continue working with the twins and Natsuki."

From her graceful appearance, he never would have guessed at the skill and speed his host-mother possessed, even knowing beforehand that she trained. Just as she had drilled him in Japanese when he first arrived, Yukiko now set to work on his body, sculpting it with exercises as she saw fit. She wielded her wooden sword more sharply than a ruler in an old nun's hand, always expecting his best.

"How come Masao-san's picture isn't with the Masters? Grandpa's was up there before he died," David asked as he held an intricate pose designed to build his arm strength and balance.

"Masao was never promoted to master before Masato-hanshi died. In this family, the master will pass on the title and final secrets when he thinks the next generation is ready. Now only the Emperor can bestow that title on Masao, and he has not," Yukiko replied as she jabbed with her stave. "Your leg is too low."

Together the pair worked in the Japanese garden while the rest trained in the Dojo. With only his fingertips touching the cold stone bridge over the pond, David struggled to maintain his balance, and keep himself from falling into the water.

"While I've got you here," Yukiko said with a gleam in her eye. "Do you like Rie?"

David missed a jab from Yukiko's practice sword. He realized his mistake only as he tumbled into the icy water.

David extricated himself from the shallow pool, his movements accompanied by Kou's annoyed growls. Yukiko invited him over to the bench.

"Umm," David said to stall, his thoughts rushing to find an answer. He realized that ever since Valentine's Day, he had lost the surety of their previous friendship.

"No matter," she said. "I've noted awkwardness between you two. The two times she summoned a spirit, she did so in your presence. Her weakness has made us question her... emotions. I am worried about her. She has yet to find the key to her power, and you are the only hint we have, yet the two of you have been avoiding each other. This is dangerous." Yukiko's gaze reminded David of Grandpa's piercing eyes.

'What should I say? I don't know what she wants, how can I help Rie? I don't even know how to help myself.'

'Rie is dangerous, but not evil. You should help her if you can. If I had known how much my stunt would affect the two of you, I would have risked another demon.'

"Well, in any case," Yukiko said, seeming to read David's conversation with Kou. "I think you need a more intimate knowledge about how swords are created. Your techniques are suffering from your ignorance. From now on, every other night, you will work in the forge instead of practicing with the Seikaku. Besides, Rie could use some help getting ready to make her first sword, and the fastest way to learn is to teach. You and Kou can still practice together at night. Tsubasa says he needs some time to work on his inventions anyway. I'm sure Natsuki and Takumi will find some constructive way to use the time as well." With a smile, she left him soaking on the bench, oddly warm in the cold air.

David came to look forward to the nights spent among the darkness and heat of the forge with Rie. After a few awkward minutes, Rie adopted her usual brusque teaching methods and began training him in the basics of sword craft. The work was so demanding, and required so much coordination and collaboration that they had to work as one or risk destroying hours or days of work.

With yet another skill to learn, David could almost feel the driving tempo of his training. Every day there were new techniques to learn and old ones to master. Still, constant pain did not fill his body, as it had his first weeks after Kou's possession. He had grown comfortable with the difficulties.

'I know I should worry more about the outside world, about Chul Soon, ōkami, and other dangers we will have to face, but each day is a challenge. I can hardly find the time to focus on that stuff, even with the random attacks from fake owls and deranged rats.'

'*A little higher with that tool of yours or Rie will make you start over.*'

'Just because you don't have thumbs-'

Rie glared at him and David aimed his hammer strokes a little higher. Since the Seikaku was David's primary weapon, Kou was interested in the process of sword making, but he spent most of the time searching out the Zodiac Tiger's memories so that David could enjoy the experience and newness of creating with his own hands. It was an amazing thrill to create something, and the satisfaction fed a part of him of which he had not been aware. Kou compared it to the enjoyment he got while hunting, an activity they had long ago decided was Kou's personal domain.

Every day, animal and human understood each other a little better, but they both agreed to leave at least some things separate.

'Sword making is like my own personal foundation. Creating is a human thing, difficult but interesting.'

'*Yes. My ground is the hunt. Our roots might one day lead to only one being, but we both needed some time to be just human… and just tiger.*'

David relaxed into the physical human aspect of the heat and rhythm of the pounding, and then suddenly he was in perfect step with Rie. His body moved with hers and together an artful weapon took shape under their direction. It was simple, easy. They fit together without a thought.

"You're not as uptight as you were. What happened?" Jessica asked in her next email. After he told her about starting to learn sword making, she began grilling him on everything he did with Rie. As usual, his little sister's questions led his thoughts in new directions, made him examine his feelings until he recognized that indeed, the stress that had grown up from the constant tension between him and Rie since the play had almost disappeared.

The extra time they spent together had other consequences as well. Just as with Natsuki and Takumi, David and Rie began to show improved coordination on the badminton court. It got to the point that no one but their closest friends would play them as a doubles team. With school going well, badminton keeping him on his toes, Tsubasa on the Estate, and the slow but continuous way he was getting to know the Matsumotos, David was almost always happy. When he said as much to Jessica, her reaction was so over-the-top he was reminded of Mizuki and her friends.

'I missed something. I've never equated her to that group before,' David thought.

'Who knows? I bet Natsuki has emailed her more than you recently. If you're not careful you are going to have me hunting Rie down and…'

"Fine, we'll go hunt, I can take a hint," David said aloud as he left the Matsumotos' computer to head outside. With a wave to Ryohei, floating in the garden, David left his clothes by the nearest tree and surrendered to the tiger within him. He regretted at once. As Kou's massive paws clawed through the silent forest, he had plenty of time to think.

十三

AN OLD MAN'S HOUSE

Reconnecting with our old haunts and… acquaintances, seemed to breathe life into my brother. While I was far from unmoved, it lit a wild, dangerous, and even reckless part of him. We moved swiftly thereafter, making our way back into China and along the old smuggling routes into Russia. In that place, things became more difficult. Though the red giant had fallen, the people were wary and few had love for outsiders…

'It's time to get rid of the bed, don't you think?'

'You almost never use it anymore, might as well.'

'It's in the way isn't it? Besides, I live in Japan. I should follow as many customs as I can, especially if I am going to be a Jitsugen Samurai.'

'I do not think it matters what you sleep on. I am sure Ninigi slept on grass. I think the whole room would be pointless if it was not for your need of clothes. If you could just stay as a tiger all the time, then we could sleep on a nice comfortable tree branch.'

'Yes, well, you have fur. While we can get away with going naked as a tiger. I don't think Japan at large would appreciate the naked gaijin.'

'A few might.'

Kou's last thought and the accompanying image he called up made David turn so red that Rie turned on him with her familiar, searching gaze. David mouthed the word "Kou" then returned to his task. The Friday before the graduation ceremony for the third years, Class 2B was busy preparing the gym. David was supposed to be holding up a red and white striped sheet that his classmates were attaching to hooks next to the stage. The mind-numbing work left his mind free to wander, or in his case, talk to Kou.

He hitched the curtain back up to its proper height and turned to see the progress throughout the gym. The first years were bringing in planters of red flowers to decorate the front of the stage, while other second years set out mats and chairs, or tried to tape red carpet into place.

In Nakano, junior high graduation was a big deal. The town was small enough that there was not a high school nearby. This meant all the students who wanted to go to high school had to go to schools in Himeji, or farther. Since the high school students went to, could affect what colleges they could get into, it was an important decision. Unlike in America, high school was not mandatory in Japan, meaning third years had to pass entrance exams to get in. The third years were anxiously waiting for news that could change their lives.

The graduation preparation work got David thinking about the years to come. While he had come as a one-year exchange student, thanks to Kou, he could no longer leave Japan for more than twelve hours without dying. Again. The Matsumotos and their contacts with the Imperial Household had already secured another year for him in the exchange program, but it had taken weeks to convince his father and sister it was for the best, even after they visited in autumn. It would be difficult to sell them on the idea of him going to high school in Japan as well.

'I wonder what kind of school I should go to. It's hard to know what kind of courses a Jitsugen Samurai will need. And what if I don't get into the same school as the twins? I bet Masao already has a plan. I hope it's not some stuffy academic only school. Maybe there's a protectors-of-Japan high school.'

"David... *David*." When he looked up, Rie sighed at his preoccupation. "We're done. You're just standing there holding onto the curtain like an idiot." Sliding closer she whispered, "You and Kou seem talkative today."

"Yep, talking about you," David said. The flippant remark elicited a strange look from her, but then Tsubasa and Kenta joined them. Kenta started asking him about one of the experiments David had helped his father with before moving to Japan. Rie slipped away as the three boys headed back to their homeroom deep in conversation about blocking radio waves.

Since the gym was occupied, they had a rare afternoon off from badminton practice. David had figured they would head back to the Estate early, but at the gates to the school, Natsuki grabbed Takumi and pulled him toward the route to her house. With Takumi stumbling after in surprise, Natsuki winked at Rie.

"Don't worry, Natsu is kidnapping Takumi for the afternoon," Rie said turning to David. She knew him well enough to expect the bemused expression on his face.

"And you're going to kidnap me too?" he asked.

"You're learning. So what's it going to be, peaceful or with a battle that will betray hundreds of years of Matsumoto secrets?" Rie's smile belied her words and serious tone.

"Who am I to argue with a scion of the famous Matsumoto swordsmiths?" David said, waiting for her to unfold the rest of her plan for him. Her smile widened in appreciation of the fact he was willing to play along. Under the early spring sun, they walked together through the buildings and fields around Nakano.

'*Don't overdo it. You...*' Kou began inside David's head.

'Shhh,' David said cutting him off. 'Let me have *some* fun. It's not like I'm going to make her summon a demon.'

"I have to say, you're a bad kidnapper. Not only am I free, but you're kidnapping me back to where I live," David said as they passed behind the police station. In answer, Rie gave him her most daunting grin, the kind she used before she gave him a sound beating in sparring matches.

With lightning reflexes, she had him in an arm lock that brought them uncomfortably close together before thrusting him forward and around a corner. They stood before the Nakano train station.

"Come on, we'll miss it." Rie ran forward, punched a few buttons on the ticket machine, threw some coins in, and retrieved two tickets. Nonplussed, David tried to look at the tickets, but Rie pushed him through an electronic turnstile and onto a waiting local train.

"Do I get to know where we're going?" he asked as they sat down.

"West."

They got off after only three stops, but since the area was so rural and mountainous, it took over half an hour to arrive. Still, since it was a short day of school it was early. Without a word, Rie led David up a steep, narrow, and winding country road.

'Okay, stop pouting. I'm sorry I told you to be quiet. It's just nice to be able to talk like a human once in a while.'

'*I shall consider your apology after I find out where we are going. I like this place, but I do not think I've stalked here before. Remember, we must stay on guard in case any more snacks… I mean attacks come our way.*'

With Kou awake within him again, David's body released the tension that had built up throughout his absence. The change was not lost on Rie, though David would not have noticed even then, except for her reaction.

"You already know about it?" she said turning on him, a bit of fire behind her brown contacts.

"What? No, it's Kou. I uh, insulted him earlier and now he's back," David replied, quick to reassure her.

"Oh, good. Hi Kou. Don't give anything away to him. It's a surprise." Again, Rie walked off.

'Do not bother. I know about as much as you, if that,' he thought. 'Humans...'

'Girls,' David agreed.

They arrived before an unassuming wooden gate and high fence. Gesturing to David, she bowed and entered the grounds through a sliding door. On the other side stood an old man with a shaved head wearing a brown, somber robe. The monk's ready smile jolted David with memories of Masato Matsumoto, the man David had known as Grandpa.

"Welcome Rie-chan, David-kun. Please come in," he said with a slight but graceful bow. He led them on a path between tall bamboo to a small, but well-built, house. There, the monk invited them to sit while he brought out an ancient tea set and poured scalding green tea. "Now, I'm always happy for a visit, but you have never brought any of your friends."

"Sorry, but are you a Matsumoto?" David asked confused by the old man and his similarity to Grandpa. David was so distracted he slipped into the casual form of Japanese used among friends. The slip got him an elbow from Rie.

Laughing, the monk waved Rie away, saying, "No, it's quite alright. I'm surprised he was doing so well. My name is Mikio, but you may call me Mickey if you like. I am not a Matsumoto but an old friend of the family. I went to school with Masato-kun. Nowadays though, I mostly sit up here in the mountains and observe life as best I can. And now, it's time for me to go and do some observing down in my vegetable garden. Enjoy yourselves."

With that, Mickey the monk was gone. It took David a few heartbeats to accept the fact he had left, so quietly had he moved.

"There's a lot more to him than you might think," Rie said. "Hopefully, we can come back again soon and spend some more time with him, but for now…" Rie's eyes twinkled as she stood. Unsure of what to expect, David followed her as she led him out a back door. There, two pairs of handmade sandals were waiting for them. With a nudge, Rie guided David around a bamboo screen.

Behind the house was a Japanese garden that put the Matsumotos' to shame. Every needle of every miniature tree had been shaped into perfection. Water flowed from a natural spring into a bit of bamboo and then spilled when the bamboo tipped over, filling the area with the intermittent sound of a low knock. The air was fresh and clean, as if washed in the purity of the surrounding mountains. In the center of a small pond, a single island of stone supported a single elegant bonsai tree. Past the garden, the ground fell away, revealing green-shrouded mountains around them and Nakano valley in the distance.

"I know how much you like the garden back home. This is one of my favorite spots to disappear to. I come here sometimes when I'm 'off training in the mountains.' I thought you might like to get away from Nakano for a little bit since we had the time," Rie said sitting down against a tree. A light breeze brushed past, making her hair dance along with the leaves. "And here we can relax. Thanks to Mikio-san's skills, we're likely safe from any possessed stuff."

They sat together, in Mikio the monk's yard, enjoying the rare freedom from the ever-watchful eyes at school and on the Estate. They spoke no words, but David felt a peace and comfort he had yet to find since that horrible night Grandpa had died. There was a constant pressure from knowing ōkami and other monsters were lurking in his future. Everything he did had to be better, *he* had to be better.

'I always figured my own life was forfeit anyway, since the day you possessed me,' David thought as the sun moved over the mountains. 'But I can't think of only myself, can I?'

'*Even before you came to Japan, you worried. I can see it in your memories. You worry about Jessica, about the Matsumotos, and about what Chul Soon might one day do. Plan. Do. Think about the future even, but do not worry,*' Kou thought, then withdrew deep into their combined subconscious.

Despite Kou's words, David felt the responsibilities that had hung over him since Jahangir had stolen Rie away. Every second of every day, there were reminders that he had to try harder, to do better, lest he fail Japan.

'No, that's too big an idea. I don't train for Japan. I'm a Jitsugen Samurai because of the Matsumotos. Grandpa died, Rie was taken, and Takumi killed. Even Ryohei is proof of the sacrifices they've made over the centuries. And you. I remember what the Zodiac Tiger told me.'

Even when on their own in the Matsumoto forest, Kou's animalistic senses kept them from becoming completely relaxed, yet sitting next to Rie in a stranger's garden with Kou withdrawn the tension ebbed from his body. Kou left just enough of a connection between them, that David could tell the young kami was delving into his own memories of the Zodiac Tiger. It reminded him that Kou was still very, very young.

David sighed and let all his worries, all his responsibilities fade from his mind. For a few long minutes, he lost himself among the raw nature of the mountains and sculpted garden trees. A dragonfly caught his attention and he watched as it flew over the water. It curved in low over a bit of grass, and then landed on Rie's knee.

With his host-sister, David had rarely found it difficult to talk. Even when there had been a language barrier, she had worked hard to understand him. Communication was an essential aspect of their training, and David had learned to read much in the small things she did, but words failed him as he watched the dragonfly's slow-moving wings. Rie smiled, and the dragonfly flew on, bobbing along the pond.

When they rose, neither consciously deciding it was time, they found Mikio waiting for them in the house. With a few words of poetry and an invitation to return whenever they wished, David and Rie left for the station. It was not until they were riding back along the two-car train that David spoke again.

"So where did Natsuki want to take Takumi?" David asked.

"What? No fifty questions about Mikio-san?" Rie said with feigned shock.

"Well of course I want to know more about him, but I was also trying to figure out the real reason you brought me out here. Certainly not just so I could see the view."

'*Don't make assumptions*,' Kou thought as a bit of the old familiar shadow crossed her face.

"Anyway, was it just me or did Mikio-san have on Hello Kitty socks?" David asked to cover.

Rie giggled and the change in her struck him. His first impressions of his host-sister had been a giggly schoolgirl, yet now her laugh seemed a jarring contrast to the Rie he had saved. It was as if he was seeing a memory of her old self, and David wondered which would fade away.

"He has a whole room of Hello Kitty memorabilia," she said from behind her hand. She covered her mouth in a way common among his female classmates. "He loves Kitty-chan, collects anything and everything to do with her. Of course, he wouldn't let it interfere with his other... duties. I assume you noticed the precision of just about everything there?"

"Not to mention how quiet he was," David added, smiling, but not sure why.

"Where do you think I learned how to be better at tracking than Takumi?" Rie said with a sly grin. "To answer your other question, Natsu wanted to have Takumi over for dinner. Her parents were home, and I needed to get away for a bit. I thought it would be fun to hangout, you know, like *real* kids for a change." The teenagers shared a sober look for the barest instant, and then both laughed at the absurdity of their lives. The lack of reaction from the other passengers confused David for a moment, until he realized they were purposely ignoring him and Rie. It made him laugh even harder as the train returned them to Nakano valley.

The others were waiting for David and Rie at the Estate. Together they worked to build their skills under Masao's strict tutelage while Yukiko dealt with a sword inquiry. After their usual practices, Masao surprised them all by agreeing to let Takumi and Kou spar.

Despite Takumi's armor, Kou's claws still found openings, requiring frequent breaks for Takumi to heal. Takumi took the slew of new scars enigmatically, and after he learned to counter Kou's power attacks, it soon became apparent the tiger had a lot to learn about fighting an opponent that fought back. David had better luck anticipating Takumi when he took over Kou's body, but his imperfect control gave Takumi the upper hand. They ended their bout early so that both would have time to recover before school.

The day after graduation was one that David had been afraid of for weeks, yet it was one that he was also excited about as well. White Day was the day where boys in Japan gave gifts back to the girls who had given them chocolate. He was limited in time and resources, but he also wanted to thank Rie for taking him to her favorite spot, even if she had never given him anything for Valentine's Day. He begged use of the kitchen from Yukiko and set to work baking his favorite cookies.

Jessica had emailed the recipes the three of them had baked every year in December. She did extract the reason first, much to his embarrassment. After mixing a big bowl of dough, he realized the Matsumotos' oven was about a quarter the size of an American one. He found an old toaster oven and used that as well.

For the classmates who had given him chocolate, he made each a small bag of cookies. For Natsuki he made one giant cookie as a way to get her back for the token chocolate and her joke in class. For Rie, he made a chocolate chip cookie, and then shaped it into a likeness of Kou, using icing in an attempt to match Kou's features. Though he offered two days of hunting, Kou was so indignant at being made into food that he refused to go look in a mirror or share his perfect memories. David left the orange, white, and black cookie with a note in Rie's room. When he returned from an abbreviated hunt with Kou that night, he found a large box of chocolates waiting on his floor.

十四

ANOTHER NEW YEAR

Going west proved too difficult, and south was dangerous. We lost plenty of what Chul Soon considered precious time back-tracking. The only advantage was that our trip had given us access to new identities that would get us to our destination if we took the right route. Of course, Okinawa would have to be our next stop...

The turn of the year might take place in January, but in Japan, beginnings had their roots in spring. It was a surreal moment for David when he looked into a mirror on the one-year anniversary of his arrival in Japan. A different person looked back, if you could call a once-dead and possessed boy a person. He was far taller. The excess childhood fat he had carried so long had melted into coiled muscle, and he was slowly gaining the balance and lithe steps he had envied so much in the twins. His mind was clear, and above all, Kou was there with him. The young tiger was a second perspective for every instant. He looked through the same eyes and yet saw things so differently. The extra opinion was a useful tool for a boy who still had much to learn about the foreign country that had become his home.

'*It makes perfect sense to me,*' Kou thought when David questioned him about all the variations in food and culture that accompanied the change in season. '*Your months are arbitrary anyway.*'

David sat with the other new third years in the gym for the opening ceremony. The second years were beside them, happy they would soon have kohai of their own. David was sure they looked forward to the first years calling them senpai.

After a bit of last minute scrambling by the student council, the vice-principal started things off with greetings and bows. It was awkward, as no one knew the new teacher, but the introductions were not until after the traditional opening speeches.

'Most of them seem decent enough. I don't know about Aramoto-sensei, though. I might go nuts in class if I have to listen to him insert twenty useless words for every sentence. I, uh, think, hmm, we should, ah, maybe fall asleep, right, in ah, his class.'

'*He does seem a bit tedious. I could bite him… Maybe stalk him through a dark alley.*'

David laughed along with Kou at the dark image both knew would never happen. Kou and David had enough rouge spirits, ghosts, demons, and gods to worry about without getting involved with annoying teachers.

With the introductions complete, the entire staff stood at the front of the gym while Principal Yogi announced each teacher's position for the new school year, including subjects and homerooms. The new vice-principal, a stern looking woman with a twenty-year-old dress and hawk-like stare, announced the most critical information. With the loss of so many students the previous year, rumors had been flying that they would change the way the third years' classes were organized, which meant David could end up in a different division than his friends. To their great relief, she announced the ABC divisions would remain the same since they were expecting a few new student transfers after the summer.

Together, Class 3B gathered to meet their homeroom teacher. Although Moriyama-sensei was still at the school, as a more senior teacher he had managed to escape the extra work of being a homeroom teacher as well. Kou growled within as David spotted a tall man who looked like he had barely made it into his tight-fitting suit.

'I wonder if he's the new P.E. teacher. He looks like someone tried to stick a young Arnold Schwarzenegger in a suit made for Tsubasa.'

'*That one is dangerous. Everything about him speaks of a life spent cutting others' short.*'

David observed the man's stiff stride, close-cropped hair, and set jaw as he approached. His manner as he walked toward them was intense enough to cause his classmates to pull closer together, as if being in a group could protect them.

"Hello." His voice was smooth and soft, belying his stiff presence and the edge around his jaw. Mizuki and her friends relaxed at the light tone in the man's voice, yet a quick look at the twins revealed they noticed the strain behind his words. "I am Takaeishi Nakamura. From now on, I will be your homeroom and shop teacher. Go to the classroom. I will meet you there."

His words were formal, but if David had just heard his voice, he would not have been concerned. Kou was so perturbed by the forty-something man, however, that David had trouble keeping his eyes from turning color.

"Something wrong Mr. Matthews?" Takaeishi asked. Although his words were like honey, his stance was a challenge, and David had a sinking feeling that his school life was going to change. With someone so observant, he would have to be on constant guard to keep the Matsumotos' secrets intact. "No? Very well. Get going."

Halfway through settling into their new classroom, Takaeishi joined them. He waved away Mizuki as she tried to give a welcome speech.

"Mizuki-san, the class representatives will limit their role to the student council forum," Takaeishi said. "Elections for this year's new class rep will be next week."

His words caused immediate murmurs throughout the class that were stopped by the look he gave them. Over the next hour, he displayed an intimate knowledge of each of them. Already he knew their names, and seemed to have some insights into the student's personalities and club activities.

'I wonder how much he knows about us. It could be trouble if he starts asking too many questions about some of last year's events,' David thought as Takeishi went through their schedule for the year.

Compared to the other teachers David had met, Takaeishi-sensei was by far the most distant. He was even quiet about his background, ignoring questions about which schools he had taught at. David was sure he was not the only student wondering about Takaeishi Nakamura as they began preparations for the first year's entrance ceremony.

"It's such a relief to be done," Takumi said on their walk home. "That was almost more difficult than a morning practice. I've never had anyone make me so tense for so long."

"I know. It's going to be tough having to deal with him every day, though everyone else seemed to like him," David said.

"That's just because they think he's handsome and haven't the training we do," Natsuki answered from alongside Takumi. "Though it was nice to see Mizuki's face."

"When he shut her up!" Rie laughed with Natsuki as the boys shared a look of concern.

Over the next few days, Nakano Junior High settled into new routines as the first years and new teachers adjusted. With Takaeishi always seeming to be around whenever they had a chance to talk, David and the other samurai had to be even more careful than usual in their conversations. They had all grown so close that it was difficult to winnow out the life they led on the Estate. Kou despised having to hide so much within David. On the Estate, he spoke freely with the others, and had his own relationships with each. Even at school, he sometimes inserted his own opinions when no one else could hear, but with the new teacher, they dared not risk revealing themselves to such an unknown.

'I guess I know how the flying dinner feels. Since Takumi is not a Jitsugen Samurai, she is unable to speak even when there are no Takaeishis around to hear. It is no wonder Reimi is so insistent that Takumi let her fly.'

Class 3B received a shock greater than the strange personality of their new teacher in their second week of class. Mizuki was disposed from her long running role as class representative. With a surprise nomination from Miu, the class elected Rie as their new representative. The other classes held their own elections and the new student council made Rie the new Student Body President, with Kenta as her vice president and Mizuki as a junior secretary.

On the Estate, David continued his morning practices with Yukiko, and alternated evening practices between working with his Seikaku, Kou, and sword making with Rie. David had felt Kou's annoyance growing, until Kou's restraint failed. In the middle of a breathing exercise with Yukiko, Kou asserted himself and made David transform into their animal form. Kou growled, pacing in agitation, his head taller than Yukiko's waist.

"David trains with his body and yes, sometimes we practice with me in charge, but you do not train us to fight with this body," he said in his growling voice as he sniffed at Yukiko. *"In the past, we have had to rely on instinct, and nearly failed to beat the ōkami that attacked us. Even the sparring with Takumi is limited."*

"I told Masao you were getting… annoyed," Yukiko said with a smile. "You are correct, Kou, we have been stalling. You can, of course, train with Takumi, and he can heal if your claws get inside his armor, but it is painful for him, and the scars are permanent. You could study the kata as David does, and you will, but until you have a proper sparring partner, there is no way to put them into practice. We were hoping that Rie would gain control over her power."

"Why would Rie's power matter?" David asked as Kou sat back to better look up at Yukiko.

"If she can master herself, she will be able to summon animals for you to fight, and over time, she may even summon more powerful ones that will allow you and Kou to improve your skills in both forms. For now, her inability to summon a target hobbles us. It has always been a difficult aspect of a Jitsugen Samurai's training. In the ancient past, well, human life was not viewed the same as it is today.

"In any case, you and Rie seem more comfortable together than you were, but there still seems to be something between you. You haven't spoken about the cultural festival yet, have you?"

Yukiko's lilting laugh rang through the garden as Kou's body struggled to give an animalistic approximation for David's embarrassment. It was not a reaction Kou's body was used to, and resulted in Kou's fur standing on end while his paw covered his nose.

Reluctant as he was to disturb the return of his relationship with Rie to normalcy, he promised to talk to her.

"Soon."

The next morning, Masao met the students behind the Dojo after their morning run.

"Instead of our normal practice, we're going to try another sparring match between Kou and Takumi," he said. "I want to do it now in case Takumi needs to heal before school. If there's time we can still do regular basics after."

Since Kou usually kept his armor on, he waited alone outside while the rest ran to the main house or Dojo to fetch theirs. Though Kou was eager to take over, David took the time to stretch a bit more after the run.

'I hate popping back into existence all sore,' he complained, as Kou's will playfully jabbed at his mind.

It was not until David had worked through every stretch he knew that he realized it was far too quiet. Distracted by a Zodiac dream, Kou growled. They shifted into Kou's tiger so that they would have access to his heightened animal senses. Kou noticed the irregularity as soon as his ears started functioning. Four hearts were beating far slower than they should be. The tiger kami recognized the flavor of the aura permeating the area as soon as he jumped to the veranda on the side.

"*Obake.*"

Wrapped in his leather and plate armor, Kou entered the Dojo with every sense alert. Masao, Takumi, Tsubasa, and Rie were sprawled around the building. Yukiko had returned to the main house, leaving two obake in the center of the room, their ghostly aura keeping David's friends asleep, just as the obake had knocked Natsuki out among the castle ruins.

'She is going to be either a wreck, or really, really pissed off when she wakes up,' David thought as he spotted his old partner. Kou growled a challenge and tensed to charge.

"Are you sure you want to do that?" one of the ghosts asked. He was thin and ragged, but with a twitch that made David wary. "My friend here can keep them under, or he can feed on them. We aren't supposed to kill them. Just you. He said all we need to do is kill one pesky tiger shape-shifter and we get all the souls we want. Let me kill you and we'll only drain your friends to the brink of death."

"Yeah," the other said. The fat old ghost kept opening and shutting its mouth as if heaving in some great effort. "A.

Present. He told us. To tell you. From your old friend." With each motion the ghost made, Kou felt another wave of the obake's aura.

"Quiet Ritsu," the first ghost said. "I'll do the talking."

Kou lunged, his long body stretching out. Sharp claws snicked out to impale the unwary ghost. Kou snarled as he latched teeth around the thin ghost's neck. Behind the fat one, Kou just caught the outline of another ghost seep through the wall as a jerk of his powerful neck sent him and the obake spinning through the air.

Enraged, Ryohei stuck two translucent fists through Ritsu's head. His gasps turned to choking coughs and the samurai began to stir. Natsuki's eyes, filled with rage, flew open. Her hand slapped the floor in a convulsion knocking against Tsubasa's bag. From within came the faint but familiar hum of electricity. Her hand closed around a strap, and although the rest of her body seemed paralyzed, she heaved it at the thin ghost.

Tsubasa's mirror sailed out of the bag and slammed into the ghost. He shrieked, sending all of them reeling from the mental and physical blows. Kou fell away, blood pouring from his sensitive ears. David transformed, his world silent as the ghost tried to shake the mirror from his body. With strong will, he summoned his Seikaku and plunged it into the evil spirit before him. Careful to keep his sword away from Ryohei, he dispatched the other obake before turning back into Kou. Together they dashed out of the Dojo to check on Yukiko and the rest of the Estate.

Aside from David, all the samurai were so ill that Yukiko excused them from school. David, however, healed in time to go. Takaeishi seemed very interested the samurai's absence, but, since Yukiko was a nurse, said nothing. When David returned to the Estate, he once again had to record the incident in his diary.

"I'm going to have to practice that technique," Ryohei said as David wrote. "It might be useful to learn how to put you humans to sleep."

"Yeah, well, just don't ask Natsuki to help you practice. I don't think Tsubasa wants any more prototypes destroyed."

When they finished, Masao sent them all searching along every inch of the wall. He had explained that such attacks should not have been possible given the ancient nature and sacred protection from hundreds of years of visits by so many kami. Sure enough, they found an odd metal tablet wedged between two rocks that formed the foundation of the wall. Masao refused to let anyone touch it until after he had donned his full priestly garb and produced two long chopsticks with intricate carvings. They were all banished from the Estate during the extraction.

Kou and Takumi got their chance to spar a week later. It went so horribly that Takumi ended up with two jagged scars on either side of his throat. Kou remained unapologetic, and retreated whenever David tried to talk about the match.

"I bet he has more than just a headache," Tsubasa whispered when they were back at school and Takumi was once again absent. Takaeishi's glare and his knowledge of what his host-brother was going through kept David from turning to answer. Knowing from experience how painful the accelerated healing process was for the possessed, made him want to let Kou bite their newest member for just the barest instant. By the time they returned, Takumi was fine and was eager for a rematch, which Kou smugly accepted.

Due to the dangers of exposing Takumi's healing abilities, and without any way to explain the scars that even high collars could not hide, Masao forbade them from sparring again. Kou had to sit through a long speech from Masao for not working with David during the fight. Instead of sparing, Masao took a greater hand in their weekend training. He worked with both Kou and Takumi so that they could better practice the various techniques that would keep them alive someday, without scaring Takumi past all recognition.

The next time Reimi appeared, she complained that they had not included her as well. Masao's explanation that the fact she was still only slightly larger than a pigeon made sparing that impossible for her, did not console her. Instead, Masao set her tasks to help hone her flying skills. Soon Reimi and Kou were spending their evenings playing hide and seek with various objects throughout the Matsumoto Estate. Their favorite version was for Kou to hide a rat, so that Reimi could search for it from above the trees and then dive and retrieve it before Kou could find and tackle her. The games were so entertaining that Natsuki and Tsubasa began betting on the outcome.

Between school, badminton practice, nights with Rie in the forge, and all the training, April flew by faster than Reimi at her fastest dive. Things seemed to be going so well, even with the random "presents" from the Jeongs that David did not want to ruin things by bringing up old issues. Despite the fact that Rie had yet to summon anything else, and his promise, David shied away from discussing anything with Rie more substantive than their latest project in the forge.

十五

A WEEK'S VACATION

Family can be annoying, especially when they are not really your family at all, except maybe by the loosest definition. There are always too many questions and they feel entitled to answers. They expect to know your business just because they share a bit of history. But then, how could they know we were so different? Chul Soon with his need for revenge, and me, well, I have always been a bit different...

Due to the way the holidays lined up, Golden Week, Japan's spring break, gave Nakano Junior High a full week off from school starting May 1. While most students spent the break going on trips or playing with their friends, the Matsumotos used the time for extended training in the mountains around the Estate. David had to admit he now looked back on the difficulties of his first trip with fondness, despite how exhausting trekking through the forests and attempting to remain quiet had been.

The value of the yearly trips was not lost on him after familiarization with the mountains and forests made it far easier to stop the ōkami that had later threatened the Nakano Festival. He was beginning to realize just how important the Estate was.

With at least an idea of what to expect, and with Kou and Reimi along to help, David anticipated an exciting week. The plan was for David, Rie, Takumi, and Natsuki to go out into the wilds while Masao, Yukiko, and Tsubasa hunted, attempting to keep them from reaching the Estate's Shrine. Everyone had agreed Tsubasa was a bit too new to the Matsumoto training to be effective alone, and that five versus two would defeat the point of the exercise. In preparation for their outing, David, Takumi, and Kou had all donned their armor. Although Kou had wanted to run, David forced himself to sleep instead. In full armor, he laid down on his new futon.

The Estate was quiet when David awoke with a sense something was wrong. Thanks to Kou, he was able to wake almost instantly, yet remain unmoving and quiet. Takumi still complained about the hours he had lost trying to wake David up the first couple of months that he had lived there. As he smiled at the stray thought, David and Kou tried to understand why they had awoken.

Though the house was silent, Kou insisted they at least take a stroll through the hallways. David padded through the corridor around the sliding doors. As usual, the tatami room doors were closed since the Matsumotos slept behind them. He worked his way around toward the kitchen side of the house. As he passed behind the main hall to the tatami rooms in the back, David felt a light breeze blow against his ankles. While Japanese houses were often drafty, designed to catch cooling breezes, the Matsumoto shut back of the house at night to keep out the insects that came from the Japanese garden.

'*There should be no northern wind.*'

'At least not at night.'

David quickened his pace, but strove to keep silent. His armor made the task more difficult as the metal and Kevlar plates tried to swish together. At the back of the main house, his internal alarm bells rang louder as he found one of the outside sliding doors was open. It took three long strides to confirm that Rie's door was open and her room empty. A flash of movement in the trees beside the Dojo caught his attention. A sudden burst of adrenaline pumped through his system as Kou's instincts awoke within him. Remembering one of Grandpa's admonitions to them before he died, David and Kou breathed to calm the rush of impulse and focus on merging their separate personalities. They needed both of their strengths, but as one.

In the distance, Kou caught the movement again, furtive, but not like an animal. With a quick look back into Rie's room, David jumped to the ground, feeling the hard gravel of a path beneath his bare feet. He picked up a trail of kicked stones and scuffmarks in the dirt that had him stalking ever faster toward the movement. The trail separated, one branch leading from the wall, another curved for the front gate.

'*The gate trail is clearer. Heavier paws.*'

'What about the movement. Shouldn't we go after that?'

David looked back to the trees, but could spot nothing else in the darkness. With a quick decision, they turned, following the trail as it led to the front of the Estate.

At the main gate, they found the doors disengaged from the inside. David felt exposed, out in the middle of the road with no idea what he was hunting. It took another second to realize he had not seen Ryohei floating above the pond, another disturbing sign. David dashed across the road into the trees. Crouching, he wove through the underbrush until he picked up the trail again. David followed the discreet tracks back along the Estate perimeter, past the stream, and toward the wilderness of the mountains.

'Is this part of the golden week challenge? Did they change it at the last minute?'

'Those were not Matsumoto tracks, I can tell the difference even with your pathetic senses. Be careful. I think the others in the Estate are still asleep.'

As the trail wove away into the woods, David began to catch more details in the tracks as they grew less confused by other feet. He was able to employ more of Rie's training in tracking. The first thing he caught was that there were several people.

'Kidnappers?'

'It looks like they took Rie. These tracks are human, but they do not walk like the humans I've seen before.'

'I don't like how there are fresh tracks over even more that are a few hours old.'

David hurried forward. He was far into the woods when he noticed another set of tracks merge with the older ones. Like the first, these too showed at least one person had a much heavier load than the others.

"You'll want to stop there," a voice said from ahead in the darkness. David sped up. A splash of reflected moonlight caught his attention as David recognized the movement from earlier at the Estate. "Stop or I shoot."

David halted. His gaze locked on a dark shadow that he was sure was the source of the voice.

"Where is she?" David asked, his voice low.

"*I* don't know," said a voice with an exaggerated tone, like a lawyer. David caught an undercurrent that warned him the whininess was only an affectation. The man was a killer. "But my employer invites you to come alone and find them. He has a use for you. Of course, if you try to get help, they will die."

"I'm already coming alone aren't I?" David asked stepping forward again.

"None of that," he said. "You'll stay right where you are until I'm gone."

"Bull," David surged forward. He heard a click, and then felt impacts on his chest. Hard rubber bullets bounced off his armor. David laughed and pumped his legs. Another gleam of moonlight and this time white-hot pain shot through him as a real bullet found a mark between his shoulder and arm fittings. Kou roared within at David's pain and the fiery smell of blood. David's vision shifted, and Kou's advanced senses caught the movement of their assailant, even in the minimal light.

Kou pounded after, their quick transformation, catching David off balance. Slug after slug exploded in the dirt around Kou's minimal armor. As he faltered under the assault of bullets, he roared in rage, his voice echoing in the forest around them. Shaking himself, Kou moved faster, fed by the rare fire of pain. The man seemed to hesitate, to panic, and then stopped just long enough to unload an entire clip on semi auto at the advancing tiger's legs. Kou's muscles gave out as too much connective tissue was torn to hold his weight. The man turned and stalked back toward them, fitting a new clip in the gun's grip.

"We will expect you shortly," he said as he aimed and fired two more shots into Kou's hind leg. He finished with a blow to the head that, while Kou could hear coming, could do nothing about.

Kou's advanced healing powers did their work. He awoke and his vision cleared enough for him to make out the dusty ground just in front of his snout. Kou growled past the pain and lurched to a standing position. The movement sent jolts of ice through his corded muscle. His whiskers twitched in agitation as his tail swept behind him. With a tentative, jerking step, they began following the trail again. Kou yowled in discomfort every time his advanced healing forced a slug back out of his muscle and skin. David tried to hide from the pain he could feel so acutely through Kou's heightened senses. He knew where each bullet lodged and could trace every painful path they took as Kou's body disposed of them. Without his own body to focus on, Kou's pain dominated David's consciousness.

'We shouldn't have transformed, my armor is better than yours,' David thought as the last slug popped out of their leg and clinked against a rock. 'We really need to avoid getting shot.' Kou's nostrils flared at the smell of his own blood.

"*When we catch him, I am going to gnaw off his leg,*" Kou growled as they limped on. "*I am going to chew slowly.*"

Kou and David struggled on throughout the rest of the healing process. Kou tracked their assailant north and west. The occasional footprints, broken branches, ferns, and other indicators made it easy to find the gunman's path. The instant Kou healed, they transformed back into a human. While it was still light out, David would be able to see well enough to follow the trail. Together, they decided to give Kou a chance to rest so that when night fell they could rely on his vision in the darkness. Even then, David could tell from the tracks they would not find Rie soon.

David walked and ran around trees and over swift streams. The forest was familiar, but the tracks led ever onward. As twilight approached, David came upon a clearing in which the man's tracks disappeared altogether. Before he could let out his yell of frustration, they turned into Kou and it came out as a growl. With Kou's eyes better suited for the night and his sense of smell, they scoured the area but found only a faint acrid odor lingering in the air.

The young tiger searched for vehicle tracks, but the clearing was free of obvious marks. With the last light of the day, Kou spotted a small glimmer on the far side of the clearing. There, plain to see was a cheap wristwatch. It had the stink of the gunman, and with its power out and both hands pointing to the north and west. In the dark, Kou moved onward.

An animalistic intensity drove them forward. It was a new feeling. They had never lost prey while hunting. David had to battle against Kou's primal side as he tried to keep him on track. The man who had shot them was gone. Whether or not he had been leaving tracks on purpose before was a mystery, but there were none now. All they had was the hope the watch was left to guide them in the correct direction.

As they stalked, thoughts plagued David. 'Who else had they taken? Why had it been done?'

Kou focused on the gunman. If they found him, David knew it would be difficult to restrain Kou. The thought of Rie's empty room floated out from the depths of his mind, playing out before them as if the darkness of the forest was a mirror for his worst memories. Other visions came soon after. With Kou so focused on trying to find a scent, David was alone and with little control in a very dark world.

He relived the moment his hand broke when he tried to punch Koji. The memory seemed to taunt him from beneath a pine tree, only to disappear as they ran past. A vision of Grandpa's mangled body replaced it, followed by the dark orbs of Rie's eyes when she was a yūrei. The horrible images sped up, and the forest around them appeared ever more unreal.

At their worst, David's troubled mind caused Kou to miss a branch and they went tumbling down a hill. The bumps and whirling ground was enough pull them both out of the darkness.

'We are in our element, the forest is our strength. We will find the prey with the gun.'

"The coward did say his employer wanted to be found," David mused as Kou shook leaves from his fur. "So be it, we will find him."

The sun rose in the sky, so they transformed to let Kou rest. David trod barefoot through the rough terrain as the tiger rested within him.

"Should have grabbed my armor boots," he grumbled as stones and branches sliced at his feet. They were forever in pain as the forest floor opened new wounds, even as his Jitsu-gen Samurai powers healed him. Although David's body was refreshed from Kou's long dominance, the steep mountains and rough footing wore on him. His armor was as comfortable as a second skin, but its weight also drained his reserves. By the time the new night came, David was happy to revert to Kou. Kou's light armor hindered him far less than David's, and his paws were one with the forest. The young tiger god was made for, made by, and even helped to make the very earth, the root of every forest. With the moon, stars, and Kou's animalistic awareness to guide them, they moved through the second night, ever north and west.

'There must be a connection between our link to the forest and the fact that my Seikaku is wood,' David thought as they hunted. Even when in their human form, David felt more awake and alive among the trees than he did in the city. He had never forgotten the feelings of lethargy and distance during the plane ride to Kyushu, or his fear at the waters of the ocean. They were meant to be among the living places of Japan. Kou remained silent, focusing on the input from his senses in the deep of night.

While they sought after Rie, Kou stopped to sate his hunger with the small animals he could easily catch along the way. If he had the time, he could have found a larger animal that would have kept them comfortable for a day or more, but with speed being a necessity, Kou gave up much of his stealth in their pursuit. As Kou cracked through a bone, David berated himself for leaving in such a hurry. Aside from the trail he had left, there was nothing for anyone else on the Estate to go on. He had no radio, no supplies, and no shoes. David also feared for his own body. Although Kou could sustain them, perhaps even indefinitely, they had never tried going so long without David eating. They had no idea how it would affect them.

With their shared belly growling again a few hours later, Kou caught the sound of quick scampering feet nearby. Slowing, Kou blended into his surroundings to the greatest extent possible. David withdrew as the tiger took over, his hunting instincts driving all else out. He became a kind of observer, with the most realistic TV in the world, complete with sight, sound, smell, and twitching tail, all seeking after its prey. His large paws moved silently over even the most difficult arrays of branches, leaves, and grass.

They spotted dinner high in a tree. A tanuki, a type of Japanese raccoon sat with its head in a hole. Its back legs kicking as it tried to reach deeper in. Kou paused to watch it.

'It's alright, this one we can eat.'

'What you only like certain kinds of raccoons? You've never had a raccoon before.'

'Some tanuki are not for eating. This one's ancestors grew stupid long ago.' Kou crept up a nearby tree.

It was over with a speed borne of hunger, even with the slow creep, the steady beat of their heart, the straining of their senses. When Kou sprang, his full weight knocked out the small animal before it ever knew there was a danger. Together they fell to the ground where, growling in pride, Kou began to eat. Though he gorged himself, his senses still sought for danger.

Just as the tanuki missed the assault from above, so did Kou. He barely had time to roll away from his kill and on to his back, baring his sharp claws as the forest around them turned to fire.

十六

THE MAN WITH THE GUN

It took far longer than we expected to leave them. There were all of those probing questions. I reassured my brother that it is in our nature to inquire. Even with the delay, we left far more prepared than we had hoped. We were finally on the last leg of our trip; soon we would be in a position to strike at will...

"We might have found you sooner, but I couldn't carry the Eye," Reimi said once Kou had smothered his singed fur. "*Takumi stopped next to a nearby village. It's got these terraced fields cut into the mountains, and I circled around and around them in case you were playing in the mud. But then I swept out over the trees and spotted a shadow so I glided lower. I worried I might swoop down on a deer again, but hey, it was you. I wish I were bigger. I bet you would have popped right out from the forest at the height I was flying.*"

"What's an Eye?" Kou asked, curious enough to talk to Reimi instead of just scowling at her for burning some of his fur.

Kou had been feeding on his tanuki when he heard a rustle from Reimi's passage through the canopy. Seeing Kou's fangs turn on her, Reimi had burst into flames just as Kou's bloody jaws snapped shut in surprise. Kou had rolled in an attempt to avoid the crackling tongues of fire roiling off the dangerous little phoenix, but she had still singed him. As Kou recovered his composure, his fur rippling and large eyes blinking, Reimi settled her wings and began to speak. The occasional spark flew along her wings.

"*Sorry, you startled me,*" Reimi said, clawing at the scorch marks on the root. "*You aren't easy to catch up to, let alone find. By the way, I thought cats were supposed to be clean.*"

"*What?*" Kou asked as he looked around.

"*Your whole muzzle is covered in blood.*" Reimi laughed. As she cooled, the darkness returned to the forest around them. Reimi reverted to her usual light gray. She danced a little on the root, fighting back the urge to transform. Somewhere within her, Takumi was impatient. "*Look, Takumi could not catch up by foot, but we left some things behind that we need. I'll let Takumi convince you, but think about how much faster we will find Natsuki if we hunt together.*"

Before Kou could respond to the news that Natsuki was missing too, Takumi appeared on the root in his stylish ash and fire streaked armor. Blinking in the utter darkness, his practiced gaze swept the night as he tried to find Kou. The faint rustle of fur on fur as Kou wiped the remains of his dinner from his jaws, brought Takumi's attention to him.

"*So then Natsuki was the other one they kidnapped?*" Kou asked.

"Yes, look, we can talk more later. I've been trying to find you since you didn't show at our meeting place," Takumi said. "I have supplies stashed about ten kilometers away. I've been switching with Reimi, but she's not big enough to carry everything we will need. If you will wait for me I can get them and we can hunt together."

David and Kou tried not to be angry at the delay. While they both understood the benefits of going into a potential fight with backup, and had been able to finish off the rest of the raccoon, it was difficult to restrain themselves during the long wait.

David was pacing when Takumi's stumbling steps brought him into hearing range. When David got to him, however, his anger died away. Takumi had pushed his body past the breaking point. Even David could see the dark blotchy skin concealing the snapped tendons, bruised muscles, and broken bones his host-brother was sporting. To do the kind of damage he saw, Takumi must have strained the limits of survival, pitting his advanced healing against the damage he did with each overextended step. Only his connection with Reimi, riding the edge between damage to his body and their accelerated rejuvenation had kept him alive.

Falling to the ground, Takumi fumbled for a radio on his pack. He shivered in obvious pain as the healing process continued, his legs jerking uncontrolled.

'We should be hunting down the coward with the gun, not playing with radios. We can show him what kind of holes our teeth can make.'

'It's too late. We made the choice to wait for Takumi, so we aren't going to catch them unless they stop as well, which they will otherwise they'll hit a major town, and if that was their plan they would have gone east.'

Kou's growl made Takumi fumble with the dials on the radio. Even as he worked the controls, Takumi's body began to relax as it healed. He bit back a growl of his own as a broken toe popped back into place with a jolt of pain. Though the radios were military issue, and encrypted, Takumi failed to raise anyone. Kou backed away as the static from channel after channel hurt his sensitive ears.

"*What's wrong with it?*" he asked, working his jaw a little. As he had grown larger, his voice had grown ever deeper, giving it a far more menacing tone than he intended.

"I… I don't know," Takumi said. His eyelids fluttered as he struggled to stay conscious. "I can't raise anyone. Someone might be jamming the signal, or none of the radios are on back home. Either way it's not good."

Realizing Takumi was about to pass out, Kou had him strap the gear to his back. Takumi finished adjusting his sword then transformed back into Reimi. The little bird hopped up onto Kou's shoulders and fell asleep. With a quick look behind him, Kou took off through the woods. Without Takumi awake to guide them toward Natsuki, Kou followed their previous course through the forested mountains.

Much later, when Kou could go on no further, he stopped and transformed. The pack and Reimi flopped to the ground as his body contorted from lithe and furry to David's corded muscles and heavy samurai armor. Falling to the ground, Reimi shuffled her wings and tail-feathers languidly. Seconds later, she too disappeared in her customary smoke as Takumi emerged in his armor.

"How come I don't get to appear in a swath of smoke too?" David sighed. Takumi's appearances were always impressive. Materializing, his armor made him even more indistinct and mysterious in the blanketing smoke.

"You aren't cool enough," Takumi said. Behind the mask, his host-brother's face twisted in pain. Takumi doubled over. David helped him sit. Though he was not tired, his mind recovered during his time in Kou's body, the lack of rest for both bodies left David's muscles sore with sympathetic pain. It was as if his muscles' cells remembered the same strain as Kou's cells.

"I guess the whole instant healing thing has limits after all," David muttered.

"Yeah, our endurance," Takumi said. With a free hand, he released his mask and took off his helmet. "It's going to be a little bit before I can move. I know you want to keep going but you're shaking too. Sit, eat some jerky, and then we can move on."

David frowned, and then saw how much his hands were jerking around. They made it difficult for him to go through Takumi's bag, but he managed to grab water and meat for both of them.

"Okay," David said around a huge gulp of water. "If we have to wait, tell me what happened on the Estate, how do you know they took Natsuki?"

"Back in Nakano, I waited for you, Rie, and Natsu at the spot. I hadn't been able to sleep well, so I left early and waited outside. As the time came and went for our meeting, I got annoyed, then nervous. I figured even if you had gone back to your old habits, Natsuki wouldn't be late without a good reason."

David threw a hunk of meat at him in annoyance for his lack of trust, but let him continue without otherwise interrupting.

"I scrawled a note and left it on the ground for Reimi."

"*I'll still get you two back for my fur,*" Kou growled from David's mouth. "*I was minding my own business, eating, and then poof, half my fur is singed. If it hadn't grown back so fast, I would have had phoenix for dessert.*"

"Anyway," Takumi said in an obvious attempt to change the subject, "my note outlined the situation and asked her to check the area. Just as I can understand some of what she's doing when we are flying, she already understood the basics of what I had been up to. I think it is hard for her to keep her full attention on me while trapped behind my senses. The note made things faster.

"I figured her better vision and Reimi's connection to Natsu would help us meet up faster. It's like the itch when Reimi really wants to fly. Natsuki feels a growing pressure that can only be satisfied by a proximity to Reimi."

David frowned at the reminder he no longer had a partner, but then shrugged the thought away. He had friends and they were in danger.

'My hands need to stop shaking.'

"I know Reimi hates the fact I have to go to school and she can't participate there," Takumi said. "I think that's why she took off so fast, but even as the wind wove over our wings minutes passed without Natsu coming to find us. She caught movement on the Estate so after gaining a bit more altitude, she rotated her wings and we were hurtling toward the ground. You have no idea what it's like. Even with the muddled senses I get, that is the one thing I feel more clearly than everything else.

"This is taking too long. Let me try something." Takumi straightened, then relaxed. His eyes unfocused and David noticed Takumi use one of the breathing techniques Yukiko had taught him. Then Takumi began speaking again, yet it was with a tone David remembered Masato and Masao had used when telling David the story of Ninigi and Amaterasu. Though not as refined as his father, Takumi's words called images to David's mind. Where the elder Matsumotos had seemed to transport him to the ancient forests of Japan, Takumi provided more of a standard experience.

David saw Masao and Yukiko sleeping in their room, as if the fact they had told Takumi about what happened enabled him to relay it to David in perfect clarity. Masao's eyes jerked open. His body remained still as his hand reached up to touch his lips. Yukiko stirred beside him. A single look passed between them before they moved, throwing open the sliding doors around their room.

David's host-parents circled the house in their nightclothes until they found Rie's door ajar. Yukiko bent down to examine what David recognized as his own foot prints, leading away.

They split without speaking, Masao heading for the Dojo, Yukiko disappearing into the house. Yukiko returned with a bundle in her arms as she sprinted after Masao. When they emerged from the Dojo, it was in their armor. Their swords strapped at their sides. In addition to the traditional wear, they had the radio equipment the Imperial Household had previously given them. Thus connected, they split to search the various tracks around the house as the sun rose above the eastern trees.

David watched as Reimi landed beside Yukiko while she examined the main gate's mechanism. After a slight jump from surprise that revealed how tightly wound she was, Yukiko radioed Masao and he joined them before the house. After learning the group's plan to meet that morning, and how no one had shown, even after changing into Reimi, Masao sent her to the Ashikawas' Estate to see if Natsuki was at home. It did not take her long to get back with confirmation that there appeared to be the same signs of kidnapping that had shown up at the Matsumoto Estate.

"Someone has been sloppy, leaving trails and marks for us to follow," Masao said, a dark edge to his smile.

"What about David?" Yukiko began. A noise outside the gate stopped her. The sound of steel swords leaving their sheaths rang through the morning breeze as a gangly boy popped his head through the gate. Tsubasa stopped short seeing the Matsumoto elders in ready stances with naked blades, and Reimi fluttering above, red in her wrath. The trio relaxed as Tsubasa stepped forward.

"Did I miss something?" Tsubasa asked as he took in the situation.

"Reimi, would you mind changing back to Takumi? It would be easier to explain what we know once," Yukiko asked, looking up as Reimi's color reverted to its usual ash gray. With a blink of her red eyes, she landed and Takumi remerged in her place. Wrapped in his armor he looked around as he regained his balance and analyzed the situation.

Masao relayed what they knew of the situation, telling them about the gas he had tasted on his lips. He spoke about how David too, had gone.

'I'm glad they noticed my tracks. It's why I avoided cross-ing the older ones. Grandpa did the same thing when he went after Rie.'

"Takumi, take a radio and see where David's trail leads," Masao commanded. "Tsubasa, you will have to stay with us on the Estate. Whoever did this may try to come after you next, and though our walls have failed, this is still the safest place."

"Wait," Tsubasa called as Takumi turned to leave. "I have something that might help." Tsubasa clawed through his bag as the four of them walked back to the Japanese garden.

"We call it the Eye," Tsubasa said, holding out a small box the size of a phone. "Thanks to Ryohei I think I've isolated the frequency and other harmonics that resonated with the ghosts. From there we were able to isolate kami by spying on Takumi and David. At first, we could not find a filter that would focus a kami, even though we knew there should be one. Masao helped us out with that of course."

Takumi turned with a surprise look to his father. David could sense the shock his host-brother had felt as the images showed the hint of a smile playing at the corners of Masao's mouth, though the rest of his features remained serious.

"We were going to use it to catch you coming in to the Es-tate," Tsubasa said with a smile. "It's like infrared. Just point it and if there's anything resonating at the setting you select it will pop up on the screen.

"This looks like an old iPhone. You fit all that into such a small case?" Yukiko asked, impressed with the object.

"Yeah, see it's pretty much just a miniature infrared cam-era, screen, nob, and a circuit board," Tsubasa said, basking in the praise. "We were able to cram it all into an old iPhone chas-sis we grabbed from the school lab."

Stepping back, Tsubasa demonstrated the Eye, first point-ing it at Yukiko. The screen remained black until he turned the nob. Faint wire representations appeared on the screen exactly where the trees were. It was as if someone had ripped them out and replaced them with a stylized metal framework.

"It seems like trees and animals resonate as well, though we haven't had time to explore what that means," Tsubasa explained. With another flip of the nob, the screen went blank again. Then he turned the camera on Takumi.

Like fire, the entirety of Takumi's body was on the screen. The edges of his body were all in orange, going to red, purple, blue, and finally white hot. In the center of his chest, though, was static. The colors swirled and pulsed as if an inferno waiting to explode on the world, beautiful and terrifying, even with the small screen.

"We don't know why the screen wont register his center, its transmitting, but we have yet to find a way to display the camera's input," Tsubasa said, looking over their shoulders. "It can spot them within thirty meters. I tested it the other night during training. It might work on ōkami as well, though I'm not sure. I need one to test it on."

With the technical presentation finished and every possibility considered, Takumi transformed back into Reimi. Masao filled her in on their plans. Masao and Yukiko would stay with Tsubasa on the Estate. Takumi would track David and stay in contact with them. Masao agreed to let them go alone after Reimi argued that she could take to the air if need be without leaving anyone else behind.

"It's up to the two of you," Yukiko said. Reimi changed back and they re-outfitted Takumi with the radio, food, water, his sword, and the Eye.

With a stiff bow to his parents, Takumi ran off in pursuit of David and Kou. Even though he was moving quickly, helped along by David's clear trail, it still took until after noon for Takumi to find the spot where the gunman had shot David. Noting the messed tracks and bullet casings, he radioed back to the Estate with the information, and with the fact that David had changed to Kou when he found the new tracks. Scanning the area with the Eye showed nothing out of the ordinary, except for one area of sickly green splashes on the screen. When he looked without the Eye, Takumi could find no explanation, but felt he had seen something similar before. He realized the splayed patterns were blood. Just as he could not see Kou's blood with his eyes, David's did not register on the screen.

"That's when I started running full out," Takumi said. "I switched off with Reimi like you did, but we had to keep going back for the supplies. Reimi can fly father and faster than either of us could run, but in the end, the distance we covered was up to me. We must have been gaining on you."

David wiped his face, as if rubbing away the last vestiges of the visions. The night was the deep darkness before the first light of morning could begin to shade it to a lighter hue.

"You've been running far longer than I have. Anyway, you will have to teach me how to do that," David said. Looking at his hands, he noticed they had stopped shaking. "Let's go see if we can't find the girls. Kou wants to snack on one particular man's legs."

Soon after starting off, they reached the peak of the mountain they had begun climbing the previous day. The opposite slope before them was bare and rocky, an unnatural emptiness that left them exposed as it plunged to a wide valley. Where the ground leveled off below them, green trees spread out in an arc that stretched into the distance. Tall sentry trees fenced in another expansive, yet quite different forest from the one they had been traveling through. The trees ahead seemed older, closer, even from their high vantage point. In the far distance, David was just able to make out the speck of a lake by the reflection of lights from the town beside it.

"Look. There's a fire to the west," Takumi said, his dark mask locked on the bare glow among the trees. With a growl in his throat, David flung his legs out, his bare feet ripping at the ground and propelling him toward the fire.

十七

DEER FRIENDS

Her memories, the little bits gleaned from her soul while my pack fed stayed with me for the longest time, but Chul Soon was there, as always, to remind me that she was a distraction. Better rewards would come soon enough. I needed the encouragement. Container ships are not conducive to comfort or happy thoughts, and a month without feeding, a sore trial. Chul Soon always got so grumpy when he did not have the chance to steal a spirit or two…

David halted just before the first outlying trees. Unlike those on the Estate, these trees were not ancient, preserved by generations of Matsumotos. Fire, floods, and lightning had provided the destruction needed for a continual renewal of fresh growth. The trees were tall and vibrant, full of a thrumming energy.

'Power washes out from them. There is life beyond the trees.'

The Matsumotos had lived on their estate for hundreds of years. The continual presence of humans had driven away the large animals that had roamed the area when Ninigi had been alive. Here, though, was an untamed land. This was a place where Kou could hunt and find no lack of prey. He could lie under the trees and not be bothered by pollution or the noise of humans.

David and Kou knew that Natsuki and Rie were beyond the trees. With such a driving desire to recover them and to hunt the wild beasts within the forest, it took every ounce of David's self-control to restrain Kou. The place echoed with an ancient presence. Despite his instincts, even Kou got the sense it would be impolite to go farther without welcome. They could tell Takumi felt the same. David and Takumi had stopped together. There was something on the wind and in the rustle of tree branches. Someone was coming.

'*Prepare to fight*,' Kou thought, his emotions beginning to surge through David. '*Let me make the challenge.*'

"Natsu is close," Takumi said. Though his face was calm, David saw determination in his stance. His whole bearing urged David to chance a bit of rudeness. With an apprehensive look, David stepped into the forest. The night was getting old, first light, the perfect time to strike would soon come. They moved as stealthily as possible, keeping to the darkest bits of forest as they neared the fire. The acrid smell of smoke hit them first, followed by the weak glow of flames below.

Takumi and David halted to observe the camp. There were several men in the firelight. Natsuki and Rie lay side by side a bit away from the fire and under a tree. The sense that something was approaching, faster now, hung over them. Beside him, Takumi's head jerked as if he too was feeling the driving will for them to *get out*. Then a yell burst from one of the men.

Natsuki was up and moving, a sharp twig in her hand and cut tape on her wrists as she pulled off a blindfold. Beside her, Rie remained unmoving.

A giant black bear, tall on two massive legs turned. Coals from the fire scattered as the bear brushed against a log. The bear had appeared behind a group of men who jerked away from the embers. David moved, but already at least two of captors were unconscious and bleeding from wounds inflicted by the bear's sharp claws. At the far end of the light three men remained standing. Like their fallen comrades, they were all dressed in black, reminiscent of the clothes the Matsumoto used for their own camping trips. With a yell, one of the men sprang at the wild animal with a pair of wicked looking blades. Dodging the massive claws, he managed to strike a leg before the bear's free paw sent him cartwheeling into a tree.

The man hit with a sickening thump and slid the better part of a meter to the ground. Seeing her awake, one of the men looked between Natsuki, the bear, and the man beside him, then turned and ran into the night. The final man stood relaxed and confident. David scowled as Kou roared within. It was the man with the gun. David was halfway to tiger before he could jerk Kou's attention back to their priorities. Covered in fur, he was just able to get his human features back to the way they should be as the bear turned on the man. Despite his anger, it was hard not to be impressed as the gunman faced down the monster. As the bear bellowed, a challenge that would have made any of its kindred run, the man smoothly drew his large pistol and aligned it with the bear's chest.

Natsuki stood in the firelight, frozen by the bear's rampage. Takumi dodged from tree to tree, trying to cover the ground between him and his partner just as David was heading for Rie. Time seemed to slow as gray smoke whirled through the air between them and the camp. As the bear fell onto his front paws to charge, the man unleashed bullet after bullet. In seconds, it was apparent to both that the useless toy had enraged the beast.

The firelight played over the dark mass of the bear's hide. The gunman turned a reluctant gaze toward Natsuki, but David caught his attention instead. As their eyes met, David saw not fear but annoyance. Then he was gone, running after his frightened partner into the night, the bear close behind.

Takumi made it to Natsuki's side just before David found Rie. His host-sister looked back with yellow eyes full of confusion as he removed her blindfold. With a quick look around to ensure the captors were not nearby, he summoned his Seikaku and carefully cut her bonds.

"Looks like your bear got them," David said as he pulled the duct tape off Rie's mouth in one pull. She winced but said nothing and kept her eyes shut. When they reopened, she had a look of relief as understanding washed over her.

"I thought I summoned you, or that you were a kidnapper for a second," Rie said as she sat up, rubbing her joints to restart the circulation. She took in their surroundings, and then smirked at how awkwardly Takumi stood beside Natsuki. "We better go. My... bear? Won't hold them for long. Let's grab some supplies."

They scoured the camp, taking a selection of useful items. Rie laughed as she checked the equipment left behind. When Natsuki asked her about what was so funny, Rie said, "They'll live. Serves them right."

With food and water, they made their escape through the woods before the kidnappers could regroup. Though Kou wanted to go after the bear and the man, they both knew they were better off with them occupying each other's time.

The feeling they were being followed grew and soon Takumi and David had the girls running, trying to reach the edge of the forest. By the time they got to where the trees began to thin, David knew they were too late.

'Listen,' Kou demanded as they stopped. David calmed himself. He knew there was no more reason to run. Curiosity seemed to come from the trees themselves. David surrendered himself to Kou and they transformed into a tiger. Kou could almost smell the excitement and anticipation among the woody forest scents.

In the evening twilight, something rustled softly as it stepped gracefully, proudly among the underbrush. Kou sniffed at the air, dumbstruck by the presence, by *her* presence. David tried to take over as he felt Kou's control over their tiger form slip away, but he too could do nothing. A silver doe, taller than a horse, stepped out of the trees. A single eye watched them as the girls moved closer together. Reimi hopped a few inches to stand between Natsuki and the kami before them.

"*You tigers are all alike. Peace for over a hundred years, then you show up and nothing but fire and mayhem.*" Her words reverberated within their minds, as her piercing eye remained locked on Kou. "*At least you had the good sense not to hunt here, that's more than I can say for that annoying sibling of mine. Since you did not kill anything, and are a youngling, I will offer you some advice. Eat more greens.*

"*Reimi, it's been so long since I've met a fire daughter. Dangerous... But a necessary part of the forest's cycle... natural, unlike some males I know.*" The doe turned its head in a way they read as a scowl meant for Kou. "*As for the girls. I have no words of censure for you. I owe you for releasing the bear on those humans. The deer truly enjoyed watching them flee.*

"*One last piece of advice. Hurry home.*"

As if released from a spell, Kou stirred as she disappeared among the shadows. Behind them, four massive deer appeared with lowered antlers. Moving in unison, they herded them past the trees and then left. Kou's pride bent to the breaking point, but somehow David kept him from attacking his natural dinner. From the edge of the trees, they moved up the mountain, away from the forest and the kidnappers.

At the top of the mountain, David stopped. Prompted by Kou, he looked back over the valley as wistful emotions boiled up from deep within. A bellow echoed from far away that was still strong enough to make Natsuki jump and pull at Takumi's armor.

"Was that the bear?" Takumi asked.

"Probably," Rie said, her face stricken as if thinking about the creature she had summoned was painful. Without a look behind, Rie stepped forward, heading down the mountain and away from the valley at a brisk pace.

With the girls along with them, the boys could neither run nor fly, so their pace was far slower than the fearful race through the mountains that had brought them to such an uncertain end. The twins figured the valley was at least a three and a half day hike from the Estate. Moving at the edge of their endurance, Kou and Reimi had made it there in just fewer than two. How the captors had moved so quickly bothered David as they made their way back at a normal pace. He felt like he was missing too many pieces of the puzzle to figure out what was going on or why.

They moved cautiously, with Reimi or David transforming to keep their heightened senses on the forest. Even with their exceptional endurance, they still had to stop to eat and sleep. David suggested trying to call the Estate on the radios again, but the twins shook their heads in unison. Whatever Rie had discovered at the camp had Takumi on guard as well.

"Well if we can't call the Estate, at least tell us what happened," David growled as he slumped against a nearby tree. The others moved slowly as tired muscles resisted both their attempts to move and relax.

"I woke up before they wanted me to," Natsuki said in a hushed voice. "I almost wish I had stayed asleep. Waking to total darkness and then realizing I couldn't move was horrible. Then there was my connection with Reimi. Being unable to act made the distance even worse. Instead of an annoying itch, it was like an almost physical pain. I knew I was in a forest because I could still feel the needles and sticks beneath me, and smell the trees. Then I heard a man curse. They stuck something in my leg and I passed out again.

"It must have been your connection with Reimi," Rie said around a rescued ration packet. "I was out until just before everything blew up. The pain and panic from being tied up built within me until something broke loose. I knew I had summoned something, but I didn't know what it was until David released me."

"How did you get loose?" Takumi asked. He squatted on the balls of his feet, his face showing a professional interest in the method of Natsuki's escape.

"The second time I woke up I stayed still," she said. "I tried to relax every muscle like Yukiko showed me. From the pain, I knew we had been there for a while. I slowed my breathing, and as I listened, I learned about what was around me. Our captors didn't speak, but they moved enough that I got a sense of where they were. It was harder to figure out how many there might be.

"After a few minutes I noticed another body close by me. I could feel Rie's presence like a vacuum of sound nearby, a warm vacuum, but I didn't know it was her of course. I waited until I heard the fewest sounds from the men, then started moving. It was hard and painful, but I moved a centimeter at a time. Along the way, my hands picked up a twig and I started working on my wrists as I moved. When the scream came, I still hadn't made it to Rie, but I was free so I ripped off the rest of the tape to make a run for it, but then you were there." She looked at Takumi with a smile that made him turn away.

"Any idea where we are?" David asked.

"Well past the Estate," Rie said. "Aside from Grandpa I've done the most exploring. We are nowhere near it."

"It took us almost two days to get here running full out," Takumi said.

"In that case, I guess we can forgive you for being late," Natsuki quipped.

In the middle of their second night from the valley, David woke suddenly from his first real rest since the gunman shot him. The forest was as silent as Kou's paws on a tree branch. His pulse quickened as Rie rolled a little in her sleep next to him. Natsuki, who had the watch, turned her head toward the movement.

He put a finger to his lips as he stood and backed away from the tree. In seconds, he was gone. Leaving Rie and Takumi asleep, Natsuki regarded every shadow as a potential enemy. Her hand touched Takumi's sword. A few meters away, a young girl stepped into the faint moon light filtering down through the forest canopy. She had long black hair and a pleased smile. She took a confident step forward, then another. In one smooth motion, Natsuki stood and drew Takumi's blade. The ring stopped the girl cold and woke the twins. With a quick look, Rie noticed David was gone, and then saw the girl.

"You," Rie said with venom. Before she could bolt, Kou appeared in a branch just behind and above the girl.

"Manami, I wouldn't make any sudden moves," Kou said. She tensed at the sudden sound, but then relaxed and smiled.

"Do you know how long it's taken me to find your cute butt?" she said, turning so her sides were to both Rie and Kou. As she took a threatening step forward, Rie's eyes seemed to glow a bit in the darkness. Manami raised her hand to ward off the movement. "Whoa there, don't need any more rabbits, thank you."

"Natsuki could I borrow that sword for a second?" Rie asked with a fierce grin. Settling deeper into a crouch, Kou watched Manami, and then blinked at David's host-sister to let her know he was in control.

"You are far from Okinawa," Kou growled. "And ōkami run in packs. Oh, that's right. You had me get rid of yours for you."

Manami winced at David's harsh tone as he took over Kou's throat.

"They really were after me. Yes, I'm an ōkami, but that's not my fault! You think I came all the way here, knowing how easily you took care of my 'pack' for a fight?" she asked with a laugh. When no one smiled and Kou growled from behind her, she frowned. "Did I miss something?"

"Why did you kidnap us? Where are the rest of your friends?" Natsuki demanded, adjusting her sword.

"Hey, I just got into town. What kidnapping?" she said with a quick look back at Kou.

"*Speak,*" Kou growled. "*Why are you here? We don't have a healthy history with ōkami. This is your one chance to convince us you wouldn't look better as a statue.*"

"You did me a big favor, saved my hide, so I'm here to return the favor. Two Akuma Clan ōkami came through Okinawa looking for help getting out of Japan. They wouldn't tell us much, but they weren't a pack, just two brothers, all alone. It was strange. I did some digging, and some eavesdropping. They have a definite beef with you, David. I don't know what they are planning but it's going to be big, and aimed at 'some humans in a town near Himeji.' I remembered you said you were from Nakano," she turned, ignoring Natsuki's sword and Rie's scowl. "Do you know the Jeong brothers?"

Kou dropped to the ground.

"*You had better tell us everything you know,*" he said. "They're the ones who turned Rie into a majo."

They listened as Manami outlined what she knew about the brothers and their plans. She told them little they hadn't already guessed, but she did confirm that they had left Japan. They were out of David's reach.

"David, the Akuma Clan is dangerous," Manami said. "Since I live on the outskirts of our world I don't hear much, but what I do hear is scary, even for me. Look—"

"*We don't have time for this,*" Kou said, cutting her off. "*There are people after us, and we can't call the Estate. We have to move. You will come with us until we decide what to do about you. If you try to escape or feed off any of us*, I'll turn you to wood and then burn your statue. Previous… help, or no."

With watchful eyes on Manami, they resumed their course back to the Estate. Their careful but swift trekking brought them to the familiar areas they used during their usual Golden Week trips. They had to be careful, avoiding the numerous traps that Masao and Yukiko activated as soon as Takumi was clear. Rie took great pleasure when her charge *accidentally* ended up in a rope trap that left her dangling above their heads.

"With any hope, they'll slow down the… people who took the girls," Takumi said with a frown. His glance told David he was concerned, but unwilling to speak about the unknown men, and lack of communication with the Estate. Still, he cut Manami down with his sword.

David caught Rie's attention. She looked as if she wanted to say something, but then turned her gaze back on Manami. Rie had taken it upon herself to follow the lone ōkami, refusing to let her stray more than a sword strike or two away. 'I think she might actually be embarrassed.'

'Why are the twins so confident yet seem so wary?' David asked Kou.

'*Yes. It is an odd mix of emotions. I would think they'd be more comfortable in their marked territory.*'

An hour out from the Estate, the sun began to rise. It was early Thursday morning, five days since the girls' abduction. They were all hungry, as the food they had brought had run out a day before, and the kami had avoided hunting so that they would not give away Takumi's ability to Manami. Approaching the Estate without knowing the situation bothered David. He was far from an expert on tactics, but even he knew from experience that ambushes were hard to avoid without foreknowledge.

"Rie, Natsuki, would you mind waiting here with our... friend Manami for a bit. I need to talk to Takumi in private," David said to the girls. While none were happy, David won out and they set about hiding while the boys jogged away.

"Want to tell me what we are up to?" Takumi asked as soon as they were out of view.

"We've been going as fast as we could, but with the girls we should have been easy to catch. I have some suspicions I think Reimi can help me answer," David said, a wide grin spreading beneath ferocious eyes.

David's orange, black, and white armor shone in the early morning sun. The metal tiger mask surveyed the men around the trees. In the spot where he had shot David and Kou just days before stood the leader of their abductors, arm out-stretched, gun pointed.

"Where are the others," the man said throwing a quick look around. Despite having his face covered by a hood and mask, he appeared rattled. His clothes were almost as ratty and torn as the girls' were after the long hike back. With no response, the man motioned with his free hand and two followers left the trees behind him to flank the armored boy. They had the easy confidence of killers, despite the armored hand resting on the hilt of a sheathed sword.

By the time the man with the gun realized his mistake it was too late. A well-aimed side-kick to one of the goon's solar plexus had him flying back while the hilt of Takumi's sword jammed into the other. With a roar like thunder, Kou flew out of the forest, claws sinking into the leader's back as he fell off his rock perch to the ground at Takumi's feet. As the man fell, Takumi finished off the two other men with well-placed blows. Kou gave Takumi an amused blink, and then caught up the man's hood with his teeth and pulled.

With the gunman and his subordinates tied up, it was a simple matter to disable the rest of the squad waiting around the Estate. It was impossible for the men to find concealment in places David and Takumi knew so well. The only one not pleased with the outcome was Manami. Rie had insisted on tying her up before they finished their sweep.

"We can't let them find out about you. They'd insist we make you into a statue right now. Not that I think that would be a bad thing," Rie had said. "But David seems to think we should keep you around. For now." David smirked at the thought as he walked back to the ambush site after retrieving his armor from Takumi. With strength born of his year training with the Matsumoto, he hefted the bleeding, but mostly unharmed gunman onto his shoulders and started for the gate.

十八

INVITATIONS

Our ship landed in the cold north, a place I quite liked. With our new identities, it was a simple matter to head south. The land was wide and open, and while border security might have been tighter since the attacks in New York, they were not looking for…

Masao and Yukiko were waiting for them at the Estate's gate. Beside them stood a man familiar in stance and bearing, but like the other kidnappers he wore a hood that concealed his features. Smiling, David dropped his baggage, eliciting a groan from the bound man. Just out of view among the trees, Takumi and Natsuki watched over their captives, listening in case he needed help. Rie had volunteered to watch Manami.

"David, you can let him go," Yukiko said, running a practiced gaze over the man, looking for wounds.

"Not until I get an explanation from the Imperial Guard," David said flatly, his attention focused on hooded figure. "There are a lot better ways to test our abilities. Some of us do not appreciate having our friends kidnapped."

"Matsumoto-shihan, since when do you allow your students to speak so crudely?" Takaeishi asked as he pulled back his hood. "Where are my men?" His homeroom teacher stared at David with tight lips. A muscle near his temple twitched.

"Oh, I'd say he has every right to speak as he will in this instance," Masao said with a frown at the man. Bringing his attention back to David, he said, "Let's get everyone into the Estate and we can unravel the explanations."

David backed into the forest. As soon as he was among the trees, he sprinted off toward Rie and Manami. It took him just moments to circle around to where the creek flowed under the Estate wall.

"You were right," he said as soon as he saw Rie. "It was the Guard."

"What do we do with her?" Rie asked looking at Manami.

In response, David summoned his Seikaku. Manami's eyes widened in fear as the translucent wood grains glittered in the hard metal of the sword. The Seikaku dropped, deftly slicing through Manami's bonds.

"David! What are you doing?" Rie asked, even as she turned to block Manami's escape. Her left foot came forward as her knees flexed in the traditional Matsumoto fighting stance. A light breeze swept warm pine scents through the air as Manami looked between the two.

"One chance," David said. "The Guard is waiting for us at the gate. They don't know about you, Manami. If you do as I ask, wait for us in the pagoda near the Shrine, and go nowhere else, then I and the other Matsumotos will listen to your story. If you leave, your trip will have been for nothing. You will have made an enemy of me and I will have to hunt you down. What's it going to be?"

"I came here to help," Manami said, rubbing her skin where the tape had bound her. "What are a few extra hours of waiting?"

Rie complained the entire walk back to Takumi and Natsuki. She had wanted, at the very least, to tape Manami to a tree while they dealt with the Imperial House Guard. As they approached the partners, he shook his head to stave off their questions and Rie's argument. Back with Takumi and Natsuki,

they helped up their bound charges. Takumi freed their legs
with his sword, but left their hands and mouths taped.

"I still can't believe you carried a roll of duct tape all the
way through the forest and back in that pack of yours," David
said as they approached the Matsumoto Estate's gate.

"Dust tape can do anything," he said.

*'I still think you should have let me bite a few of them... That
would have taught a much better lesson than being tied up by a
bunch of Jr. High cubs.'*

'This was all some sort of test. We need to be careful what
we reveal until we know what Takeishi-sensei has to do with
all of this.'

David guided the guardsmen around the old rock wall of
the Matsumoto Estate. Takeishi glowered at them as they
brought his men stumbling to a stop in front of the gate.
Yukiko delicately covered her mouth with a slender hand to
stifle the giggle that threatened to break out at the sight of the
men. Despite all the students had been through over the previous days, the Imperial Guard looked far worse; pathetic with
their hands and mouths bound and clothes worn and dirty.

"Let them go," Takeishi grumbled. Takumi obliged with
quick and careful cuts from his sword. The six men were
bruised, sullen, and tired, but showed the quality of their
training by coming to attention before their commander. None
spoke. "You are all dismissed. Return to Tokyo. I will debrief
you later."

As one, the men turned and walked down the dirt road.
Soon after they were gone, a quiet military helicopter lifted
into view above the trees in the distance and angled east.
Takeishi turned and walked past the Estate's gates without an
invitation.

The tall brooding figure of their homeroom teacher angled
around the house showing he was well aware of the Estate's
layout. David caught Masao's gate stiffen as the man walked
straight through the Matsumoto garden to the Dojo. Yukiko

disappeared into the main house's adjoining kitchen as they passed.

'*I do not think Masao-san likes Takaeishi anymore than you do,*' Kou thought as they walked up the stairs to the Dojo. Masao was scowling, an expression David had never seen on his host-father.

'I wonder where Tsubasa is. He was supposed to be here. Masao even talked to his father.'

Once they were in the Dojo, Masao turned on Takaeishi with formal and distant movements, as if welcoming a client.

"Explain yourself," Masao said, his words a high contrast to his manner. The quiet tones were the one warning Takaeishi would get. "Or are you here to test my patience."

"I do what I am told, even when my orders are as distasteful as these," Takeishi said, sitting in the middle of the room. Yukiko arrived with a tray of tea.

"You must all be tired." Masao looked to the students. "Sit but stay alert and listen. Dear, none for our guest. I'm sure he must leave soon."

With the slightest twitch at the corner of her mouth, Yukiko served her husband, David, Natsuki, and her children, and then sat with her own cup. There had been no seventh cup on the tray.

"So what brings the head of the Imperial Guard all the way to Nakano," Yukiko asked.

"I no longer hold that position," Takaeishi began. "At the Emperor's request, I have resigned so that I could fulfill the Right of Assessment-"

"There has been no Assessment in a thousand years," Masao bellowed. David was reminded of the time Masao had smashed a table in a fit of rage after his father's death. He was his calm self again a moment later. David would have wondered if he imagined it, but Kou played back Masao's face for them in slow motion.

"We, the Emperor, decided that given the unique circumstances around Mr. Matthews' possession, that he, and the rest of the Matsumotos should be assessed. After all, there is no master," Takeishi said with an almost gloating smile. When Masao did not react, the teacher gave a disappointed frown.

"We suspected as much when you arrived as Takumi's homeroom teacher," Yukiko said. "Although the Assessor might have the right to conduct the test in his own manner, was it necessary to abduct our daughter and Natsuki? We could have limited the danger if you had informed us. Your men would be in far better shape than they are now. We could have warned you how dangerous Rie can be in her present state."

"I'm going to hold you responsible for the jerk with the gun," David added as he stared back at his teacher. "Those bullets were no test."

"You shot the boy," Masao said, his body leaning forward, his eyes intense.

"From the blood I saw, it looked like a lot more than once," Takumi said.

"Someone will pay for that one day. No one shoots a tiger and gets away with it for long," Kou growled.

"Your men shot a kami!" Masao roared. "You could have killed Japan's best hope for the coming darkness. Are you insane? All for a stupid rivalry that-"

The hand was so fast David missed the movement. Takeishi went sprawling as Yukiko's palm connected with his face. Hard. David's host-mother stood, turned her back on him, and walked out of the Dojo.

"Yes. Go complain." Takeishi's voice was dead, lacking any kind of inflection, feeling, or hint of life. He wiped a bit of blood from the corner of his mouth and righted himself. "He's alive. And although things did not go as I planned, everything happened within the guidelines under which I was operating. The girl however..." Rie returned his stare. Her yellow eyes glowed brightly despite the low light. "Well, the Emperor will have to decide, I have no specific instructions about her.

"As Assessor I…assert that by surviving the test, David Matthews and Kou are indeed a potential Jitsugen Samurai. We will not dispose of Takumi and Rie at this time, though all their statuses are pending a further and continued review. The elder Matsumotos and David are invited," he said as if the words stuck in his mouth, "to stay in Tokyo this summer to meet the Imperial Family. We will also continue to search for the Jeong brothers and will pass on any information we find."

Takeishi stood and stomped out of the Dojo, stopping to slide into his boots before leaving. The wind blew over the pond just enough to create miniature ripples that raced after the man as he passed, as if shooing him away. Masao grunted in satisfaction when he was out of sight.

"Alright, Takumi go get your mother, then you can all fill us in on what happened and we will tell what we know," Masao said returning his attention on the students.

"Actually," David said before the others could speak, "I need to go take care of one last thing. I'll be back as soon as I can." Before anyone could protest, David was up and moving toward the door. He changed into Kou over the threshold, landing on big cat paws. Kou loped to the Matsumoto Shrine, his speed quick but measured.

Kou slowed as he approached the pagoda. Light trickled down through the old trees in greens and yellows. Kou stalked over dead leaves and needles as he searched for Manami with his senses. David still marveled at how weak his own eyes and nose were compared to Kou's sight and smell. He could see and sense things through Kou that no human ever had.

The forest around the pagoda was silent. Manami did not seem to be there, yet David was sure she was. Although he did not know her well, he knew she was at least practical. To have come all the way to the Estate to warn him, and then leave before she could explain herself did not make sense. Still, David was unsure what to think of the fact she was an ōkami. He had not grown up amidst Japanese culture, and thus had no personal relationship with the legends. Still, he had met and destroyed three packs of the wolves. Every encounter was fresh in his memory. Chul Moo and Chul Soon were the two ōkami he had known best. They had been different, but he had counted Chul Soon as a friend, right up until he betrayed him. Manami stuck her head above the railing, her eyes locking onto David.

"Alone?" she asked with a playful smile. Despite himself, Kou smiled, a fearful sight on a tiger, though it made Manami laugh. David exerted control and he emerged, covered in his tiger armor.

"I figured it would be better to see if you were still here before I told the other Matsumotos about you," David said.

"David wanted a chance alone with you," Kou added, much to David's displeasure. Manami laughed.

"Good," she said jumping down. "You know, I might have kissed you so that I could escape, but now that I'm getting to know you… I do like you. It's not my fault I'm an ōkami. It wasn't my choice. I've done my best with the life I was given." She moved closer to him. "Maybe we were meant to meet, you know, so I could teach you more about us."

David was very aware of how close she was to him, his mind flicked back to the two times they had kissed as his vision blurred a little with the memory. An indefinable scent seemed to wash through the air that ignited the blood in his fingertips.

"Ah-hem," Rie cleared her throat. David whirled, kicking himself as he realized his expression would give away his surprise. Manami smiled, the challenge was not lost on Rie. Embarrassed, but not sure why, David missed the looks the two girls were giving each other.

"Uh, let's get back to the Dojo," David said. He led the way back through the Shrine path with Manami following close behind as Rie watched.

By the time the trio got back to the Dojo, Tsubasa was there waiting with the Matsumotos. Manami's confident stride faltered as they approached the old building. With the doors wide, she could see Masao and Yukiko watching her with veiled emotions. Masao leaned a little to the side and whispered to Takumi. The answer was too quiet to hear as David ascended the steps and entered. Tsubasa stared at the newcomer with fixed features as he fumbled with something in his lap. His mouth hung open a little.

"Ugh, stop drooling," Rie said as she spotted him.

"You are the first ōkami to enter here. Your words will determine if you ever leave," Masao said, ignoring his daughter and even David. No one could doubt his sincerity.

"You may sit," Yukiko said with an unusual edge to her voice.

"Why are you here?" Masao asked. If Manami had expected a different greeting, or introductions, she did not show it. Instead, she kneeled in the difficult seiza position in the indicated spot and kept her eyes downcast.

"Many years ago a single ōkami came to our small island," Manami said. "Although there are just over five hundred people on Nanboku, the administrators, teachers, doctor, post office staff, policeman, all change every few years. He was cunning and quiet, and before anyone knew something was wrong, he had changed many of us. Some joined him, but the rest of us turned on him and drove him from the island.

"We were family. We couldn't feed on the other islanders, and so we almost starved. Feeding our bodies was easy enough. Fish and meat would sustain us, but our spirit half weakened to the point where a few died. Then we found we could survive off animals. There were no large animals on the island except a few goats and cats. We found by accident that if we went with the boats we could take the essence of the fish before they died, sustaining the spirit part, while the flesh kept our human forms alive. I'm sure other ōkami have done the same, but humans are so much easier, so few choose to fight their nature."

"Was it the warm fuzzy family feeling, or the fact they would have hunted you down if you had started feeding on such a small population?" Rie asked, not buying her story.

"Maybe a few were kept from feeding for that reason, but the majority of us had lived our whole lives on Nanboku," she said. "We were family, and we found a way to live together. Things might have stayed well enough, except that the ōkami we drove out never forgot us. Okinawa has become the focal point for our kind in Japan. With so many foreigners already there, it is easier for those returning, or changed elsewhere to hide and operate. The free ōkami, as we call ourselves, don't hear much but we couldn't help but sense the change over the last two years. There have been many whisperings. Then I met David."

"Why should we believe you," Rie said from the corner of the Dojo. She had refused to sit, instead watching as if expecting Manami to run for it.

"Yeah, explain what happened last January," Takumi said. Unlike Rie, he was sitting near Masao, looking at Manami with an intensity that earned him a reproachful look from Natsuki.

"Well, like I said, the ōkami that turned us and his pack remembered us. He caught my scent in the airport. They have runts stationed in most of them now. There were enough people around that they couldn't attack me. They sent a pack after me. They aren't too appreciative of our... abnormalities. Might make others realize they don't have to stay bound to the clans. Anyway, I was scared they might attack me or the other students; I was the only one my age they got. Then I saw David.

I don't know why, but he was so cute. I hoped I could play on his western chivalry to get him to distract the pack long enough to get through the trip."

David felt his cheeks start to burn, and hoped the others would miss the color rising on his face. Rie's glance and Takumi smirk gave him his answer.

'Easy. I hate it when you get embarrassed. It's too... weird.'

'I'm human, get over it.'

"So you didn't know what he was," Yukiko asked.

"No! I mean of course he stood out, aside from being very tempting, at most I thought maybe he was a shifter," Manami said.

"Tempting?" Masao asked, his face clouding in anger.

"I am an ōkami. My pack chooses not to attack humans, but that doesn't mean we don't have... attractions. I didn't ask to be turned but I won't apologize for something that was not my fault. So yes, David was, is, a temptation, and I admit I used some of my abilities on him. But I'd never feed on a human."

As Manami spoke, Rie moved closer, her stance aggressive. Natsuki remained silent throughout the entire exchange. David's raised eyebrow did not even get a reaction from her.

"Continue," Masao commanded with a frown.

"Okay, so I told him I needed his help, and then he saw me at the ski resort," she continued. "He got there just as the clan's pack got to me. I though he was a goner, then all of a sudden he had a sword and turned them all to wood. I was scared out of my fur, so I turned up the pheromones, and distracted him long enough to get away. He was so sweet, too. I didn't realize it was his first kiss until later."

David turned bright red as Kou growled within and Takumi let out an explosive laugh. Tsubasa closed his eyes as if reliving the event in his mind.

"And the statue you took?" Natsuki asked, joining the conversation for the first time.

"Well, that was a friend of mine. He had wanted to stay with us, but his twin brother forced him to go with the clan. He didn't even try to fight David, so I decided to take him home. Maybe he can give us more information on what's going on around the mainland. Plus, I was scared. I mean this cute boy turned out to be way more than I had bargained for. It wasn't until I got back that I found out there were samurai more powerful than those in the history books. The Jitsugen Samurai are a whispered legend of a painful death among our kind."

'That is the third time she's mentioned a clan. We need to know more about them and what is going on in Okinawa.'

'I know. A pack is bad enough. I'd hate to think what a clan is…what did she say? The Acura clan?'

'The Akuma Clan.'

Manami spoke until night fell over the Estate. In the midst of her warnings about the Jeong brothers and the Akuma Clan, Ryohei returned. A pair of ghosts loyal to the Emperor and his guard had lured him away. After hearing her entire story, Masao agreed to let Manami leave the Estate, though after all that had happened they stopped short of trusting her with any more of their secrets. For her part, Manami seemed reluctant to say goodbye, and Tsubasa asked Masao to let her stay so he could perfect and test the Eye.

"I think she has been here long enough," Rie said. David looked to her, surprised she was still so abrasive.

'It must be because of her time as a yūrei,' he told himself.

"Golden Week is almost up and I still have school too," she said. "Anyway, it's the digital age, hit me up on Facebook."

十九
THIRD YEAR

The road south was monotonous, yet faster and far easier than the paths through China or Russia. Here there were no checkpoints or security. As long as we did not succumb to boredom and break the speed limit, we were virtually undetectable along the wide-open highways...

With Manami away, the Matsumotos locked down the rest of the Estate. Their usual security measures were back up and working, but the kidnapping had rattled Masao and Yukiko. When they were finished, they all sat down for what should have been the end of Golden Week celebratory feast. Instead, they settled for take-out from one of the local restaurants. It was the first time David had eaten food on the Estate that was not from the kitchen.

Though there was still much they had to cover about the events of the preceding days, they were all starving. Takumi, Natsuki, and Tsubasa prepared the tables in the main room while David and Rie helped Yukiko get the food from the car.

The dishes were set out so that everyone could take what they wanted. David went straight for the fried noodles. Across from him, Takumi grabbed a strip of raw tuna over sushi rice, but before he could get it to his mouth, Natsuki lashed out with a wicked backhand that sent the fish, rice, and wood flying across the table to hit David square in the face.

"Thanks Natsu, I forgot to check," Takumi said with the sappiest face David had ever seen on him. David checked the others at the table to ensure he was not the only one that found Takumi thanking Natsuki for knocking about his food strange.

"You have fish in your hair," Tsubasa said as he turned back to his own plate. Masao did not even look up, while Yukiko had the same air of relaxation she got after the rare instances David had managed to surprise her during their morning practices.

"Idiot," Rie mumbled to Takumi around a soup bowl.

"Umm," David muttered, "did I miss something?"

"Sorry David," Natsuki said with a giggle at his hair. "Ta-kun is allergic to wasabi. You know. The spicy green stuff."

"I usually don't have to worry at home," Takumi said. "Maybe now that Reimi is with me I can eat it!"

"Best not to risk it," Masao said. "You almost died the last time you had any."

Once everyone's initial hunger had been sated, their attention turned to the kidnapping. Masao began by reviewing the historical precedents for his children and the others. In the ancient past, the Emperors would often send a personal representative to the Matsumoto Estate to supervise and test a new Jitsugen Samurai. In those days, people communicated and traveled by foot. The Emperor would not travel to observe the Estate, thus a retainer performed the Right of Assessment. The practice had fallen off as the Emperors lost their political powers and the Shogunates rose. The Matsumoto's role had grown ever more secretive as they worked to keep the Jitsugen Samurai from becoming political tools.

"Takaeishi-kun and his company are from the Imperial Guard," Masao said. "You met some of them in Kyoto when we visited the Crown Prince. Their goal was clear. They wanted to see the extent of your powers and your willingness to save others. Unfortunately, it appears Takaeishi had a free hand. I have a feeling the Emperor designed this stunt to get me to go to Tokyo."

"I thought you were friends with the Crown Prince," David asked.

"The Crown Prince, yes," he said. "We grew up and trained together. The Emperor is another matter." Masao's eyes unfocused as he looked into his past with dissatisfaction. Unnerved by the silence in the room, David bit into a cold piece of tempura. Registering the stillness of the room, Masao roused himself. "Never mind. It will have to wait. The Emperor summons you to Tokyo as well. I have a feeling your summer is going to be… interesting."

"Tell us what happened while you were gone," Yukiko said. "We know the girls were taken, and that you were shot, David, but that is all."

"Did the Eye work out alright?" Tsubasa added, his full focus hanging on the answer. "How did you escape, Rie? Natsuki?"

"David why don't you go first," Yukiko said. David went through his whole story, including the incident with the gunman and meeting Takumi. Masao seemed most interested in his encounter with the doe kami. When he got to the reunion with the girls, Rie took over and told them about their escape.

"Is there really a giant bear running around in the forest?" Tsubasa asked, leaning forward in interest.

"It's not like I did it on purpose," Rie said with a tear sliding along her cheek. "I woke up bound and panicked. Before I could do anything, there was a giant bear crashing through the camp. Natsuki woke up and then the boys were there."

"Manami showed up not long after," Natsuki added. "You've heard her story."

The discussions continued late into the evening. While the invitations were intriguing, neither was immediate. The warning from Manami about the Jeong brothers gave them little to work on. It was also clear that Masao was as angry as David and Kou were about the method Takaeishi had chosen for the assessment. Rie and Natsuki both grumbled about being bait. Tsubasa just seemed excited to be included in such interesting events for his Golden Week.

"At most I just end up playing around in the computer lab," he said. "This is way better. I got to see Yukiko-sensei smack the hell out of Takaeishi!"

When David left for school on Friday, it was with the expectation that the principal would be announcing the mysterious transfer of their homeroom teacher. Instead, Takaeishi caught David, Takumi, Natsuki, Rie, and Tsubasa in the forest just before the main road between Nakano and Himeji. He was no less intimidating without his black combat fatigues. Takaeishi looked quite capable of ambushing them in his tracksuit.

"You all get surprised far too easily," he said. "I wanted to assure the five of you that I will remain your teacher for the duration of this school year. If any of you so much as hint to anyone about my past career I will find a very unpleasant way to return the favor. I would just as soon fail you all and return to Tokyo, but those are not my orders." The corners of his mouth pulled in disgust as he stared down the teenagers.

"I don't like it when my friends are threatened," David said, his eyes narrowing as he stepped forward. His tone was as cold as he could make it. "I'm holding you responsible for that coward under your command."

'I am having a hard time deciding if he is always this repellant, or if he is acting this way as a test. He makes me want to bite him.'

'You're supposed to be the one telling me not to attack him.'

'How about a scratch?' Kou brought up an image of his right paw with a claw popping out.

Takaeishi's eyes flashed at David. Rie smiled, none of them missed the anger course through his features before he was able to clamp down on them.

"I bet the jerk with the gun will never think of bears the same way at least," Rie said.

"You're all very lucky the Emperor has given me such strict orders," Takaeishi spit. "The Jitsugen Samurai are where they should be. Long Forgotten in the past. We don't need a gaijin like you or old historians like the Matsumoto to protect Japan."

"Really?" Takumi asked as his foot slid into the familiar fighting stance his family had used for generations.

"Yes," the man said, biting off the word. "Japan has people who have devoted their entire lives to its protection. Japan has me."

He turned his back on them and walked down the road. A second later David heard a motor rumble to life, followed by the grind of pebbles spraying from spinning tires. Natsuki pulled the others out of their individual thoughts. They were late.

Takaeishi, of course, reprimanded them at school. He gave them extra cleaning duties for a week. Although he ignored David's glower throughout the rest of first period, even Mizuki started looking between Takaeishi and the samurai. As soon as their teacher left the room, Naoto was in front of David's desk.

"What was that all about," he asked.

"Huh? Oh I don't know," David replied. "He must have had a bad vacation or something. Speaking of, how was Okinawa? That's where your family went right? And new shoes?"

The tension throughout the class broke down as friends grouped together to hear about the various adventures over the last week of vacation. No one bothered to ask the twins about their vacation since they did the same thing every year. After meeting Manami again, David was quite interested in hearing about Okinawa and encouraged Naoto go on in detail. An occasional question kept him going until Aramoto-sensei walked in to start math.

"Let's uh, start shall we?" he said. "Why don't you, mm, open your notebooks, so, uh, I can check your homework, ok?"

'He sure talks a lot for a fifty year old man.'

'*Can he not say one sentence without useless words? He hurts my ears.*'

'You mean he hurts my ears. Yours are … hey where do you go when I'm here.'

Aramoto began walking around to check everyone's homework. Even with a class as small as 3B, the time it took their teacher to say even the simplest phrase meant it would be quite a while before David's turn would come.

'*They go the same place your body goes when I come forth, the same place where the Seikaku and your armor go. Everything exists, but not everything exists in the same way.*'

'Wait. You mean like dimensions? Like my body flies off to some other earth when you show up?

'*Yes and no. When you humans see something out of the corner of your eye, but you look again and there is nothing there… that is you catching a glimpse past this existence into another. This reality is where humans and animals exist. Long ago, the kami banished spirits, ghosts, and monsters past the barrier, a veil. Unfortunately, like most barriers there are ways around them. It is the reason most people cannot see obake.*'

"David. David-kun," Aramoto said. "Ah yes, I was uh, afraid you might have fallen asleep, right? Do you, uh, have, mm, your homework? This, uh, must be it, right? Ok then, umm good work and all."

Aramoto-sensei moved to the front of the class and began writing long lines of numbers on the board. The previous year's material had been simple for David since he had already covered it in Arizona. Their new math, however, was different from anything he had done before, and Kou, while helpful most of the time, was no better at figures than David was. They abandoned their internal conversation to focus on the lesson.

The rest of the teachers seemed just as interested in giving the third years headaches as Aramoto was. Every class they had contained new and more challenging material than they had ever had before. Every teacher gave the students stacks of new homework with promises of more to come. Even the English worksheets he got took him two or three readings for every question before he was certain of the right answer. In Japanese, David struggled to perfect writing the myriad characters that formed the basis of written language. His connection to Japan through Kou gave David the ability to speak and read even ancient Japanese, but Kou refused to use his indelible memory to help David memorize the difficult symbols.

'Just as we practice with our bodies, you must practice with your mind. Else, you will be forever at my mercy rather than an equal partner. Besides, I have no interest in writing. Tail and tooth are so much more expressive. You must learn it on your own.'

"I feel like my brain is dead," Takumi said after school. The others were even worse off than David was. In English at least, David could already write, and he had an internal god to translate his thoughts for him.

"At least we can blow of some steam at badminton," David said on their way to change.

"Blow off steam?" Natsuki asked, confused.

"It's an American saying," Shou said, jumping into the conversation. "It loses something in the translation. Anyway, we have badminton for now, but after second semester they are going to make us quit to study for our high school entrance exams."

"I can't believe it's so soon," Rie said.

"We still have at least one more competition before summer," Takumi said. "Maybe there will be another in the fall."

"I don't know," Shou said. "No one is going to keep you from killing at the competition in doubles this time... It's too bad it's not a mixed competition. You and Natsuki can beat any of our boys' teams. Even me and Shouki."

"*I* can beat Shouki," David said with a laugh as they entered the gym.

They were sore and tired when the group returned to the Estate, but in far better spirits than they had been around Takaeishi. As soon as they were past the trees, Takumi transformed and Reimi took wing above them through the cool twilight. Natsuki sighed and then ran after, trying to follow as Reimi dived among the high tree branches. David caught her fingering a lighter she kept with her most of the time now, just in case she had to lure Reimi back down to the ground.

That night, though he was sore and tired after a long evening practice, David took the time for a video chat with Jessica. She was getting excited for summer as her classes started winding down toward the end of semester. She spent most their chat talking about her summer plans and where she wanted to go to junior high, dropping hints that she might try for the same exchange program David had landed.

'Why the smug smile on her face.'

'I can't ask her, she knows I'm horrible at catching details.' David yawned. He was curious, but instead of questioning her, he relayed Natsuki and Rie's thanks for her presents, and then signed off so he could run with Kou.

二十
MOTHERS' DAY

This part of the plan, at least, I could not complain much about. I had expected Chul Soon to do it, but instead he took charge of the rest. Perhaps because they called for more violence. There was such a draw to my job, yet the challenge made me nervous. I was unsure if I could keep up the act for so long, after all these years. She made it surprisingly easy to smile, as long as I did not think about her future. In the end, I convinced myself it would be good practice...

On Saturday, David went through his normal morning routine. One of the days they had gotten off for Golden Week was repaid as they donned their uniforms for school. As part of the Mother's Day celebrations, the students had regular classes in the morning, with the mothers invited to visit later in the day. Yukiko came in with Natsuki's mother during third period English and watched. After lunch, many of the mothers returned so they could play volleyball with their children. David's group was one of the few that won their game.

'I can't believe how good they all are.'

'*They are fierce indeed. Maybe not so surprising when you think they used to be students like Rie and Natsuki.*'

After school, the students all went home instead of staying for after-school practice. The teachers and PTA hosted a dinner and party for all the mothers while the fathers took responsibility for their children. Masao was so impressed with David and Rie's dinner that he let the samurai choose their own training for the night.

"Let's play hide and seek," Rie said a sly smile touching the corner of her lips. David and Takumi smiled in return, but Tsubasa just looked confused.

"What rules?" Takumi asked, a bit of his school excitement leaking out.

"No buildings. Estate boundaries. All else goes of course," Natsuki said with a grin to match Takumi's. Tsubasa started looking through his ever-present bag of gadgets. "The seeker has to wait five minutes before starting."

With everyone agreed on the rules, they settled for their usual decision making tool to see who would be the first seeker.

"Jan, ken, pon!" they shouted before throwing out their hands. David lost with scissors. David and his classmates used the classic game for most decisions. They avoided letting Kou play since he always won. It was hard to convince a tiger that fang or claw did not beat any of the usual three, especially since said claws would be so close to their hands. Since he lost, David closed his eyes and began counting as the others shuffled off.

'So what do you think? Nice or Tiger?'

Kou smiled, his fangs exposed as they transformed and slunk into the darkness. Kou proceeded to stalk through the Estate. Tsubasa was the easiest. He did not know the Estate as well as the twins or Natsuki, and so was at a disadvantage. Kou spotted Tsubasa behind a tree as he tried to fiddle with a new version of the Eye. Using the darkness around him, Kou scaled one of the trees nearby and then jumped from branch to branch until he was above the oblivious boy.

Moving slowly, Kou sunk his sharp claws deep into the old pine. He could smell the rich sap as well as he could smell the boy below him. When he was above, he pushed out from the tree and spun, careful to retract his claws. Tsubasa let out a whoosh of air as Kou landed in his lap. With one big paw, he bonked him on the forehead.

"*Dead*," Kou said to him before he sprang away into some nearby underbrush.

He found Natsuki by scent. As he slid through the forest, he picked up her familiar trail. Kou heard her heart pounding beneath a thick layer of pine needles. With another fanged grin, he padded over to the pile, stopping right on it. To Kou's surprise, she did not move or let out a sign he was there. Kou carefully unsheathed his claws until Natsuki gave.

"Okay, okay. You got me, put them away before you stick me," she said wiping away the needles over her face. "You're getting fat you know."

Indignant, Kou sat back on Natsuki's stomach, making her groan and swat at him before he took off after the others.

Rie was far more difficult. She was always on the Estate so Kou could not rely on trying to track her by scent alone. Kou searched the vegetable garden with no luck.

'Try the Japanese garden, under the bridge,' David thought to him.

'*But that is your favorite place on the Estate. Would she hide there?*'

'I bet she thinks we wouldn't check there because I know she knows I like it.'

'*What do I get if you're wrong?*'

'More time to hunt her if you're right, either way a good deal.'

Together they slipped off toward the bridge. David wanted Kou to go around behind one of the islands and slip into the water to surprise Rie, but the tiger would have none of it. While Kou liked the water just fine, he refused to get his fur all wet and mangy looking for just a game. Instead, he trotted into the garden and sat on the bridge. He let his tail hang over one edge, and then pointed the tip at Rie's face.

"Uh, no fair," she said from below. "How'd you know?"

"It seems David knows you better than you thought," Kou said as he bounded away to find his last prey.

Time was almost up when Kou jumped out of the tree and tackled Reimi mid-flight. The two kami tumbled through the branches and hit the ground, but not before the little phoenix erupted into flames. Kou growled at her for singing his fur again but could not help laugh as Reimi's flame abruptly went out as she started coughing up little hairballs that ignited in puffs of smoke.

For the next rounds, they instituted a human only rule and rotated so that everyone got a chance to seek. By the end, they were all sore and tired.

The next morning, David met Rie in the kitchen well before the usual four AM. It was far easier for him to make the appointment than in the past since he had stayed out most of the night as Kou. Doing so allowed him to meet his sleepy-eyed host-sister full of energy. She scowled at his perkiness then together they began breakfast for Yukiko.

Instead of their usual routine, the family ate together, and then practiced in the Dojo. Soon after eating, David and the twins left for Sunday badminton practice. With a week before their next badminton competition, they could not miss practice, even for Mother's Day. Natsuki met them at school. She had taken the morning off from Matsumoto training to spend a rare morning with her own mother.

At practice, the way the younger students treated him still confused David. Though he had been playing badminton for less than a year, they talked to him with almost as much deference as they did with the coach. Whenever he tried to help clean up or pick up a few shuttles, a first year would run over and take over for him. He had improved since his first days of stumbling around the court, but not enough he thought, to warrant such attention.

"It's because you're a senpai now," Rie said as he stared off at one of the new first years.

"Huh?" he asked.

"You might have been able to find me on the Estate, but I've gotten to know you pretty well too. You lower your eyebrows and your eyes squint every time you're confused by something," she said with a smile. "The differences between years are important, most of all in club activities."

"Is that why they don't let me help clean anymore?" he asked. "I thought I was doing something wrong."

"Nah, well, you're making them look bad because they're supposed to get to it before you do. It's their job to take care of stuff so we can focus on practicing and winning the competitions. At the same time, they get to learn from us. It's about mutual respect and tradition."

"It's going to take me a long time to get used to that," David said.

"Don't worry about it. Let's go show the newbies a thing or two," Rie said as she took off for a court. Smiling, David trotted after, swinging his racket to loosen up a few tight muscles. Though he would prefer to swing his Seikaku at Chul Soon's beady black eyes, he'd settle for a badminton shuttle.

Rie's insistent practice after recovering from her time as a yūrei had turned her into the best female player at Nakano. As they finished warming up, a first year student came over with a clipboard to record their game. It was as fierce as their sparring match had been that morning. David's physical improvements and daily drills were still having a great effect on him. Practicing with Rie all the time and their work in the forge also gave him insights into her strategies and body language, plus Kou was there to help him focus on multiple aspects of the game. His longer legs and arms had begun to give him a distinct advantage on the small badminton courts. In the end, it all served to put him on a nearly equal footing with his host-sister, despite her years of practice.

David and Rie were sweaty and tired after their long game. She had just managed to score the last two points needed to beat him, but it had been a near thing. With Kou's help, his reactions were quickening.

"Careful or I'll have to summon another rabbit to win next time," she whispered as she slid by him to towel off.

The next morning, Takaeishi walked into Class 3B, with a huge smile and a large pile of papers. The students' faces fell as he began to describe their upcoming schedule. Most of the students were still tired from their busy vacations and the news their workload was about to double was far from welcome. His smile never wavering, Takaeishi told them about the upcoming standardized tests. While "optional," he showed them completed applications for every student.

"Any student who does not pass their tests, including the Eiken English tests, will be required to end their involvement with any extracurricular activities," he announced to a groaning audience. He dropped a pile of application receipts on David's desk. "Those of you who have neglected to take the previous levels will take every level up to the current grade. David will take Eiken level one."

Even Mizuki watched with something approaching pity. The level one tests, were late high school level and were notoriously difficult, even for native speakers. Takaeishi stood in front of his desk, daring him to complain.

"So what level Eiken did you say you passed, Takaeishi-sensei?" David asked, his voice loud enough for the entire class to hear. Their teacher's gaze turned to David, but he continued handing out the massive stacks of worksheets in every subject.

While Takaeishi was the most brutal about it, the rest of their teachers soon proved the increase in their workload would not be from a single teacher. The warnings from the first day of class were proving prophetic. The third years were about to be very busy.

At home, David and his friends had more than just their schoolwork to keep them busy. They began a detailed internet search for the Jeong brothers. Thanks to Manami, they knew the ōkami had been in Okinawa and that they were moving about. Using software obtained from the Imperial Guard, they began trying to trace the ōkamis' movements based on bits and scraps of intelligence and news. The hard part was that although they had access to government databases, none of them tracked ancient monsters. Instead, they had to try to separate the ōkami from intelligence gathered on known terrorist networks.

"You'd be surprised how many of those religious cults have a pack of ōkami at their center," Masao said as he helped David and the twin's research. "What better way is there to drain away someone's spirit over long periods of time without anyone noticing?"

Tsubasa was the most helpful in the search and enjoyed having something at which he could best the twins and David. He scoured news sites, blogs, Facebook, and Twitter for anything matching the two brothers. Tsubasa's first hit was a local story about the pair's disappearance and the related animal attacks in Nakano. The wider Japanese news had played the story, but it fell into the background.

"It doesn't seem like much," Tsubasa said, "but at least we have two references on our timeline already."

With the amount of homework they had, the group was limited in the time they had to search. Every morning they were up at four to start practice, then off to school. After school was badminton and their various evening training, then they had scant time for homework and the search. It was so bad that Yukiko began insisting they cut their evening practices shorter.

Only David and Takumi were able to continue their evening patrols late into the mornings. Their ability to switch into their animal forms allowed them to recover even as they continued their work. The same ability did not help their virtual search. Kou had tried to use a keyboard but had sent a claw straight through. Reimi was still small enough to hop around on the keys, but she became so excited that she set the entire desk on fire.

"The relics and history of this place are far too important to be destroyed in a fit of excitement," Masao said scowling at the little bird.

"*I can't help it. I'm a phoenix. Fire is what I do,*" she replied.

Masao summarily banned her from the Matsumoto Library.

FITNESS AND FALLS

She was like a young cross between Natsuki and Rie, yet so different. Since I looked a few years her senior, it was easy to impress her. There was no way for her to know how many years I had actually lived...

Naoto chuckled from beside David as he stared out at the faces of the entire school. Takaeishi glared at him from behind the sitting students, which did not help the sudden nervousness that sprang into the pit of his stomach. With the Matsumotos' training, he saw every look he got from the students. Some were bored. A few, Mizuki's friends, were hostile. Another group of girls had odd smiles on their faces. David knew all of them were waiting for him. Tsukasa-sensei gave him a prompting hand motion.

"Umm," he began.

'Great start. Epic.'

"This year's boys' badminton team has been practicing very hard," David managed despite Kou. "For doubles we have Takumi and I." They stepped forward and bowed, then stepped back. As he called their names, his team members did the same. Somehow, he made it through the rest of the introductions and returned to sit with the rest of the team. The girl group AKB48's song *Heavy Rotation* started to play and the students who had gone behind stage earlier came out cross-dressed. David stifled a laugh. The boys had all borrowed skirts and sailor tops from the girls, while the girls had on the boy's slacks and white dress shirts. To finish off the spectacle most had drawings on their faces.

Soon the entire student body was laughing at the group as they tried to follow Kenta's choreography. They finished with a short shout out to the team then raced off in embarrassment.

At lunch, discussions around David's table focused on what everyone had done for Mother's Day. The conversation seemed innocent enough until Hidemi caught his attention from farther down the table.

"Do you have Mother's Day in America?" she asked.

"Yeah, we do," David said. "It's the same day as in Japan, but it's a family thing. They don't have events at the school like we had."

"Did you do anything for your mom?" Hidemi continued. She often asked David about cultural differences and was the best in English in their class beside him. When he asked her why she could speak English so well, she always dodged with a sly smile and returned to her book. David frowned at her question.

"My mom died a long time ago," he said, trying to keep the old memories at bay. "We made breakfast for Yukiko though." With that conversation killer, the others backed away, yet Hidemi focused on him even more. She did not say anything, and David tried to think of something more to say, but when he looked back, she had joined a new conversation about a K-Pop group. David ignored Rie's glances in his direction. That evening after practice, Rie met David alone outside the gym.

"Natsuki and Takumi are going to stop by her house on the way back to the Estate," she said. "Natsuki's dad has something she thinks will help the search for the Jeong Brothers."

"The last time those two disappeared it was because you convinced them to go hangout so we could see the monk,"

David said, letting his suspicion tint his voice. It was hard to keep from smiling.

'She's up to something.'

"I have no idea what you're talking about," she said with an innocent grin. As they passed the grocery store, David could not help detouring around to look at the ruined warehouse. The whole area was clear, with weeds beginning to stick up among the foundation. The basement hole was still visible, with black scorch marks where the flames had licked out before the rest of the building had caught. "So what happened?"

David sighed. 'She wants to know about my mother.'

"There's not much to tell," he said as they continued walking. "I don't remember much and my father always had a hard time talking about it." David popped open an umbrella for the two of them as a light rain began. It had rained every day that week.

"You don't have to tell me," Rie said, huddling under the umbrella with him.

"We had just moved, I don't remember where. I think we had moved so my dad could work at a new laboratory or something. I remember being confused, sad, scared even, but even Kou can't help me remember what happened. Afterward, she was gone. We moved back to Arizona. I feel like I remember some of the drive, that or I've heard about it so much my thoughts seem like memory. I guess my dad took a few jobs. Eventually he got the job with public television. He's been doing that for a long time."

They walked without direction or hurry. Rie put her arm around his to guide him as he sank back into his memories. Kou stayed clear letting David deal in his own way. Rie led him down the Matsumotos' drive where the rain had turned the tall pines' bark into tall black walls, topped with green.

"There's no rain smell here," David said a little wistfully. It was the first time in a long time he felt even a little homesick.

"No rain smell?" Rie asked, confused.

"In the desert, the creosote bush sends out a smell whenever it rains," David said. "It's fresh and clean, and though now I know it comes from the plants, when I was younger I thought that was what rain smelled like."

They reached the Estate and headed to their own rooms to put away their bags. David headed to the computer to see if there were any new news stories for the day that might point to the Jeong Brothers. Instead, there was an email waiting for him from his sister.

> *I know it's been all of a day since I wrote, but Dad told me you are in a badminton competition this weekend. Good luck! Have you started dating Natsuki? Is that why she hasn't written me back yet? Anyway, it's all good. I have my own boyfriend now. All my girlfriends are just dying of jealousy. Take care big bro. I'm off to the movies! YAY!*
>
> *-Jess (duh!)*

David smiled as he typed a reply. He told her all about the embarrassing speech he gave that morning and the subsequent performance. He figured she would get a kick out of it, and it was something he could talk to her about without having to hold anything back. David scowled a bit at the mention of a boyfriend. For all his faults, David had prided himself on being a decent older brother. His mind conjured images of using whoever was after his sister as a target for his practice sword. Kou purred contentedly as the images rolled through their minds. With a chuckle, David smiled and sent the email.

That night David worked out the aggression thinking about his mother and sister had caused on a length of steel. Rie methodically pounded out a rhythm with a small hammer, showing David where to hit with the giant sledge he wielded. It was their night to work in the forge. Out of all the Matsumotos' training, sword making was taking him the longest to master. It was something that had to be beaten into every muscle by repetition, and a skill Kou would not, could not, help him with. Still, it was giving him a way to center himself, learn more about Rie, and was even strengthening his body past what the normal Matsumoto training had already accomplished.

That weekend, David and the badminton team met early at Nakano Station with their bags and rackets. Natsuki, Takumi, Rie, Tsubasa, and David walked together after an intense morning practice. Yukiko had decided David would focus on bone toughening. After basics, she had sent him through a series of exercises meant to fracture his bones slightly so they would regrow stronger. Even without his Jitsugen Samurai powers, this would have been safe enough, yet it was painful. She had him punch lengths of wood covered in rough rope to build callouses over his knuckles and strengthen the bones of his hand. He had to bang his arms and legs into various objects to build those up too. She kept him going so fast that the bruises outdid his body's advanced healing.

Like all the other things the Matsumotos taught him, it was another integral part of their martial art. The twins, however, were observant enough to realize David was not enjoying this new part of his training. As they walked to school, they split to either side of him.

"You broke your hand that first time you punched Koji, right?" Takumi said. "It took you out of the fight."

"You have to build your bone density and strength," Rie added. "Even with your powers, a break could cost you your life."

"Oh, I know," David said. "It's just too bad super strength and bones of steel aren't part of Kou's repertoire."

"Right?" Takumi said, laughing as they arrived at the station.

"This feels weird," David said as the rest of the team arrived. "I feel like we should be off hunting Chul Soon, even if he is out of the country. Instead, we're going to a badminton competition."

"If we stop living our lives, then whatever it is that is bringing the clans back out of isolation will have won," Rie answered.

"There's a cheery thought," Tsubasa murmured.

Before the team left, there was the usual round of speeches. Naoto ended up having to speak for the boys with Tsukasa and the head of the PTA also giving a quick word. After loading onto one of the train's cars, they laughed and joked about the upcoming match. The ride to Himeji was short, but once they were in town, they had to navigate a stream of smaller trains to get them to the junior high hosting the competition. For David the trains were still new enough to be interesting. Arizona had little in the way of public transport, though Jessica had gone on at length about the new tram in Mesa he would never see.

Himeji East Junior High was a crush of humanity. Hundreds of students had arrived from the surrounding schools for the daylong competition. In addition to the students, teachers, and even a few parents, roamed around, finding seats on the second floor gallery in the immense gym. Unlike Nakano, which only had three courts, Himeji East had two gyms with six courts apiece.

David stood with his teammates through the welcoming ceremony and the subsequent explanation of the rules. As soon as it was finished, they began to warm up. David and Takumi's first match was the second game on court three. The girls waved goodbye and headed to the second gym for their doubles games.

Their first game was against a local team of third years. They made a show of yelling before every serve. David could not help smiling. Their shouts of "Hai!" in Japanese translated for him as "Yes," though Kou's presence within him enabled David to understand its meaning as closer to "ready." The difference in phrases was still entertaining. There were often instances like that, where the phrases used to express an idea were completely different between the two languages. Most of the time he did not even register them because he always thought in Japanese, but with the adrenaline pumping through him his mind was buzzing with intensity.

'Cut it out, they're about to start,' David thought as he realized the buzzing was just Kou showing his annoyance at having to stay cooped up all day just because David wanted to hit a shuttle around the court. 'You know I have to keep up appearances. It's not my fault you don't have thumbs.'

'*I prefer my own kind of badminton, thank you,*' Kou said as he played a memory for David. He had to struggle to pay attention as the game began since Kou insisted on playing out the entire memory of the bird he had caught the previous week. David had his own memories of that particular meal.

'Too many feathers.'

David caught a high clear and sent it smashing back at his opponents. Even with Kou trying to distract him, David was able to concentrate enough on the game that he and Takumi won by a high margin.

They progressed through the competition at a steady pace. Takumi was near perfect. David was good, but had room to improve. Takumi had been playing badminton for years and was in peak physical condition. He had fine control over his muscles, hard won from his martial arts training. He could put the shuttle exactly where he wanted it. When he smashed, he jumped over a meter into the air. For his part, David was almost as fit, and although he had far less experience, had gotten to know Takumi rather well. David could move around the court without thinking, and while his return shots were not always perfect, they were strong. His height gave him an advantage as well, even though he could not jump as high as Takumi.

Yuji and Ryu were the first Nakano team eliminated. Since both were first years it was no surprise they did not make it to the finals, though they did make the top thirty-two. Tsubasa's team lost in the next round to a team from Kobe. Shou and David's teams both made it to the top eight. Students and teachers crowded around the last two courts for the top four competitions after Shou and Yuki lost by the barest two points.

David saw Natsuki and Rie enter the throng as he prepared for his match. They both had radiant smiles.

"We got second," Natsuki crowed. "We're going to the regionals in Kobe!"

"You lost?" David asked.

'I thought they would have it in the bag. They've been killing during practices.'

'I agree. It is odd they did not succeed in the hunt.'

David tried to catch Rie's attention but she pretended to be interested in the floor.

"Don't worry about it, Rie," Natsuki said. "It was completely understandable. We did well enough."

'That must have cost her a lot to say. Natsu is so competitive.'

The announcer called the boys' game, and David put aside his concern for Rie. They were in the finals.

Later that night, Rie explained what had happened during the competition. With the intensity of the game, she had summoned a cockroach, thankfully not the giant kind, which had freaked out the other team. She had felt so bad that she had thrown the game.

"But it was an accident," David said. "Takumi and I won the competition. Does that mean our win was unfair because Kou is within me?"

"No! Of course not." She smiled as she tucked her legs into a tree branch and flipped over to meet his gaze. They were in David's favorite tree after a long stint in the workshop. "Your improvements have all been your work. Sure, maybe you can heal faster, but you still get tired. Kou hasn't started to affect you physically, so it's still a fair fight. Distracting them with a magical animal wouldn't be right." She sighed as she swung a little on the branch. David smiled as her hair dangled in front of him. "I have to find some way to control this."

Her yellow eyes seemed to glow in the dim light of the tree. At first, a pang of regret surged through him as her eyes reminded him of his failure to stop Chul Soon before they changed her. Then he noticed the slight curves at the corner of her mouth, the subtle smile that always seemed there ready for him. David noticed other things about her he never had before as well. Something shifted within him, and David saw past his familiarity, taking in every detail of her face as if for the first time. It sent shivers racing through him.

'No ideas, nothing in all that ancient wisdom of yours?' David asked Kou, a strange need growing in him to find a way help her. David could sense disapproval from Kou, but could not lock on its source.

"*I've never met any other majo,*" Kou replied aloud. "*It seems like you summon the animal spirits when you are emotionally charged. I'm not an expert on human emotions. All I have to go on is my memories and David. My guess is that until you can find a way to focus your power, you will have to learn to use your emotions to smash through the barriers between layers.*"

"But how do I control my emotions?" she said with a sad sigh. "Maybe we should have kept Manami around. She was good at pissing me off."

As he saw the idea spring into Kou's mind, David tried to clamp shut their mouth, but it was too late. Kou sensed the shift in David, and unlike his other half, Kou was all about action.

Kou took full control of David's body. As Rie swung in, Kou did something more embarrassing than anything David had managed on his own, and given his history that was incredible.

Kou made David lick Rie's cheek. Inside, David just about died from humiliation as Rie's face froze in shock. She was so surprised her legs loosened and she tumbled out of the tree. A very confused rat fell alongside. Kou reacted with lightning reflexes. David's body jumped out of the tree and bit into the rat before David could re-exert control. As they fell, David caught Rie with one hand and flung the other against the trunk. His fingers ripped into the bark, slowing them as his legs flexed beneath him. There was a resounding crack as his right leg broke under their combined weight and speed as they landed.

David staggered, spitting out the rat with disgust as the pain sped up his spine and ripped fingers. Rie laughed high and clear. Rie grabbed him before he could fall, helping stretch out. When he settled, she started checking his legs.

"This is going to hurt," she said. Before he could steel himself, Rie grasped his leg just above his ankle and jerked. A scream caught in his mouth as she set the leg. He just managed to avoid blacking out as the painful healing process began. Rie adjusted his torso, so that his legs were flat, and then sat against the base of the tree. She tilted his head up and placed it in her lap. David was just conscious enough through the shooting pain in his leg and hand to see Rie wipe her cheek above him.

"David, um, people don't go around licking each other," she said, with just enough of a smile to tell him that she knew who had been in control. David's eyes turned orange as Kou growled through their shared pain.

"It seemed like a good idea," he said. *"I just wanted to see if it would provoke your connection to the deeper levels. I didn't expect you to fall out of the tree."*

David's vision started to fade as his body's resources focused on healing.

"Hmm. Well maybe next time leave the kissing to the humans," she said.

When David woke the next morning, it was in his own room with his usual blanket over him. His thin Japanese futon was spread out on the tatami mats below him, and the room was still dark.

'Tell me that didn't happen,' he pleaded.

'It worked didn't it? She summoned a rat. Too bad we did not get to eat it. I wonder why it wasn't as big as the rabbit the first time she summoned one.'

'NO. MORE. LICKING.'

He threw off his blanket and rolled, testing his leg. With a grumble, he folded up the futon and put it in his closet. David threw the blanket and pillow on top and slammed the sliding door shut.

It was still well before their training hour, so David used his old escape route under the floorboards in his room. Dressed in a light tracksuit, he took off through the Matsumoto forest. He extended his morning run well past the usual five kilometers. The memory of the incident had awakened more emotions than just embarrassment, and he worked hard to rid himself of them as his legs pumped over trees and rocks. David ignored Kou.

He almost thought he sensed her moving toward him. It was impossible to decide what tipped him off to her presence, but soon he was sure Rie was running nearby. She caught up with him just as he turned down a steep incline that led back to the Estate. His legs, longer every day, pumped just fast enough to give him a taste of the speed he had enjoyed on his snowboard.

"Try not to be too hard on him," Rie said as she appeared a few feet away. She nimbly avoided an old log, springing over it to land beside him. "Kou was just being a tiger, if with your body."

David saw her smile, and could not help but return it, despite the fact he was sprinting down the woody hillside.

"Well if you liked it so much, I'll let Kou do it again," David said. "Did you know that a tiger's tongue can rip the skin off an animal?"

"In that case, maybe we should just stick to me and you." Rie bobbed in, his hand rose to defend, but she dodged and kissed him fleetingly on the cheek. He barely registered the tree as he smacked into it. "Now we're even," she called as she disappeared along the Estate's wall.

FIRE AND WATER(MELON)

*The awaited day finally came. Over long weeks, I had almost
forgotten why we were there. The lie had been a pleasant one.
Chul Soon had finalized his own plans though, and the day
of 'our' revenge was at hand. I write it that way because as
much as he used words like 'we,' 'our,' and 'clan,' it was never
more than…*

The days swept by for David. The quick pace broken by lingering memories and the often-crippling uncertainty they
brought. The unbidden thoughts seemed to slow time for brief
periods, though not all were disconcerting. The high from
winning the doubles badminton tournament with Takumi,
who had also taken first in singles, was slow to fade, but David
still remembered every second of *the run* as well. Kou had suggested returning Rie's gesture as a way of helping her to focus
her powers, but David pushed the thought from his mind.

He had been horrified enough when Kou had licked her,
but he was still in shock from Rie's reaction to it. He could not
tell if it had been her revenge on him for Kou's actions, or if she
might actually like him. The question filled his mind, but he
quailed at the thought of bringing it up with her. He was just
glad she did not hate him.

'Takumi is going to kill me.'

'Probably.'

'There is nothing worse than a tiger who thinks he has a sense of humor.'

It took him a week to get over being awkward again in the forge. Rie seemed to enjoy his difficulties, and unlike after the cultural festival, made things worse by refusing to act awkwardly herself. Her giggles were distracting as they worked over the hot metal of a sword. Her smiles drove him nuts at badminton practice. Finally, he had to admit to Kou, and to himself, that he liked Rie. Kou was no help.

'I don't think hunting a deer and bringing it back for her is the smartest way to ask her out.'

He spared a glance as Rie ran through the sand with Natsuki. David splashed more water as flames shot out of the grill. As with the previous year, the Ashikawas hosted a barbeque at Matsuyama Beach for the entire 3B class. Their spirits soared as they realized Takaeishi had not come as he had threatened to the previous Friday. David and his homeroom teacher had had another battle of wills over the cleaning schedule. He was sure that Takaeishi would have his revenge soon enough. David had managed to keep from changing to Takeishi's cleaning section by pleading his case to Aramoto-sensei.

'I know we cannot provoke Takaeishi, but must we deal with the old man instead?' Kou complained by playing one of the elderly teacher's more inane speeches back for David.

At Matsuyama Beach, the sun was shaded by thick clouds, but it was not cold. Since Kou could not be near the ocean, David kept his distance and helped Miu with dinner. It was not because Kou was a feline that he had problems getting close to the vast gray sea. Kou had no problem swimming in the pond or stream at the Estate, providing his fur had plenty of time to dry out. It was because the ocean was not part of Japan. No treaties about fishing grounds mattered to a kami. Kou was bound to the land.

David splashed more water, and then helped stir the massive pile of vegetables. They were making yakisoba. David managed the flames as Miu wielded long chopsticks around frying vegetables and noodles. Pulling his gaze away from where Rie and a group of her friends where playing in the ocean, David eyed Takumi.

His host-brother had even more problems than David did. Thanks to Reimi, Takumi could not enter the ocean, but worse she also made his eyes turn whenever he got too close to the cooking fire. David knew she would love to jump right in. Reimi was, after all, a phoenix. Takumi resorted to playing volleyball, which to David's amusement turned out to be one of the few activities in which he was not naturally gifted.

As another glut of flames leaped out from under the frying pan, David brooded on the latest email from Jess. Her endless small talk about her new boyfriend reminded David that Takumi would most likely not appreciate the feelings toward Rie that had taken David so long to define. His daydreams of hunting Jess's boyfriend made him feel guilty about not telling Takumi about what Kou had done. The only thing worse than someone dating his own sister, was if they tried to do it sneakily.

'I'm surprised Dad is letting her date. She must have talked him into it.'

'*The meat is burning.*' David vigorously poked at the coals, and then growled back at Kou when he noticed the meat was still red.

'Just because you eat everything raw doesn't mean my classmates want uncooked meat.' Kou responded by pulling away from their combined mind.

When the time came for watermelon smashing, the entire class turned on the boys, separating Takumi and David from the rest of the class. Left alone, they sat on a group of rocks watching various students send up gouts of sand as they missed.

"Kou licked Rie," David said once the rest of the students returned to the spectacle of Mizuki trying to break open the big watermelon with a stick.

"Why," Takumi asked as he watched Natsuki dodge past a group of students. David followed his gaze as another group crowded around her to keep her from getting to the melon before everyone had a turn.

"Umm,' David said losing his nerve.

"Whatever, he's a kami," Takumi said. "Must be some ancient tiger thing, you'd know better than I."

"*I was trying to help her summon a spirit,*" Kou said. "*I noticed how she was making David feel-*" Kou's voice cut off as David put his entire will behind keeping his mouth shut. He flinched, sure Takumi was about to attack him.

Takumi laughed so hard he rolled off the rock.

"Kou was trying to kiss Rie?" Takumi gasped as he crawled back up. Kou growled within as Takumi recovered. "Wow. Well I don't know what you see in her but good luck."

"You don't care?" David said, surprised.

"Look, Natsu and I are partnered right? It's not like that has made things any easier between us though…I mean, you know I like her. Girls," Takumi said with a curse. "Just do me a favor, don't go giving Natsu any ideas. I know you western-ers are all about holding hands or whatever, but remember its Japan and-"

"Um, that's ok," David said. "I don't have any plans or anything, and I don't know what Rie thinks, just thought I should tell you, you know. Umm, yeah."

The boys glanced at each other, and then inwardly sighed as a commotion by the melon gave them an excuse to shift their attention. Most of the class had gone, and still had not broken the watermelon open. Rie winked at David, and then spun past a few students. Grabbing the stick out of Kenta's hand, she twisted past Kaeda as she tried to trip her. With unerring accuracy, she broke free of the mob and split the melon in two.

"Good, now we can eat," she said with a smile. "You all were taking forever."

Most of the class laughed, Kaeda and Mizuki were the exceptions as Kaeda tried to brush rocks and sand away from her friend who had fallen in the tumble. She scowled and even refused to take any of the melon when Rie offered her some.

'Strange,' David thought as Kaeda stormed off toward the awnings.

Rie and Natsuki landed in front of the boys with knowing smiles.

"So what have you two been talking about?" Natsuki asked. Her smile widened as David squirmed. "I see." With quick reflexes, Natsuki grabbed Takumi's arm and pulled him up. "Come on bird boy, they're about to start lighting off fireworks, we better disappear for a bit."

Rie took Takumi's place next to David. He was hyperaware of her as she handed him a slice of watermelon. The last rays of summer sun disappeared behind them as David took a bite. Rie smiled and together they watched as their classmates lit off sparklers and mini-rockets. Relieved at the comfortable silence, David enjoyed the rest of the evening beside Rie.

Back in Nakano Valley, David was always busy. Despite the reputation he had developed with Kou in his head, he had never been a woolgatherer, and had no time to become one. Still, it was impossible to keep his thoughts from turning to Rie. He looked forward to spending time with her, but he was even more nervous around her. He felt ever surer she liked him, but he had no guide to tell him what to do next. David kept his distance, trying to find a balance between his fears and hopes.

Takaeishi revealed his next strike against David on the Tuesday following the barbeque. From the girls' expressions, David was sure Yuka and Kaeda had been behind it. Takaeishi made a big point of moving David to the front corner of the desks, and then moved Rie to the opposite at the back of the room. He then went into a long speech about focusing on schoolwork and not dating while looking pointedly between them. He did not even try to stop the class from giggling at the pair. David hated the fact he turned bright red. They were of course the center of gossip at Nakano Junior High.

After a quick glance at Rie, who refused to do anything but look straight ahead, he turned his attention to Takaeishi, who seemed to enjoy David's glare. To his surprise, Takumi avoided David as if he was infected.

David waited until the end of the last class. While everyone filtered out to their team or club activities, David remained in his seat. Takaeishi also stayed at the front of the class, flipping through homework rather than returning to the teachers' room. When only David, Rie, and Natsuki were in the room, Rie trying to get David's attention, Takaeishi looked up.

"I believe you have student council business to take care of Rie-chan, you too Natsuki," he said. They both tensed, but Natsuki grabbed Rie's arm and pulled her out of the room. She sent one last, unheeded, look of warning at David. David and Takaeishi were alone.

"What the hell is your problem?" David seethed as he stood, his chair flying into the desk behind him.

"You," he replied in a dark voice. "You are my problem, one I don't want. Do you know how trying it is, having to deal with all your classmates' inane problems? I was the head of the Imperial Guard, but am here because of you, so please, go ahead and attack me, that way I can kick you out of here and go back to my important duties."

Kou and David were in near perfect harmony. The anger and hate they felt for their smug teacher boiled away at their combined self-control. It took all of their willpower to keep from leaping at his throat with claws and fangs bared.

Takumi threw open the sliding door with a crash. He took in the standoff in an instant, and then dashed into the room and dragged David out, by his tail. Takaeishi's harsh laugh followed them down the corridor.

They stopped just long enough for David to be rid of Kou's tail, and then David stomped away from their homeroom. As Takumi followed after, David let the tension leech out of him.

'Things are difficult enough without that jerk making things worse.'

"Just don't start dating publically to get back at him," Takumi said. "Please? If you think everyone is bad now, just think what they'll say if they see you two together."

"Whoa, Rie and I haven't said anything," David said. "You and Natsuki are more together than we are. I noticed he didn't say anything about you two disappearing."

"Yeah, strange huh?" Takumi's tilting head told David he was not giving the whole story, but he was too annoyed to follow up. Instead, he put his frustrations into badminton practice. David played with such intensity he broke the strings on one of Takumi's best rackets. The badminton team knew David and Rie well enough that they did not comment on the gossip. If they had anything to say on the subject, they said it where David could not hear.

With a broken racket and a barely controllable rage running through him, David gave up on practice and headed for the Estate early. Just to ensure no one followed, he took the path Natsuki always took when she headed straight home.

He had barely made it into the forest before Takaeishi appeared before him on the rugged trail through the trees. David's training and anger merged into a well-balanced Matsumoto fighting stance.

"You are so not going to give me any crap about leaving school early," David said, his hands coming up into guard positions.

"As much as I'd like to go a few rounds with you, that's not why I'm here," Takaeishi said. His words made David tense even more. There was none of the animosity that had filled his voice just a few hours earlier. "I did not want to be the one to tell you this, but the Crown Prince insisted you be informed. Now." David took a step back. Takaeishi's eyes refused to meet his. He had adopted his full military bearing, staring straight into David's neck.

"There was a fire-"

David was gone. Kou leapt, his claws dug into the bark of a tree next to him, and then he was over Takaeishi's head and running for the Estate.

A small pink truck almost hit them as Kou raced out into the main road to Himeji without looking. A loud horn blared, but they dodged it and ran on. On the other side, Kou took to the tree branches. His four strong legs pounded along the thick upper branches, his claws propelling them toward the walled boundary of their home. Kou raced into the Estate looking for fire. Instead, he spotted Yukiko walking back from the vegetable garden with a basket of onions. Kou sprang at her.

For most people, seeing a tiger paw toward them at top speed would be a major cause for concern. Yukiko smiled when she spotted them running over the short grass around the main house.

"What's the hurry, Kou?" she asked. That brought him up short. "I think Masao wants you to work on your katas this evening. And there's a letter from Jessica for David on your desk."

"*A letter?*" Kou asked for David. "*We did not know she could write. She always sends emails.*"

"Well you might as well go read it before the others show up... I know Masao will want to start practice as soon as everyone is here."

"Nothing wrong at the Estate?" David asked, confused.

"Not a thing," she said. "Why?"

'Damn that Takaeishi,' David thought. "Nothing. Thanks."

Kou jogged around the house to the veranda where his room was. Kou wiped his paws on a fresh patch of grass then leaped up. He took a second to ensure his paws were clean before nudging the heavy sliding door open to his room. He had grown far more conscious of tracking dirt in after he had started sleeping on the floor with his futon. Once Kou shut the door again, he transformed and David threw on a spare gi. Since he planned to change back into Kou in a few minutes, he did not bother with a more substantial outfit.

As promised a regular envelope was waiting on his desk. As odd as a letter from his sister was, the shipping label brought him up short. She had sent it express, with a specific delivery day. With a shrug, David ripped open the corner and pulled out a single sheet of heavyweight paper. Jessica's lettering was easy enough to recognize. It was the neat printing many elementary students seemed to prefer right after learning they did not have to use cursive. The words, however, sent a chill through him.

May 31st,

David. Oh, how I hope you have been enjoying yourself. Things had been quite difficult for a while now. Ever since you showed up, I've been annoyed with you. I had, of course, noticed you. Who couldn't? Such a bumbling, uncoordinated idiot, making things more difficult. I was the special one, the foreigner everyone liked. It was going to be so easy to feed on them. I was even going to do them a favor and get rid of you. Surely, Rie would have been happy to be free of you. Then you

had to go and get possessed. You had to go and mess up my
plans. I am very cross with you, David. You got in the way
of something too big. A stupid gaijin who never should have
even been in Japan. Do you have any idea how long the pack
had been together? Do you know how important Jahangir
was, how hard it was to get my brother back? The least I can
do is return the favor. After all, what's a little more sacrifice?

Kisses,
Jess

Every word instilled a new level of terror in him. His rage
was so strong, Kou pulled away from his mind, leaving David
alone with the nightmares that raced through him. His feet
started moving. The sun was sinking behind the western trees
when he found Takaeishi standing before the main gate,
Yukiko blocking his way into the Estate.

二十三

REVENGE OF
THE AKUMA CLAN

Whatever my feelings toward Chul Soon's motivations, I could not fault his success. He had planned every blow with precision. The letter was the first strike in a battle that would break my brother's only real competition. I was rather surprised how well I made out from the deal. It made me suspicious…

David hoped she was dead. The alternative was just too hard to bear. Having her soul devoured by ōkami would be bad enough, but what if they tried to turn her into a yūrei? He was not sure if he could handle having to cut another corrupted kami out of someone he cared about. Worse, he was not sure he would be able to.

'Do I even know her well enough? Would I be able to distinguish between the kami and my sister? If I miss, I would kill her. And if I succeed, look at the pain it's caused Rie, and that's without the shock.' The one thing that kept him rooted to reality was the certainty he would see the Jeong brothers very soon. He knew what he would do to them. Then David remembered Takaeishi's words. 'The fire.'

"Talk," David said as he stomped toward his homeroom teacher. His despair, grief, and pain were burning within him as hot as the metal had been at the Matsumotos' Shrine, almost as much as the pain of having his mind ripped into two beings when Kou was born. The pain fed his rage. Takaeishi's face hardened as his hands came up palms out. Despite being wary of Takaeishi's sudden appearance at the Estate, Yukiko backed away, giving him room to escape if needed.

"We have just been contacted by the American Embassy. The Crown Prince is using every available backchannel to get more information. Our LA consulate has already sent a representative to Phoenix," he said. David stopped, glowering down at Takaeishi with a disturbing intensity. "There was a fire last night. It took them a while to find out who the next of kin was. They're having trouble confirming what, who, they've found."

The main gate, ajar from Takaeishi's entrance swung wider. Rie, missing Takaeishi behind the door, ran to David. "I did it! I finally did it," she called to him, brandishing a small crane. The live bird flapped in her palm. David ignored her. His mind blanked by the internal scream of rage within him, his full attention locked on Takaeishi. When Takaeishi remained silent, he turned and stalked deep into the Estate.

The destruction David reigned through the forest surprised the small part of him that was still conscious of his surroundings. In his blind anger, he felled giant, ancient trees. Underbrush and saplings all but disappeared. It was as if David had set out to mark a new path to the Shrine, for the damage did not end until he collapsed into emptiness in the clearing.

By the time he recovered from the injuries he had received from his rampage, it was deep into the night. David sat propped against a severely leaning tree staring at the ornate stonework above him, just visible by starlight.

"What do I do? They're dead."

David's voice was answered with silence, and then a few chirping insects. It took him several long seconds to realize no answer had come, that Kou was silent. He turned toward the

Estate, intending to sneak back for a quick change of clothes so he would not be too conspicuous on the train, then he saw the trees. Guilt ripped through him as he saw the destruction his Seikaku and fists had caused. A scar more ugly than any of Takumi's had been ripped through the Estate.

"This is going to hurt," David sighed aloud, his rage gone in an instant. With practiced ease, he summoned his Seikaku in its wood form and began repairing the worst of the damage. He started with the tree leaning over the shrine. The true sword gave David the ability, but the results were limited by his mind. It had always been easier to destroy than create, since destruction was wild and free and required little concentration. Creation, however, required David to imagine every aspect of the rebuilding process. Without Kou to help him, he had to strain for the most basic changes. It took him ten minutes just to fix the single leaning tree.

A big part of him was happy with the difficulty it took to undo the damage. It kept his mind off what might have happened back in Arizona, while also helping to assuage the guilt he felt at the damage around him. The forest had stood for centuries, and it would be impossible to put everything back the way it had been. The major damage began to disappear with each thrust of his sword, but Kou remained silent.

The destruction was so prevalent that David knew it would take days. With a solemn promise to return, David whipped through the Estate and beyond. He arrived just in time to catch the first local train to Himeji.

If one of the Matsumotos was following him, they gave David no hint. He arrived in Himeji and transferred onto an express to Kyoto, following the route they had taken the previous year when looking for a way to save Rie. The solitary train ride gave David the time to come to grips with the reality of what had happened, but also gave his imagination time to work on the unknowns. Without the certainty of proof, his mind created ever-worsening scenarios.

The letter stuck in his mind. Jessica wrote the letter before the fire. Would they make her into a yūrei after all? Could they? Chul Soon would remember the lengths David went to save Rie. Would they risk becoming puppets again for the power? It was clear the Jeong brothers' desire for revenge outweighed any fear of David. Would they give him the chance to save his sister in their hopes they could take him? He had to find out, and to do that, he needed more information.

Kou roared. David had heard the kami within him growl often enough, but it was the first time he had unleashed such an unbridled wave of fury within David. The passengers across the aisle stared at David as his mouth hung loose in shock at the power that washed through his mind.

'I am part of you, yet you endangered my very being. Do you realize how very close to the edge we came back in that forest? I am an earth kami. Such wanton destruction of the forest is a corruption that goes against the core of us. You could have created something far worse than a yūrei. Where would Japan be then?'

'But'

'We are going to put every tree back. I don't care how long it takes. You might have felt guilty, but not enough. Just what do you expect to get from the Crown Prince that you can't get from the Matsumotos? The Matsumotos care about you. They are your family now too. Yet you abandon them when you need them most.'

'Screw your trees. They have my sister. My father may be dead.' David choked on the thought but his rage was back. 'I fixed some of your trees but now I'm going to get answers, and if you don't like it shut up and leave the Jeong brothers to me.'

David exited the train with a crush of people into the crowded late-morning station. Past the turnstiles, the buildings rose up around a massive square. David ignored the shops and restaurants as he moved to a long line of taxis. Part of him knew Kou was right, but the tiger's long silence and the accusatory tone in his inner voice was not something David could deal with.

David tried to ignore the cab driver, who kept looking into the mirror to check on him. He could not tell if the driver was afraid David could not pay, or if he was concerned David was traveling alone. He stared down the driver's look whenever it appeared in the rear-view mirror. Although he was in a hurry and rage still ran through him, David still knew he had to be less direct than he would like to be. He walked from the corner of a busy shopping intersection until the taxi was gone. Out of sight, he turned down a wide street toward the same gate they had entered during their last trip.

A long wall surrounded the palace grounds, much like the ones outside the Kumamoto Castle he had visited with his class earlier in the year. On the eastern side, there was a small gate used by the staff and the Imperial Family. David walked right up to it and began looking for away in. The old wooded doors looked quite solid, but he knocked anyway.

"This way please, Mr. Matthews," called a man's voice in Oxford accented English. Backing up from the gate, David noticed a guard in a simple black suit staring at him from a doorway beside the gate. David shrugged and followed him in. The small door shut behind them and locked with heavy metal bolts. "We have been told to expect you. The helicopter is waiting."

"Helicopter?"

"Yes," a familiar voice said. David stiffened, that dangerous flame within him rising again. "The Crown Prince has requested an audience, but he is not here."

David's hands rose away from his sides as his fingers balled into fists. His feet spread apart into a fighting stance as he half turned to face Takaeishi as he walked down an intersecting path.

"I do not agree with Masao-kun," Takaeishi said. "I refuse to let you wander around on your own. My instructions, unfortunately, are to bring you to Tokyo so that you can receive the latest news as it comes in from the Embassy. When you disappeared, the Crown Prince thought you might seek an audience, but he is not here, so he sent me to bring you to him."

"So you're my driver then?" David said. "Good. Get me on a train."

"The helicopter is not optional. You do not waste the Crown Prince's time," he spat. As if realizing there might be others watching, Takaeishi paused to calm himself. "I thought you'd want to hear what we learned about the fire."

David had never been so tempted to hit someone. He wanted to erase Takaeishi's superior, taunting smile. Even Natsuki and Koji had not created such a strong desire within him, but where his control had broken then, things were different. David was different. His sister was in danger and Takeishi would not get to him. Thanks to the Matsumotos' training, he knew he could probably beat Takaeishi in a fight, but after what he had just done to the forest, he knew he could never let himself lose control again. As much as it grated to let Takaeishi's attitude slide, he needed his help. David was supposed to be a Jitsugen Samurai, a protector.

David never found out if Takaeishi knew anything more about his father and sister. Despite Kou's attempt to withdraw, David found it impossible to concentrate while they were in the air. The whole time felt as if he was having a huge anxiety attack. The attack turned the annoying buzz he remembered from the previous trip into a painful headache as the view from the helicopter jerked in a bit of turbulence. It was so bad he ended up retching, though he at least managed to direct it toward his teacher.

His pain and nausea lasted minutes after they touched down at the Imperial Palace in Tokyo. Even with the beautiful gardens around them, David felt weaker without the forests and life of the Matsumoto Estate. He had no idea how long the flight had taken, but he vowed to get a train back, no matter who was waiting.

The Tokyo Imperial Palace had some similarities to the palace in Kyoto. There were manicured gardens and paths surrounded by high walls. Old buildings stood around the gardens, and security was everywhere. Takaeishi rushed David from the helicopter, before its blades even stopped, into a low building. The way Takaeishi's head moved from side to side it was almost as if he was afraid someone would see them.

David still felt sick as they hurried through modern, but isolated corridors and halls. If it had not been for the lack of people, he probably would not have noticed the other boy his age and the little girl standing next to him peering out from a doorway. The boy's eyes narrowed as they stared back at David.

'Great, one more person who hates me,' David thought. His small laugh stopped Takaeishi. He turned around and David caught the surprise on the boy's face as he tried, unsuccessfully, to avoid notice. Takaeishi surprised David even more by bowing low to the door before pulling David on through another corridor. 'I've never seen Takaeishi bow to anyone.'

They met the Crown Prince in a conference room that could have been any successful company's boardroom. Plush chairs surrounded a long, rectangular table. Around the room, screens showed various video feeds from international news to other conference rooms with other Japanese government workers. Aside from Crown Prince Nakahito, a few aids were leaning over the table to discuss something in whispers, while more fiddled with controls or checked the headlines streaming from the televisions. David stopped as he recognized the woman next to the Crown Prince.

"The cake lady."

"David-san, you're here, good," Nakahito said. David was surprised enough at the lack of ceremony that he almost smiled. Instead, he flicked his gaze to the screens. One showed a familiar news logo. Its focus was on what had once been his childhood home. "I am so very sorry we are meeting again in such a difficult time for you. Yes, you've met my assistant before. Please, sit." Nakahito indicated one of the chairs. David relaxed a little as Takaeishi left the room.

"What happened?" David asked in a small, dead voice. Nakahito looked uncomfortable as he shifted around a file in front of him. He gestured slightly to his aide.

"David-san," she said. "Your father is alive, but… someone called your 911 last night in Phoenix. When the first responders got to the house, flames were already coming from the roof. They were able to search most of the house and did not find anyone in it as they tried to battle back the flames. Unfortunately, it seems your father was near the center of the inferno. By the time they found him… his chances are not good." She looked to Nakahito who nodded. "There are indications he was injured prior to the burns."

"My sister?"

"They put out an Amber Alert," she said. "I'm not sure what that is, but I think they are looking for her."

"I'm sorry to intrude your highness," a voice said from one of the screens with a conference room in it. "There has been another development."

"Go ahead," Nakahito said.

"Witnesses report seeing the girl's boyfriend and one of his friends as the last visitors to the house before the fire," a suited man said. "Subsequent investigations have found she has been dating a boy for a few weeks, but the boy cannot be found. No one seems to know who he is or where he came from. Phoenix police have just issued a bulletin seeking two boys for questioning in the fire and attempted murder of Dr. Sydney Matthews.

"As you may have noticed, the news companies here have caught wind of the fact that Dr. Matthews had a son and that he is in Japan. We feel it will not be long until they start pressuring NHK for an interview with him."

David felt sick, as if the room had a cloying evil smell. The faces on the screens seemed to blur, and all he could see was a mirror-house nightmare of Chul Soon's smiling face mocking him from every screen.

"Is there any way for me to get to Arizona? Any way at all," David said as he fought down the vision.

"No David-kun," Nakahito said. A look passed between him and his assistant, and his voice cracked. "I'm so sorry. The fastest flights take almost ten hours one way. Even if you made it, the trip would kill you. Do you have any idea who could have done this? Not even the local police think it was an accident."

"It was the Jeong brothers," he said. Somehow, he had kept the letter with him throughout the destruction of the forest and even after changing his clothes before the trains. David realized he had been fingering it the whole time he had been sitting in the room. With a shudder, he threw it onto the table and slid it over to Nakahito. A guard caught it and checked it before handing it over.

"If I'm reading the English correctly, it doesn't sound like your sister wrote this," Nakahito said.

"She didn't think up the words, but it was my sister's writing," David muttered. Remembering whom he was talking to, he shifted a little in his seat and tried to speak more politely. "Chul Soon used the letter to tell me he is in control of my sister. They must have been around her, maybe even feeding off her for some time. I think he is going to turn her into a yūrei. That way she will either kill me, or I will have to hunt and kill her. It is his revenge for my rescue of Rie and the destruction of his pack. According to Rie and some other sources, we might have delayed the plans of the Akuma Clan, a much larger group of ōkami based in Okinawa."

"This is very bad news," Nakahito said with a grave frown. "If they are trying to revive the Akuma Clan things are far worse than we anticipated." He turned to one of the men sitting around the table. "Find out why the Matsumotos did not tell us about the connection, and then send a scouting party to Okinawa."

"David-san," the woman began, "There is no way for you to get to America. Even if we could get you there, you know the Jeong brothers will not stay."

"No. Chul Soon will come back, if only to gloat," David said. His grief and guilt was draining away as he sat in the big leather chair, staring at the next Emperor of Japan. One by one, David wrestled with his wild emotions, just as he once battled against his unruly muscles. Every passing second left him more in control of himself than ever before. A single train of thought was beginning to eclipse all the pain and anger from the news of his sister's disappearance and father's condition.

'My sister is alive. They will bring her to me. I need to be stronger.'

"I'm sorry to have intruded," David said, standing. "I need to get back to the Estate."

"You don't want to see if the Americans track down your sister?" the woman asked.

"No. It doesn't matter anymore. They will come for me. I need to be visible, vulnerable. That is when they will attack."

"That may be true, but we cannot risk you so openly," Nakahito said. "The media will want to interview you as well, not to mention your relatives. They will likely attempt to bring you back to America."

"I have no other family," David said, his voice cracked as he realized he was alone. His mother had died so long ago that he could not remember much of her. Although he had been away, his father had stayed with him through the videos of his show he sent every week. Now he was so close to death and David could do nothing to help.

'Everything I've learned. Every broken bone, every shaped tree, and I cannot help my father.'

'Not alone. I am still a part of you. I understand your pain.'

'What do you understand? You have the Zodiac Memories. You're a part of him and he is still stalking around out there somewhere.'

'*No David. He is dying out there. His sacrifice… for us.*'

David shuddered, and before he could stop himself, he began to cry.

He awoke in a dark room that reminded him of the first hotel on his school trip. The room was much larger, but decked out in the same kind of neutral design and furniture a hotel might have.

'What are we going to do? They have her. I have to be stronger. I have to lure them in before they change her. If I go hunting and miss them, they might turn her rather than come for me.'

'*You are already strong enough to face the Jeong brothers. Takumi, Rie, Natsuki, and even Tsubasa will all be there for you. The Matsumotos will fight with you again. They have all met your sister. They have fought the Jeongs. They are as much a part of this fight as we are.*'

David sighed. Part of him wanted to crawl into a little hole, a much bigger part wanted to wrap his hands around one particular wolf's neck. Instead, he crawled out the bed and slipped into his freshly laundered clothes. Despite the very early hour, outside his room he found the boy from the hallway waiting for him.

"I can't believe they picked you," he said. "Such a whiney baby. They should let me train with the Matsumotos. It's my right after all."

Before David could respond, one of the house guards came into view. The boy took off down a corridor. The guard bowed at the empty hallway then beckoned to David. After ensuring he was not one of Takaeishi's group from the kidnapping, he followed him back to the conference room. The man halted

David outside the door, but he was still able to make out the tired voices inside.

"Crown Prince, if you remember, I suggested something along those lines," the woman said. "It could help us take care of that pesky citizenship issue of his as well."

"Yes, I think we should go ahead with that," Nakahito said. "But based on Takaeishi's most recent reports, I don't think the Matsumotos will be the best choice. I know the other way will cause a great commotion, but it might help us with the press, and will make their education more discreet."

"It is only for another few months, after all," said a third voice. A few moments later, they ushered David in again. Even as he sat, a new determination rushed through him.

"David, once again, we are so very sorry for your losses," the woman said. "Unfortunately, I have to inform you that while your father's condition is uncertain. Even if he wakes, he will likely never be able to walk. His legs were badly injured before the fire. In addition there has been no luck in tracking down your sister or her abductors."

"I do not know if you remember, David, but I once promised you would never have to worry about a place to live. That has not changed," Nakahito said. "For now it would be best for you to stay here."

David straightened in his chair. He had already decided his course, and it was not comprised of hiding behind the Imperial Household while Chul Soon had control of his sister.

"If I do that, then Chul Soon will know I am protected. He might just kill Jess if he thinks the Imperial House will start hunting him too. If I go back, even get on the news, make it easy for him to attack, we can be ready for him. We can save my sister. I would humbly request the Crown Prince's people observe all ships and planes going to and from the Japanese mainland. If you can give me a hint when they arrive, I might be able to figure out when they will attack."

The Crown Prince stared at David for a long moment. His eyes, intelligent and probing searched David's face. For his part, David reached out to Kou. They had come to an uneasy agreement in the night, but there was still a lot to talk about.

"Very well. Takaeishi will escort you back to the Matsumoto Estate. He will continue to be my father's observer. On that note, the esteemed Emperor wants to meet you, but will not intrude at such a difficult time. Please return during the summer. By then our plans should be in place for your future."

"Thank you," David said with the lowest bow the table would allow. "I have two more requests. Will you fire Takaeishi?" This elicited a few laughs from around the room. Nakahito smiled, but it was clear from the way he stared back that it was not an option. "OK, then can we at least take the train back?"

"*I don't do helicopters,*" Kou said.

二十四

THE POSTER CHILD

With Jessica under my control, we slipped out of Phoenix with minimal difficulty. The border between the States and Mexico was easy enough to cross. By the time the news noticed there was more to the incident than yet another fire, we were long gone. With his prize in sight, however, Chul Soon was that much more determined, controlling, and insistent...

Masao met them at the Nakano station. David threw a final glare at his teacher, one of many during the long trip, before walking over to his host-father. David bowed low. Tensing as he anticipated a verbal barrage from the strict man.

"We can talk in the car," Masao said. David kept his head lowered but could not resist glancing up at his host-father's kindly tone. David followed Masao to the car. "I noticed you began repairing the damage to the forest. I expect you will continue with your work?"

"Of course Masao-shihan," David said as he entered the family car. "Look, I'm-"

"No need to apologize," he said. "I know how you must have felt. I am of course disappointed you felt the need to seek out the Crown Prince's advice before ours, and as for the forest, well, after destroying that table with the ōkami statue, I should not lecture on losing one's temper, should I?" His chuckle made David smile, despite the hairpin turns Masao was putting them through. His smile turned a little more genuine as he realized they were taking the long way back to the Estate.

"Do you have a strategy? You were not gone for very long," he said.

"I'm going to be bait," David said with a grin very similar to an oni's when anticipating a particularly destructive afternoon.

"Your plan is to be bait?"

"Nakahito, I mean the Crown Prince, did not like it either," he said. "I'm sure they have Jess, they are either going to kill her or turn her. Either way Chul Soon is going to want me to see what they do to her. They will come here. My plan is to make myself as visible as possible. Hopefully, the Imperial Household will be able to figure out when they make it to the mainland so that we can be ready with an ambush."

"You will need a lot of help to pull off an ambush," Masao said, slowing the car fractionally to turn onto the unpaved drive into the Matsumoto Estate.

"Yes. We are going to need everyone's help."

David spent the next ten days repairing the damage he had caused in the forest. Every night after his regular training and homework, he summoned his Seikaku and helped the trees and plants grow back to their original ancient splendor. Kou's indelible memory was the only thing that made it possible. With a perfect picture of every tree from Kou's memory of their times slinking around the forest, he was able to guide the branches and bark back to their original configuration. The task left David exhausted each night, but he welcomed the fatigue as a reminder of the potential within him.

'There's so much power in the Seikaku. I've just started to learn its secrets,' David thought after his second night of restoration.

'*It will become as much a part of you as my claws are to me. We must both be careful not to scratch the wrong things.*'

'Evil classmates, check. Trees, no. Got it.' David yawned. 'I just hope the TV cameras assume my exhaustion is pain and grief rather than me practicing an ancient martial art and fixing trees I blew apart with a magic sword.'

The Japanese news, NHK, had called the Estate the day after the news about the fire. Although as wary as Nakahito, Masao and Yukiko had relented at David's insistence, and allowed the reporters to interview him.

"If they get their fill then the news shows will be over and done with soon enough," David had argued over breakfast. Yukiko had frowned over her tea. "If we refuse, they will start looking at why we won't talk. Besides, it will help lull the Jeong brothers into a sense of security. They will think they have already won."

After NHK, one of the Phoenix news shows picked up the story and had an affiliate in Kobe travel all the way to Nakano. They caught him after school. It was like magic. The twins, Natsuki, and Tsubasa were gone before the camera was even level.

"David! Can we have a word?" an eager dark-haired woman asked in perfect English. She looked like a new reporter trying to make her first big story. David put on the most pained face he could manage. It was easy. The responsibility he felt for the damage done to his father was an icepick in his side, painful, cold, and his own fault. His work in the forest was not just to fix the damage, but was a cathartic process, helping him to avoid thinking over much about his father and sister. David had spent so much time with his father among the trees in northern Arizona, however, that they served as their own painful form of absolution as well. He gave a slight nod and walked over so the cameraman could frame him with the school behind.

"I'm here with David Matthews, the young son of Dr. Matthews, star of the popular public access television show *Crazy Science*, who remains in critical condition after last week's fire in his Phoenix, Arizona home. David, we have learned that Phoenix Fire Investigators are not ruling out arson as the cause of the fire and that your younger sister is still missing. There are whispers your sister might be a suspect, but like the boys last seen at the scene, she cannot be found." That surprised him. It was the first he had heard about his sister being a suspect. "Your reaction?"

"It is very difficult. Of course, my host-family has been as supportive as possible. I never thought I would be so separated from him, my dad." David's eyes hardened a little as he looked up to the reporter. It was obvious from her eager expression she had been the one to suspect Jessica. "I was contacted by the US embassy, there is no way my sister could have been involved in the fire. I only hope the Phoenix police can find the boys who took her. There is no doubt in my mind they are responsible for both my father's injuries and the disappearance of my little sister."

If she was annoyed, the woman covered it. She continued to ask inane questions about his old life, which he answered with appropriate reluctance and difficulty.

"Is there anything you would say to the criminals who have taken away so much from you?"

"Yes. My sister is Jessica Matthews. My father will never walk and may never wake up. He may die. Isn't that enough? Bring her back to me." He did not have to fake the tears, even though his emotions ran closer to a slow burning anger.

'I will get her back, and no wood chips are going to keep us from destroying the dogs this time,' David thought.

NHK dubbed the interview and played it in the slight lull between breaths as people tried to comprehend the bombshell announced the next afternoon. David had all of thirty minutes to contemplate the information in a letter hand-delivered from the Imperial Household before it rocked Japan.

Crown Prince Nakahito planned to adopt David.

After the formal letter was a separate, more personal note explaining the reasoning behind the Prince's move to David and the Matsumotos. It was a very long note.

They had decided to take David's strategy to an extreme. While the story of Dr. Matthews's and the disappearance of his daughter were still playing on national news shows in America, the news in Japan had run the highly edited interview with David only once. Even the notion of having a foreigner adopted by the Crown Prince was already causing a huge stir. They hoped that the ignited debate would be intense but burn out quickly. It would also mean an in-depth investigation into everything David Matthews. Everyone would know where he was and what he was doing.

The Imperial Household thwarted the first round of distractors by painting a tale of heartbreak by the Princess at seeing the news of such a young boy, the same age as her own nephew, essentially orphaned and with his sister still missing. She was a picture of motherly concern as she answered questions.

"Of course, young David will stay with his host-parents for the time being," she said, sitting opposite an attentive and appropriately senior journalist. She was composed in a smart suit that seemed to balance tradition and modernity. "The Matsumoto family has been a wonderful support for the young man, but I just could not let the boy get caught up in citizenship issues during his time of need. By adopting David ourselves, we can ensure he has a home. Our lawyers assure us, of course, that as long as necessary declarations are made affirming he has no right to enter the Imperial Household itself, he can stay with us. Of course, he will spend most of his time in school, but what an opportunity to show modern Japan's hospitality to the world."

The anchor was, of course, sympathetic. Then they showed the new dubbed clip again, a lonely boy asking for the return of his sister, complete with Japanese translations. The opposition was fierce, but the loudest arguments came from those who were against the Imperial House in the first place. Their arguments solidified David's place as a narrow majority rallied behind the establishment.

The Crown Prince finalized his public stance with an interview for the major papers. Most of Nakahito's words focused on Japan's past, on the role adoption played in Japanese history, of the spirit of inclusion that had kept Japan strong in difficult times. He spoke of how Japan had become so withdrawn as a society that they had forgotten one of their greatest strengths.

"Being Japanese is not, nor has it ever been, about blood or the way we look," he said. "It is time to acknowledge that to be Japanese is…" The article was accompanied by criticism, analysis, and comments on Japan's growing geriatric populations in various proportions depending on the bent of the newspaper, but overall David realized the tone of all of them were subtly guiding the issue away from that of a lone boy. The Prince, or one of his advisors, had made it into yet another political question, one that could fade into the background of discussion and almost certain obscurity.

Nakahito's note also sparked David's suspicions as it expressed the various political, legal, and social reasons behind the adoption. It was long enough that David questioned just whom the note was supposed to convince.

'There still seems to be something missing, why not just ask the Matsumotos to adopt me?'

'*The answer is in that envelope the courier gave to Masao. I think Nakahito liked the way this is going to make the constitution's limitations on the size, scope, and role of the Imperial Household look like a crude and outdated bit of legislation. You cannot escape the irony behind the fact that America wrote it, and yet it causes the only question to whether they can go ahead with it.'*

'But why didn't they just have someone else adopt me. They said I'd stay with the Matsumotos already. The bit about it being a perfect cover for my summer in Tokyo seems a bit short sighted.'

'Yes, there is more at play, but it is working to our advantage. Chul Soon will see you as weak, needing rescue, and relying on help. I doubt he will realize our resolve. As long as no one uncovers the true historical ties between the Matsumotos and Imperial House we should be fine.'

For David, the hardest thing to deal with after his sister's disappearance was school. At first, there was sympathy, then, when the news broke about the pending adoption, it all went to hell. Most of his classmates were only vaguely aware of the Imperial Family. Instead of seeing them as the symbol of Japanese nationalism, most of his friends gave them the same attention as pop stars. The gossip hounds followed what little news leaked about the ins and outs of the family.

David went from the resident gaijin to someone of national renown. It was as if he was doing his first day all over again, for the third time. Even Naoto and Shou watched him as if they did not know him. Every girl who had given him chocolate on Valentine's Day was suddenly there again, waiting to talk to him. Most smiled sadly, as they asked again about his sister and father, hanging on every word he muttered. Fewer asked if he had met the Emperor. Twice David had to get Takumi's help to escape from a girl that had started a rumor they were dating. A few came to him to tell him they did not care about his adoption, but hoped he found his sister soon.

Most of the time David was floundering in awkward social situations, Rie was off to the side in conversation with

Natsuki, often with a smirk that had become a new trademark for her.

'I'm not sure why, but I'm beginning to suspect she is *happy* about the adoption news. I know she cares, *but she is also enjoying herself.*'

As the Crown Prince had suggested in his letter, the story peaked after a few days and died off as NHK returned to the usual game shows and celebrities eating various foods and shouting some variation of "*Delicious*" for the audience. At school too, things quickly quieted down after a few days of nothing changing. David continued coming to school with the twins every day, no one but media arrived in Nakano and spot nor speck of the Imperial Family was seen.

Class 3B had other problems to deal with. No one but the samurai knew why, but they all had to deal with increased homework and difficult assignments. Takaeishi was furious. Yukiko had explained that since David was to become a member of the Crown Prince's family, Takaeishi would be honor bound to follow David's instructions.

Thanks to the Matsumoto training, it was easy for David and the others to spot the reporters and various investigators that began following them around. In accordance with David's strategy, they all made themselves visible. They stayed later at school after practice, and even began making regular stops at the one of the nearby convenience stores, giving the reporters plenty of time to see them as normal junior high students. The only major change was to keep their morning runs to within the Estate's walls.

With a sheer lack of anything interesting to report, David noticed ever fewer unfamiliar faces. Eventually, even the most cynical journalists gave up. The second day after David noticed the last reporter was gone, Rie celebrated by ambushing him on his way to the forge.

"Um, thanks," he said as a baseball cap covered his eyes. Frowning, Rie stepped away from her hiding spot behind a tree and pulled the hat back off. She replaced it with a wide straw monstrosity.

"You have too much hair," Rie complained. After a bit more adjusting, she gave up and ditched both hats. "Your skin would give you away anyway. We will just have to risk it. Let's go, my co-conspirator is waiting."

David stumbled a bit as she pulled him toward the Estate wall, but smiled to see her determination. Together they climbed the ancient rocks.

'I hope she disabled the sensors.'

'We'll know if Masao or Yukiko show up.'

Without a word, Rie led David through the forest, heading back to the main road. As he watched her weave through the trees, David remembered Kou's words from days ago, but they now had new meaning for him. The thought hit like one of Masato's old tree branch traps.

'The Matsumotos aren't going to adopt me. Rie's not going to be my sister, is she?'

'Took you a while, didn't it.' Just then Rie looked back, and he seriously hoped his face had not turned as red as it felt.

About a mile from the Estate, they ran into an overgrown trail that David assumed had once been some kind of road. Rie turned onto it, heading straight for a bright pink mini-truck.

David almost laughed aloud when he recognized the owner of the bald head in the front seat. Mikio the monk sat snoring, his arm dangling out the open window. Rie jumped in the back, and David followed suit.

"Ready!" Rie called.

Without warning, the truck stared up and they were moving. Rie laughed as David studied the cab warily. With a shake of his head, he followed Rie's example as she lay below the bed's sides.

"Just in case any of those reporters are still around," she said.

"It is a risk," David said. "Though it should take the Jeong brothers longer to get back anyway. Tatsuya-san, Nakahito-sama's aide, assured me it would take even Takaeishi-sensei awhile to get Jess into the country without sending off every alarm."

"Let's hope they set off at least one."

They spent the rest of the trip bouncing along with every bump as the little truck sped along as fast as Masao drove. From the very brief views of the trees he got, Kou figured they were heading toward the small village where the monk lived.

'*She's going to notice if you keep glancing at her,*' Kou warned.

'*Fine. Distract me.*'

Kou proceeded to play a newly unlocked memory from the Zodiac Tiger. It was a battle from the warring states period that their history class on the subject had awoken. Kou almost succeeded.

Mikio welcomed them into his home, but unlike before, he did not leave straight away. They shared uncomfortable cups of tea as the old monk watched every sip.

"You're quite the famous one nowadays," Mikio said with a smile. "Next time you see your new dad, tell him he still owes me."

David's smile faltered at the painful reminder that his father was stuck wrapped up like a mummy in some hospital bed. Mikio stood and left the room.

"That was strange," Rie whispered as they walked toward the back.

By the time they made it outside, the sun had set somewhere behind the house, the stars just beginning to show in the sky. The night was warm, but David's mind had strayed to memories of building solar ovens and frying eggs on concrete with his father.

Guided by the last of the fading sunset, Rie led David around the side of the house, away from the pond. There, a thick bamboo forest blocked their way. David followed Rie between two towering stalks.

"I thought you might like a little peace and quiet after everything that's happened," Rie said, her voice melding with the quiet atmosphere and serenity of the place. "It always helps me." A low thock reverberated around them as the pond's bamboo cup tipped in the distance.

There was little for him to say. Rie was well aware of his situation in all its intricacies. He laughed a little; their walk might have been a romantic stroll except he was dressed in his worst clothes having expected a night in the forge. Rie was in a comfortable outfit that she had somehow made stylish. Kou brought to his attention the fact she had done something new with her hair. David tried to relax and enjoy the simplicity of the bamboo stalks around them, but he was exhausted. Rie let him be. She walked beside him as they wandered various paths. Before long, they came to the same overlook where they had stopped at their last visit. David sat.

"Dad was annoyed when he read the Crown Prince's note," she said. "He stayed annoyed right though the second one. He smiled when he read the last one. I tried to get a glimpse but he wouldn't let me see it. He burned it after I tried to steal it." David laughed at the image of Rie getting caught trying to get a peek at the letter. David was also impressed Masao had caught her. After all, he was the sneakiest of the Matsumotos. "He figured I wouldn't let it go. He was waiting for me, of course."

"Kou and I have some ideas about what it might have said. But hey, things have been so busy. Tell us about your summoning."

Rie giggled and produced a small square of red origami paper. David watched as her hands began graceful folds. Her long slender fingers marked each crease. Soon she had an elongated diamond. With a brief flick of her eyes at him, she opened the tips of the point to reveal the wings of a paper crane. As soon as Rie completed the bird, it disappeared and an actual crane sat flapping in her hand. It was far larger than the paper had been.

"Maybe someday I'll be able to do it without the paper, but for now it helps me concentrate to bridge the gap between, what did Kou call it? The layers. I was making cranes at Natsuki's for a sick relative and it popped out. Over the last few days, I've tried a few other basic shapes. You might find a few new frogs in the pond back home."

David's eyes shaded orange as they watched the flapping bird.

"How convenient, bird on demand," Kou said. Rie punched David.

"It's not your dinner, go hunt a deer," she laughed.

"Can you make deer? Ooo, I've always wanted to try antelope."

"Hey cut it out," David said struggling back into control of his body. "Sorry, we haven't hunted in a while, he gets a little testy. But that's awesome! Can you summon them at will?"

"Watch this," she said with an eager smile. Rie threw the bird into the air. It spread its wings and flapped hard, its long legs tucking behind. Rie closed her eyes and the bird turned through the air and dive-bombed David. He barely had time to duck before the bird was airborne again and circling overhead. The red-feathered crane spread its wings wide again and glided down to the pond where it started to peck after small fish in the shallows.

"You can control it!" David said with a laugh.

"Yep. Next time we are in a fight you'll have some back up. From what I've been able to read about the animals, they are real enough. It's like a vacation for the spirits that occupy the creatures, they're already dead so if something happens it's just like going back to sleep for them. Of course there's still a danger I could summon something from beyond the Devil's Doorway, but I think I would have to consciously do that."

Talking to Rie, seeing her so excited as they watched the crane play in the pond, David forgot about his own worries. His plans for the Jeong brothers faded from his mind and he relaxed in a way he'd been unable to for days.

"Thank you," he said with a sigh as the crane flew off into the night.

"Well, it's been hard to get the famous Mr. Matthews alone." Rie smiled, her face was calm, but her eyes were bright behind the colored contacts. "And if you ever leave me behind while you get to go to Tokyo again I'll pull a Natsuki and hunt you down with a pack of paper animals. If you think getting adopted by the Crown Prince is going to-"

David could not stand it any longer. Beside him was the girl who had helped him when he was at his worst. The friend who always seemed to know what to say to him. Where minutes ago, he had been depressed and on the brink of tears, his life now seemed filled with potential and purpose. He knew it was a mistake, he felt a thrill of fear, but acted anyway. He turned, and before his nerve failed, kissed her gently on the lips.

Seeing her stunned face was worth every bit of the nervousness he had gone through steeling himself for the move.

"*Now* we're even," he said, his cheeks coloring red in embarrassment and thrill.

They were both quiet during the drive back to the Estate. David was happy he had acted, if only a little. There was a sense of peace between them again. The tension that had built up over the last weeks, the tension he had not even realized was there because it had grown up so slowly, had passed. Rie sighed beside him as Mikio's pink truck bounced over a rut in the road.

"We can't tell anyone," she said.

"Tell anyone what," he asked, his eyebrows raised. She punched him. He knew what she meant. They were going out. Then a thought caught him unaware, and it was as if the ice-pick had been stuck back into his heart.

'Yes, the Jeong brothers will strike at anything they think will hurt us.'

"Definitely can't tell anyone," he choked.

二十五

THE EMPEROR'S GRANDSON

Back in Japan, back on the main island, back in the place where I endured the inescapable fire, trapped in that shell no better than my hide. At least this time half the company was good. Jessica was fun to date, and her new life seemed to suit her well. She took to it with an unexpected enthusiasm that I could see made Chul Soon ecstatic. Unfortunately, the more pleased he was with her, the less he was with me. The closer we got, the more guarded he was with his plans. The vaguer he became about my concerns and his promises...

Kou leapt back, dodging Takumi's bamboo sword. It was the evening after their trip to Mikio's house. Kou and Takumi had opted to try for another bout of sparing without telling the elders. Though Masao had forbidden it, Takumi did not want to let the last disaster keep them from practicing. Kou had promised not to use his claws or teeth. Despite the concentration they had to exert on the fight, David could not help but think about Rie.

'It's crazy. I'm happy, excited, thrilled. I mean, she likes me too. In all the movies and TV shows, boys ask girls out and the girls turn them down. Except now it's out there, that we like each other, I'm so freaked out I can't think straight.'

'Tigers do not get so attached, though all I have is the Zodiac Tiger's memories to go on. We bonded with Natsuki but that was different from what you feel. Natsuki saved us. Your relationship with Rie has been slow to form, but long in coming.'

Takumi took advantage of Kou's distraction, smacking him in the side. The roar of indignity shook the trees as a ferocious orange paw swiped the bamboo out of Takumi's grasp. Natsuki threw him another.

'You're afraid Chul Soon will find out and take her like he took your father and sister. Be silent for a second.' Kou growled again as Takumi smacked his head.

"Distracted much?" Takumi taunted. Together, David and Kou lunged, bringing their full weight on Takumi. Takumi grunted as he fell back. "Ugh. Lose some weight."

Kou opened his jaws wide, fangs flashing, Takumi flinched as Kou ripped the red helmet off him. Pinned, Takumi could do little as the blue-eyed Kou smiled over him. A long string of tiger drool began to leak down toward his face. Just before it could hit, Takumi disappeared. Reimi popped into place and ignited the underbrush all around Kou, singing his fur. Natsuki and Rie dashed out of the way, giggling as Kou ran growling after the flaming bird.

"Boys," Natsuki said with a laugh.

"Yeah," Rie answered with a sigh. Kou caught Natsuki look at David's new girlfriend in suspicion as he circled around a tree after Reimi. Rie covered her lapse by pulling out a square of paper from her pocket. "Let's see how they deal with this."

Rie's hands began to fly as her slender fingers made the complicated folds for an origami animal. When she finished, a slightly misshapen but very large hawk, popped into her hands.

"Hmm, still needs work," Natsuki said. Rie released the bird, which dashed into the trees overhead. Soon it was high above the forest, swooping to attack both Kou and Reimi.

Kou scaled the closest tree while Reimi flapped to gain altitude. The bigger bird was faster. From above the trees it dived, catching Reimi in is sharp talons.

"*Now Kou!*" Reimi called. From out of the tree, Kou sprang catching the big bird in a puff of feathers.

"Nife," David mumbled around the bird as they plunged toward the trees. Reimi flapped once then plopped onto Kou's back as they tumbled. Kou twitched his claws out, slowing their fall as they dug into the wood. David cringed within Kou as long gashes opened in the bark. At the bottom, Kou sat and started enjoying his hawk. Rie and Natsuki found them just as Takumi transformed back into his armor.

"Dang, that didn't take you very long," Rie complained. Takumi looked around confused, and then made a face at the flying feathers.

"It was two on one. Reimi left herself as bait," Natsuki said. Kou ignored them, preferring to focus on Rie's plump hawk.

"*Compliments to the chef,*" he said between bites.

"You're impossible," Natsuki said as she readied another sword for Takumi. It was hard for David to smile along with the others, even Kou, as they finished practice. His dad had stabilized, but each message made it more certain he would be in a prolonged coma. He had yet to get any news on Jessica's whereabouts, and he had immediate concerns for Rie's safety.

His eyes kept betraying him. David tried not to watch Rie. He was determined to keep her safe, but that meant staying both close enough to act if something happened, and far enough away so he did not give Chul Soon's spies any ideas. Worst of all, he could not abandon the impulses from his unruly mind. Kou was absolutely no help.

'*I could pounce on her if you want,*' he thought. "*Or lick her again.*'

David caught a glimpse of a smile from Rie, as if she knew exactly what they were talking about as she walked back to the main house with Natsuki. Takumi stopped him with a serious look.

"Don't forget to clean up your bird."

As June ended, Nakano's first semester started winding down. The tests approached as they had every semester before. Teachers began reviewing and handing out worksheets, while badminton practice was put on hold with the expectation that they all study instead. David spent as much time as he could with Rie. She provided a sense of comfort and a ready smile despite the fact he expected an attack any day. The Imperial Household had yet to find any trace of the Jeong brothers or Jessica, but he was sure that every day brought them closer.

The difficult thing about spending time with Rie was that there was always someone else around. David's fame had created an unlooked-for side effect that did not disperse with the reporters.

'I can't believe I have groupies,' he thought, reminding himself to keep an outward smile for those around him. He wanted to yell at them, or better yet escape into the forest for a walk alone with Rie as he had planned. 'It's like someone replaced them. Mizuki is like my biggest fan now. I've used the Eye on her twice. I was sure she'd been possessed.'

'You're legally the Emperor's grandson now. Even you got all gooey when you met the Crown Prince the first time. You can't complain. Being bait was your idea.'

'Watch me.' Kou obliged by forming a perfect mental image of his eyes looking back from the mirror in their room.

'If you were to go grab her hand and walk off like you want to, everyone would know you are together. That means Chul Soon would know you are together and that would put her in even more danger than she is now.'

With a shudder, David clamped down on his impulse to run. Instead, he went back to his English notebook, writing out the answers before those around him could even finish one. His work complete, he settled into the stiff library chair to field questions about the homework. David figured Takumi's suggestion they study in the school library was part strategy, part entertainment for him. David translated the brief look Takumi gave him from his secluded corner as a smirk though few others would have been able to tell. Natsuki of course, knew Takumi well enough and punched him.

When he was finally able to escape the library, it seemed everyone who lived in the area had waited just to gather around him. It had gotten to the point that Tsubasa and Natsuki walked home on their own and then snuck onto the Matsumoto Estate after the crowd dispersed.

"I'm getting nervous," David said a few days later during morning practice with Yukiko. His hands flexed so that only his fingertips touched the rough bark of the tree. He balanced on a branch high above the ground. His host-mother sat below him, composed as ever.

"That I'll notice how much time you and Rie have been spending together?" she asked. David blinked but maintained his balance. He was past letting Yukiko's piercing questions distract him. "Ah, then a there's a more troublesome problem for you than my daughter?"

"We haven't heard anything from the Imperial Household. Too much time has gone by. Chul Soon gave up his chance for surprise. They must want to lure me out or just cause me pain. Still, they should have come by now. I figured being vulnerable would bring them, but what if it scared them away? The Crown Prince's announcement…"

"Yes I had a few choice words for my cousin about that, though I cannot fault his logic," she said. That revelation almost knocked him out of the tree.

"You're related to the Crown Prince?"

"Of course. Why do you think Masao doesn't get along with the Emperor? Now, the best advice I can give is for you to prepare for a fight anywhere you go. Of course, you should try to avoid fighting if possible, and limit any bystanders' involvement."

From a perfectly relaxed sitting position, Yukiko sprang at David, a metal blade glinting in the early morning sunlight. With a grin, David summoned his Seikaku. The involuntary rising of his arms caused him to plummet toward the ground below the tree in which he had been practicing. He caught the gleaming metal sword just in time to block Yukiko's slash, halfway up the tree trunk.

David used the blow to spin away and land, throwing the Seikaku up behind him to block Yukiko's quick strike to his back, before reversing into a series of attacks on his own. David opened himself to Kou and the forest. Drawing on their strength, he focused on controlling every movement of his sword, willing it to go exactly where he wished. The sparring match led them farther into the forest, green light barely filtering down through the thick trees. Mid-swing, Yukiko whistled as she jumped back. Rie jumped into the fight, a sword David had never seen before in her hand.

"Have fun, you two," Yukiko called. David just registered her words as Rie attacked. The pace of the fight was quick as deadly metal edges flowed around them. It reminded him of that first match between Natsuki and Takumi, the match he had watched in such awe. Now, David was the one moving with near blinding speed, egging Rie on even as she stretched his imagination to its limits.

"You finished?" he asked as the match's momentum brought them close together.

"Mom thought it would be a… fun… way to test it," she answered.

"Congratulations, it looks great," David said as Rie's new sword flashed past his face. Kou inserted himself just enough to improve David's eyesight to full tiger HD. As Takumi had the previous year, Rie had completed her first sword. It was a major accomplishment for a Matsumoto. Rie's radiant joy washed through the fight as she moved more fluidly than he had ever seen before. He did not want to hurt her, but neither did David hold back. He trusted her, and knew what she wanted. With a wide smile, he kicked off a tree and attacked again.

First semester tests ended with a week to go before the beginning of summer. Every teacher, but especially Takaeishi, seemed to revel in the massive amounts of summer homework piled on the third years.

"Look, my bag is ripping from all these handouts," Naoto complained.

Even though they had a week of school left before the five-week vacation began, all the students' spirits were high. The next day was the third-year-only party thrown by the PTA. Yukiko had explained it as a way to encourage them to work hard over the summer and last two semesters until their high school entrance exams.

Before heading out the next day, David placed a secure call to Nakahito's staff, checking to make sure no one fitting the Jeong brothers or his sister had entered mainland Japan. With reassurances from them that they had checked for any groups with an American girl and one or two boys and found none, David helped with preparations for leaving. Just in case, Takumi strapped on Kou's armor before they left.

"You've gotten fat," he grunted as he struggled to loosen a strap. The comment left him with a new scar on his leg.

"*I'm a growing kitten,*" Kou reminded him.

"Tigers do not lack pride," David added by way of apology when he transformed back. Takumi knew the tiger well enough to understand Kou would be annoyed if David apologized more plainly. Takumi settled for a knock to David's head before running out of the Dojo.

Though they did not expect a fight, David insisted they all bring as much protection with them as possible, no matter where they went. Natsuki readied the concealed sword Takumi had made for her, while Rie and Takumi both put their own metal blades into a cutout section of a giant cooler. Masao and Yukiko had offered to provide drinks for the students so that they would have a convenient place to stash weapons for those who could not summon them from thin air as David could.

Since the party was for all the third years, including three classes, the PTA organizers had selected a camping site just south of Nakano that everyone was familiar with. David rode with Natsuki and the twins in the back of the Ashikawas' pickup with the cooler.

The campground was a wide clearing on the edge of a small clear lake tucked between two of the mountains that surrounded Nakano valley. In the center, an area was open for cooking fires. Nearby, several concrete tables sat in a square around a central fire pit. Tall trees running up to the rocky beach surrounded the clearing.

David scowled as the truck parked off to the side of the road. Takaeishi stood alone in the middle of the area, staring back at David. Mr. and Mrs. Ashikawa smiled, walking over to greet their daughter's homeroom teacher as Takumi and David started dragging the weighted cooler to one of the tables. Not long after they got it in place, David heard the hum of another car. Mizuki's parents dropped her off in the clearing right before Kenta appeared behind her in his father's white mini-truck.

Car after car of students came through the narrow forest road dropping off third years. About half the parents stayed to help with food and activities. To David's surprise, many of their teachers came as well. It was a little awkward, having them all come and greet him outside of class, joking as if they were family friends. Back home, he never spoke to teachers outside of class. In Japan, he had gotten to know Tsukasa-sensei during badminton competitions and practice, but he had not spoken much to the others.

Takaeishi of course he knew all too well, knowledge he felt he could have done without. Their English, science, math, and Japanese teachers were soon all there smiling and talking as if they were as interested in how he was doing as his friends. Rie ran up to him and saved him just as Aramoto-sensei started walking toward him.

"Let's go for a swim before it gets too crazy," she said with a smile. "If we hike over to the cliffs we can dive."

"Thanks for the save," David said. "But what if Kou cramps up like with the ocean?"

"If you jump then there won't be any chance for him to stop you." Rie covered a smirk with a face so serious David turned to check behind him. "Besides, I got a new swimsuit," she whispered, running off into the woods before he could turn back. David checked the area once more, and then ran after.

'Real difficult decision there.'

'The water won't be a problem for you?'

'Who knows? But I'd rather face a thirty foot drop into the ocean than listen to your teacher try to make small talk.'

Rie's tracks faded and David smiled. She was not going to make it too easy for him to find her. With a laugh, he put on a burst of speed and ran after. If he hurried, they might even get some time alone before Takumi and the other third years found them.

二十六

THE DANGERS OF CLIFF DIVING

Chul Soon's plan seemed good enough, but it grated on me that he would not reveal the whole thing. His promises, though, his promises made all the waiting and all the sacrifices worthwhile. I could have that most important thing back. After innumerable years of life, I would have a partner...

As the trees thinned, David noticed bits of Rie's outfit left like a crumbs for him to follow. As he prowled forward, he scooped up her shirt and shorts so that Takumi would not get the wrong idea if he followed.

David found her sitting just back from the top of a tall ledge. She was cross-legged and staring down in her lap. Slight movements in her arms told him she was folding paper as David approached silently from behind her. A clear sky overhead set the lake shimmering far below them. The cliffs were just out of sight of the clearing, though David was able to see a few students playing in the water.

"Just a second," Rie said. "Almost finished."

"How'd you know?"

"You still breathe too loudly."

"If so, it's your fault."

Her smile blanked his thoughts as she turned, her hair flipping around in the light breeze. The simple power her gaze held over him was impossible to deny. He was just about to comment on her cute one-piece when she whipped around and stood. She held a giant freshwater carp in her hands that she promptly heaved over the cliff into the lake. With a wink, she followed it with a graceful dive.

David struggled out of his shirt and shoes, and without giving himself a chance to back down plunged headlong down the steep fall. He wished he had taken a second to right himself as the cold clear water rushed up at him, his body far too flat. David hit with a horrible slap of rushing water. His belly flop stunned him, pushing the air out of his chest, and blanking out his vision with red blotches. As he sank, the panic welling up in him had nothing to do with Kou's revulsion of the ocean. It seemed he was safe enough within lakes. Instead, the panic was from the pain and inability to breathe or see. He tried kicking but had no idea of his direction.

Something slimy bumped into him, and then pushed with a light, constant pressure. David's head broke the surface and he gasped in half a lungful of air, the rest, water. Coughing, he opened his eyes to stare at the thing that had saved him. The carp's mouth gaped wide at him, as if wondering if it could eat his head. Rie popped up beside it, holding a hand against the behemoth's scales.

"That had to hurt," she said.

"That was a special American dive, ten points." Her stare told him bravado wasn't working. He winced. "You have no idea. I feel like a drowned rat."

"Look like one too," Rie said, her smile widening as she took his hand. With her other, she grabbed onto the carp's wide tail. As her eyes closed, the carp turned and pulled them through the water to a small inlet below the cliffs where they could sit.

It was hard for David to keep his gaze from wandering back toward Rie as they crawled into a shallow cave out of the sun. She smiled at him. The carp turned in the water and with a giant splash that washed over David, took off into the lake.

"Hey! You did that on purpose!" David said.

"Yeah, so what? You want to fight about it?" Rie's smile said she would be quite happy to have a sparring match right then and there, but the thought embarrassed him as he realized he was in nothing but his ratty old shorts. David had never seen Rie wear anything so stylish. She always looked stunning, be it in her school uniform or training clothes, but her one-piece made her look like a movie star just getting out of the pool.

"No? Well then sit," she said. "It should be a few minutes before the others find us, and I'd like to talk." Rie's shift from aggressive to almost uncertain made him think of the quiet girls in his class, and how she was so not one of them. David sat, watching lest she unleash any more surprises.

"Sure. What about," he asked, the skin burning on his cheek again as he remembered the light brush of her lips there.

"I know this is not the best time, you're still worried about your sister and dad, but well, I want to be with you when they come." She moved a little closer to him. "Not just fighting beside you, but with you. I've tried to keep my distance, but I don't think I can. I want to be with you when you save your sister, and every day after that. I don't want to lose you if they make you move in with the Imperial Family."

"They'd make me leave?" David asked. "I thought it was all just part of the strategy, to get the Jeong brothers, they aren't going to make us leave are they?"

"I don't think so, but I'm not going to let you go. I know you have a stupid chauvinistic fear Chul Soon will try to get to you through me, but I can help you. I want to be your partner, just like Natsuki is for Takumi. I have the same feelings for you."

David looked into the eyes of the girl that had introduced him to Japan. Who was more fierce and capable in combat than anyone else he knew. He looked into the eyes of the girl who had once been possessed by an evil kami but had fought her way back from despair.

His laugh echoed around the small cave as Rie recoiled in shock and hurt. Seeing her reaction, he reached out a quick hand. Catching her chin in his hand he drew her close and, though he had no idea where the will to fight through his fear came from, he kissed her.

"I can't speak for Kou about you becoming our partner. I don't know how that all works yet. But as for me, I know I like you and no one else more. I can see it was stupid of me to try and protect you from Chul Soon, it's just that with my sister-"

"Shut up." Rie leaned forward and kissed him again, this time on his lips. All his worries, concerns, and fears faded away, replaced by the simple reality of the girl beside him. They sat together for a while, listening to the waves wash against the nearby rocks. The pair huddled close together and basked in the comfort of each other's presence.

"So, um, no dating other girls or I might have to attack them. Or you."

"Fair enough. You aren't seeing any wolves at the moment are you?" Rie punched him. He rolled with the blow, but stopped at the boisterous approach of their classmates.

"Well that didn't take very long," Rie complained, lowering her hand from a blocking position.

"I guess we better go make our presence known before they get the right idea," David said.

"Oh, they are going to be horrible. The rumors were bad enough."

"After the whole adoption thing, being able to call you my girlfriend will be easy, I might even get to like it, eventually." David jumped and was back in the water before her kick could connect.

He was just in time to spot a dark gray blur weaving through the trees along the shoreline.

"David! Where's Rie?" Takumi called from the top of the cliff. David threw Rie a quick look.

"They're here," David said, just loud enough for both twins to hear, then struck out for the shore. He heard Rie splash into the water behind him. When he looked back up to the cliff, Takumi was gone.

"David, head for the cliff top," Rie called. His toes brushed the lakebed. Two powerful strokes brought him far enough that his legs were able to push him out of the water and onto shore. He ignored the pain from rocks that slashed into his bare feet as he ran along the base of the cliff to where the forest met the rise to the top. The shore was silent around him. No birds or animals sounded, no one called him, only Rie's quick movements from behind registered in his ears. David winced as he realized she would have no protection for her feet.

"Don't stop," Rie hissed coming up behind him. Kou agreed.

"Get on." Without waiting, David grabbed Rie and slung her onto his back. He ignored the scream of pain through his own feet, and tried very hard to ignore Rie. He took off again, running cautiously up the rocky path to the top of the diving ledge. There, at the very top, Natsuki, Tsubasa, and Hidemi were huddled behind Takumi, who held one hand back, as if to keep them from advancing. His whole body shook with the effort to keep from changing in front of the uninitiated Hidemi. Before Takumi, and between David and his friends, was a large gray-haired wolf.

David stopped short and let Rie down. Despite Hidemi's presence, he summoned his Seikaku. Beside him, Rie reached for her non-existent pockets. The realization that there was no paper for her to fold made her frown even more at the wolf. For his part, the gray-haired Chul Moo's full attention remained on Takumi until the Seikaku materialized in David's hands. The change in his bearing and attitude was so abrupt it made Natsuki jump and Takumi transform into Reimi and take flight. Hidemi stood a bit off to the side, watching the others with interest and a naive lack of concern for her own safety.

Chul Moo turned to face David, but instead of attacking, began backing away. His ears lay flat along his shaggy head, his tail tucked firmly behind him. His dark eyes, fur, and sounds betrayed his fear before the big head turned to the look of revulsion on Rie's face. With a mastering sigh, Chul Moo shuffled his fur and sat back on his haunches.

"You have minutes," he said through the wolf's mouth. "I'm not sure how many. I know you'll want to turn me back into a statue, but let me talk first, and if possible let me live so I can start to make amends for the pain I caused Rie." He glanced at her, and then returned his features to David. "This is a separate matter, however, one about your sister."

David's sword, raised high for an attack slid forward for a few unconscious inches before he could jerk himself to a stop. Reimi continued flapping nearby, maintaining her altitude for a quick dive attack should Chul Moo's words be a trap.

"Talk."

"As far back as I can remember I have been nothing but an ōkami. I used to be proud of the fact, as my brother is. Over the years, however, things have changed. I came to Nakano and someone I cared about was almost lost to the horrible nature to which I always thought there was no escape. Chul Soon is mad, David. He will stop at nothing. He does not want to destroy you; he wants to chip away at your soul... It is part of our nature as ōkami. We attack slowly, covertly, we worm our way into your societies, then your minds."

"WHERE IS MY SISTER," David demanded, his blade jerking as his self-control flagged in the face of one of her captors.

Chul Moo cowered under the rage pouring off his old classmate.

"I don't know the whole plan," Chul Moo said. "They've been hiding things from me since Okinawa. He made promises, but Manami warned me of the lie so that I could talk to you."

"You know Manami," Rie asked, suspicion coloring her voice.

"Yes." His voice smoothing as he turned to Rie. "I was the one who talked to her. I had no idea there was another way for us to live, but I was still wary. Chul Soon was always there driving me, but as his plans progressed he told me less and less." Chul Moo turned back to David. "He said if I seduced her, he wouldn't kill her or Rie-"

David leapt forward; his Seikaku stopping bare inches from Chul Moo's head as Rie wrapped her arms around David's bare chest, holding him back from the killing blow. Enraged, David ignored everything but trying to impale the ōkami before him.

"Better hurry," Rie gasped, straining against all of David's rage.

"They are coming here, I don't know how many, they mean to kill you all. You need help, save who you can." Chul Moo's eyes closed peacefully as Rie lost her grip and David's sword ripped straight into the creature. It stuck there until Kou reminded him to turn the blade to his wood form. Chul Moo shrank into a small wooden statue. No sign remained of the violence except David shaking in Rie's arms.

Even as Reimi landed, Natsuki pulled one of the military grade-radios from the pocket of Takumi's clothes.

"It will happen here," she said into the speaker. "Bring Ryohei."

二十七

THE ENTIRE THIRD YEAR CLASS IS POISONED

Going into the shadows was almost peaceful this time. There was no pain. I had accepted it as my fate the instant I made the choice to betray my brother. There would be no missing piece to keep me locked in a prison. The fire would release instead of torture. If only I had been able to talk longer with Rie, or tell David that last, most important piece of information...

David recovered a little with each blink. Looking into Rie's eyes, yellow since the strain of keeping him in check had melted her cosmetic contacts, David found his center. He stood, and with a final squeeze of her hand, let go to face the others.

"Tsubasa, watch over Hidemi. Get her back to the campsite then grab a radio and watch the road in," David said with a clear voice of command. "Reimi meet with the Matsumotos and explain things. They should have Takumi's armor in the cars. Natsuki, go with him. Rie and I will follow."

"*There will not be time to evacuate everyone,*" Kou said. Although he had kept from intruding before, his observations were too important to keep quiet. If Hidemi was concerned over the sudden change in David's voice and manners, she did not show it. "*The cub-mates and their parents will be safest where we can keep watch on them. We need to consolidate them, make sure there is no one that might tempt a lone ōkami.* Let's move."

Natsuki and Reimi were away in an instant, their swift legs and wings carrying them out of view among the trees. Tsubasa followed after, pulling Hidemi behind him.

"I'll make sure you don't come back to bite us a third time," David said picking up the wooden statue. He hesitated a second, then turned to Rie. "Be careful." He stepped in and kissed her once more in farewell, and then handed her the statue. Seconds after, Kou dashed off in a blur of fur.

When they got back to the clearing, it was full of third years, teachers, and a few parents. Natsuki was a bit away from the majority of the students talking with Takaeishi while Takumi dragged the cooler toward a group of trees. Kou had passed Tsubasa and Hidemi on the way, and Rie was still behind him, so, he continued past the campground. Out of sight, Kou kept every sense focused on the search for the scent of wolves. As he neared the road, a familiar roar sounded as Masao's sedan slid to a stop on the gravel road. Masao jumped out, clad in his full armor. Ryohei glided out from the front of the car.

"Do you have any idea how hard it is to stay in the car when you drive that fast," he complained. Masao ignored him, pulling more armor from the cramped cargo area. Kou grabbed David's armored skirt in his teeth and dragged it back into the forest. There he transformed and attached that bit of armor, so at least he was decent before running back over to the car. As he started buckling greaves to his legs, Takumi, Rie, and Natsuki showed and began sorting through their own armor. Rie came over and began lacing his chest piece. Every time her fingers brushed his skin, a shiver raced through him. He hoped Masao was too busy to catch his involuntary smile.

Natsuki moved to help Takumi don his gray and red streaked armor as well. David attached his own sleeves and

gauntlets, and placed his wide helmet on his head before helping Rie struggle into her armor. Tsubasa showed up just after
carrying the swords from the cooler.

"What? You said to keep an eye on her," he said as everyone turned on him and Hidemi.

"You can kill me after if you have to," Hidemi said, "At
least that way I don't get eaten by some crazy wolves with revenge on their minds."

"Awww, come on," Takumi complained as Natsuki slid a
bit of armor over his head. "How much did you tell her?"

Hidemi's eyes darted between David and Rie, a frown
forming on her usually pleasant face. Natsuki jerked Takumi's
armor into place. "Be nice, she's a friend," she said in a biting
tone. David could not complain. With adrenaline rushing
through him, he had to remind himself just how dangerous the
coming minutes would be for all his classmates.

"Ryohei!" David called. "I think you know what we need.
Good Luck. Tsubasa, Hidemi, go with him, and drag any
stragglers back by the fire pits. Take a radio and give a shout if
you see anything strange."

Ryohei gave a grand bow, complete with rolling arms before floating after the pair.

"Yukiko is staying at the Estate in case this is another feint
and they want to turn Jessica into a yūrei using the Shrine,"
Masao said. "Of course, you need to be prepared in case they
have already done that. I don't understand Chul Moo's timing.
Even with the time it took to get here, there is no way he
should have had time to make her into a yūrei and give her
time to strengthen enough to summon oni. We have to be very
careful."

Within twenty minutes of Chul Moo's warning, they were
almost ready. Masao, David, Natsuki, Rie, and Takumi were all
armor clad and armed. Ryohei was using his ghostly aura to
knock out the Nakano Junior High students, while Tsubasa

used the latest version of the Eye to screen the surroundings for kami, ōkami, or worse.

The barest sound in the woods behind him sent David spinning away from Rie. His Seikaku appeared in an instant. Takaeishi stepped onto the road, clad in the same black armored fatigues his men had worn when storming the Estate. In his hands, he held two wickedly curving blades with a perpendicular handle a quarter of the way from one end. They were like the tonfa David had begun practicing with in the morning, except they were no wooden nightsticks. The curved blades glinted in the late morning's light.

"So what's the plan then," Takaeishi asked.

"Form a perimeter around the students," David said without hesitation. "Reimi will watch from above, and Tsubasa will plant himself in a tree with Hidemi to keep watch as well. The rest of us will spread out around and hope they are attacking here. If you see my sister, call me."

"I'm surprised," Takaeishi said. "Nothing you've shown in class so far this year hinted at the kind of intelligence needed to concoct such a dynamic strategy. Make a perimeter. Very clever." Before David could reply, Takaeishi turned and walked down the road. Rie's hand, light on his arm, kept him in place.

Takumi handed his sword to Natsuki, and then disappeared. Reimi emerged and jumped into Natsuki's arms. She began explaining the situation as she walked off after Takaeishi. Masao looked between David and Rie. He stopped, as if he wanted to say something, but instead walked off through the forest to cover the western approaches.

David reached for his mask, but the contoured metal piece was gone. He turned, and Rie was there, staring into him with such intensity that she reminded him of the way Masato Matsumoto, her grandfather, had seemed to look into his soul.

"Do what you have to, then come back to me," she said as she attached the snarling tiger image to his helmet.

'She's ready to run off and face the same things that turned her into a yūrei, all to save my sister and protect her classmates,' David thought. 'She's stronger than I am.'

'*Chul Soon is going to tuck tail and run when he sees the three of us together. Don't forget, Rie said she's been practicing some very interesting origami just in case. I'm looking forward to seeing what she has in store for that furry mutt.*'

'She did grab a lot of paper from the car...' David sighed as they embraced. He smiled, and then remembered she could not see. He helped adjust her mask, and then checked to ensure every fastening was in place.

"Don't worry, we will get her back," Rie said. Then she was off, running after her father.

David transformed into Kou, secure in the knowledge that if he needed it, his armor would reappear with his human form. Before running off, Kou padded over to a gadget Tsubasa had made for him. Kou bit down on a foam case, which contained one of the encrypted radios. Tsubasa had designed it to sit on Kou's lower fangs, so when he bit into the foam, his jaw came away with a mini waterproof receiver in his mouth so that he could talk hands-free if need be. With the last of the preparations complete, David and Kou immersed themselves in their animal instincts and began the hunt.

Kou made a quick circuit to the east, checking back along the paths through the forest to the diving cliffs. Halfway to the edge, he picked up Chul Moo's trail and began following it away from the mountains. It curved back through the forest toward the main part of Nakano Town. David frowned as they neared the southernmost buildings. The trail was easy to follow, as if Chul Moo had made it obvious on purpose, yet if he turned to look back at the way he came, the trail disappeared among the forest's underbrush.

'Looks like he didn't want anyone following him to the lake.'

'He did not expect to return. He left the trail for you to follow back, but guarded against leading the pack to us.'

To David's relief, the trail did not lead into town, but instead skirted it back to the west. Kou followed the broken branches and lingering smells that marked the last steps of Chul Moo.

'Bet you wish you had let him finish talking. We could have found out how many friends to expect, or where they are keeping Jessica.'

'You weren't exactly a restraining influence you know. Besides, he already said Chul Soon had left him out of the plans. Either he was sent to lure us, or he wanted to warn us and Chul Soon was smart enough to keep anything that important from his brother.'

'They will hunt as a pack, but if they are a newly formed group, perhaps they will not be organized. Think back on the attack by those five ōkami we ambushed outside of Nakano. They had a scout, but the rest moved together. The others are protecting your classmates. We should swing wide, go through town, and come at them from behind and the side. Perhaps we can find a greedy wolf or two among the outer houses.'

'Fine, but only as long as we don't get too far from the others. We don't want to alert them we know what's coming if Chul Moo was telling the truth.'

"*Swordsmith* this is tiger," David called over the radio. He let Kou have full control over his movements as they turned north in order to concentrate on talking with his own voice.

"Go ahead, David," Takaeishi replied. David cut off a growl at the fact his homeroom teacher was butting in.

"We need you to make it seem like the party is still going on, at least from a distance. We don't want to tip off whoever is attacking in case Chul Moo was telling the truth. Start some music, throw a ball around, things like that," David said as Kou cleared a fallen tree in one lithe leap.

They found their first target as Kou curved away from town. His keen ears picked up another animal moving through a field on approach to a farmhouse. Kou pawed toward the sound, confident in his ability to remain undetected. Passing around the edge, he followed the bank up a divide between fields, stopping at the top. Below and a bit ahead, a mass of plants and trees used as a privacy hedge and windshield surrounded a farmhouse. Kou just caught a reddish brown backside squeeze through a hole between a bush and tree as he passed.

Moments later, Kou jumped, clearing the distance between the bank and an old pine where he was able to watch the clearing between the trees and the house. The wolf below him was cagey, keeping to the shadows. Its jerky movements, constant looks behind, and reluctant steps told David it was not where it was supposed to be. Despite the giveaways, Kou recognized the posture of a predator on the hunt. The ōkami was torn between his orders and his nature. What ōkami could resist such an easy meal as a lone farmer far away from prying eyes? Kou, and David through him, knew how easy it must have been for the ōkami to make the quick detour.

One hundred and fifty pounds of muscle and bone tipped by two-inch razor-sharp claws fell from above to land on the unsuspecting ōkami. Kou flexed the muscles in his paws, driving his claws deep into the ragged fur of his opponent as his long fangs sank into the wolf's neck. The fall alone was nearly enough to subdue the unwary creature, but Kou shook his powerful head and put a quick end to his prey. Before it could begin to recover, Kou reluctantly drew back and let David take over. Emerging once again as a human, they summoned the Seikaku and turned the ōkami into a wooden statue. David hid the statue among the trees, and then Kou was off again.

'Great, now I have a leaf stuck in my teeth. This friend-caller I have to carry in my mouth, it is easy to put in the first time, not so much the second.'

'At least Tsubasa was able to make the radio. Without it we'd be cut off from the others.'

Kou was able to ambush two more ōkami before calls from Takaeishi and Masao sent Kou back toward the campsite. Both men had been able to subdue ōkami closer to the mountains, but without a Seikaku, could do little more than hack the still-snarling bits of wolf to keep them from reforming in a nightmarish parody of David's own healing abilities. They found Takaeishi first.

The second he spotted David, the ex-head of the Imperial Guard disappeared into the trees, leaving him to dispose of what had once been a brown wolf with dark beady eyes. Those orbs still shone with hate as David plunged the wood form of the Seikaku into it.

'I don't like how easy this is,' David thought as they headed for Masao.

'They are like the young ones we caught in the mountains, not like Jahangir. They are undisciplined, yet dangerous. Did you notice Takaeishi was injured?'

'Ha! Is that why he ran?' Kou followed the curve of a rock wall protruding out of the ground as it bent toward the mountains.

Kou found Masao on the far side of the river from the campsite. His host-father fought a thin framed canine that was surprisingly fast, even for someone accustomed to the speed with which animals could move. Alone, it was no match for the elder Matsumoto, but another ōkami Masao had already dispatched was wielding a heavy length of wood, making it difficult for him to finish off the newcomer. With a smile as they decided a course of action, Kou leapt into the air, David taking control as they flew. Kou and David's thoughts melded and they imagined tightening their stomach muscles. There was no longer fur and claws flying through the air, but a boy in striped armor holding a long and deadly sword.

David landed in perfect unison with Masao's graceful slashes. Every strike from his Seikaku was a counterpoint to the forged steel his host-father wielded. Overcome by the intensity of the renewed attack, the ōkami snarled and tried to back away. The Seikaku, glimmering and translucent slid just under Masao's arm to catch the ōkami in the shoulder. He followed the cut under his host-father's blade, which skimmed the top of his helmet before striking the wolf full in the throat.

David twisted, pulling his blade away from the bloodied ōkami just in time to stop a slash from the other at Masao's back. The maimed wolf spun, as its injured leg buckled. It snarled and snapped at him, but like the others, was no match for David and his Seikaku. With precise strikes he immobilized the ōkami, and created another statue. A few steps away, Masao stood atop the other, his sword pinning it to the ground through its neck. The ōkami tried to rip away the sword, so Masao drew his shorter wakasashi and hacked at the hands. David rushed over to finish it.

"Something is wrong with all of this," David said, handing Masao the two statues. "I'd like everyone to go back to the campsite. I'm going to take another look to the east. I haven't caught a sign of Chul Soon and while there have been several single ōkami through this area, there is no pack. Kou's radio fell somewhere among the trees when I transformed. Would you please let the others know?"

"Very well. How many have you found?"

"These make at least five that we've seen."

"Good. Your form is looking excellent. Go. Today we take back your sister."

David smiled, heat burning his cheeks as pride suffused through him. Pride was an emotion Kou was quite capable of. He could feel their thoughts align as the emotions brought them closer together. David transformed and with a growl and quick flick of their tail, they were off.

二十八

AMONG THE TREES
OF NAKANO VALLEY

With all my plans coming to fruition, the moment of my revenge soon at hand, it was annoying to have that whining failure cause me so much concern. I had found someone worthy to be at my side. One to witness and bring about the long awaited rise of the Akuma Clan...
—Part of a journal recovered
from the ruins of Nanboku Island

Kou ran just inside the tree line as he circled the lake. From between the brown blurs of tall tree trunks, David and Kou could see the campground on the edge of the eastern shore. Movement around the site made it look as if the teachers and students were still active. Even with Kou's excellent vision, they could not see anything to warn away the ōkami. As they ran, their tail stretched out behind them, helping to balance their lithe movements. David was still surprised how much Kou relied on it. Their tail was one of the reasons David had yet to master moving as a tiger. Kou used it almost like a rudder, and the human had yet to adjust to the extra appendage.

A shadow to the left caught Kou's attention and they veered toward it. David grinned at the power he felt coursing through Kou's lithe limbs. Within two lengths of his body, as

Kou counted, they realized the shadow was Takaeishi and turned back for the campsite.

'Just let him try...'

"*To keep up*," Kou said, finishing David's thought. Despite his pace, they both took pleasure in the brief moment of clarity as their thoughts aligned.

They made a quick circuit around the campsite to check everyone's positions. Tsubasa, Hidemi, Natsuki, Rie, and Takumi were all back and manically running around to keep up the appearance a party was going on, all the while arranging themselves around their classmates to protect them. The effect was enhanced by what seemed to be about ten of each of them. Copies of Hidemi seemed to stare around bookishly while others of Tsubasa jerked around with quick inquisitive movements. Ryohei floated over the mayhem, his face twisted in concentration.

'It must be almost impossible for him to maintain his aura at just the right level. Powerful enough to keep everyone asleep, but not so much as to horrify them or draw on their souls,' David thought. Seeing Rie smile at him as he shot past, Kou flicked his tail at her in greeting. 'I don't think she reads tail yet.'

'*Then maybe you should teach her to read tails. I had no idea she could copy humans with her paper trick. I wonder how they taste. Fine. No humans.*'

'I still don't know what all your twitches mean. Well I do, because I can feel it, but it's not like I can see our tail when you think those things.'

'*Not my problem. It is not as if you help me with all the strange hand signs or face twitches you make.*'

'What. A thumbs up? You so know what that means.'

Their internal conversation continued right up to the point when the light shifted in the trees ahead. Kou slowed so that instead of barely touching the ground as he passed over it, at least three paws connected at any given moment. Ahead, there was a single fallen tree, leaving a space in the canopy through which sunlight flowed. Below, a small area around the trunk of a once proud tree was awash in light. In the very center, balancing on top of one of the massive roots was a handsome boy with long black hair, stylish shirt, and a satisfied grin.

Kou's fur rippled from his head to tail in the two seconds it took for David to exert control and revert to his human form. Summoning his Seikaku, he stepped into the light and strode toward the feral boy above him. In the months since he had last seen Chul Soon, David noted he was thinner, less the innocent and outgoing boy David had counted as his friend. His cheeks were higher, his face more angled, and his eyes were dark and wild. When he spotted David in the trees, he smiled as if he had just received a present. He took no note of the blade that had impaled him the previous year.

"David, my old friend," Chul Soon said in his sonorous voice. Every inflection was full of charm. "It's so nice of you to come to me alone. I was afraid this was going to take most of the afternoon, and well, I have other priorities of late. In fact, if it was not for the fact I spent so much time getting to this point, I would have just left things be. Well, no, you are quite right, that was a lie. The Akuma Clan can't have an actual Jitsugen Samurai running around, now can it?"

David ignored the words. His focus was tight on Chul Soon, though he did not ignore his surroundings. He saw the three other ōkami lurking in the shadows behind his old friend, even though they were trying to hide. As multi-opponent scenarios ran through his mind, David opened himself to Kou, merging his human and animal side. He could feel the orange and black striped fur begin to grow from his body, but he ignored the strange sensation. The physical change was insignificant compared to the sense of mental strength and confidence Kou imparted. Kou seemed to encompass him with his strength and speed even as his knowledge and tenacity came out from within. As their anger and desire to hunt grew, they took another step.

"Oh, come now, none of that." Chul Soon twitched his head and two other human shapes stepped into the light. They both wore loose, comfortable clothing that could have passed as a casual outfit for any of his classmates. Like the others he had dispatched earlier, these ōkami looked to be about his own age, which meant they were young by the wolves' standards, but much older than David. The female had pink hair, her almond skin shining in the patchwork light around the fallen tree. The male beside her was similar, but with spikes of black hair. Their faces revealed little. A fourth shadow stayed hidden among the trees, though slight, restless movements gave it away. David took another step.

"Fine, have it your way." Chul Soon jumped from the branch, landing behind the tree. When he came back into view, he dragged the fourth hidden figure forward with a tight grip. She was taller than Chul Soon, and her long blond hair had leaves and pine needles stuck in it. Chul Soon smiled as he pointed a gun at Jessica. David stopped.

David's hands fell, his sword limp in his hand beside him. His sister was dressed as stylishly as any Japanese student, which was extremely odd for him to see. Just two years younger, she had changed in the few months since she had last visited Japan. There was a gag in her mouth and her sad eyes seemed to plead with him. David sighed in relief, though his anger was kept hot by Kou.

'Her skin is still normal. They didn't make her into a yūrei.'

'*David. We can't let them get away, and we can't let them kill us.*'

'She's my sister.' David tightened his grip on the Seikaku. Though his ears were not as good as Kou's, even he heard the unnatural brush of leaves and branches in the forest. Several bodies were moving in behind him.

"Ah, good, the rest of them are here," Chul Soon said, smiling as he jerked Jessica closer to him, his fingers digging into her arm. "If I were you, I would wait right there unless you want to set my finger off. It is very twitchy. My friends are coming up behind you right now. They all came for the same thing. To watch me have my revenge on you, to watch me kill the scary gaijin who plays at being a warrior. With you out of the way, the Akuma Clan will have its first taste of revenge on the Jitsugen Samurai. The Master will reward me very well. Though, to be honest, I'm already satisfied on our personal score."

David's mind whirled as he tried to figure a way out for him and Jessica.

'Three ōkami in front, how many behind? Didn't we get them all? The others should at least be able to ward off any strays we missed from the west.'

'What if they are not ōkami?'

David smiled and readied his Seikaku. He brought it up before him, Jessica's eyes widening as she followed the blade. David wondered what she was thinking, seeing the ferocious tiger mask and armor, her older brother holding a very long, very sharp katana.

Chul Soon growled at the woods behind David. His two fellows, drawing close, pulled wicked looking claw gauntlets from bags by their feet. In a semicircle behind him, Rie, Masao, Takumi, and Natsuki entered just within the barest edges of the light filtering from the hole in the canopy. Chul Soon let loose such a howl of anger that the very trees themselves seemed to vibrate at the power behind it. David smiled.

Chul Soon's calm assurance, so pervasive just a minute before, was gone. He looked among the faces advancing before him and growled again.

"How?!" he shouted.

"Simple," Rie said. David could just imagine her smiling sweetly as she spoke, though he dare not look away from Chul Soon.

"Chul Moo," David said aloud. "Your brother decided to warn us about your visit. If you were expecting help, well..." The ringing of metal matched his shrug as the others drew their blades.

Chul Soon's face was as bestial as his wolven form. His arm with the gun quaked and his eyes blazed with more hate than anything David had seen before. He cocked the gun.

"I might not get to kill you this time, but I've already had my revenge. I killed your father myself, David. I took away from you what you took from me. You can have my brother. He's no loss, though I doubt you would think the same of your little sister. If you value her life, you will stay right there, or else my friend here is going to shoot her in the head."

Chul Soon moved to toss the gun to one of the other ōkami, but with a swift movement, Jessica snatched the gun from the air and turned it on the ōkami.

"The Master is angry," she said in Japanese. As her head turned, the gun began firing. The entirety of her attention fell on David and there was more hatred and fury on her face than he had ever witnessed before. All directed at him.

Jessica fired at close range into Chul Soon. He stumbled off the tree, howling in pain. Then Jessica turned and unleashed the rest of the clip at David. With each bullet strike, David fell back from the force of the lead on his armor. When the gun clicked empty, Jessica disappeared. In her place, a white wolf with deep blue eyes snarled back at them with the hate of centuries and then sprang away.

The howl of pain and rage and loss poured from two throats as the other ōkami attacked. Rie and Takumi met the ōkami's clawed gauntlets, but even as David stepped to follow his sister, a swarm of possessed souvenirs flew into the clearing and blocked the way. Looking around, Chul Soon howled again, this time changing into the familiar form of a black-haired ōkami. He lurched after Jessica but a giant kendama toy that looked like a crazy cross between a ball catch game and a hammer smacked him back into the clearing.

'An ōkami. They made her into an ōkami. She's one of them and she hates me. He did this. Chul Soon.'

David convulsed and transformed, even as the rest of the Matsumotos engaged the ōkami, miniature statues, and flying rice balls around him. He lunged at the black-haired wolf, but despite obvious injuries, Chul Soon proved he was not going to give up. He snarled and bared his fangs as Kou's heavy paw lashed out with claws extended. They rolled out of the clearing, a snarling growling mass of fur and sharp points.

Rie's sword sparked against the male ōkami's gauntlets while Natsuki and Takumi wove in and out of each other's paths as they advanced on the snarling pink-haired ōkami. Masao spun, striking with Matsumoto steel at every stray souvenir that crossed his path. A pair of glass pipes smashed into him and exploded in a shower of glittering shards.

Rie sliced down with her sword, energy and focus returning as she let go of the myriad spirits she had summoned at the campsite. Her foe was young and lithe and caught her sword between the claws of his gauntlets. Rie cringed, worried her first blade might snap, but it held. She let the monster pull against her, then let go. As he fell off balance, she quickly drew two smaller blades from her side and stabbed them into his sides.

Takumi ducked as Natsuki leapt high into a badminton smash, except instead of a racket, she held the blade Takumi had made for her. Half the girl's long pink hair fell away. Below, Takumi's blade caught her in the knee, driving halfway through her kneecap before she spun and ripped the leg away.

As soon as they were away from the main fight, Chul Soon tried to flee. He raced off through the underbrush, but Kou would have none of it. Overcoming the wiry but beaten down wolf was easy compared to playing hide-and-seek with Reimi. Kou sprang from a tree branch, and they transformed again mid-air. David summoned his sword, but at the last instant, Chul Soon spun, his wiry doglegs knocking David off target enough that the tip of David's sword hit the ground. Immediately, it disappeared. With a growl of hate, the wolf snaked its jaws past David's arms inside of the flared helmet to bite at his neck. The armor protected David from the teeth, but a snap from the wolf's powerful muscles sent David flying into the nearest tree.

Dazed, he slumped against the tree trunk. Chul Soon glowered and shook himself, turning his black-furred face to his foe.

"You are a pathetic thing to fear," he said. "Your father was so easy to take. Your sister so willing. She's a wily one. Didn't you like how she shot me? Revenge lives in her blood. The Master must want her more than I thought he did. Perhaps he has taken her for his own. My brother did such a good job with her."

David looked with hate and rage as the dark wolf spoke. His mind was as blank as when he ravaged the Matsumoto Forest, yet he could not move. Something had gone wrong with his legs. They jerked beneath him, yet he could feel nothing. The lack of feeling jerked him out of his anger as fear flooded through him.

'We will heal, but we need time. The forest is our home, it will help us.'

"You see, David. Even if somehow you get rid of me. There are always more. We are the Akuma Clan. We have planned for centuries to return. Our Master will have his revenge."

Chul Soon stepped forward again, a big black paw kicking leaves off an old root.

'A root.'

David closed his eyes and called forth his Seikaku. As he caught it again, Chul Soon paused, suspicious, and then as if realizing David's legs were useless, he growled an evil wolf laugh and lunged.

David drove the sword down between his useless legs into the root beneath him. As his Seikaku connected with the wood, David called forth his powers to shape the living wood to his will. As his will began to change the tree, his back arched as his advanced healing began to reknit the nerves in his spine. David shrieked in pain, but Kou joined him and together they willed the root to grow in a spark of thought. Even as Chul Soon attacked, the root shot tendrils up into the wolf. Chul Soon's howl echoed with David's scream of pain as shoot after shoot of sharp new root drove through the ōkami and branched into new leaves above him.

Though it seemed like he hung in a world of pain for an age, David recovered and stood. Chul Soon hung thrashing several feet above the ground in the midst of a newly grown tree. A thought entered his mind then, to leave him there to suffer, but David remembered his brother.

"You won't ever be coming back," David said. Chul Soon foamed at the mouth and tried to bite him.

'We must hurry. Turn him so that we can check on the others. Perhaps Reimi can track your sister.'

With a shudder, David cursed himself for allowing Chul Soon to distract him for so long. He took hold of his Seikaku, and with the knowledge that Kou would always be able to re-play this moment, drove the point in between the two dark pits of evil.

When he made it back to the fallen tree, David had to dodge a smiling cat statue with a paw like a slot machine lever that kept trying to whack him. He analyzed the scene as fast as his Matsumoto training allowed. His heart nearly stopped when he saw the blood covering Rie. David leapt, his jump taking him clear through the air until he was atop the fallen tree.

His leg buckled, but he managed to stand. His mind blanked by rage he grabbed the male ōkami's head with his gauntleted hands and twisted. Far stronger than any human, the neck did not snap, instead, under the massive force, its whole body spun to the ground. Rie followed up with a quick strike, which did little against the tough hide.

"It's not all mine," she said. Despite failing to stop the wolf, Rie's presence brought David out of his rage. She cleared his mind like a fall into the Matsumotos' pond.

David took the barest instant to calm himself and reconnect with Kou. It was all the time the ōkami needed. Seeing her partner fall, the pink haired ōkami whipped out another gun and shot a quick succession of bullets at Takumi and Natsuki, forcing them off the attack long enough for her to lunge at David with the sharp, glimmering blades of her gauntlets.

Rie tackled David, pulling him out of the way. They spun through the air together, ripping the clawed gauntlet from the ōkami's hand as it stuck deep in Rie's back.

David summoned his sword as they rotated through the forest air and smashed into the nearest tree. The wood form of the Seikaku anchored them into place and stopped their roll. An entire branch of the tree disintegrated into a shower of splinters that drove themselves into the ōkami's hide. While the ōkami were distracted, David had one of the roots grow up and envelop Rie to keep her safe. Standing, David swept his gaze around the clearing. Masao was just outside the light, fighting a latecomer. Like the other two, the ōkami was young, but had light skin and brown hair. Instead of quick movements, the foreign ōkami hacked at Masao with a broad double-edged sword.

"Reimi, go after Jessica please," David shouted as he stalked forward. Takumi disappeared in an instant and took wing. Natsuki tried to shout to the little grey bird, but the pink-haired ōkami attacked again. She raised her sword in defense.

"I." David sliced viciously at the flailing male ōkami. The boy had several wounds from the tree, and his legs seemed to have been damaged by Rie's attack. "Have." Ducking, David slipped inside his opponent's guard. "Had." The sword, containing part of David and Kou's very beings sliced deep into the ōkami's joints, disabling him even as he tried to attack. "Enough." David whirled, changing his blade with the speed of thought into its wood form. As his eyes met the ōkami's he plunged his blade deep. A howl rent the thick forest air as a small wooden statue replaced the human shape.

Within minutes, David had helped dispatch the remaining two ōkami. As soon as they were all statues, they made short work of the few remaining snacks and statues. He returned to the tree where he had stashed Rie. Furious pounding sounded from the thin but hard surface of her enclosure. He had to stop. His arm trembled, and his warring emotions made it dangerous for him to attempt her release.

"What's the idea locking me up in a tree!" she yelled when her head was free.

"Um, you're hurt," David said, embarrassed, but very conscious of Masao and Natsuki's presence.

"If you think because I'm your girlfriend you can lock me in a tree every time I get a scratch, you've got a lot to learn," she said as she struggled to extricate herself. Despite the pain stabbing through him, both from the loss of his sister and the remaining pain of his mending back, he could feel a smile starting to pull at his lips.

For an instant, David forgot everything that had happened. Despite the grime and scowl on her, Rie had just proclaimed her feelings for him. He forgot that her father was standing right behind him with a very sharp sword. He pulled off his mask and kissed her, awkward as it was with his helmet. Kou purred within.

"*It's about time,*" Reimi said, gliding down in a tight spiral. She alighted on one of the tree roots. "*I'm sorry David. She was too quick. I saw her at the station. She got on one of the express trains. By the time you do anything she will be in Himeji or beyond.*" The little gray bird landed and cocked her head at David.

Takumi emerged a few moments later. With a glance at the others, Masao retrieved the new ōkami statues and disappeared back into the shadows. Soon, only David and Rie remained in the clearing.

"David," she said, her yellow eyes flashing. He turned back to smile at the dangerous tone in her voice. "Get me out of this tree!"

二十九
A GIRL AND A TIGER

I was afraid. I had expected a quick death, a blazing finish to a lifetime of pain. Was David that sadistic? Would he leave me for all eternity as a wooden statue, just as he had left me in that police warehouse? Chul Soon would not return for me again. The thought that I had risked it all for nothing…

It took a better part of an hour to find all the ōkami statues and pile all of them except Chul Moo into the campsite fires. The young tree confounded them all. From the root, a new tree formed from the twisted shoots that had impaled Chul Soon. Two meters off the ground, Chul Soon's wooden features snarled from center. In the end, David had to stab the tree with his Seikaku and will the tree to release the statue. For good measure, Masao had him fell the tree so they could burn that too.

With a call to the Imperial Household, Takaeishi was able to get a contingent of his men brought in with Japan Health Ministry suits. They carried the students down the road away from the campsite, and then marked off the area with ropes. When everyone awoke, fake doctors checked them over, telling them they were suffering from a widespread case of tainted water, but that all would be fine.

"It seems every time something happens, someone else finds out about secrets they are better off not knowing," Masao grumbled once they arrived back at the Estate. Tsubasa chatted with Hidemi about the various wolves they had seen with the Eye.

The final events had finally affected Hidemi. Where she had taken the initial changes in stride, ever since David and Rie had returned to the campsite holding hands she had begun to show some of the strain they would have expected from any classmate. For her it meant becoming very quiet and watching everyone closely while fingering one of the small books she always carried.

David and Rie were quiet during the ride back. He was still processing the fact that Chul Soon had turned Jessica, that he had taken out a disturbing number of wolves, and that he and Rie were together. Rie seemed content just to be beside him. She was there for him, but did not intrude on his brooding. David was pretty sure she was still more than a little angry at him for trying to protect her.

They all spent the next several hours writing their experiences for the Matsumoto library, ensuring the incident would never be lost. When they finished Yukiko allowed them to talk amongst each other so they might understand the full extent of what had happened.

The Jeong brother's initial plan had been to encircle and attack the party. With David alone, they could have killed him and then gone on to take out Takumi and the rest of the Matsumotos.

"Is there any way to save her?" David asked tiredly. Rie sat next to him, she had not left his side since the fight, and her presence was a tangible comfort.

"This is something our family has studied at length," Masao said. "Once a human is made into an ōkami there is no going back. Her best hope will be for you to get her to Manami and her friends, to teacher her to overcome her natural tendencies. It may be very difficult if this Master is goading and guiding her."

"The Akuma Clan will know they have a power over you for as long as he holds your sister," Yukiko added. "Even if Chul Soon had kept you secret until now, if Jessica is cooperating they'll soon piece things together."

"Yes, but Chul Moo may be able to help us get to her," Masao said. "We should take his statue to Manami in Okinawa. If we revive him-" David and Takumi both frowned at the thought. "If we revive him, he may be able to get us closer than you could get alone."

"He did warn you, didn't he?" Yukiko said.

"I don't know how helpful he will be once he finds out I'm with David though," Rie said. "He thinks he loves me, but I don't think he knows what love is. Still, if it will help Jessica, I'm all for it."

Their discussion lasted well into the night, far after Tsubasa and Hidemi had gone home. After learning she would have to start coming to the Estate to train every day, she left more excited than David had ever seen her before, despite Masao's dire warnings.

They also received a late warning from the Imperial Household that three people matching the Jeong brothers and Jessica's descriptions had purchased airplane tickets. The delay was due to the fact they had traveled as part of three different tours with other young people. There were not yet sure, but one of Nakahito's aides suggested they might have snuck into Japan by taking a fishing boat to a small outer island, then worked their way toward Okinawa on a ferry.

On the Monday after the attack, the third year's homerooms were full of complaints over the missed party. Their teachers were ready, however, with a promise from the PTA to redo the party in the early fall.

David spent most of his classes trying not to stare across at Rie. He failed so miserably that Takumi, smiling in a way that let David know it was in return for the picture during the school trip, informed everyone that indeed the two were dating. Despite the annoying comments and gossip that again brought him back to the center of attention at school, David decided he had other things to worry about.

'Why didn't you partner with her when she saved us? You like her too.'

'I do not know David. We both like her, but we have known her for such a short time. Perhaps we need more time together, maybe it is because she has a separate link through the layers.'

David spent every minute that he could with Rie. It helped that she was quite adept at keeping up with Kou during his evening runs through the woods. One of the most surprising outcomes from their public dating was that Masao and Yukiko changed their training. In the mornings, David and Rie worked together with Natsuki and Takumi while Tsubasa worked with Yukiko.

Instead of practicing with them, Hidemi had explained she would not train and began studying the Matsumoto diaries. Both the elder Matsumotos tried to talk her into joining, but she was resolute. She arrived every morning, but refused to do more than watch and learn. Her obvious interest in the library, and the way she was able to pull helpful and obscure bits of information from almost any text soon had her in charge of researching a way to help Jessica.

In the evenings, Kou and David alternated practicing with Rie and working with her in the forge while the rest pursued their own training. David feared she would get sick of him, but her smile always made him forget his worries. The last week of school barely registered in David's mind, though Kou remembered.

'I'd say this is the happiest I've ever been, except for Jess and my dad.'

'*At least you know what happened to her, and that she is still alive. Who knows what might have happened to her as a human or a yūrei.*'

'You're right. At least now she has some protection, and my father is stabilizing.'

David sent an email to Jessica's account every night, hoping she might someday read them, and that he would be able to reach the part of her that was still human. Rie sat with him as he wrote. Mostly, she did her homework, but her presence helped to remind him that there were paths back from darkness.

The junior high students' last day was a recreation day. Instead of classes, they spent the first period cleaning their homerooms for the summer, then the next three periods playing soccer out on the field. All the A classes, 1A, 2A, 3A were one team. The same was true for B and C. Together each group mobbed their opponents with masses of students in a game so thick that all skill levels were equalized. More interested in talking with Rie than playing the game, David hung back from the center of the action.

Takaeishi was waiting for David just off the field when the games finished. Rie stood beside him as he stared down their homeroom teacher.

"Let's go for a walk," he said. He spoke to David, but Rie moved with him, invitation, or no. If Takaeishi was annoyed, he did not show it. David almost laughed as they walked behind the gym to the very spot he had fist fought with Koji. Takaeishi's restraint failed, and David was sure he missed Reimi glide into a nearby tree. "I don't know what is so funny. You continue to fail, yet you and the Matsumotos seem fine with it." Rie glared at him, David smiled in defiance.

"I am not here to fix your mistakes. You will leave for Tokyo in two days. You will spend the summer there. Rie

Matsumoto may accompany you as the Matsumoto Family's representative. You will both receive instruction on the Imperial Family and David will take his place as the adopted son of his highness the Crown Prince."

Finished, Takaeishi turned and walked into the forest. Reimi glided down and landed on David's head, her sharp talons scraping his skull.

"He's always so cheerful isn't he," she said.

"It could have been worse," Kou said.

"Oh?"

"Yeah, he could have said you were going too!"

Kou transformed, making Reimi fall before she could open her wings and glide to the ground. Kou chomped at her, and then ran off into the forest with the two kami playing tag as the end of day bell rang through the school.

The next few days were full of packing and preparations. Masao decided he and Yukiko would also travel to Tokyo to meet the Emperor and observe David's formal adoption. From a few stray comments Kou was able to pick up, David was sure that Masao also wanted a few words with Japan's figurehead. Yukiko fussed over David, insisting they make a trip to Himeji for new clothes for both him and Rie. Takumi and Natsuki seemed to alternate between jealousy and happiness, for they were being left in charge of the Estate in the elder Matsumotos' absence. The responsibility weighed heavily on Takumi, but he seemed rather happy about it to David.

The media got wind of the impending trip and showed up en masse at the Estate. Their reporting led to a stream of wellwishers and students coming to see David so that his preparation time was cut to almost nothing. He spent most of the afternoon before he was supposed to leave assuring his classmates that it was just for the summer, and that he would indeed return to finish his third year of junior high in Class 3B.

When Mizuki came, Rie made a point of sitting with David for the brief interview. Instead of taking the obvious seat on the other side of the table, she came all the way around the table and hugged Rie.

"Oh, I'm so happy for you Rie-chan!" she giggled in a high-pitched voice. He watched in fascination as Mizuki knelt beside a horrified Rie and took her hands. "I can't believe you snared the adopted grandson of the Emperor! I can't wait for you two to get back. We are going to be such good friends. Just like Elementary school!"

When she finally left, David lost all decorum and rolled along the tatami floors of the main room laughing. It went on so long Rie almost turned red herself, and then gave up and started laughing with him.

"It's going to be an interesting year," David gasped. Rie punched him.

"*I could use a new playmate,*" Kou growled. David's eyes lit up at Kou's amusement. Rie swatted at David again.

"There are still bones in the forest from your last playmate, Kou," she pointed out.

They left early the next morning, escaping all but the most tenacious reporters. Masao drove them to Nakano Station, where they all met members of the Imperial Guard. David was pleased to note none of them had been in the group that had attacked the Estate.

The Crown Prince had decided on public transportation so that people would have an opportunity to view David as a normal boy, taking a normal trip. Masao and Yukiko planned to follow along after. The fact they received no special transportation would solidify the idea he was just a regular boy taken in by a kind public figure. It would feed the cynical analysis from talking heads on the various news stations, that the adoption was for purely political and public relations reasons.

David enjoyed the trip. He made an effort to stay respectful, and avoided speaking with Rie too informally. Their guards sat apart and quickly blended into the other passengers as they transferred in Himeji to a faster train.

It was entertaining to catch bits of news broadcasts in various stations, complete with his picture or a scene from his departure. Rie went through it all with seeming ease, but her confession before they left that such public spectacles made her nervous let David know they were both in new territory. Dressed in her school uniform, as he was in his, they both looked polite yet not too formal. Their baggage, including their armor, had been shipped ahead, so they had little to carry.

"Where do you want to eat?" David asked while they waited for their next train in Kobe.

"How about that one? We can take the bento on the train."

When the little lunchbox store owner realized who they were, and saw the cameras that mysteriously appeared around them, he insisted they take a fresh box for free and bowed them all the way back to their train. David followed Rie's lead for responding to the situation. The scene reminded him of all the food shows and references he had seen on Japanese TV.

"I bet that bentoya-san loves us right now," he said with a smirk when they started on the beautifully arrayed box of rice, vegetables, and fish.

"I love him right now. So good."

David struggled to smile, feeling Kou fade within as they moved farther from the rural areas and into the cities. As always, the loss was a physical and mental blow. Rie gave him the smallest of nods to show she understood. He sighed and pushed away his empty bento box, staring out the train's window.

The tall buildings of Tokyo rushed by, and David looked in amazement at the sprawl of the modern city. The train slowed for a final time and he readied himself for the new challenges awaiting him. With Rie beside him, David stood and walked toward the waiting Imperial Guard.

ACKNOWLEDGMENTS

I am pleased to work with the team at Tuttle Publishing again, especially with William and Rowan, who have worked so hard to bring these stories to the world. The people of Kitadaito and Kumejima have inspired me throughout the writing process. Many of the names used in this series are borrowed from my students, friends, and teachers, but the characters and personalities of the real people are not attached to the names. I have to thank the JET Programme for providing me the opportunity to live and work in Japan over the last five years. Japan is an amazing place to learn and grow, and I firmly believe that the best way to learn is to teach. I would also like to thank my beta reader Natalie for taking the time to give me a fresh perspective. Thank you to all who have taken the time to read my work.

Benjamin Martin is the author of *Samurai Awakening* and the blog *More Things Japanese*. He graduated from the University of Arizona and has been studying Japanese history, language, and culture for more than ten years. Benjamin has spent the last five years living on remote islands off the Okinawa mainland, teaching English as a second language. He currently lives in Okinawa.

Join the Awakening. Visit www.SamuraiAwakening.com to learn more about the books and connect with the author.

The Tuttle Story: "Books to Span the East and West"

Many people are surprised to learn that the world's largest publisher of books on Asia had its humble beginnings in the tiny American state of Vermont. The company's founder, Charles Tuttle, came from a New England family steeped in publishing.

Tuttle's father was a noted antiquarian dealer in Rutland, Vermont. Young Charles honed his knowledge of the trade working in the family bookstore, and later in the rare books section of Columbia University Library. His passion for beautiful books—old and new—never wavered through his long career as a bookseller and publisher.

After graduating from Harvard, Tuttle enlisted in the military and in 1945 was sent to Tokyo to work on General Douglas MacArthur's staff and was tasked with helping to revive the Japanese publishing industry, which had been utterly devastated by the war. After his tour of duty was completed, he left the military, married a talented and beautiful singer, Reiko Chiba, and in 1948 began several successful business ventures.

To his astonishment, Tuttle discovered that postwar Tokyo was actually a book-lover's paradise. He befriended dealers in the Kanda district and began supplying rare Japanese editions to American libraries. He also imported American books to sell to the thousands of GIs stationed in Japan. By 1949, Tuttle's business was thriving, and he opened Tokyo's very first English-language bookstore in the Takashimaya Department Store in Ginza, to great success. Two years later, he began publishing books to fulfill the growing interest of foreigners in all things Asian.

Though a westerner, Tuttle was hugely instrumental in bringing a knowledge of Japan and Asia to a world hungry for information about the East. By the time of his death in 1993, he had published over 6,000 books on Asian culture, history and art—a legacy honored by Emperor Hirohito in 1983 with the "Order of the Sacred Treasure," the highest honor Japan bestows upon a non-Japanese.

The Tuttle company today maintains an active backlist of some 1,500 titles, many of which have been continuously in print since the 1950s and 1960s—a great testament to Charles Tuttle's skill as a publisher. More than 60 years after its founding, Tuttle Publishing is more active today than at any time in its history, still inspired by Charles Tuttle's core mission—to publish fine books to span the East and West and provide a greater understanding of each.